Life's

Captivity

Sharon A. Aricol

BOOK PUBLISHERS NETWORK

Book Publishers Network
P. O. Box 2256
Bothell • WA • 98041
Ph • 425-483-3040
www.bookpublishersnetwork.com

10 9 8 7 6 5 4 3 2 1

Printed in the United States of America

LCCN 2008943470
ISBN10 1-935359-06-1
ISBN13 978-1-935359-06-7

Author's portrait was done by artist Noel Torrey. Some of Noel's other works include *The Road to Emmaus, The Virgin Mary, Mother Teresa,* and *Blessed Juan Diego of Guadalupe,* displayed in the sanctuary of St. Phillip Neri's Church in Midwest City, Oklahoma.

Editor: Julie Scandora
Cover Designer: Laura Zugzda
Typographer: Stephanie Martindale

This book is done in memory of Greg Colsch, Mike Duncklee, Dean Miene, and Glenn Wachter, whose lives were far too short, and they were never far from my thoughts in the years it took to write this story. They will never be forgotten.

Acknowledgements

I want to thank God for all the people He has brought into my life in the times and places He chose. The many conversations over the years and small acts of kindness have all done their part, and when the time was right, my eyes were opened to the true gift from God.

I would like to thank my publisher, Sheryn Hara, for encouraging me to "write, write, write," never doubting that in all the years, fifteen to be exact, I would eventually produce from all that writing. Thank you, too, for the selection of Julie Scandora to do the very important job of editing, and Julie what a fantastic job you have done, taking all the meanderings and ponderings of thought and sculpting them into a true work of art. Thank you so much for your insightful understanding of the message I wished to share.

I would also like to say special thanks to Laura Zugzda for her inspirational cover. You assailed my fears so I could boldly proceed.

Last, but not least, I would like to thank my husband and best friend, Donald, and my children, Gabriel, David, and Laura Mae, for so patiently giving me all this time over the years to walk and run. This time was most precious in that I spent it with the Lord in reflection and prayer, allowing me to draw ever closer to His greatness in His merciful loving kindness to us through His only Son the Lord Jesus Christ.

Chapter One

Michael

Had four years really passed? The scenario played the same as it had four years earlier, only this time the greyhound bus was heading in the opposite direction. Another two hours and Michael David Calhoun, age twenty-two, would be home, a civilian again. Into his head, the headset drummed the tune "Take the Long Way Home": "When you look through the years and see what you could have been, oh, what you might have been, if you'd had more time." Michael smiled at the irony. He was finally heading home, the long way… His thoughts became reflective as he stared into his own questioning eyes in the tinted glass of the bus window.

What had it all meant, those four years? He felt the same, and the landscape sure hadn't changed much. Farming communities usually don't. Farmers come and go, but the land, even at the toiling hand of man, does as it's commanded by a higher being.

Life, sighed Michael. *What's it all for? Things seem to change, but upon a wider glance, nothing ever really does. Each man's lot is the same: You're born, you work, and then if you're lucky, you acquire a family that means more work, and in the end you die. Nothing changes; no one ever seems to make a difference. It doesn't matter who you are. Even the great men die. And people still keep being born, one day awake with hopes and dreams and the next burdened with the realization of only work and death ahead.*

Michael peered hopelessly out the bus window and scanned the horizon near and far. Despite his moodiness, the beauty of the passing countryside moved him to great appreciation for where he had been born and had grown up.

The closer the bus brought him to his birthplace, the more beautiful the land became. The steep and terraced hills displayed the strip cropping used to prevent soil erosion. The contours only magnified the depth of the valleys, leading the mind to wander to the days when the wagon trains crossed the great expanse of the continent. How had they ever managed such heights and drops in the terrain, time and again, until they had come to the vast, flat, open plains? In some spots the treetops were right at road level as the bus wound around and through the limestone hillside. The cool dark of the narrowed vales opened up in areas to small meadows where clear streams meandered alongside the road, sometimes widening to reveal fishing spots where the locals sat on the tree-covered banks. The scenes held such peace one could almost imagine what it would be like if there were no evidence of man and God's creation remained quiet and serene, beauty undisturbed.

But man had made his stamp in and among all this amazing beauty. An abandoned and grey-weathered house, with sagging roof and glassless windows, peered at passers-by amid the surrounding overgrowth of trees and shrubs once meant to cool and now concealing. The aging building reminded Michael of man's brevity and nature's patience—man marks and nature recovers. Places Michael remembered as open were overgrown, and other areas he had driven through with friends were built up. It almost saddened him. *Where does life go?* Modern pole barns gently mixed with centuries-old red barns, and new homes intermingled among old white-washed three-story farmhouses of yesteryear. Even the fence lines were a mix of new galvanized steel wire running tight and taunt between steel posts and rusted barbed wire looped on time-rotted wood posts. Time passed, but life still operated on the sameness of years previous. The cows in the fields stood as they'd done for numberless years, going as obediently to and from their pasture and into the hand-crafted red barns of his grandfather's day as into the manufactured pole barns of today.

Structures that had provided activities to draw neighbors together, such as barn raisings, had been replaced with modern, steel-constructed buildings put up by outsiders. A sense of community had given way to expedience for today's time-constrained landowners. Though Michael appreciated the modernity of his world, he couldn't help but wonder what had been lost.

He rested his head upon the tinted glass and peered ever harder at the passing fields. As far as he could tell, the same crops grew today as they had in his father's and grandfather's days; only the methods had changed. Remove a few modern innovations, and you wouldn't even know into which era you peered.

Had four years really passed? He felt no different now from the day he had departed. These thoughts made him feel weary, weighted by an insightful knowledge he was too young to be troubled with. He brushed his forehead and leaned back into the headrest of the bus seat.

His eyes continued searching. He gazed at the big old farm houses, handed down from generation to generation, and thought of the lives of those who lived the sameness of each farm day, rising early, working in all weather to till the soil. And for what? Surely, they knew for all their hard work they were just going to die as had all their ancestors. What made them keep going, day after day, with this knowledge? The people were, and then they weren't; but the land and the work remained and always would.

Oh God, how this thinking tired him. Where came this slumbering giant that stirred his subconscious, asking if life offered more than what appeared? Thoughts rose, questions formed, but never did the answers come. Only a tired wondering filled the blanks.

Where Goes My Road?

Where goes my road?
My soul knows not.
The way has become obscured,
yet on I walk.

I know, dear Jesus, that You are
with me for I have faith.
But yet my ears hear You not,
and my eyes keep seeking;
for where do I stop?
Which way to turn?

I look and listen.
I read and search.
Do I task in vain?
Am I at my post
and know it not?

If so, then why, I ask,
is my heart so timely restless?

No one seeing the tall, young man of medium build, with the deep brown eyes and close-cropped hair of the military, would ever guess behind a quick smile lay such depth of thought and weight of soul. With a deep sigh and a slight shake of his head, Michael cleared the questing from his conscious mind and stretched his cramped six-foot-three frame in anticipation of release, physically and mentally. His gaze, recaptured by the newly planted fields in eastern Iowa, took him back to happier times of youth.

The tragedy remembered flashed from deep within. Four years earlier, he had boarded a Greyhound bus to run and forget the nightmare of death. One can never outrun it, but run he had as so many do. His mind screamed, *NO!* at the memories flooding to the surface. Again he cried an inward and soft, *Oh God, how had it happened? What…WHAT was it all for?* The thoughts brought unshed tears from the past to his trauma-aged eyes, and he became lost in the surfacing memories life had wickedly dished out.

The passing scene outside blurred, and the droning bus engine covered all noise as the present slipped away.

Saturday had rolled around like so many others before it. Michael had served the five-o'clock Saturday evening mass with his two best buddies, Glen Haloran, a friend since kindergarten, and David Connor, whose friendship had been made in the testing waters of the seventh grade. Both boys had been like brothers to a boy whose closest sibling was eleven years older than he was.

David, the youngest of the trio of friends, had lived the farthest from town on a ramshackle farm that had been in his family since his Irish ancestors had arrived during the potato famine in the late 1800s. They were staunch Catholics with a love for the drink surpassed only by the desire for the procreation of more Connors. David had joined four siblings, and he now had seven below him with another on the way. They were good church-going people, bringing all the family to weekly mass, filling more than an entire pew. It was a prideful moment for a family that had nothing much else to offer. With so many mouths to feed and little energy to spend on so many, discipline was rare if not entirely absent, as was care and maintenance of the aging farm. David had been as unpredictable and untamed as the farm and family he had come from. His shocking red hair and pale blue eyes had drawn almost as much attention as his small wiry stature. He had been a smidge under five feet tall and barely tipped the scales at 110 muscled pounds. Most people who had encountered the young David Connor had seen a youthful boy, not the somewhat loud, unruly teenager, bursting into manhood his two friends had known him to be and providing the ideas and antics that most often got the trio of friends into trouble.

Glen Haloran had been almost the exact opposite of David. He had been a full foot taller than David and of big bone structure, solid, his face angular and long with piercing blue eyes and dark wavy hair. Glen's family were of German/Irish heritage and equally proud of their ancestry. They were strict in adhering to the rules of their faith. Where David's family was chaotic, Glen's was ordered and meticulous. His father ran the family farm with tough discipline and a heavy hand, which Glen had felt many times over his youthful years. Glen had been obedient but hadn't hesitated to join in when fun and adventure had lain before him. The family farming operation ran like clockwork. As his father had preached to Glen many times, it was their livelihood; it kept the bread on the table. Hard work had anchored Glen, giving him little time for goofing off, as his father had termed Glen's free time. Time had purged the elder Haloran of his memory of his own youthful spirit of risk-taking, and he had often wondered how his son, working from sunup until sundown, had had any energy left for the troubles he had managed to get himself into.

Glen had enjoyed David's lively spirit and wild ideas and had admired Michael's innate sense of solitude or seemingly inborn wisdom. The three boys' friendship had been solid and mutual.

They had sat side-by-side in the sanctuary, trying not to fidget while Father Joseph Deeny had finished his no-fuss sermon. One thing all had agreed upon: Father Deeny knew how to deliver a mass, quick and simple, and the parishioners had appreciated his efforts. At most spring masses, Father had always drawn a good crowd of farmers whose time was precious during the planting season.

Michael had sat between David and Glen and had tried to stifle the yawn he had felt rising. A cool spring breeze had blown in the open sanctuary window, carrying Father's closing remarks. "So to love thy neighbor as thyself, one must first love thyself by believing oneself loved by God who created us and gave His only Son to be sacrificed for us, so that we may live eternal life. With that knowledge alone, we should all believe we are truly loved and should show love to one another."

Michael had defeated the yawn, revitalized by the chill and scent-filled spring breeze of newness of life erupting from the grounds around the church and carried in through the window of the stuffy sanctuary. He had smiled at having caught the gist of Father's homily. *Good old Father Deeny, he never failed. He must really know people.* A person had never had to pay real close attention to his homily. Just catching the end of it had always revealed what you were supposed to get from the whole of it. The Monsignor, on the other hand, could put the pope to sleep.

Standing now with the others and fighting the urge to stretch, Michael had recited the Profession of Faith, stealing a glance at David whose eyes had been elsewhere. Before he could follow his friend's gaze to see what had so transfixed him, the business of continuing mass had overtaken his attention.

A full forty minutes later, the boys had horsed around in the darkening vestibule, hanging their serving clothes and combing their hair for their pre-planned Saturday night outing. With thoughts of the unfolding evening, Father Deeny's words had slipped into Michael's subconscious mind for further examination at a later date.

"Hey, David," Michael had chided with a wicked gleam, "what had your eye during the homily?"

"Man, didn't ya see it, Mike? You must either be blind or paying too much attention to the padre. For your sake, let it be the first. Ya ain't got the calling do ya?" David had replied with mock horror.

"I listen out of respect, turd–breath. What were you staring at so intently? Did you have a vision?" Mike had questioned in jest.

"Yeah, a vision, that's what it was, and oh, what a vision. You must be blind. Mrs. O'Toole had on the lowest-cut dress I ever seen in a church." With a gleeful laugh, he had added "Man, is she stacked. Imagine them things without a bra; they must be big as pumpkins!"

"God, David, she must be eighty. You can really disgust me. What a pig! How can you think such things in church? That must be a double sin to even talk about Mrs. O'Toole like that. She's like a grandma to half the town. You need help."

Mike had shaken his head in disbelief. He hadn't shared his own sinful thoughts of the perfect backside of the lovely Jennifer Ryan. She had been a hauntingly beautiful fellow classmate, but he hadn't wanted to take any ribbing on the impossibility of his having a chance with the aforementioned young lady. He had been sure that every living, breathing, sight-blessed male in all of New Haven, Iowa, had wanted to be with the beauty named Jennifer. She had indeed been lovely, but it was her backside that had always caught Michael. At mass, he would scan the crowd to search for her, and if he found her, he would watch as she left the Communion rail, his eyes transfixed on the gentle sway of that most symmetrical roundness.

With a friendly shove and an equally demeaning jab at him, Glen had interrupted David's private vision. "Get off it, Mike. He's just more juiced than us regular guys, all balls and no pecker." Glen had laughed at his own putdown.

"Yeah, you two go ahead. Maybe I'll be the next Hugh Hefner," David had shot back with a glare at Glen.

"Dream on, ya pig."

"Hey guys, want to see if there's any wine left?" David had piped up, his eyes alight with mischief.

"You've got to be kidding," Michael had almost squeaked in shock, "Wouldn't that be like stealing?" In all the time he had known his friend, that had had to be the worst idea he had ever come up with. He had shaken his head and recalled the event that had cemented the boys' friendship in their beginning days of seventh grade when another of David's ideas had landed them in some pretty serious hot water.

David had met Glen and, with Glen in tow along with a couple of rougher second-time seventh graders, had talked Michael into joining them into lifting their basketball coach's small car onto the school sidewalk during fifth period when all the boys should have been in physical education class. David had reasoned with his cohorts that if they were caught, they could simply say they had been exerting their physical limitations against a stationary object all the while trying to determine if the dimensions of the car would cover the sidewalk and if the sidewalk would hold the entire mass of the car if it didn't. Physical education *and* physics at work at the same time. His application of science to the endeavor had drawn in Michael's intellect, and Glen had just liked a little excitement now and then. The two other boys David had brought along were known troublemakers and had looked at the idea as a way of getting even with the coach. Michael still couldn't believe he had been persuaded by David's savvy. The boys had been caught and, even though David had argued that his idea had resulted in exercise for all with some application of physics to boot, they had not been excused from cutting physical education class.

No real harm had been done, but they had been "nailed," and each boy had received punishment in a form fitting to his individual circumstances. All five had been suspended for a week. Glen's father had made sure Glen had had enough extra chores at home so he would have no energy left for "car moving." David had heard lectures long and hard by the school guidance counselor for wasting his inventiveness on stupid pranks when he could have been using his mind to improve his academics to secure a brighter future. And counselor and teachers alike had shamed Michael. They could only shake their heads and with disappointment wonder how someone of his maturity and intellect could have been hoodwinked into such juvenile delinquency. They, likewise, had reminded him of his class standing and promising academic future, that he shouldn't throw it all away running with the likes of David and the seventh-grade repeaters who never had come back to class after their week's suspension. Aided by the monthly junior high paper and its published photo of the car on the sidewalk, word had spread throughout the school. The boy's notoriety and the prank had followed them all their junior high days, where they had remained "those boys."

And now, once again, David had presented his buddies with another ridiculous idea. Michael had added, "It seems it would be against God, too."

"Naw, I'd say it's more like having seconds, and we'd be getting rid of leftovers. Even God would like that," David had replied with an innocent look of a young child eager to please.

"You are in need of serious help," Glen had agreed with Mike's earlier pronouncement but added to alleviate David's astonished look of hurt, "I don't think it would hurt." He had smiled conspiratorially at David. "But only if it's still out; no snooping. It's kinda eerie when no one's here. Come on." The quiet and the ever-growing darkness of the church interior had lent a solemnity Glen had found unsettling.

The boys had gone in for a quick search and had found the wine still out.

"Hey, maybe someone's still here," Glen had said softly, licking lips that had suddenly gone dry. "I mean, they usually don't leave this stuff out, do they?" His voice had risen in pitch, and he had nervously looked over his shoulder.

"Naw, it's Saturday. They're probably leaving it for tomorrow's sunrise mass," David had reassured Glen and then Mike, who had suddenly looked as nervous as Glen.

"Well then, I.Q. man, do you think we should drink it if it's for tomorrow's mass?" Mike had asked with scorn.

"Sure, why not?" David had shrugged indifferently.

"Think, stupid. If it's left for tomorrow, what do you think will happen if it's gone?" Mike had finished with a look of incredulity.

"Well, I didn't say we had to drink it all," David had retorted in defense of his intelligence. "We could each take a drink apiece." His eyes had brightened at the cleverness of his idea.

"Oh, all right." Mike had given in. "You first."

"Hey, maybe we should make the sign of the cross first," Glen had suggested with honest appeal to the holiness of the wine.

David had burst out laughing. "Oh, that's good, Glen. Sure. Why not?" With a big grin, he had made an elaborate sign of the cross and drunk deeply from the decanter.

"Gee whiz, David, I'm glad you said only a drink apiece. You almost emptied half of it." Mike had looked a little shocked at the brazenness of David's actions.

"Well, it's blessed," David had smiled. "It goes down quicker." He had set it down and had turned to Glen, saying, "Have at it."

At the same time but unbeknownst to two of the boys, Father Deeny had walked in. David had gone ashen and then deep red, his eyes as big as saucers. "Father Deeny, I…"

"Oh, come on, David. Cut the crap," Glen had almost snapped. "This place is getting to me enough without you giving me the willies."

"No, guys, I'm serious," David had pleaded in earnest.

"Well, boys," Father Deeny's big baritone voice had boomed, causing both Glen and Mike to visibly jump.

With terror-stricken eyes filling their youthful faces, the bravado gone, Glen and Mike had turned, and with a peaked squeak, had stammered, "F-f-f-ather D-d-deeny."

Father Deeny had presented an apparition all his own. At thirty-eight years of age he had been fit, standing a solid six feet, with broad shoulders and chest. One had had the impression that not too many men could have moved him or would even have attempted to. His dark ebony skin and equally dark brown eyes had given his strength more depth, making him a man to be admired for his internal presence of power. He had smiled while advancing, the whiteness of his teeth lighting his face, and had given the look of a parent, surprised at the audacity of naughty children.

"Yes, it is I, in the flesh. And what have we here?" Father Deeny, in the midst of the parting boys, had shaken his head.

"Ah…we…uhmm…," the boys had stuttered at once.

"Relax, boys," he had said as he had laid a hand on David's shoulder, "Do you think I was never young?" With the softly worded question, he had looked intently, searchingly from one to the next. Shaking his head again, he had sighed. "Some things will never change, I guess. So you decided to have a final nip, hmm?"

The boys had only been able to nod, too full of fear and embarrassment at their actions to speak.

"Well, I can see by your expressions you all know what you were doing was sinful and wrong in so many ways and I'll be hearing your confessions," Father Deeny had stated and looked each boy fully in the face. Then he had added in a tired tone, "So I'll let that lesson sink in all on its own. Let me wipe this off and replenish it for tomorrow." His gaze had gone directly to David. "Then maybe we can all have a little toast to the evening ahead in my home, if you'll oblige me," he had added, peering over his glasses while bending to get the cloth to wipe the flask.

The boys had relaxed a hair and had only nodded, fearing that maybe the worst was yet to come.

Upon refilling and wiping the decanter, Father Deeny had motioned the boys to proceed ahead of him out of the sanctuary. Fear lingering and guilt weighing heavily, the boys had moved slowly and silently, unsure of what was to become of them.

Entering the cool corridor of the rectory, the priest's living quarters, they had looked curiously and hesitantly about, none of them ever having seen the inside of the building. The freshness of the spring day had still filled the air as Father Joe, like most people, had left a window open to enjoy the hints of life bursting forth from the sleep of winter. A few pictures hanging on the walls had given a hominess to the hall, and a floral print rug had softened their steps on the hardwood floor. At the end of the foyer, a doorway's light had shone like a beacon in the dark. The entrance gave way to a small but fairly modern kitchen lit by the last bits of fading sun creeping in the west-facing window.

Father Deeny had motioned the boys to the chairs around the table, and they had quietly slunk into them, not quite believing what was happening, wishing only to become one with the furniture and disappear.

"I presume you are all eighteen?" Father Deeny had questioned in a warmer yet not too familiar tone. They all had nodded dumbly, disbelief in their innocent-looking faces.

Father Deeny had shaken his head with a melancholy smile at their shocked silence and still somewhat fearful faces. With a softer tone and the look of a conspirator, he had set glasses before them, pouring a small amount into each. "Just a touch now, except for you, young David," he had admonished, sending David's face into deeper shades of red, "seeing as you've had such a blessed portion already."

Father Deeny's words had revealed he had been in the sanctuary quite sometime before stepping forth and making his presence known. The fact he had observed David's great blessing over his nip in the sanctuary had made Glen and Mike grin in spite of their fear, relaxing them a little more.

"That's better. I thought maybe someone had died." Father Deeny had looked innocently from boy to boy, with full knowledge of the lameness of the tired old joke. It had removed further the heaviness of fear from the room. "Here, David, how about a soda? Will that do?" Father Deeny had offered.

"Yes, Father, thank you." David had gratefully nodded.

"We all do irresponsible, even stupid, things," he had said and continued, "in our youth, but no great harm's been done, so we can forget it. Here's to one fewer stupid thing you have yet to do before becoming mature young men." Father Deeny had toasted with a friendly yet sarcastic smile in his eyes. "May all your actions be as harmless," he had added as a caring afterthought. His eyes deepening with concern, he had thought, *It's a miracle anyone ever survives the stupidity of youth.*

The boys had relaxed with raised glasses, yet they had only sipped their drinks.

"Father Deeny," Mike had piped up with surprising courage at his own voice, "will you tell our folks?"

"No, Michael, I don't think that's necessary. Do any of you?" Father Deeny had asked.

"No, sir," they had all replied with great relief.

"Well, drink up, and remember sometimes it's better to ask first before you help yourself." With a smile, they all had nodded silently, knowing there was a lesson Father Deeny wanted them to take with them from their little act of irresponsibility.

"I'm here most evenings if any of you need a sounding board." And he had added on a more personal note, "I like company. Feel free to come by sometime. It does old people good to be reminded of being young." He had smiled, knowing that in their youth, they saw his thirty-eight years as quite old.

"Sure, Father Deeny," Mike had said for the group.

"Thanks, Father Deeny," Glen and David had added, being clearly relieved at the reprieve, as they had risen to leave, drinks unfinished.

"You boys have a good time tonight, and don't stretch that indomitable youth too far. Even young people can get hurt." Father Deeny had tried to sound stern though his eyes had belied his imagining their enjoyment in the night ahead.

"Okay, Father Deeny," the boys had chorused. They had extended their hands in gratitude to his generosity and forgiving spirit, and had left as quietly as they had come.

Father Deeny had sighed softly, shaking his head as the door had softly closed upon their forms, retreating into the quickly darkening twilight. Quietly, as someone used to conversing to himself, he had said, "Good boys, God be with them." In the quiet of approaching evening, he had raised his half-empty glass and finished his drink. Slowly rising, he had pushed away the feelings of loneliness that had reached from within the emptiness of the silent and dim interior. It had been his home since he had come to this small community fresh from the seminary, filled then with the eagerness of servitude to his Church. As he had set his glass on the sideboard, he had reached for the wall phone to dial the Ryan family to see if they had planned on attending the monthly bingo game. He hadn't wanted to sit alone the rest of the evening.

The boys had walked in silence from the rectory to the back of the church where Glen had parked his car.

"Whew!" Mike had expelled.

"Did you ever guess?" Glen had added in awe. "I mean, I never thought of Father Deeny as anything but…you know…a priest. He almost… I always respected him and that but…"

"He almost seemed human," David had added in an equally awed tone. "Kinda gives ya the creeps. I thought they were, ya know,…well…I dunno.. I just never thought I'd sit at a kitchen table and toast with a priest." He had let loose a small nervous laugh, tossing off tension as the evening's events had caught up with him. To lighten the mood, he had weakly added, "He actually has a kitchen and a table."

His attempt had failed, and Glen had added quietly, "Do ya suppose it means anything?"

Mike, beginning to rouse to normalcy, had shaken his head and with forced lightness had asserted, "Naw, Father Deeny is just one in a million, a human priest." And he had laughed uncomfortably.

"Yeah, I'll agree with that." David had nodded quickly, and dispensing with any further contemplation, had gently shoved Glen, asking, "Ya driving this heap or pushing it?" Then, he had reminded his pal, "The night's young, and chores are calling."

"Yeah, we better get going. Dad'll be fit to beat me if I ain't home soon," Glen had said, surfacing back to the present and shaking off any premonitions the events might have stirred within him.

"Okay, I'll see you guys at nine at the bowling alley," Mike had replied, also returning to normal. "Just don't make any side trips on the way back to town without me. Last time I waited like a stooge till 9:30!"

"Quit your nagging, prissy boy. We showed," David had shot back. "This time we'll take your sorry ass with us."

"You better. I'm the brains of the bunch, remember," Mike had goaded.

Glen and David had gotten into the car, flashed Mike a high five, and driven off to Glen's father's farm to help with evening milking, or what was left of it.

Father Deeny had sat in the somewhat dilapidated rented bingo hall and had looked out the huge plate glass window at the approaching families. He had always enjoyed people-watching, but these people were his family—or the majority of them were for, though it was a church-sponsored game, anyone of any faith could play. He had smiled inwardly as regular parishioners had gathered in the slowly filling parking lot, greeting each other with hugs and laughs, the children in tow breaking away to join up with friends. Any other night, he would have greeted the arrivals in the parking lot, too. But tonight he had chosen to take his regular seat and watch for his usual bingo partners to arrive, the evening's earlier events still heavy in his subconscious. To distract himself, he had noted how most of the town had dressed comfortably, the men in overalls or jeans with pressed cotton shirts and the majority of the women in homemade dresses. Their hands full, they had carried baked goods from home or surplus homegrown produce to share with elderly patrons who had retired into the town and no longer gardened or had someone to bake for them.

A fairly regular crowd had played on bingo nights, the first Saturday of the month, as the town hadn't much to offer in the way of affordable entertainment, and the Church had used all profits to help the less fortunate in the community, faith not considered. Cards had cost a nickel, and the refreshments had been almost given away as the donors had brought them primarily to share among each other. People had come to socialize and had played the game as an afterthought, something to keep their hands busy while the communication had flowed. Many elderly and quite a good showing of middle-aged parishioners had often attended to share stories or events that had occurred since the last game. The children tagging along had aged between six and fourteen, old enough to have carefully watched the cards of the talking adults, the younger ones feeling ever so important when they found a number before the card-holder, sometimes even given the privilege of marking the card. The older youths, too young to be out without supervision, had simply hung around for something to do. They had sat in their own little groups, talking of events they had been sure their parents were clueless about, sometimes buying cards among them "just for the fun of it," to see if they could win. The prizes had been modest, but the companionship priceless.

Small farm communities tended to mind each other's business. Families, once settled and established, grew close over time. Everyone in the town commonly knew the entire family history of neighbors and most of the community's founding families. What would appear to be nosiness and gossipy busybody behavior to outsiders was just a larger form of family care for the entirety of the community. Through marriages across families over the years and school-aged friendships surviving down through the generations, bonds between members were loose to allow growth and yet strong to ensure survivability of the whole in times of tragedy or misfortune. The age-old saying, "strength in numbers," played true in what "city folks" might label quaint or passé practices.

The building itself was an interesting mix of the town's existence. It sat in the center of the town and primarily held meetings of the local chapter of the Veterans of Foreign Wars, or VFW. It had originated with the town and still displayed the Romanesque-style door from the original entrance. Peering at the ancient looking stone building from across the street, one would see the heavily tree-shaded, aging, arched entry with its weathered wooden door and wonder what was within.

When the facility had been remodeled in the early sixties, the local patrons had argued with the designing architect to leave the front half of the building as it was, voting to shore up any decaying parts of the stone and timber structure from within to keep as much of the original appearance as possible. A heated battle had ensued, and in the end out of respect for the sacrifices given by the men for whom the structure had been built, the architect had left the front half of the building intact, inspecting and repairing decay from within. The back entrance to the building was now the main entrance used by the majority of the community, in part due to the proximity of the new parking lot that had been constructed along with the remodel. The interior was paneled in the style of the sixties, and the floor had an ocean blue carpet that had, over twenty years, worn quite thin in the more heavily trafficked spots. A little dust always covered the florescent ceiling lights. Although the funds had been plentiful during the remodel, it was hard to keep housekeeping paid, and volunteers filled in when funding was scarce. They did their best to come and care for the now aging facility, but during the planting and harvesting seasons, the dust was always a little more apparent, adding the atmosphere of home to the large gathering room.

A loud commotion had drawn the good priest's attention back to the gathering outside in the parking lot. An aging station wagon had arrived, filled to the brim with a majority of the Connor clan, which at last count had numbered…well…. Father Deeny had smiled as he had tried to think just how many Connors there were at present. They certainly had followed the faith in the sex-for-procreation teaching. Yes, he had believed they numbered either eleven or twelve, and the missus was expecting in a couple of months with either number twelve or thirteen. Good gracious, the number had caught him by surprise. Were there really that many of them?

He had watched in fascination as the car's contents had emptied and relieved the pressure from within. Out of the back seat had popped a girl of maybe twelve. Following closely on her heels, two smaller youths, a boy and another girl, who appeared to be between four and seven had tumbled forth. Then a preteen boy between ten and thirteen, who was carrying a toddler of about two or three, had come running from around the rear of the car. He had seemed overly eager to deposit his small person into the arms his older sister. The two smaller children had made an attempt to join friends across the way, and the preteen boy with lightning speed had discharged his load and made off after the two escaping youths. These two, possibly with prior experience from similar attempts, had shrieked in delight at being pursued. Their talk had been loud, and their shrieks had filled the parking lot as the children had rushed to the sanctuary of their friends. These small ones, seeing the alleged frightful fear of their approaching friends, had taken off for the far reaches of the parking lot, which caused more of a ruckus as parents had called to the growing number of fleeing youths to come back. This unloading and chase scene had happened most every bingo game, and how they had ever managed to get the children rounded up and settled down had always amazed Father Deeny.

His glance had then gone to the adult Connors as they had slowly exited out of the front seat of the old vehicle. They had moved slowly, not with age but with no outward cares. Life was to be lived for what it was, take it or leave it. They had never seemed bothered by what they didn't have or what they may have needed. Their children were born, and they, too, lived. Discipline required effort, and they hadn't believed too much in that either. It had always appeared to the good father that some of the older children had given more parenting than the two who had brought the whole clan into existence. They had been a happy bunch despite their lack of motivation or funding. Their clothes had been mostly clean but usually rumpled and had had noticeable wear from being passed from one growing sibling to the next. But they had been a lively group, with the older ones looking after the younger ones. Their arrival had always brought kids running from all directions for then the fun would begin. With ten or eleven more to play with, a party had begun, and no one had been left without a playmate.

With his attention focused on the developing scene in the parking lot, Father Deeny had failed to notice his companions' arrival. After they had quietly taken their usual seats, Hazel O'Meary had broken into his thoughts, gently intoning at his side, "They always do grab one's attention with their arrival, don't they," more a statement than a question.

"Oh, pardon me, Hazel." Father Deeny had apologized for his inattentiveness as he had turned his attention to Hazel, who had been, at his guess, just a few years under sixty and had been widowed early in life. Of quick humor, she had been loved and sought out by all in the town she had lived in her entire life. Many who had looked for her company had often found their spirits lifted and their outlook brighter after having spent time in her presence. Her blue eyes had always been lit with laughter, and her stylishly coiffed blue-gray hair had framed a complexion kept flawless from a lifetime of protection from the sun. Many of the younger generation had considered her the town's grandmother for she had been involved in many civic and social gatherings. Tonight she had brought along her teenage niece, Jennifer Ryan, and her seventy-five-year-old cousin, visiting from a nearby city, Claudia Chiffon. They had made quite an entertaining trio. Hazel was a former one-room schoolteacher and a highly respected member of the Ladies of St. Mary's. She was so well liked that Father Deeny, alone, knew of her personal loneliness. He had learned her story shortly after he had joined the parish. As the only other priest in the parish, he had found ready acceptance into his new community. He had felt as if he had been born and raised there his whole life. The tragedy of her story had moved him, and he had often wondered if she wouldn't have been happier if she'd given in and married the grocer who'd courted her so many years ago after her husband had passed. *Then, too,* he had mused, *she lives with her brother and had an excuse not to accept the marriage proposal.* Alas, Catholics of her upbringing often felt it sinful to marry out of the faith, and poor Charles was Protestant. The crosses people chose to put upon themselves!

"Do you think this will be their last, Father? That poor woman," Hazel had said with great compassion and concern. "She certainly has her hands full, and I hear she is possibly carrying twins."

Jennifer, across from her aunt, had exclaimed, "Twins, oh how exciting! I'll have to ask Beth. Surely she would know." Beth had been the Connor below David in the family line-up, and Jennifer had shared a class with her in school.

"I don't know, Jenny," Hazel had cautioned, "she might be embarrassed. You know how you kids are, and you yourself have told me their family takes a lot of ribbing for their size."

"You're right, Aunt Hazel. I probably shouldn't. But I think that would be so neat—twins. It would be so much fun, even for them," Jennifer, an only child, had added with a small note of envy.

Hazel and Jennifer had been very close due to Jennifer's own family circumstances, and she had shared much of her life with her aunt. Upon Jennifer's birth, her mother had taken seriously ill, and Hazel, who had recently lost her husband to illness and had had to sell their farm to pay medical bills, had moved in to help with the care of her brother's wife and his new daughter. After seven months of Hazel's care, Mae had recovered, and Hazel's position in the family had been made permanent.

"Twins! Good gracious, are you sure, Hazel?" The news had caught Father Deeny off-guard. He had told himself he would have to ask after Mrs. Connor's health; she hadn't been young, and all in town had known Mr. Connor, though a family man, hadn't contributed much to the family's support. They had very often been recipients of the bingo receipts, and twins would certainly need more care than one addition.

At the father's great surprise, Hazel had been a little abashed, feeling more like a gossip than the concerned person she felt herself to be. "Well, I'm not for certain, but Mrs. Connor herself told her sister she felt bigger this time round and thought she might be carrying more than one, or at least she said she hoped it was two rather than one for as big as she felt. They haven't much for medical, and they don't know for sure."

Wondering privately who in town could possibly help determine the truth in her condition, Father Deeny had replied to Hazel, "We shall have to see if the Ladies of St. Mary's might say a rosary for Mrs. Connor; don't you think, Hazel?"

"What a wonderful idea, Father. I'm just ashamed I didn't think of it myself. I'll approach the ladies at Monday night's rosary. I feel better for her already. God bless you, Father." She had clutched his arm with a thankful squeeze.

After silently listening to the exchange, Hazel's cousin had interjected, "I think it's a shame, a shame, I tell you. Those people are like rabbits, and poor as church mice. If you ask me, people shouldn't have more children than they can afford to properly dress and care for." She had continued with much disdain, "They should be made to stop their...." She had colored deeply when she had realized what she had needed to complete her sentence and had finished in frustration, saying, "They should just stop." Her lips had pinched the words out of her selfish soul, and she had sat with her judgment, waiting for their approval of her pronouncement.

Father Deeny had looked sadly and quietly at Claudia and then had directed his attention to Jennifer. "You'll remember, too, Jennifer, to be there for Beth. She has so much responsibility for one so young."

"Yes, Father Deeny," Jennifer had assured him, "Beth and I have Home Economics II this semester. She and I are lab partners. I'll be there for her." She had often thought of Beth as a younger sister, or, more, Jennifer had wished she had had a younger sister.

Jennifer was Hazel's only niece. She had just turned eighteen some months back, and she had been a lovely young girl, kept on a tight leash by her almost militantly religious father, Shaun. Father Deeny had felt almost positive the man had been a hell raiser in his younger days, and that had explained his strict over-protectiveness. A Midwestern beauty, she had been almost five feet eight, tall for a young girl, with a small frame and bountiful, thick, wavy blond tresses that had fallen just below her shoulders. Jennifer's clear hazel eyes had been filled with youthful innocence and trust, and she had been uncommonly modest for someone so lovely. Not to be aware of her own good looks had made her even more attractive. Her natural God-given beauty had attracted the attention of passers-by, but the beauty within that had reflected outward had made her even more stunning. She had been a gift from heaven; one could hardly blame her father for having been so protective.

As the shuffling, noisy clan had entered the bingo hall, Father Deeny had pondered on Claudia's harsh words and the person from whom they had come. She had been a woman of another culture, prim and starch, almost snobbish. She had seemed to visit her cousin Hazel to reaffirm her own belief in her self-appointed station. Born into wealth and fairly intelligent, she had made a point of informing those she met she had gone to college when most women were barely educated. The inherited wealth combined with her education had inclined her to the opinion of self that she was better than most. This self-appointed "fact," when announced, had been followed with her demand for instant respect and adulation from all she encountered. Had she known her actions had the entirely opposite effect on those around her, one could only hope, she wouldn't have pushed her self-importance. Very few people had kept company with her for any length of time, and she had rarely been asked back after a first visit. Why—or how—Hazel had put up with such callous rudeness had been a miracle. It had truly revealed Hazel's own good heart. Lord bless the dear.

"The first number for the night's games is O-67, O-67." The bingo caller had broken into Father Deeny's thoughts, and his night had begun.

✳

"Michael, is that you?" a voice from somewhere in the house had called out. "I wish you wouldn't let the door slam like that; you'll knock it off its hinges," had followed without waiting for a reply to the question.

"Yes, Mom, it's me. Sorry about the door!" His voice had become lost as he had headed into the hall closet in search of his bowling ball.

"There you are, dear," Mrs. Calhoun's words had become clearer as she had entered the front hall from the living room. Mrs. Calhoun was a small woman in structure but considered tall for her time. At nearly five feet seven, she had often towered above her peers. She may have been fifty-eight years old, but the liveliness in her fading brown eyes had often belied the harshness life had dealt her. Her hair once brown was generously sprinkled with white as she had liked to correct those who termed it gray. She had had a quick wit and had often used it to Michael's delight. It had helped them through his turbulent teens.

"How was mass? Did Glen and David serve with you? Was there a good crowd?" She had directed her queries to Michael's crouching form in the closet.

"Huh, Mom, where's my bowling ball?" Michael, sitting on his haunches, had addressed the interior of the closet with a perplexed frown.

"I put it in the garage now that the weather's warmer. It takes up so much floor space I can't get my sweeper out," Mrs. Calhoun had replied to her son's seated form, not minding that her questions had gone unanswered. They had developed an odd form of communication at the start of Michael's teenage years: She would express her concern for his comings and goings with unlimited questions, and he would have no pressure for giving exacting answers. Michael, aware of his mother's need to know, had given out answers only to the most important ones, reserving the need for independence on matters he felt too personal for mothers. To an outsider, their "exchange" would have appeared to be one she was carrying on with herself.

"The family's coming over for Sunday dinner. You won't be out late, will you? The last time you boys seemed to get home pretty late, I recall." She had finished her statement as she had headed back down the hall to the kitchen from where she had come.

"I won't stay out late tonight. Glen and David have to be home to help in the fields tomorrow." Muttering, he had said to himself, *Sure wish I had something lined up for tomorrow.* He had headed into the kitchen and had snatched a bite of food from the table.

He was immediately rewarded with a resounding *slap!* "Michael! Wash up first before you grab!" she had reprimanded him.

"Mom, I just came from church, and I served!" he had exclaimed in complete exasperation. "Doesn't that count for something?"

"Mass was over at six, and it's almost seven," his mother had stated matter-of-factly. "There's a lot of space between here and the church." She had smiled sweetly and headed him into the washroom just off the kitchen.

"Mothers!" he had groaned and complied.

"Sons!" she had retorted to the closing door.

In the small bathroom, Michael Calhoun had contemplated his empty Sunday with mild despair. He had lived alone with his mother, the youngest of eight children. His father had been a farmer and had died in a farming accident when Michael, a late-in-life surprise, had been only two. Upon his father's untimely death, his mother had given the family farm to his oldest brother, Joe, who had already married and had been living and farming elsewhere. In return, Joe, who was now forty, had purchased his mother a house on the outskirts of town with two acres of land, enough to have a good-sized garden, a few chickens, and a couple of fruit trees. But in a farming community, those responsibilities had hardly qualified him as a farmer. Heck, he hadn't even wanted to be a farmer anyway. Who wanted to get up at five in the morning everyday of his entire life to milk and care for cows? He had spent a week one summer with Glen, and though he didn't really mind getting up just before the sun peeked over the horizon, being in the barn with the cows and cleaning up after they had been milked hadn't appealed to him at all. It had amazed him his friend, who at the time had been twelve, hadn't seemed to mind this daily chore. Ugh! He had wanted to fit in with his friends, and yet he had no desire to share their kind of work for the rest of his life. What had he been complaining about then? He had splashed some cold water in his face and had sighed to himself, *Sometimes life just plain sucks.*

"Michael, supper's getting cold. You sleeping in there?" His mother had begun to sound anxious. "Michael?"

He had opened the door to his mother's face, startling her, "Goodness, Michael."

"Sorry, Mom. Just daydreaming."

"Scared me half to death," she had said, calming herself. "Let's eat. You okay, son?" his mother had asked with true concern tingeing her voice, her brow puckering.

"Yeah, Mom. Just preoccupied," Michael had sighed.

Michael and his mother had sat down and bowed their heads to say grace. With the blessing completed, Michael's mother had proceeded to dish up his supper as if he'd been the first in a long line of eaters. Old habits die hard, and he'd long ago stopped trying to serve himself his food.

"Hey, Mom, not too much tonight. I'm not that hungry." Michael had looked for a noncommittal reply, hoping his mother wouldn't become overly anxious. The scene at Father Deeny's had suddenly come sneaking back and was weighing in his subconscious. His stomach felt heavy.

"Are you planning on going out tonight?" his mother had asked, with pointed sarcasm and a touch of a smile in her eye.

"Yeah, David and Glen are meeting me at the bowling alley again." Michael had tried to sound disinterested in his own planned evening to discourage a barrage of parental questions he didn't have the energy or patience to answer.

"Well, if you're going out, you need something to run on." With a tone a little more stern and a look of "I'm still your mother," Mrs. Calhoun had firmly set his plate before him.

"It looks good, Mom," Michael had responded, and seeing no way out, he had dug in, eating with more gusto than he had felt. *Moms, who can figure them?*

Mrs. Calhoun had eaten in silence, not bothering to question Michael on the mass. He had seemed all tied up in his own thoughts. *So much like his father, God rest his soul.* And bless her; she'd done her best to raise him. Gracious, when Patrick had been killed in the tractor accident in '61, she had wanted to die at his side. The memory still had brought tears to her eyes if she thought too hard on him being gone. She had missed him with a depth that would catch her in the oddest moments. At the time of his death, with Michael being two, she couldn't have given up. Her little son had needed her, and Patrick wouldn't have wanted her to give up. She had vowed the day she buried him she would never stop loving him, but she would go on, and strongly. So she had, but a little of her laughter and passion had died with the death of Patrick. She had given the farm to Joseph with the excuse it had been too much for her. The truth was she couldn't bear to be in the house with all those memories of Patrick. Selling hadn't been an option either. To sell the farm would have been like selling a piece of herself. She had felt she had done the next best thing by giving it to Joe. She had gone freely to the farm and enjoyed the memories at her choosing. The purchase of the house with a few acres, little Michael, and the activities of the town had kept her busy that first year after Patrick's death, and she had survived. The sound of Michael's chair brought her thoughts to the present. She had glanced at Michael who had pushed back, making room for the last couple of bites from his plate. She had smiled at him. She'd done her best; she'd hoped it was enough.

"Would you like a piece of rhubarb pie, dear?"

"Is it fresh?"

"What, is my freezer rhubarb not good enough anymore?"

"Okay, but just a little piece. I feel my jeans are getting tight."

"Nonsense. The Calhoun's are big men; you've still got some growing to do."

At six feet even, Michael had rather doubted he would grow anymore, but who had he been to argue with his mother? Look how he'd eaten his supper. Mrs. Calhoun had cleared their plates as Michael had finished off his pie. "What are you doing tonight, Mom?" Michael had asked.

"I think I'm going to curl up with a good book and read until the wee hours of the morning when you come dragging in," she had said and shot him a knowing look.

"Mom! I only got in late that one night!" had Michael emphasized.

"Yes, and I'll remind you till you're my age to prevent another recurrence." His mother had smiled sweetly.

"Do you want some help with the dishes?"

"No, go ahead. I've got the whole night—till the wee hours of the morning," she had added in final jest.

"You're awful, Mom, just awful." Michael had kissed her cheek. "Thanks. I'll do them tomorrow night."

"Be safe, and take a jacket."

"Okay, 'night." And his mother had smiled at the sound of the front door closing without a slam.

※

At nine o'clock, Hazel had yawned. The VFW hall had grown warm over the past two hours, and she had felt sleepy. *Must be due to the garden work this afternoon*, she had thought.

Jennifer, sitting across from her aunt and beside Ms. Chiffon, had noticed her aunt's zeal had begun to dissipate around eight. Her yawns had started at eight thirty, and now Aunt Hazel looked positively sleepy. She had felt a small laugh rise at the sight of her favorite aunt but had stifled it so as not to embarrass her. The bingo games would continue until ten. She had nudged her aunt's foot under the table and caught her sleepy gaze with her own questioning one. They had spent so much time in each other's company they sometimes needed no words to communicate.

Jennifer had known Aunt Hazel forever. The timing of Jennifer's birth and Hazel's need for a home couldn't have been better planned. Hazel's brother, Shaun, Jennifer's dad, had offered his oldest sister a room, and she had become a permanent part of the family when Jennifer's mother had had a long and slow recovery after almost losing her life with the birth of Jennifer. She had loved her aunt dearly. She had been so soft compared to her father with his strict ways. Aunt Hazel's room had been her refuge, and for this reason she had taken special interest in her aging aunt's health. Jennifer had known her mother had felt pity for her under her husband's strictness, but she had felt helpless to deflect it lest he redirect it towards her or become even more controlling of Jennifer in retaliation. Keeping the home life pleasant had been Jennifer's mother's goal, and Aunt Hazel had had a big part in keeping things smooth. *What would they do without Aunt Hazel?* Jennifer had shivered at the thought.

Hazel O'Meary had felt the nudge and caught Jenny's questioning look. *Bless you, dear girl, yes,* she briefly, almost imperceptibly had nodded, *I am tired.*

Jennifer had cleared her throat, "Excuse me, Father Deeny?"

"Yes, Jennifer?"

"Do you mind if you drive us home now? I'm feeling a little tired." She had ended softly with a practiced sigh of fatigue.

"Oh, forgive me. Guess I was caught up in the game." He had smiled warmly. "Ms. Chiffon, are you ready, too?"

"Well, even if I'm not, I'll not stay among strangers alone," she had retorted sharply and strongly for the slight woman she had appeared to be.

"Ladies." Father Deeny had stood and helped Hazel to her feet. As Hazel had risen stiffly on Father's arm, he had commented with genuine concern, "Someone did a little too much gardening today, huh, Hazel?"

"Oh, yes, I guess I may have overdone it a bit today." Hazel had tried not to sound too tired and pained. "This arthritis is finally getting to me."

"Catches most of us sooner or later," Father Deeny had sympathized.

"That it does," she had replied wearily.

Once in the car, Father Deeny had turned on the heater, and Hazel had visibly relaxed into the cushioned vehicle, enjoying the warmth as it had soothed her aching back muscles. "Oh, but you've got a good heater, Father Deeny. Who works on your car?"

As Father had maneuvered out of the parking lot, he had told of the new mechanic from Minneapolis who was just opening shop in the neighboring college town a ways down the road. "He has high recommendations and seems like an honest man, though he's Protestant." He had shot a quick wink at Hazel, who had given him a friendly glare back at the old jest. "The heater's worked like a charm all winter. Jenny, you'll have to remember to tell your dad the next time his Olds is acting up."

"Yes, Father Deeny," had come Jenny's reply from the back seat.

"Spring is such a wonderful time of the year with everything bursting with life," Father Deeny had remarked as they had headed out of town to the Ryan farm. Jenny's mother had driven Jenny, Hazel, and Ms. Chiffon in for the bingo game with the usual understanding Father Deeny would bring them all home. Her mother had been a nurse's aide at the local hospital and had been working the night shift. She had worked only part-time and had chosen the weekend shift to give a bit of freedom and family time to the younger girls who she worked with. The arrangement with Father Deeny had become a fairly regular routine.

Father Deeny had enjoyed the Ryans' company on these occasions and had welcomed the opportunity to lend a little male laughter in a household where the only male presence had been so domineering. Jenny's dad had seemed so tied to his work that he had seldom seemed to get any pleasure out of life. Father had sighed. *Some people truly work themselves to death. What happens that they acquire such tunnel vision?*

"It all smells dank to me, and the ground is just mushy," Ms. Chiffon had interjected in a clipped and crisp tone from the back seat.

The lights of the town had disappeared as they had rounded the curve in the road leading out to the Ryan farm. Ms. Chiffon's remark had hung in the air, no one responding, and the silence had been oppressive.

Father had remained quiet, respecting Hazel's tiredness and not wanting to encourage further comments from the pinched Ms. Chiffon in the back seat.

The Ryan farm was only ten miles out, but it lay at the start of the steep bluffs that ran along the way to the river some ways further. The rise and fall of the hills and sharp curves had taken Father's concentration, as an occasional deer had been known to dart into the road to surprise the unwary driver.

Glen and David had finished milking and had downed the supper Mrs. Haloran had left warming for them as quickly as manners had permitted. With the kitchen clock staring at them from the wall, loudly ticking away the missed minutes of their night like sand leaving an hour glass, both boys had rushed upstairs to clean up so they could head into town for the evening ahead.

"Glen!" Mrs. Haloran had hollered up the stairwell.

"Yuh, Mmm," Glen had muffled back as he had pushed his head through his shirt.

"Don't leave without speaking to me first!" his mother had called back.

"Okay, we won't!" Glen had shouted down through the first floor as he had bent to pull on his sneakers. "Hope it's nothing long-winded," Glen had commented to his shoestrings.

"Well, it's eight forty-five. Cut the talk and we'll make the bowling alley by nine-fifteen, and ol' Mike shouldn't whine too loud," David had suggested.

Both boys had grabbed jackets from off Glen's bed and had hurried out the room he had shared with his younger brother. They had tromped down the stairs, bringing Mary Haloran out of the living room to her fourth child. Shaking her head at all the commotion, she had looked at dark-haired, blue-eyed Glen with a mix of love and irritation at the racket in his rush to leave. It had seemed he was always in a rush those days.

"Where's the fire, young man?" she had intoned a little more fiercely than she had intended, mildly upset that her son never seemed to be home lately.

"We're ready to go, Mom," Glen had responded with light irritation. *Surely she knows it's Saturday, the one day I'm allowed any time to do to what I want.* "What did you want to see me about?" Glen had asked a little more respectfully, not wanting to start a scene.

Resisting the urge to get into it with her son, Mary had lightened her tone and smiled as she had handed him some money. "Here's some extra money to put gas in the car. No, it's not for you," she had lightly laughed as his eyes had lit up with surprise. "Your dad and brothers are going fishing early in the morning, before field work. He said for you to gas it up before you head home so he has a full tank. You know how he hates it to drop below half a tank." His mother had looked pointedly stern but had smiled about her husband's little quirk.

"Sure, Mom. David'll remind me. Won't you, David?" Glen had nudged David in the side and had reassured his mother that, with two of them to rely on, her request would be fulfilled.

"Just don't forget," his mother had said a little more sternly, thinking back to all the times Glen had forgotten and been punished.

David had chimed in, "I'll remind him, Mrs. Haloran." And for emphasis, David had jumped up and grabbed Glen around the neck, knuckling his head.

"Okay, okay." Mrs. Haloran had nodded, satisfied the message wouldn't be forgotten and that the car would be sufficiently gassed to please her husband. "Be home by one, Glen," Mrs. Haloran had added firmly and then with more concern, "and drive safely."

"I will. Love you, Mom. 'Night." Glen had kissed her cheek and headed out the door.

She had snuck in a quick kiss on his cheek and an "I love you, too" as the screen door had banged and David had echoed through the screen, "Goodnight, Mrs. Haloran. Thanks for supper."

"Goodnight, David. Tell your family hello." With a wave, she had shut the front door to the chilling spring night air and had headed into the kitchen.

"Let the night begin," David had almost squealed with anticipation as the boys had settled in the car. "The night is young, and it's ours…and look what I've got." He had faded into the back seat as he had reached behind him.

"What have you got now, slime ball?" Glen had asked, accelerating down the road to town, expecting anything and being surprised at nothing. David had been the wild one of the three of them, but he had been true, and that's what had mattered.

"Okay, so what's your surprise?" Glen had repeated.

"Hold on!" David had strained. "Ah, here we are. One for you," he had said as he had shoved something hard and cold into Glen's side, "and one for me." He had popped his tab to drink deeply. "Now, that's refreshing." David had belched his satisfaction.

"Beer! Come on, David. We're smarter than that," Glen had softly retorted and continued, "Where did you get it? It's cold. Did you take it from the fridge? Hey, if my old man notices it, we'll be doing chores till we're bald," Glen had responded in disgust.

"Relax. I took it from the back. No one's gonna notice, asshole. Drink up. Who's out here to catch us?" David had smarted back. "Just us—me, you, and the cows, and they don't give a shit. I'll have yours if you won't," David had offered more hospitably.

"Naw, one ain't going to hurt, but put your window down. If we see a car, we'll pitch 'em out your window."

Glen had popped the tab and lifted the can to get his first swallow when headlights had appeared over the top of the hill directly in his lane. With one hand on the wheel, Glen had instinctively reacted and sharply turned the wheel to the right, dropping off the asphalt and onto the shoulder, soft under the thawing of spring. It had given under the weight of the car, sending it veering out of control over the edge. The car had skidded down the steep embankment into a stand of trees, sending the two unbuckled boys through the windshield and bringing a sudden end to this Saturday evening and all to come. The blare of the horn had harshly penetrated the otherwise silent night, and a trickle had begun to leak from a rupture in the car's gas tank.

At the top of the hill, a shaken Father Deeny had slowly pulled his car back to his side of the road and had brought it to a stop. Surely what had appeared to have happened hadn't. The deer had appeared from nowhere, and he hadn't seen the oncoming car, or he never would have crossed into the other lane to avoid hitting the animal. *What... how could...what...happened?* His mind had been all a-tumble; the events all had mashed together and hadn't made sense. He thought he had heard screams, but all was quiet now, except for the awful, annoying blare of a horn. He had looked at Hazel to see if she was still there. Maybe it had been a dream—*Please, let it be a dream*—but she had looked back at him with a deathly pale face and eyes that spoke of shock and the truth he had been afraid to admit.

From the back seat, Jenny's shaky voice had finally sliced the silence. "What happened to the other car?" She had looked behind them and seen only blackness. "I don't see anything."

Father Deeny had slumped at Jennifer's words. It had happened; there had been another car. "It's not there?" Father Deeny had asked, turning to look behind them on the opposite side of the road, then checking his rear view mirror for taillights in the dark. He had seen nothing.

"You don't think it ran off the road, do you?" Jenny had asked, her voice rising a notch with sickening panic.

"I'll go check," Father Deeny had said, putting on his emergency flashers and moving a safer distance off on his side of the road.

"Can I come?" Jenny had asked.

"No, you better stay here with your aunt," he had said with more calmness than he had felt. Quietly to himself, he had pleaded, *Oh, dear God, please let there be no car down there,* as he had crossed the road and walked back the way they had come. With each step forward, he had heard the sound of a blaring car horn more distinctly.

Father Deeny had dreaded the inevitable, what the blaring horn must surely reveal. Yet, he could not go back until he had gone the complete distance. He had wished with all his heart that the darkness before him would be all that lay beyond. And then as he had rounded the curve into the crest of the hill, he had spotted the illumination in the night's blackness.

Oh, dear sweet Jesus, had risen within, and an anguished cry had escaped without. Father Deeny had started to run, crying to the heavens, "Please, let whoever it is be okay! Please, dear Lord, please!" He had prayed in earnest into the night air, pleading and begging. Anxiety and fear had come to him in waves at what he had seen down a ways off the road's steep embankment. What could he do to help? He had stepped as far to the edge of the road as he had dared so as not to lose his footing in the soft spring soil. A sick feeling had risen in his stomach, overcoming him with weakness. He had not been able to see anything below into the darkness but the illumination of car lights in a stand of trees. His fear and anxiety had become tangible panic. "Please, dear Father, let it be just one," he had wailed, knowing someone might be in need of help and realizing he couldn't get to them. He had let out a small cry, followed in frustration with a soft, "Damnation!" His panic had risen further with the sickening truth that he could do nothing but leave the scene to go for help.

"Father Deeny, what is it? Are you okay?" Jenny had asked as he had approached the car at a run, breathless and shaken.

"Jenny, move over. Hurry. We must go for help." He had gasped out the words, pushing Jenny over, as she had gotten out and taken the driver's seat to move the car should there be a need. "I don't know who's hurt or if anyone is. I couldn't see anything but the car's lights. Oh, God, please help them!" Father Deeny had begged in desperation. His eyes had showed shock with his discovery heaped on helplessness in abandoning someone in need of help. Jenny had quietly started to cry at Father Deeny's distraught state.

Despite his call to hurry, Father Deeny, fearing another mishap, had driven cautiously off down the road in search of the nearest farm. No voices so much as whispered from within the car, and faces showed only shock.

Five miles and an eternity down the road, lights had appeared, and Father Deeny had breathed relief. Help could be summoned at last. *Please, dear God, let it not be too late,* Jenny and Hazel had both prayed.

Knocking on the door, Father Deeny had felt ill. The hardness of the door's wood had verified that all had not been a horrible dream. He had hollered at the door in urgency, setting off a dog who had rushed the door with vicious barks as he had impatiently pleaded, "Help, please, there's been an accident. We need help!" He had hated that someone else would also have their pleasant night forever changed. *Oh, God, please let someone answer.*

"Coming!" had sounded from within. The dog had been pulled away from the door with, "Shhh! Lady, good girl, shhh." As the door had opened, the porch light had hit Father like a spotlight.

"Father Deeny." A familiar voice had come from out of the light. "What is it? Did you say there's been an accident? Are you okay? You don't look well. Are you hurt?"

Falling a little forward, Father Deeny had shaken his head. "No, I need to use your phone." And he had repeated again, "There's been an accident." Strong hands had supported Father Deeny and led him into the house and quickly to the phone in the kitchen. Mrs. Haloran, who had come down from upstairs and followed at a close distance, had addressed her husband's back, "Is anyone with you?"

"Ah, Mr. Haloran, Mrs. Haloran, it's you. The light, it blinded me." An anguished look and then disbelieving words had tumbled out, "What a night it's turned out to be." Father had spoken with shocked disbelief as he had dialed the number to the local sheriff.

"Are you alone, Father?" Mrs. Haloran had asked again out of concern.

"Oh, no, dear me, Mrs. Hazel O'Meary and… Hello. Is the sheriff there?… Yes, there's been an accident." He had exhaled the words into the receiver.

Mrs. Haloran had headed out of the house as she put on her sweater to offer refuge to Hazel and whomever else may have been in the car.

"This is Father Deeny, and I'm at the Haloran farm. There's been an accident, about five miles south of here on the west side of the road heading into town, down a hill off the roadside." Silence had followed as he had listened for the sheriff's questions. "I don't know. The other car went down the embankment. I couldn't see it from the road. I could see light; the headlights lit up the sky." He had paused, and tears had sprung to his now terrified eyes. "Fire? I…I don't know." He had swallowed with much difficulty, fighting fresh tears and waves of nausea as the reporting of the accident had brought the reality of the event deeply to life. "It could have been." The thought of someone trapped in a burning car had overwhelmed him, and the tears had run freely down his face, and his body had sagged against the wall. "Okay, sheriff." Visibly shaken with shock, Father Deeny had hung up the phone, turning to see Lawrence Haloran getting his coat and hat.

"Father, I'll follow you in the truck. We'll see what we can do until the rescue and fire units get there." He had briefly stopped, turned, and hollered over his shoulder to his oldest son he knew was somewhere in the recesses of the house, "Larry, get your shoes on and come with me. We may need your help." Then he had clamped a firm hand on Father Deeny's shoulder, imparting strength and compassion, knowing that the best thing to do was to keep the poor guy moving. He had looked so torn with disbelief. Mr. Haloran had liked Father Deeny. He had marveled at how the priest had always seemed to reach him and answer his silent questions of faith. Once more, he had gripped Father's shoulder in a show of support, and together they had left the house.

Mrs. Haloran had led the shocked women from the car up to the porch and into the house as the men had left.

"It'll be all right, Father," Hazel had said and had given his arm a reassuring squeeze in passing. Jennifer had followed Mrs. Haloran close behind and had carefully guided the pinched Ms. Chiffon into the warm interior of the Haloran home, for what would be a long prayer-filled night.

At 10:10 p.m. the only bowling alley in town had been buzzing with activity. *Shit!* Michael had thought in impatient anger. *Where the hell are Glen and David?* He had reserved their lanes at nine, and at nine thirty, he had agreed to share them with two classmates, Lisa and her closest friend, Robin.

Both girls were a year younger than Michael and had had Algebra II with him last semester. Lisa, the more out-going of the two, had been short and voluptuous with shoulder-length, coppery red hair and bright blue eyes to match her cheery personality. Robin had been very quiet, almost reserved in her personality and of average height, with short dark hair and equally dark eyes; she was slight and slim. Lisa had promised they would start a new set of games when Glen and David finally decided to make their appearance.

The three had already bowled a complete game, and though Lisa and Robin had been nice girls, he had wished Glen and David had been there, too. He had wondered angrily, *Where are they?* The sounds of the fire trucks and ambulance screeching past the bowling alley around 9:45 had stopped everyone's bowling, and the kids had rushed to the windows to watch the emergency vehicles race out of town. Michael had followed Lisa and Robin to look out.

"Where do you think they're going?" Lisa, the chattier of the two, had turned and asked Michael.

Michael, wishing even more that his friends had been present to observe this new development, had shrugged with disinterest and offered, "Probably some little kid stuck in a railing somewhere." He had thought back to when his little nephews had done the exact same thing trying to catch a glimpse of what they were sure was Santa one Christmas Eve. "Some parents panic. My brother's wife just got out the can of Crisco and greased 'em up." The memory had brought a devilish grin to his handsome features, and both girls had been glad to see their unplanned bowling partner lighten up. They both had liked Michael more than a little and had started to think he wasn't too happy sharing his lanes with them.

A loud crash and shouts had drawn the kids from the windows back into the lanes as a fight had just broken out. Talk of the ambulance's destination had evaporated as kids had scrambled to get a good view of the ensuing fist fight. The kids involved had been local trouble-makers and known bullies who were dirty fighters. As the owners had rushed the lanes, Michael's frustration had returned. *Glen and David should be here.* He couldn't believe they had missed the fight, too. A scowl had returned to his youthful face.

The scream of sirens had alarmed everyone, and they had turned back to the windows as a patrol car had arrived. The officers had burst into the alley and quickly helped the owners break up the fight. The two youths had been handcuffed amid shouts and led out the door. The importance of the whereabouts of the ambulance racing from the small town had been replaced and forgotten in the excitement of the fight.

"Oh, my God." The quieter of the two girls, Robin, had grabbed Michael's arm and stared into his face. With nervous excitement she had continued, "Can you believe this? What a night!" She had searched

Michael's face, looking for agreed disbelief—that so much could happen on one night in such a small town.

Yet for all this excitement, Michael's anger had returned for his real friends hadn't been there. His scowl had been unexpected, and Robin had released his arm, somewhat embarrassed. To hide her chagrin, she had grabbed Lisa and said over her shoulder, "I think it's your turn, Michael." And the game had resumed.

Still not fully engaged in bowling, he had reflected on how his friends had promised they would take no more side excursions without him. The last time they had been late, they had given the excuse of passing a party on the way in and stopping to swipe a few beers in the cover of dark. Young people held most of their country parties off seldom-used roads near field entrances. They were last-minute gatherings to keep adults and local police from preventing the underage drinking. No one kept tabs on the booze or who was or wasn't there; most anyone was welcome. His friends had arrived forty minutes late that time. His anger had been so intense they had sworn they would never party without him again.

High-fiving Lisa for his strike, he had smiled and sat down hard, wondering if he should have called Glen's house. But that would have been almost like ratting him out, and he hadn't wanted to get him in trouble. Michael had fumed, *Son of a bitch!* His mood had darkened, and he had gotten truly pissed. The girls had been nice, but he had known things would have been better with Glen and David there. The night had been fast slipping away, and tomorrow had stretched ahead with nothing but emptiness. *Where were those two? Dammit!*

Father Deeny had slowed the car some distance from where the other car had appeared to leave the road. The dark of the night had concealed any evidence of its path. His only guide had been the faint glow in the night sky of what was the wreck down the embankment, and he hadn't been too sure of that either. He had been mindful to leave room for the emergency vehicles on the way and had parked carefully, not wanting to get too close to the softened embankment, yet needing to leave safe passing distance. He hadn't wanted to be the cause of another accident. Leaving his emergency flashers on, he had walked back to where the Haloran pickup had slowed and pulled over.

"I think it went down just ahead," he had offered to Mr. Haloran through his open window. He had turned to walk slowly back in the direction of his car. It had been all he could do just to keep walking; he had known he had to see this thing through.

He had completed the short distance. Mr. Haloran had followed, driving slowly forward and maneuvering around Father Deeny's car. The crunch of the tires and his own steps had made the only sound, save for a few brave crickets. The coolness of the night had invaded his subconscious, and he had shivered. At the crest of the hill, Father Deeny had stopped, and so had the pickup. It, too, had carefully pulled off the roadside. Father and son had gotten out. The wail of sirens had barely become audible in the distance.

Mr. Haloran had carefully taken a couple steps down the embankment to try to get a better look at exactly where the car was. The glow of dying flames had provided the only marker through the broken brush barely visible in the deep dark of the country. The car had seemed quite a ways down the embankment. He had felt helpless to do anything, yet he had hollered into the emptiness, "Hello, is anyone there? Help is coming!"

He then had turned and said to Larry Jr., "Get that rope and let's hook it round my belt. We need to get down there." Knowing the steep hillsides of the roadways and how they often times dropped off without warning, he hadn't wanted to add any accidents of their own to the rescue efforts.

"Dad, why don't you let me be the one to go down?"

Father Deeny had agreed, "Yes, Mr. Haloran, maybe Larry should go down; it appears it may drop off."

"All right, Larry," Mr. Haloran had consented. "Here's a flashlight. We'll turn it on and hook it to your belt. Be careful, son." As Larry Jr. had secured the flashlight, Mr. Haloran had quietly said, "I sure hope the fire trucks have a spotlight. That's a hell of a spot to go off the road. Give a yank when you get to level ground." He had lowered his voice and added, "Flash the light on and off twice if you think there are survivors. If there are, we'll alert the fire squad when it gets here."

In the still of the night, Father Deeny had heard the quiet instruction, and the idea that there might not be survivors had made him visibly ill. Mr. Haloran had steadied him, "I'm sorry, Father. I didn't mean to…." And Father Deeny had interrupted him with a weak nod. It had had to be said. The illumination in the night sky had waned, and with Mr. Haloran's words, his hopes for whoever had been hurt had dimmed with it.

The sirens had become deafening as the emergency vehicles had drawn up. The two men had been spotlighted, and the sirens silenced. Father Deeny had stepped closer to Mr. Haloran as if to draw strength from him, and he had unconsciously pleaded, "Mr. Haloran…."

"I got it, Father." Mr. Haloran had given his arm a tight squeeze and stepped forward to talk to the approaching rescuers. His night had just begun.

At 11:30 p.m., Michael had finished his third game. He had turned to Lisa and Robin. "Hey, thanks for the challenge." And he had smiled good-naturedly. They all had known he had beat them soundly. "Maybe next time we can bowl teams, even out the odds."

Both girls had chimed in, "It's been fun. Thanks for letting us share your lanes."

Lisa had added, "We're sorry Glen and David didn't make it. They sure missed out on a night of action."

Robin, seeing Michael's eyes darken, had jabbed Lisa secretly from behind and had bravely butted in, "Do you want to get a shake or something? We'll treat, seeing as we lost so horribly." She had smiled her brightest.

Fighting the anger at his friends, Michael had looked at both girls and said, "Naw, I think I'm just going to head home. How about I take a rain check on the shake?" he had added for Robin as he had seen her starting to blush with self-consciousness at her boldness.

Turning bright red and feeling the heat of embarrassment, Robin had responded, "Okay." Totally at a loss for words, she had just smiled.

"Catch you later." Michael had turned and left.

Walking home in the cool night air, Michael had reflected on the evening's events. Lisa and Robin had been nice girls, not overly bright, but he had had a couple of classes with both of them on and off over the years, and they hadn't been stupid either. He had hated stupid girls, or girls that had acted stupid. Neither of the girls had been unattractive, but they hadn't been eye-catchers either. They had been nice. Geez, what the hell had he been thinking, and why had he pondered Lisa and Robin? They had been just two nice girls. Subconsciously he had known he was avoiding thoughts of what could've kept Glen and David this time. His anger had returned with a rush. *Whatever it was it had better be damn good.* He had slowed his walk and trudged home, not wanting the night to end; tomorrow had offered nothing while tonight…well, tonight…and he had walked on, muttering to himself. How could his two best friends have done this to him again? *It had better have been a damn good party. Shit!*

Approaching the dark house, he had remembered to be quiet. The last thing he had wanted was to wake his mom and answer her questions about his disaster of an evening. He had quietly let himself into the house and softly dumped his bowling ball and jacket in the hall, not even bothering to put them away. He had shut the door and tried to decide if he should go upstairs to bed or…what? *Damn! What a waste of a Saturday, and tomorrow is Sunday.* His friends had had obligations to field work, and the day had stretched out long ahead of him. *Damn them!* He had wandered quietly but angrily into the kitchen, frustrated and tense. In a flash, the thought of his mom's homemade wine had burst into his conscious thought. *What the hell. It might make me feel better. At least I can forget about my so-called friends.* He had gotten out his mom's flask and had quietly turned the radio on to his favorite pop station, pouring himself a drink and letting his frustrations run with the tunes flowing from the small radio. *Life can sure suck!*

Mrs. Calhoun had woken at six a.m. like clockwork. Some habits just don't die, and forty-two years of waking at six a.m. as a farm wife was quite a habit. She had gone to bed at eleven, her spring cleaning had gotten the best of her, and she had found she was too tired to wait up for Michael. She had been sure he had preferred it that way anyway. *Youth*, she had thought, *always wanting their freedom.* Still, Michael was a good boy—she was lucky, considering.

She had heard the sirens about ten p.m. and had grown a little nervous until she had heard them head out of town. She had breathed a small sigh of relief and sent a short prayer to whoever was in need. She had hoped it wasn't serious. Spring always brought accidents. She reasoned it must have something to do with the rejuvenation of life; people got careless.

She had quietly walked past Michael's door, which he always left slightly open, and, out of habit, had peeked in. *Sound asleep; no need to wake him.* The family dinner wasn't until two. He had still been a growing boy in her eyes, even if he had turned eighteen in April. Lord how she had loved him. She had gone to the window at the end of the hall and slowly opened it to let in the morning breeze. *Nothing like waking to the sounds of the song birds in these trees near the house.* She had paused for a moment and had enjoyed the view and the scent, watching the little birds flit from branch to branch, their colors of brown and black vibrant against the shoots of green among the branches. This time of year, she appreciated even the homely little sparrows. She had loved their antics. It would be weeks yet before some of the more colorful birds reappeared. After drawing in a deep breath of the morning air, she had turned back down the hallway and descended the stairs.

In the kitchen, she had headed to the window over the sink to open it, too, and she had spotted the glass with the remains of some of her wine. A small smile had lit her lips. Michael had understood the dangers of the drink. Andrew, one of his older brothers, had had a serious drinking problem, and Michael had learned about responsible drinking from watching his older brother's struggle.

It hadn't been but an hour later that Michael had roamed into the kitchen.

"What's for breakfast?" Michael had yawned sleepily.

"I didn't expect you up this soon. Did you have an early night?" Mrs. Calhoun had inquired.

"Yeah. Can I have eggs and sausage, Mom?" Michael had requested and added, "Where's the paper?"

"I haven't made my way out to get it. Why don't you do that, and I'll start the eggs and sausage.

"Yeah, the fresh air will do me good," Michael had agreed and turned to go get the paper from the porch.

"How many eggs?" Mrs. Calhoun had asked to Michael's back.

"Four over easy," he had said over his shoulder as he had left the kitchen.

Upon his return, Mrs. Calhoun had picked up where they had left off. "How was your night? Remember I like all the details." She had smiled conspiratorially.

"There's nothing to tell, Mom. The guys didn't make it to town," he had said with bitterness in his tone as he had made small work of his eggs and sausage.

"Now, Michael, no plans are set in stone. Maybe something came up at the farm," Mrs. Calhoun had offered in good faith of Michael's closest friends.

"Yeah, something better have come up. Last night was a waste, and so is today!" Michael's anger had returned grudgingly.

"It's not like you to be so down in the mouth, Michael. Did you boys have something big planned?" Mrs. Calhoun had questioned with her back to Michael, as she had poured herself another cup of coffee. She had turned and remarked, "Why is today such a waste? It's just begun."

"Naw, we didn't have any big plans. It's just that it was Saturday, and Saturday's always the best day of the weekend 'cause Sunday is too close to the start of the week. I hate to see a Saturday wasted." Michael's tone had revealed his full exasperation. "It only comes once a week!" he had added with some resignation and a weak smile.

"Saturday, only once a week? Really, Michael, how very observant of you." Mrs. Calhoun had smiled in return at his attempt at humor. "Do you want more eggs or sausage, and what about today?"

"Naw, I'm full. Today, the guys are busy with farm stuff," Michael had sighed.

She had risen to take his plate and silverware and had suggested, "You could set up the volleyball net and croquet game in the yard this morning. It'll give you something productive to do, and they'll be ready when your nieces and nephews come this afternoon." Seeing his still dark look as she had turned with the cloth to wipe the table in front of him, she had tried to think of a better solution to his boredom. She had added with a cheerful request, "Maybe you can find some lilacs for me off the side of the old country road when you're done setting up the games. You know how much I love them, and they'll bring some spring into the house."

Michael, hating the effort his mother was making to brighten his mood, had agreed with a nod. He had abruptly shoved himself from the table. "I think I'll go get the lilacs first; it'll give the yard a chance to dry," Michael had suggested, suddenly feeling the need to get out of the house and vent his newly rising resentment toward his friends' betrayal of last night. "I'll set up the games and clean up my room when I get back," he had injected quickly before his mother had ordered him upstairs to do his morning chores.

"Fine, Michael. Are you okay, son?" Mrs. Calhoun had questioned with a concern that shadowed her previously youthful and lively countenance.

"Yeah, Mom." Michael had softened. "I just need some of that fresh spring air." He had given her a quick hug to show her he was quite his old self.

Mrs. Calhoun had looked at him intently for a moment and shaken her head to clear the worry from her brow. "All right. See you in a while." She had bitten back, "Take a jacket," as she had sensed his acute need for independence at the moment.

Michael had left the house by the back door and walked through the back yard to the worn dirt path that had paralleled their property at the edge of town and had wound through the fields that had bordered the town.

Sounds of the robins and meadowlarks had interspersed the soft silence of the still early Sunday morning hour as they had flitted from the brush hedging the age-old path. Michael had slowed his steps and relaxed. Eight a.m. hadn't found too many farmers in the fields this close to town. Most of them had been part-time farmers, hiring help to do the fieldwork during the week. Holding nine-to-five jobs in the larger cities an hour's drive from town, they had enjoyed farming part-time, proudly making the claim of "farmer" in their communities and having the best of both worlds.

The solitude of the morning had seeped into Michael's being, and he had sighed. The beauty of the countryside had brought a small light of pleasure to his face. The antics of the birds had lifted his spirit. And the cool air had carried hope to him in the scent of freshness and new life unique to spring. Like a young maiden opening herself to the supplications of her lover, the soil yields to the plow of the farmer, releasing her ripening life-giving scent. Breathing deeply, Michael had felt himself relaxing even more as he had begun to absorb the beauty of the morning unfolding. As pleasure had filled him, he had let go of the anger that had so filled him. He had sighed again and unfurled the tendrils of frustration, the feelings of being young and restless and not in control. With another and now audible sigh, his body had sagged, and he had paused a moment to perch on a time-worn rock. He had had time: Home would be there still.

As morning had just begun to break, Sheriff Ralph Andersan had observed the younger man seated before him. Ralph had lived all his life in New Haven and had been sheriff for the past eight years, running the first time at the tender age of fifty out of exasperation with the younger sheriff who had been up for re-election. He and many of the local residents had grown tired of the "by the book" dogma by which the out-of-towner had been operating. Though Andersan had agreed with the young sheriff that the laws must be enforced, he had felt there had to be room for small breaches of human error. People made mistakes, and sometimes they just needed a firm but gentle reminder that the laws were made for everyone to follow for the safety of the entire community. In smaller communities where everyone's business was everyone else's, this method was often more effective than slapping heavy fines and short prison stays on absent-minded farmers or spry, water-testing youth. Sheriff Andersan's first term of two years had gone so smoothly he had been re-elected without an opponent the following election cycles. His reputation was one of fairness and equal justice for all offenders. His age had never been an issue for he held a straight and tall posture and looked far younger than he should have for a man approaching sixty. He had given all credit for his youthful appearance to his wife's good cooking and his Nordic heritage. In his eight years in office, Ralph had seen many things, but last night's event had been one of the hardest he had had to deal with.

Being a man of few words, Sheriff Andersan had looked compassionately at the drooping figure of the young priest. He had remembered well when Father Deeny had arrived in New Haven. It had been right before his first run for office. The priest had been the first Negro to come and dwell in this farming community. The town had been abuzz for weeks when the news had broken, and the talk had been wild. The elder church-goers had had concerns that the new priest would be one of those "civil rights" upstarts. Many had vowed never to set foot in St. Mary's again. Others had pondered how a black person could be a Catholic. Was there such a thing? Weren't blacks all of the Bible-thumpin' southern breed?

When Father Joe Deeny had actually arrived, the townspeople had been more than a little embarrassed. Expecting a loud, brash, pushy youth like the sheriff that Ralph Andersan had replaced, they had been more than pleasantly surprised when the priest who had shared the welcome picnic had appeared to be an older man, somewhat reserved and genteel. Without a doubt, he had presented a formidable figure. His dark ebony color and broad shoulders had silently demanded respect. When the monsignor had given the podium over to the newcomer, the town folk had been impressed with his deep voice and his calm clean words of gratitude toward the hospitality they had extended. They never would have imagined their new priest had not even reached thirty years, for he had been one who, even at a younger age, had looked far older than his true years of living. Father Joe, as he had been lovingly dubbed by the younger set, had been a wonderful asset to the growing community. Sheriff Andersan had even called him a couple of times to help convince some of the town's more lively youths their road of travel was anything but the right path to be on. He had felt a special friendship toward Father Deeny, who he had sensed was a man of true moral strength and great wisdom. Yet here he had sat, beaten by the unfolding night, literally a broken man.

Not being of the Catholic faith, Sheriff Andersan had spoken informally with Father Deeny. "Look, Joe," he had said compassionately and quietly as he had gotten up from his chair and come around to where Father Deeny had sat, "this is just a formality, but this is one of those times the paperwork has to be done. I doubt charges will be brought. Last night was an accident. I'll talk with the legal people personally." He had given Father Deeny's shoulder a squeeze.

Father Deeny had looked up from the spot on the floor where he had been staring. *What a nightmare! How could this have happened?* He had felt bad for Sheriff Andersan and had mentally roused himself from his silent musings. *No need to cause more grief. I've done enough already.* The sheriff had become a friend. They had worked through some tough cases together, helping some of the local kids out of bad choices.

"I'm sorry, Ralph, it's just…," and his voice had trailed off. Words had escaped him. What could he say to relieve his friend of the burden of concern for him, that he himself had placed upon him?

"How about I give you a lift to the rectory and I'll have your car sent over later?" Sheriff Andersan had offered, glad to see some of the old Joe still there.

"No, thanks," Father Deeny had said, shaking his head. He hadn't wanted to trouble his friend anymore. "I think I'll walk." And then he had agreed, "But if it isn't too much trouble, the car…," and he had faded off with a pained look.

"Sure, I'll get the car over to you before noon." He had taken a step back to allow Father Deeny room to rise.

"Thanks, Ralph…Sheriff." Father Deeny had slowly lifted himself up from the chair and had offered his hand.

Sheriff Andersan had taken the priest's hand and clasped it firmly in an attempt to instill strength and comfort. Then he had walked him the short distance to the door.

As Father Deeny had closed the door and left the sheriff's office, the sun had been full over the silent horizon. He had looked at its reality and drawn a slow breath to try and steady himself. The sheriff's words still echoed in his ears.

Sheriff Andersan had shaken his head sadly as he had watched his friend cross the street and head back in the way of the church. He, too, had taken a deep breath as he had turned back into his office, thinking that if Joe weren't a man of the cloth this would have been his undoing. He had had faith that his friend would be all right. He had assured himself Joe was a man of great strength. Yet the sheriff had sighed. *Fate how cruel and humbling you can be.*

Father Deeny had quietly opened the door to the rectory, and the memories of the previous evening's events had flooded the hall: the boys quietly preceding him down the hall to the kitchen after he had caught them sipping the wine for today's mass; his sitting with them in the kitchen; and God forbid, his warning them to be careful. Could it really be true? He had dealt with death so many times, yet this time he was…what? He had known the boys personally; they had touched his heart. He had made a connection to them, with their youth, and he had felt alive with their spirit. How could they be gone? They had just been here sitting with him. Again he had tortured himself. Their lives had been so young and waiting to be filled. His mind had raced, and the thoughts had screamed at him. A final question had had his heart pumping: How could he or they have known that their future was only hours from being completed? He had had to stop this madness of thought. He had been a servant of God and had presided at so many deaths and funerals. Why had these deaths become so much harder to get a handle on and accept? Then the reason had hit him full in the face: The blame had lain with him! Oh God, it was all his fault! With the weight of this revelation, he had staggered down the hall into the kitchen and collapsed in sobs on the nearest chair. He had vowed to make amends. He had had to. He had had such remorse. If only he had done the right thing and called their parents. They would have been punished, grounded, or something, and they would be alive this very moment. Heaven help him. Their deaths, they had been all his fault.

Two hours later, Michael had climbed the back stairs to the entry off the kitchen. The small thud of the screen door had announced his return. "Mom, I'm home. I got you a bunch of lilacs! Mom." He had hardly needed to make such a noise as he had stood just off the kitchen, but in wiping his feet, Michael had tried to let his mother know he had returned to his old self. He had walked into the cool interior of the kitchen wondering why his mother hadn't answered his boisterous arrival. Not noticing her standing at the kitchen sink, he had tried again. "Mom, where are you?"

Mrs. Calhoun had remained quietly standing, her hands in the cold and growing colder dishwater, pain visibly etching her face.

She had started the dishes shortly after Michael had left. She had had lots to do to get the early afternoon meal ready for her growing family. She loved their Sunday get-togethers. They hadn't done them every Sunday, but she had tried to have one a month. She had been wiping off the stove top when the phone had rung not but twenty minutes after Michael had left.

"Mrs. Calhoun," she had answered into the phone as she had scrubbed a bit at the grease from making breakfast.

"Catherine, what are you doing this morning?" had come across the line.

"Francis, is that you?" Catherine Calhoun had replied to the almost rude inquiry.

"Oh my, yes, Catherine. I'm so sorry. Where are my manners? What with the news of the accident and the boys' deaths, I'm just not thinking this morning," Francis, the president of the Ladies of St. Mary's, had rushed on.

"Francis, what accident? Whose deaths?" Catherine had asked into the receiver, abruptly stopping her work at the stove top and wandering back to the kitchen sink.

"Surely *you* know. There was a terrible accident north of town last night. The Connor and Haloran boys were killed."

"Wait. Which boys, Francis? Both families have more than one son." Catherine had immediately felt bad for asking such a thing, as if loosing one child over the other would be easier; yet she had thought of her son who was close friends with boys from both families. She had silently sent up a prayer they wouldn't be Michael's friends. *Dear God, he needs those boys. They are all he has.*

"Why, Catherine, I believe they were the ones just about to graduate. At least that was the talk at the café. The ones that are in Michael's grade? You're so lucky Michael wasn't with those two. It seems the car ran off the road and burst into flames. Nothing anyone could do. The greater tragedy is the elder Larry went to help assist. Oh, Catherine, that poor man. When the rescue squad came with a vague description of the car, the poor soul just about collapsed." The silence on Catherine's end had allowed Francis to run on until she had wondered if Catherine was still there. "Catherine? Catherine?" Francis had inquired into the silent receiver.

Taking a slow, deep breath to hold off her tears, Catherine had quietly replied, "I'm here Francis." Words had failed her. The news had devastated her, and her heart had begun to hurt.

"I was sure you would have known. I'm sorry to be the bearer of bad news. I guess with them being Michael's age and all, I just thought for sure you would know. Again, I am sorry. Does Michael know?" She had tried to sound more compassionate, and yet not hearing a reply, she had gone on, "The Ladies of St. Mary's are going to have a rosary for both families this Wednesday, and the funerals will be held on Thursday. They want to allow time for family from afar to attend. Do you think you will be able to help serve after the service at the graveside?" Francis had softened her question with, "We understand if you don't feel you are able to."

"Francis, may I have a day to get back to you, please?" had been all Catherine could manage to squeeze out without bursting into tears.

Hearing the strain in Catherine's voice, Francis again had apologized. "I am so sorry, Catherine. I really thought you knew. Yes, how about we just find someone else this time, okay?"

"Oh, Francis, I think that would be best," Catherine had said with relief both immediate and audible.

"I'll call you later in the week, Catherine. Take care."

Putting the receiver back in the cradle on the wall, Catherine had slowly returned to her now lukewarm dishwater. She had leaned heavily into the countertop and looked at the barely visible suds as her tears had gently rolled down her cheeks into the still cooling water. She had lost all track of time as she had stood in her grief.

The slamming of the screen door had announced Michael's arrival home. She had slowly attempted to remove the tear stains from her face with a shrug of her shoulder, wondering how long she had stood there. She had been so lost in her thoughts. *Why did accidents happen? Dear Heavenly Father, why must life have to be so full of pain? How am I going to tell Michael?* She just hadn't wanted to. She had known his life would never be the same. *Why can't he go on as he is, untarnished by such a horrible reality? He's too young to have to go through such tremendous pain. Why, Lord, why?* She hadn't even heard Michael's greetings from the back porch, just the soft thud of the screen door. She had hoped she hadn't looked too grief stricken. She had wanted to compose herself, to lend him some support. How had he gotten home so soon?

Noticing his mother's quiet form at the kitchen sink, Michael had felt the heel for his sour attitude before. His mother had looked so small and vulnerable all of a sudden. "Mom, are you okay?" Michael had asked. She had been so quiet, and yet she seemed so visibly upset. "I'm sorry I was so rotten this morning." He had given her a gentle hug from the side and had repeated, "I'm sorry."

At his words, Mrs. Calhoun had started to cry, "Oh, Michael, it's not you."

"Mom, what is it?" His mother's free-flowing tears had scared Michael.

She had removed her dishwater-wrinkled hands from the sink and had dried them on her apron. Gently taking Michael by the upper arm, she had guided him to a chair. They had both forgotten about the lilacs Michael had brought in and had laid on the counter.

"Michael, sit down. I don't know what to say…how to say…." She had sat down across from her youngest son, absorbing his fear and knowing it would turn to anger upon his hearing her words, and she couldn't still the tears that had slipped from her soul. She had wrung her hands, wishing one last time for this to be a horrible nightmare.

"Come on, Mom. You're really scaring me. What is it? Did something happen?" Michael had started to feel very panicky.

"It's Glen and David, hon. They…." Mrs. Calhoun had stopped. To say it to another person would make it so real, and she had not been ready for that force of reality.

"What, Mom? What is it? Are they okay?" Michael had begun to feel a little sick. Something had gone very wrong.

"Michael, there was a car accident last night, and both boys were…they didn't make it. Hon, I'm so very sorry." Mrs. Calhoun had reached for Michael to extend strength across the table as her own strength had left her in a flow of new tears.

With shock and disbelief on his face and then anger at her words, Michael had pushed away his mom's hand and had shoved his chair violently back with such force it fell over. "No! No! Come on, Mom. That is just sick. An accident?" he had shot out, running his hand nervously and angrily through his short hair. This just couldn't be. Life didn't do this, not today, not today! He had taken a deep shaky breath as he had looked angrily and sickly at his mother. He had stared intently at her, silently demanding that she take back the words released into his day.

Catherine had looked through tear-filled eyes, wishing she could give in to his demand, but all she could offer was, "Michael, I'm so, so sorry."

Her apology with the truth and her refusal to grant him his irrational demand had sent him back out the screen door he had moments before entered and on a blind run across the yard to the very path he had just come from.

Catherine had sat silently as the screen door had reverberated his departure, crying quietly for his introduction into the harshness of life and the risk of caring for others.

✳

Four days later, in the same church the two boys had served mass, their funeral had been held. The entire senior class and most of the high school had come to say farewell. The faces of many had shown the streaks of tears. Some had worn the look of shock that life could be so harsh. And others had held the stare of disbelief that a life could go so quickly, without forewarning.

Monsignor Riley had taken the podium to give the homily. Funeral homilies are never easy; death is a fact of life people have a hard time accepting or never do accept, no matter what the age of the person that dies. With these thoughts in his mind, the monsignor had begun:

"Many of you may be questioning the why of the death of these two boys. It's only human to question in this way. I implore you not to judge the why. Don't come to conclusions that are humanly reasoned out. Is their death a punishment for something they did or did not do?"

Michael had looked up, his thoughts of his anger at his friends on the night of their accident topmost in his mind. His face had reddened as he had realized he had also been thinking they had been punished for drinking the wine for the next day's mass.

"These boys were young and good to so many who knew them. I implore you to try not to be angry with God who blessed our lives to know these two boys. Instead, turn to God for His comfort, and He will guide us through this passage of rough and unfriendly waters to the calm and peace on the other side.

"We are all here by God's will and by His plan. We are His, and as we so frequently pray, 'Thy will be done,' we must come to accept what has happened and remember the joy and good these two young men brought into the lives of so many. They lived the lives they had according to God's will not ours. Let us stand and pray for their eternal happiness as they go to be with God. Let us pray also for those whose lives will be forever changed by their departure, that they will turn to God for the comfort, strength, and guidance to go on and live the life God has planned for them. In this, we pray. Our Father, who art in Heaven…."

Upon the conclusion of the Lord's Prayer, Monsignor Riley had cleared his throat and said, "Please be seated. At the request of the bereaved families, I would like to share with you a note left by Father Deeny for them.

"'Dear Mr. and Mrs. Haloran and family and Mr. and Mrs. Connor and family, I shall be eternally filled with sorrow, grief, and remorse for the pain my careless action has inflicted upon your families. The depth and pain of your loss can never be removed; for that I am at a loss. I cannot undo what I have done, but I am giving my entire life savings for daily masses to be said for the repose of the souls of Glen Haloran and David Connor that their time in purgatory may be made shorter and they may receive the joy and comfort of heaven with our Lord and Savoir. I will spend every waking moment for the rest of my earthly life praying for their early release. With my deepest sorrow, Father Deeny.'

"To honor this generous act of contrition, each day starting tomorrow, our early morning mass other than Sundays will be offered in memory of David Connor and Glen Haloran for the repose of their souls from purgatory. The families are thankful to Father Deeny for his offerings in memory of these two young men."

Michael had sat in controlled shock. He himself had done the exact same thing. His guilt over his anger directed toward his friends when they had not shown up and then the news of their deaths had caused him untold agony, thinking that he may have had some small part in their demise. He had, without permission, emptied his entire savings account, put it in an envelope addressed to the church, and requested prayers be said for his friends' early release from purgatory. He, personally, had known all their antics had earned each one of them a long stretch of suffering in purgatory, and he had felt the least he could do would be to help his best friends into heaven sooner. He had still felt guilty over his anger, but he had felt better knowing he had contributed in the only way he had known. The thought of who would pray for his sinful self when he left this world had been pushed from his conscious.

The change in the motion of the bus, slowing and turning, bumping its way from the state highway onto a country road, reminded Michael of where he was and the home he would soon see. But his thoughts continued to waver back and forth between the present and the pain of the past.

The last six weeks of his senior year had been a nightmare. Luckily, for him, he had had good grades for most of his high school years, and his teachers, realizing the personal loss he had suffered, had been very forgiving of his lack of attention to his work. The plans he, Glen, and David had made for the summer had vanished with them. Where he had been looking forward to the long idle time of summer's days, he now couldn't comprehend the months ahead without the two people he had spent so much time with. Not wanting to have time to think, he had done the only thing he could: RUN. He had had to get away from all that had happened. He couldn't think about the loss life had suddenly dealt him and all that it meant. He had visited the same army recruiter who had almost talked all three boys into enlisting in the fall after graduation. He had signed up on the condition he could leave as soon as graduation was over, taking any position that would get him in immediately. Michael hadn't cared. He had just wanted to be gone, gone like his friends. His decision had aged his mother overnight. She could hardly bear the fact that he would leave so soon and especially under the circumstances. This time he did not think of how much he was hurting her but about how much he needed to run from his own pain. But he just hadn't run fast enough or far enough—and never could—for his pain came from within, and it would not be run from.

Escape

I run so hard and fast, escape is my plan.
To keep from seeing the disillusionment
that life's not what I envisioned.
For if I pause too long to look,
reality seizes me in its unjust hold.
How much easier to run with dreams
than to keep company with truths
and life's molded monotony.

Michael had spent four years with the army and hadn't come home once during that time. He had immersed himself in his training, doing his very best to keep his mind from the memories and their implications from which he had fled. When his time wasn't spent working, he had either attended college classes or partied as if his life had depended on it. He had made many friends on the surface but hadn't let anyone close enough to see or touch the pain he was carrying around inside. That pain was his, and he would deal with it in his own way.

Six months had remained on his first enlistment when he had received a call from his mother, this past Christmas, asking him when he thought he would be coming home. He remembered the call well.

+⹀⹀+

He had been sleeping in, as he had done every weekend as it killed hours of boredom and made up for the sleep he missed when he partied into the wee hours of the morning. He had been rudely awakened by the constant and yet intermittent ringing of the phone in the shared hall that Christmas around noon. Finally, out of anger that no one else would answer the damn thing, he had gotten up. He had known there were very few people still in the dorm. Why did he have to be the one? *Shit.* He had dragged himself out of bed into the hall and answered with a bleary and unfriendly, "Hello."

"Hello, and Merry Christmas. This is Mrs. Calhoun. I'm calling to speak to my son Michael Calhoun. Could somebody please get him?"

"Mom," and then again, "Mom, it's Michael." All of a sudden, Michael had been wide awake. His mother had never called in all the time he had left home. He had felt an old fear rising. "Is everything okay? Are you all right?" The voice had sounded so small.

"Michael, oh Michael, Merry Christmas, son. Is it really you? Goodness, you sound so grown-up." Catherine Calhoun couldn't help the tears that had come; Michael had sounded so like Patrick. She could hardly believe he had answered the phone. What a Christmas miracle. She had missed Michael so much and had done her best to respect his need to be the man God wanted him to be; but Lord help her, she was only human, and she couldn't help herself. Today she had given in and had called. Her happiness had overwhelmed her.

Michael had detected her obvious joy, and he had heard the tears as they had formed. "Yes, Mom, it's me. But how are you? Are you okay?" He had quickly stopped the words, "Why are you calling?" from leaving his lips as he knew they would only wound her. He hadn't called in the three and a half years since he had left, and she had respected his need for distance.

"I'm fine, Michael. It is so good to hear you. Is it really you?

He had almost sensed her effort to feel of him. His buried emotions from the events he had run from had come flooding to the surface. In his attempts to run from his own pain, he now knew without a doubt he had deeply caused pain to the one person who had loved him unconditionally all his life. His guilt had overwhelmed him as he had heard his mother's joyous tears and apology for causing him to think there was anything wrong.

"Michael, I'm sorry." Catherine had fought for control. "I'm fine. The family is fine. It's just I wanted to wish you a Merry Christmas." And her throat had clogged with tears. "Do you think you will be coming home any time soon?" She had tried hard to make it a question and not a plea. She had fought the question for so long, and today the battle had been lost. She hadn't intended to ask him, but she had missed him so much. And then to her own surprise she had added, "Staying away from home isn't going to change what happened, Michael." She had spoken very softly and gently so as not to tear open wounds she had known still needed time to heal. Nevertheless, time was passing, and Michael somehow had to come to terms with life that didn't seem fair by human expectations. She hadn't pleaded; she had just stated the obvious—that staying away from home wasn't going to bring Glen and David back.

Leaning into the wall of the hall, Michael had felt the weight of life and sagged. She had been right, and he had known it. He had been tired, and he had then realized how much he had missed his family. He had been running from feeling for so long he had been surprised at the intensity of its reappearance when he had heard the emotion in his mom's voice. He had felt sorrow with such depth he had barely been able to speak, but he had. "I'll be home, Mom. I promise. I miss you, too, and the family." He had thought of the changes in his family his mom had written to him. He had a few new nieces and nephews he hadn't even met. What a selfish schmuck he had been.

On the other end, Catherine had heard Michael's sorrow. But she had missed him terribly. How she had wanted to see her youngest son. And so she had pushed the point. "Do you think you could be home in the spring? You know, it's my favorite time of year."

She had sounded like a little kid. "Oh, Momma." He had smiled at her plea. "I'll do my best." He had drawn in a deep breath and continued, "I don't know when I'll be home, but it will be this coming year, okay?"

Knowing he would do his best, she had accepted his indefinite terms. "Oh, Michael, it'll make me so happy. Thank you, son. What a wonderful Christmas present. I love you."

"I love you too, Mom. I'll see you. Bye, Mom."

Her call had made him realize the tragedy had caused him to run not only from his pain but also from someone who had truly cared about him. Death had chased him from his youth, and he had tried to run from all of life. He had buried himself in his work and heavy drinking with friends, all to prevent himself from reaching out to others and risking getting hurt again.

Like a disaster, his friends' deaths had affected many lives, forcing people to face issues they preferred to have kept buried. The finality of death comes to all at some point in life. It brings with it no acceptable reasons and seldom gives warning of its approach; yet it screams to the survivors of the departed loved ones that life is so short. Tragedy brings some people to changes they didn't think they were capable of making; others hide in alcohol, drugs, or work; and some carry on and live one day at a time, never fully understanding but going steadily forward with faith in the One who is the Master Planner.

Lady Fate

She's a lady of stealth, waiting in the wings
on the stage of life; playing her hand
at the most fortuitous time.

The casual conversation, on a bus with a stranger,
blossoms into a deep and lifetime friendship.

A magazine picked up in haste, an article read,
gives needed insight to a troubled spirit.

The tragic loss of human life
reveals strength and compassion
and a course of life forever changed.

Some fear this lady called Fate
and beg her to keep her tragic hand at bay.
Others thank her and call upon her
to lighten troubled thoughts over decisions of weight.

Who is your master, oh Lady of Fate?
I think the hand of God must deal your cards
and the dates that they be played,
be they tragedy or fortune.

Michael had made up his mind to leave the army at the end of his four-year hitch and return home to whatever was meant to be. He had finally acknowledged he still carried the deaths of Glen and David in his heart, but he had realized staying away from home was only hurting his mother and not helping him. Maybe going home was the thing to do. He had known staying away sure wasn't. He hadn't told anyone, not even his family, of his plan to leave the service. He had decided, since his mother had never seen him in uniform, he would wear it home. She had been so proud of him, and he knew it would make her happy.

◦──◦

He had about thirty minutes before the bus pulled into his hometown. He hadn't told his mother when he would be coming. He didn't want a welcome-home gathering or anything special. He just wanted to get home. It was funny how, now that he was going home, he really was looking forward to being there. *But what was home?* he wondered. *And what was I running away from?* He had fled in such a hurry that he didn't even know. *Was it death or life?*

"New Haven, next stop," the driver called out. Michael gathered his belongings and did his best to straighten up his slightly wrinkled uniform. Bus rides could make one feel disheveled, and he certainly did.

As the bus got closer to town, the changes over the last four years were unmistakable. Life didn't stop for anyone. For a moment, that realization gripped him with an intense sense of alarm. *Are we all so inconsequential?* He quickly brushed the thought from his mind and continued noting all the physical changes the town had acquired in his four-year absence.

The bus finally came to a stop at its destination. Michael stepped off the bus and adjusted his eyes to the bright midday sun. Immediately to his right he felt a presence and turned to see a smallish woman gasp, clutch her chest, and turn ghostly white. Instinctively, the gentleman in him responded and went to her aid and then realized this little white-haired woman was his mother. The sight of her shock and her aged appearance pulled so strongly at his heart that he released a small cry. Only four years of burying his pain saved him from clutching to her and weeping like a small child at what his absence had done to her. He quickly regained his composure and gave her a gentle but strong hug, wishing he could give her back the years he had taken from her in his flight.

Mrs. Calhoun had nearly had a heart attack when she recognized that the young soldier she had been admiring stepping off the bus was her Michael. She had purposefully gone to the local store every week since he had left home on the scheduled day the bus pulled into town, hoping he would one day step off. Her answered prayers were almost too much. She could not stop the gasp of joy or the shock at his physical change. With tears gently falling, she pulled back and looked up into the face of the towering young gentleman who had come to her aid. At just over six foot three, her son in four years had grown from a boy on the doorstep of manhood into a young man hardened by the harsh realities of life. She felt such joy in seeing him. But what had time done to her innocent son? Who was this strong young man with a look of hardness to his eyes, eyes that, upon recognizing who he was assisting, softened with long-held emotion, eyes that revealed strength as they regained control before total loss?

She grabbed him to her again just to be sure he was really here before her. "You're home, Michael?" She again pulled back and questioned, looking up into his face, "Are you home?" A pained look came to her eyes as she searched his again for that small glimpse of the boy who had left, and she couldn't stop her tears.

"Yes, Mom, I'm home, for good." He gently wiped the tears from her cheek and forced himself to be strong. He refused to get caught up in whatever was fighting for release. "I was discharged before I left Germany. I only wore the uniform so you could see me in it." He caught her hand and squeezed it reassuringly.

She held him to her once again, snuffed loudly to stop the tears, and hugged him most ferociously. "Oh, Michael, I am so glad I came to town today. You're my best bargain yet." And she laughed at her poor attempt at humor.

Michael laughed, too, and put his arm gently around her shoulder. He felt relieved to see she was no longer crying and she still had her sense of humor.

So began his introduction back into life and living. He still had a distance to travel, unknowns to face, but they would wait. With his duffel bag on his shoulder, he walked home, slowing his pace to match his mother's.

Chapter Two

Jennifer

*F*our years later and hundreds of miles away, Jennifer walked into her bank in California, heading to the teller line to cash what she was contemplating to be one of her final paychecks from her days in the world of modeling. Thoughts of who she had been, the turn in her career, why she was thinking of leaving, and what she was going to do raced through her mind. She felt a sudden chill run down her spine and a sense of unease flow over her whole body; she shook her head and focused on extracting her bankcard and driver's license from her wallet, failing to notice at first the sudden commotion exploding behind her.

The resounding pop of what sounded like a loud firecracker quickly snatched her attention to her immediate surroundings. Whirling around, she caught sight of one of the bank security officers slumping to the floor in a pool of spreading blood.

Muffled shouts of "Everyone on the floor!" jolted her to her knees, pressing so quickly and solidly to the floor she didn't even feel her purse or car keys beneath her. She only wished she could become one with the floor or that she would wake up in a cold sweat, reassured it had all been a nightmare.

Another shot rang out, making Jennifer all too aware the night-mare was reality. Just as forcefully, the truth hit her: She did not want to die here, away from her real family. And she did not want to die with her daughter left in the care of anyone but the only people she really loved. *Oh, God.* She immediately started a whispered litany of fervent prayers to Jesus. "Save us, Lord Jesus. Deliver us from harm, dear Lord Jesus Christ. Help us, Lord Jesus Christ." Almost as quickly as the fear had gripped her, she felt a comforting calm. Her breath slowed and she relaxed. She now felt the cold marble of the bank floor and the sharpness of her keys digging into her abdomen. She listened intently. No more shots rang out, but she heard the quiet sobs of fear and other whispered pleas of "Help us, Lord Jesus" from those on the floor around her. The wails of the approaching sirens shattered the solemn stillness that had enveloped the bank.

One of the robbers, whose intent was to fill the bags with money, cursed angrily, "Who the fuck called the cops?" He practically spit the words at the teller in front of him, pointing his weapon accusingly at her. She fell uncontrollably to the floor, weeping in fear.

Another shot echoed inside the bank's interior, and at the same time, the jarring ring of a phone in a loan office took the attention of the thief from the teller. Leaving the empty money sack on the counter, the robber turned his weapon from the teller back to the terrified people silently molding themselves to the floor, sparing the teller's life for the moment.

Scanning the scene for his partner, the man with the gun shouted, "No one move!" Then he saw his friend lying on the floor a few feet from the security guard, neither one moving. That brought forth another burst of anger. "Aw fuck, Bruce," he hollered at his friend. "Bruce, get the fuck up, man!" Panic and terror set in. This wasn't how it was supposed to be.

Meanwhile, the ringing continued. Firing one shot over the cowering customers on the floor to show his seriousness, he turned his attention to the phone and advanced toward the office. What was he going to do now? This wasn't the plan.

With the robber's departure to the phone, the weeping teller cautiously crawled to a coworker provoking the incensed robber to fire another shot over the patrons on the floor and scream, "I said, 'NO ONE move!'"

Keeping his eyes on the people on the floor, he backed toward the source of the irritating ringing. Never letting his eyes leave those on the floor, he lifted the receiver and was immediately confronted with the seriousness of his situation. His mind went blank, collapsing under the overwhelming complexity of the plans run amuck. His life had become a nightmare, and he saw no way out. It hadn't always been so. What had happened to him that he had stepped into this quagmire of wrongness?

For just a moment, no more than a blink of an eye he became, once again, Ken Adams, just the average kid in high school, about five feet eight, medium build, not a bad student, but a hard worker and a guy who looked out for others less fortunate. He had his whole life ahead of him, no worries, no real concerns, just homework and a part-time job. Then he was blessed with a beautiful girlfriend for whom he would give his life. He loved her so, and she him; or so he had thought. How quickly his ordinary life had gone awry with an unplanned pregnancy and her hard-hearted parents. Their upper-middle class standing had not meshed with his background, and they had hated him from the start. It had seemed society itself had turned its back on the love he and his girlfriend had believed in, love he had put his faith in. Even the systems that were supposed to help had abandoned them. Life had proven to be cruel and unfair. God, how had he gotten here? His heartache and anger returned with a vengeance.

Without having heard a word of the offer, he screamed into the phone, "No, *you* listen. I need time. I'll let you know when I know!" With that he slammed the receiver into its cradle and stormed into the main bank.

Ken went back to where he had left the bag for the money. It was still empty, as empty as he felt within. Feelings of nausea swept over him. He'd known this was a bad idea, and here he was stuck in the middle of the biggest screw-up of his life. He hung his head. His anger at the unfairness again filled the growing hole of the nothingness inside him. He stormed among those lying on the floor, stopping briefly when he came to where Bruce lay on the floor just inside the door, fatally wounded. His anger raged free, "Fuck you and your fucking plan, Bruce! 'Easy,' you said! Fuck! How easy is this? What! Just what the fuck am I supposed to do now?" He unknowingly implored the Lord, "Oh God," and his voice dropped a note in despair, "What the fuck am I going to do now?"

"Everybody up. Now. Get up. On your feet!"

Slowly the few customers, two tellers, and a few loan officers moved into a single-file line to stand before him as he paced. Shaking his head and quietly cursing, Ken stalked back and forth before the line of nine people. His emotions rolled up and down, his anger flagging and raging, as he muttered in undertones to himself. "Christ, what the fuck am I going to do?" His anger at Bruce came to him in a wave. "You stupid fuck head. This was your plan, and you cop out on me, too." His shoulders drooped. "All these fucking people. God help me." He rubbed his face in exasperation.

One young man on the end made a small move as Ken approached the opposite end of the line. Upon seeing motion as he turned to head back down the line, Ken fired, hitting the man in the shoulder. Releasing his anger with the shot hadn't helped much. He still wished he could hurt his partner for getting him into this mess, but he was dead upon the floor. *Death, now there's an idea.* He was too pissed to think rationally.

The gunshot had sent the line instantly to the floor along with the young man who was now bleeding and pale. Making his way to stand over the young man, he pointed his weapon at his head and savagely kicked him with misplaced rage, then ordered everyone up, including the injured man. "The next person who moves won't be so lucky," he warned ominously. The ring of the phone again diverted his attention.

"What the fuck!" he yelled as he again backed to the phone, all the time keeping his weapon trained on the line of frightened people. He answered without hearing, "I told you not to contact me. I'll let you know when I'm ready!" Hanging up, he called to the bleeding man, "You. Come here." *Death, that's an idea,* again spun around in Ken's troubled mind.

Fearing for his life, the young man hesitated to move. Ken noted his reluctance to respond and was filled with rage. "Over here now, or I'll kill you where you stand!"

Fearing the worst, the terrified man couldn't hold his fear. "Please, sir, please," he pleaded as he put his hands forth for mercy, his panic visible as he inched forward.

Ken noticed the bleeding from his mouth and nose where he had viciously kicked him and roughly shoved him forward to the teller cage. All the while keeping the gun on his victim, he reached through and grabbed a slip of paper and scribbled on it. He shoved it into the man's hand and said, "You make sure this gets to the cops out there."

"I will, sir," came from the fellow as Ken pushed him forcibly toward the entry of the bank. Stopping fifteen feet back, well out of sight of the police outside, he shoved the bleeding man forward to the doors, sending one more shot behind him, making him scramble faster than possible through the outer door, rolling into the street to waiting officers.

Those left in line gasped and some sobbed with fear at the horror of Ken's deliberately shooting at the wounded man as he fled. Hands unknowingly reached for hands, squeezing quiet strength from one to another, keeping them all locked in silent terror as the robber turned to them in frustration.

"I ought to kill all of you and just be done with this shit!" he screamed, his anger escalating, not knowing if the note he had sent out would make a difference. "Damn! This is so piss-ass screwed up!" He looked angrily again at his dead buddy and then for the first time to the bank security officer, equally dead. "Aw fuck. When did that happen? God, will this never end?" Then he followed more quietly, "What the hell does it matter? My life is over." He eyed the line. "Yours should be, too." He waved the gun at them. "Piss! Why the hell couldn't this work? Just this one time, why couldn't something work? Damn you, Bruce, and damn you, too, Rachael," he screamed into the bank, followed almost inaudibly by, "wherever you are." He appeared close to a breakdown, but with a quick snap of his head, he repeated in renewed anger, "Damn it! *Damn it!* **Damn it!**" After a few more emotionally strained cuss words, Ken focused his attention back to the frightened line before him. What was he to do? "What the hell are you looking at?" he bellowed at one of the customers who was intently watching him.

Jennifer, sensing the desperation of the situation, ventured a small, "Sir?"

Not sure if he had imagined the sound, Ken walked slowly to where the word seemed to have originated. "Did you say something?" he asked in true shock of the gutsy nerve of the lady who had been staring at him.

Risking further uncontrolled madness, Jennifer lowered her eyes to find her voice and again tried, "Uh hmm, yes sir, excuse me," she continued very bravely. And as Ken put the gun beneath her chin to raise her face, she looked straight into his eyes, offering…what? What was in her gaze?

Standing before her, Ken was caught off guard by the clarity in her eyes. What did he see—no fear, just a deep openness. The incongruity of her peacefulness and the madness of the scene he had created hit him, but he couldn't let such thoughts sidetrack him. He vigorously shook himself free of her focus. With his anger shaken and the gun under her chin, his words struck out. "What do you want, bitch? Did I say you could talk?"

With the cold metal of the gun jabbing her in the soft flesh of her chin, Jennifer fought to retain the calm she had felt earlier on the floor. As quietly and calmly as she could, she made the simple query, "What do you want, sir?"

The simple polite question hit Ken like a pin in a balloon. "What?" He strangled out a short laugh and sagged from the effects of the intensity of his maniacal anger. The hand holding the gun under her chin dropped to his side. "'What do I want, *sir*?'" he repeated in a sweet sarcastic mimic while waving the gun in the air, and this time he let his laughter ring. For a moment he turned from the line. This was insanity. But such had been his life the last few years. He turned back. "Oh God. Really, lady. 'What do I want, *sir*?'" He hated everything at this moment. Nothing ever went right for him, not one damn plan. God, life sucked; even in error, his life sucked. He had tried so hard to be the man his stepfather had told him he needed to be, that since he was man enough to be a father he should be man enough to take care of what he had done. It hadn't worked out, no matter how hard he tried. Then he had screwed up when Rachael had left him with their son and he had lost custody of him because the help that was supposed to be help wasn't help, and now Bruce fucking died and left him holding the bag, and he was screwing things up with life's stupid insanity.

Ken straightened up. "What do I want? What do I want?" With each question his anger and frustration at the desperation of his situation returned. "I'll tell you what I want, little missy bitch," he spit into her face, "and the rest of you, too." He looked to the rest of the silent line. "I want the hell out! How about that? God, I just want the hell out of here!" His screamed words hung in the silence of the bank for a moment as he glared at her.

Then a quietly whispered, "Me too," arose from Jennifer. The people who had been holding her hands had let go when the robber had made his way to come and stand before her. They now dared to take a few steps away from her. She was a target they did not want to be a part of.

Taken aback with Jennifer's new brazen action, Ken paced a few steps and astonishingly implored to the stunned line, "What the fuck is this? Where the hell am I? Anybody, please? Somebody tell this stupid bitch this is an armed robbery, a bloody armed robbery! Lady, are you even here?" He tapped the side of her head with the end of the gun. "Do you not see my buddy lying in his own blood? How about the old dude? He ain't sleeping. He's dead! DEAD! Do you hear? Do you see!? My fucking life is over! It wasn't supposed to be this way. FUCK this shit!!"

With more strength than she could imagine, Jennifer quietly repeated, "I want out, too."

"Okay, you sarcastic little bitch, I'll blow your head off right now!" he screamed in angry frustration, pointing the gun directly at her.

Oblivious to her imminent danger, Jennifer tried again. "I just want out, too, and I'll tell you how." She stood in complete calmness.

"Don't dick with me, lady. You know a way out of here?"

Jennifer took a shaky breath and nodded yes.

Ken grabbed her from the line. "Show me."

"Please, first let everyone else go," she requested as he shoved her further apart from the others.

"NO!" he screamed in her face. "Why should I?"

"Why not?" Jennifer quietly asked back.

"What if you're lying?"

Jennifer, for the first time, looked him straight in the eye and said, "I'm not."

Her complete peacefulness of person and simple clarity of statement disarmed his anger momentarily, and he hollered at the now frozen line of customers waving his gun, "Okay, you heard the crazy bitch. Go! Get the hell out of here!"

Remembering the fleeing young man and the bullet that followed him out the door, they briefly hesitated and then, as one, rushed the front door, tumbling out into the street, leaving Jennifer with the robber.

As the last person fled with his gaze intent on Jennifer, Ken took her upper arm and said,

"Okay, lady, let's get this show on the road. How do we get out of here?"

With a deep shaky breath Jennifer calmly exhaled, "Through Jesus Christ."

"What! What the...!" He took a swing and hit the side of her face, sending her to the floor, letting loose with, "Lady, I ought to kill you!" and he gave her a quick kick while she covered her head with her hands.

Feeling the blood flow from the blow where the gun had torn her flesh, Jennifer silently prayed, *Help me to see the way, dear Lord Jesus Christ*, as she lay on the floor.

Ken, seeing the blood spill over her fingers, suddenly wondered if he had killed his last chance for freedom. Still raging yet filling with fear that he had possibly killed someone, he nudged her with his foot and ordered her on her feet with, "Get up," more a statement than a command. He was surprised and relieved as she struggled to sit. To show continued authority, he gritted out, "I should kill you now."

Jennifer calmly replied, "You won't get out then."

That she had just repeated his own thought brought his anger back. He laughed with insincerity. "God, lady, you're crazier than I am. What do you think? Jesus Christ is going to just walk in here and escort us to safety and utopia?"

"In a measure, yes, yes, I do," Jennifer offered.

Totally perplexed and now fully off-guard, Ken stated sarcastically, "Give me a minute while I check to see if I'm still alive. Maybe I'm the one that's dreaming." He then muttered, "That would be a miracle."

He took great pains to physically hurt himself to insure he was indeed awake. Once the realization was complete, he dropped to the floor, exhausted, all the while keeping the gun trained on Jennifer, and came to a sitting position a short distance from her.

The mental expense of the morning and the weight of the situation subdued him some, and he truly and quietly implored, "Oh God, what am I going to do?" His heartfelt plea rose from deep within his soul. In the greatest depths of desperation, one's soul calls out to God, its maker. The person may not even acknowledge God, but the soul created by God cries out in unbearable anguish all on its own as Ken's did then. It was the merest whisper of a plea, just audible enough for Jennifer to have heard, yet not registering to Ken himself.

Moved by this almost silent request, Jennifer dared to suggest, "You could make a phone call and make a nearly impossible demand. That would buy us some time."

This incredulous statement further amazed Ken, for he had earlier sent just such a message out with the first man released. Could his day not get any crazier? It was all supposed to be so easy, and yet everything had gone totally awry. How would her plan be any different? Why should he make any more plans with anyone?

"Buy *us* time? Lady, just who in the blazes are you?" he asked, looking at her incredulously.

"Who am I? Nobody, just...," Jennifer said and then softly repeated, "nobody."

How long ago had it been when Jennifer herself had felt such despair and the need just to be free, free from everything? The question sent her reeling back to a time when she had felt so alive and blessed, on the edge of the world, and then it had all come crashing down. No one would ever guess that she could relate so deeply to the desperate and lost young man sharing the floor next to her. Thinking back now to the tragic event that had changed her life's course so radically, she shivered. Her memories of the turn her life had taken came flooding back.

Jennifer had loved her new life in southern California. It had taken great courage to leave her small town the end of summer the year she graduated, but with the sudden death of two classmates, she had found a determination she hadn't known she possessed. Her surprise decision had hurt her mother deeply and dangerously angered her father, but she had stubbornly left home, setting out to live her life.

Jennifer hadn't liked introspection about anything then, and the battle to push the hows and whys of deeper thoughts had become more difficult as her life had unfolded in sunny California. Maybe living in the land of fruits and nuts was affecting her more than she had thought it would. She had chuckled at her own joke about the state she considered home. It had been amazing how rapidly a new place could feel so right. She had to admit to herself she loved her job. The idea that it had come at a great personal cost to her remained unexamined. Unaffected by such disturbing thoughts about her move, she had walked with purpose and confidence down the sidewalk into the high-rise to her photo session with the fashion photographer.

She remembered back to that fateful day she had stopped by the booth in the mall attracted by the catchy ad over the top, "See the world, live a life of excitement with a career in modeling." Jennifer had driven the hour and a half to the nearest mall the weekend after the funeral for her classmates, David and Glen. She hadn't been particularly close to or known either boy all that well, but they had been her age. They had been here, and they were gone in the blink of an eye. The glimpse of the transitory nature and fickleness of life at any age had troubled her deeply. She had felt she had needed change. She couldn't have imagined herself sitting in a classroom for the next four years. She had wanted to live fully before the possibilities escaped her.

Shouldering the remembered heaviness of death, Jennifer had been drawn to the prospects of a new life in an ad she had seen posted in the school. Someone had put up a flyer announcing a top modeling agency would be at the local mall searching for "a new look." With all that had happened, Jennifer had thrown caution to the wind and on a whim driven to the mall by herself. She had been too self-conscious to tell any of her friends and had felt if it was meant to be it would happen and then she would share her good news.

She had approached the stand and cleared her throat. "Excuse me," she had voiced to an attractive and smartly dressed "older" woman seated at the makeshift counter.

Hearing the tentative young voice, the agent from Horizons had looked up. "Hello," she had directed to Jennifer and had stood up. "I'm Ms. Canton. Are you here in response to our ad?"

Jennifer had been so relieved she hadn't needed to state the obvious that she had immediately relaxed and her confidence had risen. Her youthful excitement had lit her face, and Ms. Canton had seen a potential "new look," just what the company had been looking for, freshness and youth. With barely contained excitement, Jennifer had replied, "Yes, I am, but I was wondering…," and she had taken a deep breath and asked the one question most important to her, "The ad said something about traveling to exotic places. Is it true?"

The wistfulness of the question had Ms. Canton smiling. She herself had started in modeling for the very same reason. "Why don't you take a seat, and as you fill out a couple forms, I will answer all your questions." She had motioned Jennifer to a chair and had sat down also.

Jennifer had taken the offered chair and relaxed even more with the realization that her dream was starting.

As Ms. Canton had placed the proper forms in front of Jennifer, she had started her sales pitch. "Right now we are looking for the fresh faces of middle America to promote health and skin-care products. If a person should have the right look and things go well, other jobs suited to her individual strengths may come along. This can lead to a career in fashion, and to be totally honest, fashion is where the travel is. Fashion is dictated by the designers, and it changes every season. The possibilities are there."

Jennifer, still of the mind "If it's meant to be, it'll be," had smiled back.

"You need to complete this application," she had nodded to the one Jennifer was working on, "and include a black-and-white photo of your face with no makeup and a full-body photo. Send the photos and the application to the address listed on the bottom of the form. The application and photos will be reviewed by our photographic staff. If they find you photogenic, or if they determine you have the qualities they are looking for, you will receive an appointment for a personal interview. Here is some detailed information on our company. If you are under eighteen you will need your parent's signature." She had smiled as she had finished the required statements.

"Oh, I'm eighteen," Jennifer had reassured the sales representative and had added, "I'm graduating next month." She had beamed at Ms. Canton.

Ms. Canton had returned Jennifer's smile and had stood, concluding, "Thank you for coming by, and congratulations on your upcoming graduation."

Jennifer had stood, too, and gladly picked up all the information, pushing it into her handbag, hardly believing she had done what she had barely even contemplated. To act upon a whim had not been Jennifer's style, and the thoughts of the possibilities from her daring action had filled her as she had walked away from the stand.

Ms. Canton had watched Jennifer as she had blended into the fast filling mall. She could still see her youthful excitement. *Yes*, she had thought to herself, *I've found just what the company's been looking for.* Jennifer had had such a fresh and innocent look. She had had a feeling Jennifer's application, stamped with her employee identification number, would not only be accepted but also warmly welcomed.

Back at home, Jennifer had excitedly removed the application form from her purse and laid it on her desk. Looking at it, she had taken a deep breath to calm herself and think about her plan. Graduation had been just a month away, and the future that had once lain before her, a vast expanse of uncertainty, had then seemed clear. She hadn't believed she had dared to choose such a path. She had felt the excitement and…what? She hadn't grasped exactly why she had felt so certain she had to go that way; the reason had lain just below her subconscious, just out of reach, so she had pushed the budding thoughts away and concentrated on the form before her.

She had had enough of thinking after the deaths of her classmates, David and Glen. She hadn't wanted to think any more. She had wanted to live life and see the world. She had completed the form, and having turned eighteen in February, she had decided not even to bother to tell her parents about the application. She had sat back in her desk chair. All she had needed then had been the black-and-white photographs so they could determine her physical stature. She would have a friend help her take the photos and put everything in the mail before the week had passed. She had felt a rush from the thrill even as she had reminded herself she had yet to be hired, but just the thought of doing something so "out there" and without anyone knowing had made her feel so alive. She hadn't realized she had felt so buried by life or, in this case, by the loss of it.

The days up to graduation had passed in a blur of studying for finals, sending out graduation announcements, preparing for her graduation party, and waiting for acceptance letters from prospective colleges. Jennifer had sent out applications to three local colleges in the early weeks of January and was expecting replies any day. Where she had once anticipated word from these institutes of higher learning, she now had no interest. She had felt continuing in school would have been more of the same, and now she wanted something more from life. She had wanted…no, she had needed a change, and a different, exciting one.

She had kept her promise to herself and told no one about her application to the modeling agency. She couldn't bear the thought of being teased about doing anything so daring. If the agency had rejected her, the whole process would always have been her little secret.

With graduation set for the upcoming Saturday, she had even forgotten about the modeling application as graduation cards started arriving from distant friends and relatives. Retrieving the mail after school the week of graduation, she had been surprised and nervous to see a reply from the Horizon Modeling Agency tucked in with two replies from colleges she had applied to. Her mother hadn't been home, and her dad had been out in the fields, so she had had the house to herself, other than her aging aunt who had shared their home with them. Jennifer had felt relieved to be alone and thankful her mother hadn't been home to get the mail. Now she wouldn't have to explain anything to anyone, and no one would know if she had been rejected. She had picked up and looked at the envelope. Normally not one to ponder, she had hesitated. Only two, almost three, weeks ago, she had dropped the letter in the post office. Such a quick reply. She had been too afraid to contemplate what it had implied. Holding onto the thought that her future could be greatly altered by the contents of the envelope, she had delayed opening it. She had clutched the letter a moment longer, biting her inner lip, embarrassed she had even sent in her application, sure of a rejection.

Goodness, I'm getting as crazy as dear Aunt Hazel. She had mentally shaken herself and torn open the envelope. She had let out a little squeal of excitement as she had read the letter. *Oh, my gosh! Oh, my gosh!* She couldn't believe it. She had been offered an interview, and resting within the contents of the letter had been information on whom to call to set up airline travel arrangements and hotel lodging at Horizon's expense. What a surprise, a dream come true. She just couldn't believe it. She hadn't even looked at the rest of the mail but had raced to Aunt Hazel's room in the back of the house and rushed in with a gust of youthful zest.

"Aunt Hazel!" she had spilled out in breathless excitement.

"What is it child? My goodness, you're a whirlwind today," Aunt Hazel had chided. "What has you by the tail?"

Going quickly to her side, Jennifer had shoved the letter forward. "Look."

"What is this, a college acceptance?" Aunt Hazel had asked, puzzled about the intense emotion. She had known Jennifer had been less than enthusiastic about four more years of study after high school. She had confided to her aunt, who was more like a friend to the only child than an aging aunt, that she hadn't wanted to go right to college. She had grown weary of academics and hadn't even known what she wanted to study. Aunt Hazel had been sympathetic but had tried to assure Jennifer college wouldn't be as bad as high school. Hazel had never been to college, but she had read and heard from others it was a more relaxed atmosphere. In her heart she had hated the idea of Jennifer leaving home, but she had also realized Jennifer needed to go to become the person she was meant to be. Jennifer couldn't have been this excited about a college acceptance, unless she had had a change of heart. "Let me see, dear. Please hand me my reading glasses."

Specs in place, Hazel had read the letter and soon realized the reason for the great exuberance of her dearly loved niece. She had also surmised Jennifer had not told her parents about the application. Restraining the need to grab Jennifer to her and admonish her to burn the letter and pretend she had never had an interest in such a life, she had looked up into the smiling face and said with as much enthusiasm and support as she could muster, "Oh my goodness, what a surprise, Jennifer. What are you going to do?" She had known Jennifer all her life, and she had understood that Jennifer had needed a sounding board then, not another parental figure. Filling that role had been part of the reason Jennifer and Hazel had remained so close. Hazel had somehow managed always to refrain from passing judgment and yet be honest in her opinions of Jennifer's decisions. They hadn't always agreed, but they had managed to discuss Jennifer's reasons, and Hazel nonjudgmentally had helped her through her poor choices. So far, none had caused her any serious eternal damage. Hazel had always been more concerned for Jennifer's spiritual future than her physical one. The career in that letter had presented a great fear to Hazel. She hadn't known if even she could bear to see someone she loved so greatly embark upon such a road. *Oh dear Mother Mary, how could this have happened?* Hazel had silently queried. *Why my Jennifer? Dear Blessed Virgin, help me to help her not do this. Please.* Keeping her deepest fear and concern from her face, Hazel had listened intently as Jennifer's words had rushed forth like a river filled with youthful excitement. It wasn't long before the rush of words had stopped. Jennifer had sensed her aunt's misgivings about her decision, and Hazel had intuited her niece's concern. The quiet regard Jennifer had held for her aunt's opinion had given Hazel pause for hope.

"Dad and Mom won't be happy, will they? Dad more than Mom," Jennifer had suggested in all seriousness. "What will I do, Aunt Hazel? I really want to do this, but I don't want to upset Mom and Dad. Will you help me?" Jennifer had begged.

"We both know what a lot of good that will do, dear." The simple statement had brought a smile to both their faces. Over the years, Hazel had always gone to bat for Jennifer, often finding herself facing her brother's wrath. It wasn't something Hazel had done to spite her brother, but Jennifer's dad had been so irrational in matters concerning his only child. His need to protect her had almost approached the insane. The poor girl had needed someone to support her. Jennifer's mother couldn't stand her husband's loud ranting and had never challenged anything Shaun had said or done. Hazel had felt if Shaun had had his way poor Jennifer would have been sent away to live with cloistered nuns. She had inwardly giggled at the thought of her niece as a nun, one she and Jennifer had shared between them from time to time.

"You're right. I'm sorry, Aunt Hazel. Dad is going to be real angry, isn't he?" Jennifer had stated more than questioned.

"Yes, dear, I must agree with you. He most certainly will be." She had sighed tiredly, knowing there definitely would be a big scene if Jennifer were to tell her parents she wanted to go to California to try out for a modeling job. The fact that Jennifer had considered her dad's reaction had told Hazel of her niece's intent in pursuing the road the letter had opened before her. Hazel's heart had sunk with a heaviness it hadn't known since the death of her own husband so many years before. Oh life, you are truly a wicked mistress. "Why don't you wait to tell them after you graduate? That way they can enjoy your accomplishment and the party they've planned. They can be angry at a later date. Don't you agree?" Hazel had settled for a partial solution, making a suggestion she had known would keep the peace only for a short time more. She had feared the reaction from her brother would drive her beloved niece from her sheltered home. The fight to keep her true feelings of fear from Jennifer had tested her almost too much, and she had closed her eyes. She had needed time alone for a moment, to compose herself and gather her thoughts. "Jennifer, how about a cup of tea for us? Could you, please, fix some?"

"That's a great idea. I knew you would understand. Thank you so much, Aunt Hazel. I love you." She had given her aunt a hug and a quick kiss on the cheek as she had retrieved the letter and headed to her bedroom. With the letter hidden away, she had gone to the kitchen to make them both a cup of tea.

Upon her exit, Hazel had given way to the quiet tears that then trickled down her softly lined face.

"We are all nobodies, you whore," brought Jennifer quickly back, as Ken screamed in renewed rage at the insanity of the situation. Just tell me how 'buying *us* time' is going to get us out of here alive? Damn! One more inane statement out of you, and I'm taking my own worthless life you stupid, stupid bitch."

"Make the phone call first," Jennifer insisted, "then I'll explain."

Ken went to the phone and made the same impossible request he had sent out with the wounded man. He glared at Jennifer as his request revealed the painfulness of his past. The officer on the other line assured Ken they were working at locating Rachel but informed him they had no jurisdiction over his son. He sagged but angrily replied, "I don't give a damn about jurisdiction. I want to see my son! Just do it, or the bitch is dead!" he screamed into the phone, slamming it into the cradle.

"Okay, I did my part," Ken said as he turned to Jennifer, his look defiant, as if daring her to make mention of Rachel and his son. "Get me out of here if you want to live." His tone was hard and bitter. He motioned for her to rise.

His choice of words, "if you want to live," stirred in Jennifer. She slowly shifted not to rise but to reposition to relieve the numbness in her backside. Taking her time, Jennifer took a deep breath and stated matter-of-factly while looking him full in the face, "We need to talk."

Thinking things couldn't possibly get any crazier, he looked at her seated figure, acknowledged her steady gaze, and dropped all defenses. His energy was spent. In its wake were despair and mild exasperation as he replied weakly, "What?"

"I need to explain how Jesus will get us out of here," Jennifer gently offered, and she politely made a motion to the spot on the floor next to her.

Refusing her directions, Ken sat across from her, keeping the gun pointed in her general direction. His anger had abated, and in mild disgust he replied, "Sure, lady, why not? What else can I do?" He finished with a small laugh. The total absurdity of her offer and the mess of the entire morning pushed him heavily to the floor. He couldn't go anywhere without her. His weariness of the whole messed up situation rose from within, and he rested his head on his bent knees. The motion released his feelings of dejection and failure, and he fully relaxed physically for the first time since he had entered the bank, what seemed like years ago.

With a deep breath, Jennifer quietly began. "I know what it is to want to be free from this life." Her voice took on a small note of bitterness formed from hurt, anger, and disappointment. Ken looked at his hostage with fresh interest, seeing her as more complex than at first she had appeared and maybe—was this possible?—able to understand him. As he looked on, Jennifer continued, her voice growing in strength as she became lost in her own mental anguish, unaware of the effect her tortured words had on the struggling soul in front of her.

"This life sucks, and it's not fair!" she released from the depths within. "Those who love you, love you only when you do what they want, and if you cross them, they throw you out. And the rest of the world does the same." The words surged forth with an anger Jennifer had not realized lay within as Ken sat frozen, staring in astonishment.

She continued with pent up frustration as she thought back to her struggles over the past eight years. She thought she had let go of her hurt and anger from love rejected and denied when she had met Caroline, but as she lay on the bank floor realizing her life could be gone in an instant, all that had been buried came bursting forth.

"Those who are *supposed* to be there to help you help only if *they* feel you are deserving of their help. Even when you try to fix what you've done wrong, no good ever comes of it. When you try, there is no help. They want you to bow to their greater standing, their right-eousness, their piousness. The programs they've established help only those who have no dignity left, those who only want a hand-out, not a hand-up. That way the people in charge can maintain their self-importance and continue to believe that they are so much better than you, that you owe them recognition and all manners of honor. If you keep trying on your own, your situation just gets worse. There is never enough time or money to make it all work. They only help those they deem worthy of help, not the ones who are having a spot of bad luck, but the losers they like to rule. God, this life is so damn unfair." Jennifer's remembered shame and anger rent forth, and she added, "I hate this place."

Losing the hope that this woman could help him, Ken began to wonder if she was as lost as he. Trying to halt the angry rant, he said, "Look, lady, why do you think I'm here today? It's not because my life is a picnic. Let's get out of here now." He made a motion to rise.

Jennifer grabbed his shirt. "No, if you want out of here, you must listen."

"No, you're the one who needs to listen. I've got the gun." He swung the pistol into her face.

"That gun won't get you out of what you're looking to escape." She challenged him, "Use it. I don't care. I'm free, and you won't be unless you listen."

Seeing she really didn't care, Ken sat back down. He had nothing left to lose. As long as she remained alive, he had bargaining power. "Can we make this quick?" he added on an impatient note and then quietly muttering to himself, "For someone who is free, you don't seem too happy."

Jennifer heard Ken's sarcasm, and she caught herself. "I'm sorry. You're right. I guess I just wanted you to know I've been where you are, feeling trapped and hopeless. It wasn't until I met someone who showed me the way that I was freed. It is so easy to get caught up in this world that we lose sight of the way."

Ken came back at her, "This world—I live in it," and he waved the gun in a small circle, "and money does help."

"There is more to living, though," she urged. "It's not about things or jobs or even the love offered by humans." Jennifer ended on a soft and subdued note. Her gaze fell and her eyes again took on that mysterious look that had caught his attention the first time.

When Ken remained silent, Jennifer continued in a quieter and calmer voice, her eyes drawing him in.

"There is only One who will ever love you as you truly are, only One who will ever understand all that you are, and until you see and say yes, the wiles of this world will always obscure and overshadow any happiness." She looked into his gaze and saw that he understood. Drawing in a deep and tired breath, Jennifer added with sincere sadness, "Don't you see? We can't get sucked into the desperation others want us to feel. We can't allow ourselves to think for one moment this world is all there is to life."

Life a Game Is Not

The weapons you amass,
Whose capabilities you'll never experience,
With monies you hoard

In amounts incomprehensible,
Mean nothing to the Almighty who created all.

The futures you steal,
As you dabble with lives of millions
Whose individual identities
You've lost, so far removed from life are you.

World leaders you're called.
Power and titles you've been given.
You're playing at God,
And life a game is not.
We are people of infinite individual value;
And life a game is not.

"Well, then just what are you saying and how does any of this get us out of here? Ken asked, perplexed and impatience seeping back into his voice.

With a deep sigh, Jennifer apologized. "I'm sorry. I guess I'm just tired of it all," she said with a weary sigh. "And I sometimes forget what matters in life. I get wrapped up in all that's wrong with this world and the unfairness I've experienced. I get so angry. And then I remember God is real, and I am so thankful. The one thing no one can take from us is the freedom to choose what God has promised to anyone who will believe the truth. The truth is this: God gave His only Son, the Lord Jesus Christ, who taught us to love one another as you would be loved. He died so all who believe that He, Jesus Christ, is God's only Son will receive eternal life. We will live forever in paradise with unconditional love. We will never want for anything. Most important, we will never want for love."

Jennifer reached for Ken's arm and searched his face. "The one true way out, out all of this…," and she searched for the right words, "…this world of injustices and inhumane treatment is to accept the

Lord Jesus Christ. Only in the Lord Jesus Christ will you find the peace you really seek. With Jesus Christ as your Lord, what happens here is bearable. We still have to live here but, believe it or not, you will actually come to enjoy your life on earth a little more because the baggage of the material world will not burden you in this physical life. The spiritual life has fewer wants. You won't feel compelled to possess because you'll have all you could ever want: You will have the perfect, unconditional love of the Almighty who created you. He made each and everyone of us, and He loves us so much He gave His only Son to die for each one of us so we could come back to Him when our time here is over. Every time I think of this, I am so moved with thankfulness. I don't have to do anything to earn this wonderful gift of unconditional love except *believe*, and that I can do."

Ken looked at her as if she has just told him the moon was really made of cheese.

Seeing his look of shock at her revelations of the way out, she knew she had to take a different tact. She had to make real what she was saying, find a connection he could embrace. "Think for just a moment. When you made your demand on the phone to the cops, what was it based on?" Jennifer paused to let him consider his demand.

He had only ever wanted to make things right with Rachel. He wanted the life he had dreamed of. Love, that was what he had lost, Rachel's love. Then it hit Ken fully; his and Rachel's problems had started when she had lost her father's love. Love, love was all he really wanted, and it was taken from him through no fault of his own. He still loved, but his love was not returned. He hung his head in sadness. From all his efforts to recapture that which he had lost, he had jumped into his worst nightmare.

Jennifer watched as the emotions rolled over Ken's tired features. She continued, "If you really want to be free, really free, accept Jesus Christ as your Lord and Savior. You will have a love that will never be withheld, and this world will lose its power over you. You must of your own free will tell God you want to be His child through His Son the Lord Jesus Christ. You are then His forever and free from the futile rat race of seeking and searching for answers and peace from this world. The answers aren't in this world. In this world you will forever want; you will never truly be satisfied."

Her words for the better part of an hour had touched on some of the very same issues he had struggled with the past few years. She had reminded him of his own mortal exhaustion. He again thought how he had tried so hard the past few years to do what was right, and everything he had done had gone wrong and horribly so. The remembered weight of his struggle pressed upon him, and tears leaked out. He responded weakly, "Yeah, I see. There is no other way. Oh, God, I'm just so fucking tired of trying and failing. This is not," and he waved his gun around the empty expanse of the bank, "going to satisfy anything. Is it?" He posed the question to no one in particular and raggedly sucked in air. With tears slowly coming down his cheeks, he continued, "I see what you're saying, but," and with a huge indrawn breath he asked, "can it really be so simple? I just want out." He was reasoning more to himself than to Jennifer. He repeated, "I'm so fucking tired of the constant struggle. I don't want this. There really is no other way, other than death. And what is that? That's giving up." With another deep sigh, he let go. "I want…I want…." He was visibly sobbing. "I am so sorry. I have done so much wrong and failed so horribly at everything. I thought I had it all under control. I had plans—a family, a job, all the stuff you're supposed to get. None of that matters anymore. I didn't really know. It's really all about love. That's all it ever is for everyone, even Rachel. God, poor Rachel. I didn't know. I wanted to give her things and what I thought she wanted, but I never could get her what she needed." He looked up into Jennifer's eyes. "Do you really think after all I've done I can still have the Lord Jesus Christ? I've done so much wrong, and so much bad has happened in my life."

"Hey, it's not about what *you* have done or can do. It's about believing that Jesus Christ is God's only Son and that His death on the cross forgives you for all your sins today and those you might commit tomorrow," Jennifer assured him.

"What? I can still do wrong and have this eternal love?"

"No." Jennifer smiled at the question she once had asked not too long ago. "You can't knowingly do wrong and think Jesus will forgive you. Once you accept the wonderful gift that Jesus Christ gave you when He died on the cross, you will receive the Holy Spirit, which is God's very presence within you. When you are tempted to sin, you must remember to fall back on God's presence, the Holy Spirit, and God in you will not sin. It won't be you resisting temptation; it will be the very power of God in you: God rejects sin. This world is full of temptations. Jesus Christ knows how hard this world is, and because of this, when Jesus went back to heaven to be with God the Father, God sent all of us who accept Jesus Christ as His Son the gift of the Holy Spirit. The Holy Spirit does the Father's will through us, and when we are being tried, he steps in if we remember his presence within us. There are times when we forget and don't give God our lives; we sin because *we* choose not to remember God in us."

"What do you mean, 'being tried'? I thought you said all we have to do is have faith and believe?" Ken asked desperately, wanting so much to understand and be free from all he had struggled with.

"Yes, that is all we have to do. But think about what you came here to get this morning—money and hopefully lots of it—because you thought it would bring you all you hoped for. Right?" she gently reminded him.

"Yeah, I guess. Only now I know there would never be enough money to do that. No, I mean, I guess money isn't the answer." And he smiled with sheepish embarrassment.

"In trying to take this money and what you perceived as happiness, there were those who were trying to stop you. Right?" she offered in continued explanation.

"Yeah," he replied expectantly, wanting to know.

"Okay, now once you accept and believe in Jesus Christ, the devil—and individuals who live for this world—don't want you to be successful in your belief. They don't believe in this 'religious, born again' stuff, in eternal happiness, and they don't want you or any-one else to have it. But what if they are wrong? They certainly don't want the rabble beneath them to spend eternity in a wealth they don't understand and won't have any part of. In service of this world, they try to steal you from the Lord with temptations of this life. Everyday we live here, we are faced with 'or tested by' choices. The Holy Spirit is here to resist the pull of this world for you. You must have faith and accept this truth. God gives of Himself to those who believe and accept this truth. He gives the Holy Spirit, His very presence, to do the job of resisting and saying no to the temptations this world puts before those who say yes to salvation. God cannot and does not fail. Every test will only strengthen God in you. If you do make mistakes on occasion, but not intentionally, you are forgiven. What I'm trying to say is you cannot knowingly keep doing wrong and then ask Jesus to forgive you. But we will stumble along the way, and it is for these mistakes we are forgiven."

> JOHN 1:10-13 He was in the world, and though the world was made through him, the world did not recognize him. He came to that which was his own, but his own did not receive him. Yet to all who received him, to those who believed in his name, he gave the right to become children of God—children born not of natural descent, nor of human decision or a husband's will, but born of God.

Comprehension filtered into Ken's open, seeking mind. More composed but with the streaks of tears still apparent on his face, he asked with a new light to his once desperate countenance, "So all I have to do is believe that Jesus Christ is the Son of God, and Jesus...," his voice started to break up and become small, "died for me? If I do this, I get to have unconditional...," once again he began to cry, "love, forgiveness, and eternal life?"

"Yes," Jennifer softly whispered, not surprised at the overwhelming emotion taking hold of the once angry, desperate man facing her.

"I do want Jesus Christ to be my Lord and Savior," he stated through his tears. "I don't want this life I've had. I want to be forgiven," and, ever so softly and with slight embarrassment, he added, "and loved." He raised his eyes to Jennifer, and the vulnerability of this most basic and innate request caused her to cry with him.

"Jesus Christ is your Lord and Savior. You are now His, bought and paid for with His precious blood on the cross. You are no longer...I'm sorry, but I don't even know your name."

Ken smiled weakly and responded, "I'm Ken. Ken Adams."

Jennifer continued, "Ken, you are no longer the Ken of the past, the robber who came in here with bad intentions, hurt, and resentment. The robber Ken, the old you, was nailed to the cross with Jesus Christ, and a new you was born again in the resurrected Jesus Christ.

You are now 'born again' a child of the God of Abraham, the God of Isaac, and the God of Jacob."

Ken, unable to speak, hung his head, nodding acceptance to Jennifer's pronouncement. At last, he drew a deep breath and exhaled agreement, "Yes, I accept Jesus as my Lord and Savior."

At those words, Jennifer burst forth with her own joy, "Oh, thank you, Lord Jesus Christ. Thank you, thank you, thank you," as she hugged the weeping man.

After a few minutes, he straightened up, and with a fresh look of new life and hope and the light of salvation and determination to start over in his eyes, he said, "Now what?"

"We pick up the phone, and you tell them you are ready to come out," she stated matter-of-factly.

"I'm scared," he blurted out before he knew it, and then dropped his head sheepishly, his determination so rapidly fleeing in the face of the world.

"Me, too. But remember to believe and trust, have faith in God's love for you. You will have to face the consequences for what you have done, of course; for we still have to live in this world. But now the Holy Spirit is with you. You can do whatever is before you for you are not alone and never will be again."

"Will you help me?" he asked with all innocence and honesty.

"Yes, I will," Jennifer stated without any reservation and reached for his hand as they rose together for Ken to make the phone call.

Chapter Three

Joe

The security doors and locking chambers of the Foster Medium Security Prison for Men clanged shut one last time on Joseph Deeny. The prison had been his home for the past ten years. No more. Joe had no bitterness, or even anger, only resignation. He'd served his time, taken his human punishment.

And, although that experience stayed behind him, he just couldn't forget what had occurred four months ago. Just a few more steps, and he would be free. Or would he? He had received some form of release from the guilt he had carried with him the greater part of his prison sentence. Now though, upon his re-entry back into society, he felt—no knew—he had no freedom from life, and the weight of the unknown that lay ahead pressed on him like a yoke. He had never been without a plan or an idea of what he should or could do. He was almost free again. But just what was he to do? His fear stood before him, barring his path.

With a bewildered shake of his head, he stepped through the last portal into this freedom. A shell of what he had been, Joe drew a slow deep breath and mentally pushed back at the immense fear of the unknown that tried to weigh him down. He looked out the windows of the doors ahead and resolved to follow the road before him and just take one day at a time.

The guard, who held the last door for him to pass through, interrupted his thoughts. "Don't you have someone coming to meet you, Joe? I can call you a cab."

"No, I'll be fine. Thank you," Joe reassured the guard. "I'm looking forward to the walk." Joe smiled his appreciation at the prison guard's genuine concern, but he'd spoken the truth. He wanted this walk without walls, and he nodded his head in a polite good-bye, took the envelope the guard had pushed into his hands along with his personal phone number, and left the prison behind.

As he headed down the road to town, he realized that the old Joe received into prison was gone. But what of the new Joe? Thoughts circled round him. Where would he go once he got into the town that lay ahead? What would he do with the remainder of his life? Fighting the rising fear, Joe remembered the peace of Jesus Christ, and he settled back into the newness of trust and faith in God's plan for him. The intangible—his faith—he held onto tightly. An unregistered smile lit Joe's face, breathing life into a soul that had been almost smothered in years of quilted sorrow and guilt. Joe's spiritual growth, through the presence of the Holy Spirit, had just begun, and this growth is unmeasured to him who has received. The light of salvation, once acknowledged and received, takes root and grows from the grace showered down from God.

Sgt. Henry Wynegarde watched as Mr. Deeny headed off down the road to town. He wished with all his heart he could have convinced the large yet frail-looking man to take his offer of a ride. He understood a newly released inmate's need to feel freedom, but this just didn't seem to be the case with Mr. Deeny, or just Joe, as he liked to be called. Joe had been a model prisoner the past ten years. Sgt. Wynegarde would never forget him.

He had been in the corrections system for fifteen years when Joe had arrived. Some pretty hardened hearts had passed through his gates when he first transferred from walking among the general prison population to his present position. They would come in, shackled, most of them cocky, with eyes that shone with "I'm not done yet" devilishness. Very few came in humble and filled with remorse or anything near sorrow for the acts that had brought them to his post.

Over time he came to see those who should have been counseled and, though punished and set aside from society for a time, didn't belong in a prison. They lacked the selfish attitude that most of the prison population wore like a second skin. These people, most often guilty of tragic manslaughter cases, would spend their entire sentence behind bars, whereas the inmate who truly lacked the empathy and compassion to be a structural part of society usually received early release for good behavior. These were the very same to arrive back in three years tops with an even bigger ego and chip of "I'm still not done with society."

Joe was one of those who should have been released early. Sgt. Wynegarde felt such pity for the inattentive drivers and—he guiltily acknowledged—even the drunk drivers who killed without thought. Some were repeat drunk drivers, but most were just regular people who got caught in life. He often pondered the waste of such events. It happened so often everywhere, in every state. Why couldn't more be done to prevent this loss of life, on both ends? Life behind bars for some was such a waste.

Sgt. Wynegarde had struggled with his overwhelming compassion his first few years. He couldn't help but feel man wasn't made to be caged but created with the right to life, liberty, and the pursuit of happiness. Yet he had to hold on to the truth that most of the inmates were in prison because of choices they had willingly made and heartless actions against others they had brutally committed.

Yes, he knew the prisons, most of them, provided opportunities for inmates to better their situation in life so when they were finally released back into society they could be more productive members. He also knew the majority of the prisoners who deserved their prison sentence cared only about themselves and what life could do for them. These people were often clever enough to take advantage of what was offered and then use these skills to do further damage to the society that had given them their new and improved skills. To these individuals, society's locking them away enforced their feelings that they did not belong, they were defective, and they lacked the character to be among everyone else. In his own uneducated way, Sgt. Wynegarde often wondered if there couldn't be a better way to reach out to these people, to help them change their outlook, and to show them how to look beyond themselves and their own needs and wants. Wasn't there something that could get through so these people, too, could feel? What were they lacking that they thought only of themselves and their own selfish wants?

He thought of prisoners of years gone by who had worked on chain gangs. *The system worked so much better back then*, he mused, conveniently forgetting the abuse suffered by those men who had no choice but to toil under the whip. Those prisoners had contributed to society, sometimes constructing something that they could feel proud of. They had provided something good for others, not just themselves. The hard, sometimes back-breaking work had left them with little energy for fights. Often times their work had been outdoors, and these people had had the opportunity to be in God's creation with nothing but the sounds of nature, God's call to be acknowledged as the creator of the beauty in which they toiled. They had labored under heavy guard, yet they had been productive members of society. They weren't societal rejects sitting in man-made cell blocks with man-made diversions.

Sgt. Wynegarde wasn't much of a God man, but his last twenty-five years had made him more reflective about life in general. When someone came in with a sentence of fifteen to twenty-plus years, he couldn't get past what his own life had been for him—living free, creating a family, spending time with loved ones. In trying to train his compassion, he had grown to feel such hopelessness for some who walked through the prison doors. That had led to apathy, which made room for hate. The degeneration of his empathy had been one of the reasons he had had to remove himself from the general guarding of the prisoners. He had felt himself become hardened to the humanity he was guarding. Before it could take hold, he shook off the old apparition of hatred he had felt his last few months working in the general population. He was still embarrassed about the depth of hatred he had felt toward people whose lives had gone wrong. His new position afforded him some space from them, and he could look at them as individuals who somewhere, somehow had taken a wrong turn on the road of life. He was never more thankful for the life he had been blessed with.

His new position also gave him the opportunity to see that some of the released inmates truly appreciated the freedom before them. They were happy, their faces alight with a second chance to be with loved ones. Some still reflected a tinge of anger, for life had gone on, and time had changed those who were now waiting with open arms to welcome them back into the world. The sergeant wasn't much in the way of talking to God, but he always said a little prayer that they wouldn't be back and their life would be better. Some would turn their lives around, even share their experiences and help prevent others from falling into the circumstances that had brought them to prison. And here he had returned to his original thought—that some shouldn't be incarcerated to begin with.

Joe was one of these, and Sgt. Wynegarde was surprised he had had no one to greet him. Reflecting on Joe's arrival ten years ago, he remembered his curiosity about the priest who had been sentenced for involuntary manslaughter. Rumors had indicated Joe had refused an offer to shorten his prison time due to the special circumstances of his case; it was almost as if he had welcomed his sentence. The story had spread fast through the prison population, and upon Joe's incarceration, no one had bothered him. Even the toughest and most hardened and cruel prisoners had walked a wide circle around the new guy who had seemed detached from life in a haze of mental anguish. At first Sgt. Wynegarde had assumed Joe's attitude was because he was a man of the cloth, but it soon became apparent that Joe had wanted nothing to do with his calling. Some of the most violent men made every attempt to cheer the poor self-imprisoned man up. All wondered what actually "had gone down" to bring the man to welcome prison time. No one had been crass enough to ask for details. Joe's demeanor had deflected all attempts at curious questions. The overwhelming sorrow and sadness that had hovered around Joe was so pronounced no one had wished to burden the poor guy further. He had never spoken of his feelings and hadn't worn them as badges begging for acknowledgement. Yet sorrow, sadness, and unbearable guilt had enveloped him so profoundly they had emanated from him as a heavy cologne and had warded off all outsiders.

One lifer, Bjorg, a big man like Joe, doing life for possession, distribution of a controlled substance, and negligent homicide of his partner when they had run from the police, pretty much ran the yard. Upon Joe's first appearance there, Bjorg had approached Joe with a shove. Nearly unmoved, Joe had turned and met his challenging gaze full on. "I never see a man so fucking full of hurt and agony," Bjorg had told his henchmen. "He looks at me and damn if I want to take some of it." Bjorg had never apologized in all his memory, yet he immediately had told Joe, "Sorry," and turned away, trying to decipher what he had seen and felt.

Joe had never said a word to the big fellow with the bald head and arms full of tattoos. He had been lost in his own agony of guilt. The apology had never been acknowledged for he was still too new to the circumstances that he had brought into his life.

Other prisoners who were exposed to Joe, however slightly, became reflective and left questioning who they were and why they were there. The prison atmosphere around Joe, wherever he happened to be, became one of solitude and heavy quiet, not peace but a silence leaden with thought. Everyone knew how to deal with fellow criminals, but a genuinely good guy who accepted his punishment had puzzled everyone.

Over time, the truth had slowly surfaced through bits of overheard conversation Joe had with his legal counsel. The facts themselves revealed the most tragic of accidents and had sent waves of understanding and compassion through a population of people who had never dealt with such emotions for the greater part of their life. The entire body had looked forward to Joe's first parole board date nearly twenty-two months into his sentence. If ever a prisoner should be paroled, Joe was such a case. To the disappointment and shock of the prison population, Joe had declined parole. Ten full years from the day he had entered, Joe walked free.

Sgt. Wynegarde wondered as Joe's form disappeared on the horizon, *Was he truly free?* Shaking the clouded thoughts from his heart, Sgt. Wynegarde was thankful Joe had accepted the envelope of gathered donations from fellow inmates he had shoved into his hand along with his own telephone number. And before Joe had set off through the last door to the world, Sgt. Wynegarde had implored, "Call me if there is anything I can do to help, Joe, please."

Without any intention of taking the guard up on his offer, Joe had relieved Sgt. Wynegarde's conscience and put the telephone number and envelope of money in his pocket and passed through the door to the world awaiting him.

Joe sat up at the sound of his six a.m. alarm. The ticking of the minute hand resounded loudly in the darkness of the little room. As he readied himself for his job of almost five months, Joe sighed. One more day dawning. Nothing to make this any different from the one before. And just more of the same to come after. *How many more of these days lie ahead?* Joe wondered.

He had felt forgiveness, freedom, and peace earlier, just before his time in prison was up. Yet, now, two short years later, he felt the world and all he had been raised to know come creeping back in to trouble him and cover over and bury those gifts and him in the process.

He searched for the freedom he had felt, but upon his release from the confinement of prison, his old habits of living in the world had resurfaced. Lacking outward guidance and facing the stark reality of the unknown, Joe had stumbled and faltered on his path toward growth. He had lost what he had gained and slipped, for a time, into the shadow of what he had been.

Joe felt torn—pulled in two directions. Upon being absorbed back into the world, Joe wanted what he had left before his imprisonment—the security of belonging. And yet he did not want to let go of what he had received shortly before his release—the recognition of a higher truth. Why couldn't he have both—security and a higher truth? This tug of war weighed upon Joe daily.

Not wishing to return to the church he had left upon self-imprisonment, he had nothing to replace it. In addition to Catholic churches, the community of Cornell where he had settled claimed mostly Lutheran, Methodist, and Presbyterian and a few other smaller religious establishments of the Latter Day Saints and Seventh Day Adventists. But their presence only added to Joe's longing for fellowship; none gave him any satisfaction.

Joe realized he had a need for human dialogue and contact. As he settled into his job, his compassion for his fellow man and a desire for community awoke. Coworkers invited him to their services, and he did attend two or three of these houses of worship where he was warmly welcomed. Nevertheless, he had to admit he only felt uncomfortable and traitorous. These were not the Church of his upbringing; they did not feel right. In all honesty, he missed what he had left.

He still rejoiced in the forgiveness he felt he had received while confined, but he longed for the traditions, ceremony, and the celebration of the mass of his rejected religion. No other would do for him. Joe had truly loved and embraced everything about the Catholic faith of his youth. Its majestic ceremonies had comforted him, beautiful and steeped in centuries of intellectual symbolism and mysticism. He wouldn't, he couldn't have another. There was no other organized form of religion that was grand enough. His realization there would be no other house of worship left him unsure and full of doubt over his choice in the full gift of being born again and newness of self. He had never felt so utterly alone. Yet he sought no help or direction.

As much as he longed for belonging, he could not go back to the Church he had left. And as hungry as he was for ceremony, he could not now accept all the teachings of Catholicism. His eyes had been opened. He had too many questions, and the answers he had once accepted as truisms he now knew were compromises of truths made by man to unite all for the purposes of man—the need for control of wealth and power. How readily he had accepted the Church's teachings—that worshippers and priests, alike, need the doctrines of Catholicism and the hierarchy of the intellectually superior men to properly worship the heavenly Father and His only Son. He now felt so lost. He no longer felt real comfort in who he had been brought up to be or what he been brought up to believe in. He could not make what he now understood work with what he had been taught to believe, so he drifted alone.

Joe got up and dressed in his janitor's uniform. He enjoyed his job at the Cornell Independent Living Center. As janitorial supervisor, he oversaw four men and five women who did the daily upkeep and cleaning for the fifty residents that lived in the small retirement facility. Most of the people he knew on a first-name basis, and he could not deny he felt a certain closeness to those in his supervision, but something was missing. He just couldn't put his finger on his restless, aching need for truly belonging to something greater. At times, his neediness made him angry. After all, his life was comparatively good. He was in good health for a man of fifty-one years, and his home, though rented, was comfortable. By all means, he should have been happy; yet he wasn't. He angrily buttoned his last shirt button and heavily walked into his small kitchen to eat a bite of breakfast. Why did such a thought have to greet him this morning?

He poured himself a cup of coffee and, while waiting for his toast to pop, made his lunch for his workday. Thoughts of his past came back. He had been a well-loved priest and a good one, too. He had had many invites to home-cooked meals, had often been asked to attend birthday parties, retirements, graduations, and had been preferred to the higher ranking monsignor to perform most weddings and baptisms. Joe had had a way with the congregation. Before he had accepted forgiveness, he had had no problem rejecting all this love. In the effort to make reparations for his wrongdoing, he had felt undeserving and needing punishment. Love was not his, and he should not and could not have love for he had sinned. Once Joe's eyes had been opened and he accepted forgiveness, he knew how dearly he had missed and needed human love and belonging. But how to return to receiving love, he knew not.

Joe sadly reflected on his last visit with someone whom he had felt so endeared to, and he almost wept at the remembered loss of friendship.

He and Hazel O'Meary had corresponded from the start of his incarceration. Although he had thought to reject any letters, during that first mail call, something inside him had forced him to extend his hand. The letters had sat in his cell for a time before he had decided he was punishing an old acquaintance and not himself by refusing even to acknowledge her efforts. He had been shocked with her compassion and concern for his general well-being and grateful for her offerings of rosaries and prayers being said for his "situation." She had assured him everyone in "his" parish felt he shouldn't have accepted his prison sentence; what had happened was an accident, pure and simple, a tragic, tragic accident.

He had been courteous to write her back and thank her and ask her, please, to extend his thanks to the community for its generosity of forgiveness and especially for the offered prayers. He had gone on to add that she needn't write him for he felt his prison sentence most appropriate, almost lenient, compared to the loss the families had suffered due to his negligence. He had sealed the envelope and dropped it in the mail, never expecting anything more. To his surprise Hazel had kept up a regular correspondence, writing every few months. And try as Joe might, he couldn't refuse her letters. They had provided the one bright spot he had allowed into his self-imposed isolation. Near to the very end of his prison sentence, her depth of care and concern for his spiritual well-being had come through in an unannounced visit. Remembering her care expressed in letters throughout the years and in that visit, Joe realized how much he needed that connection now.

Why did giving up Catholicism mean giving up the love of his former community? He knew in his heart why: He couldn't face the criticism and ostracism of some of his most devout parishioners. Steeped in theology, he had struggled to let go of the doctrines he had cherished and the rituals he had found comfort and solace in. And he now lacked the strength to defend his newness of faith, day after day, to those he loved. They would never understand. So he had left the only family he had known since his seminary days. He had tried connecting with other church communities, but he had only felt incomplete and unsatisfied with their doctrine. Still he yearned for something more. He felt so very alone and lost.

And, now, why did Hazel have to come to mind, in this moment of weakness? His thoughts went back to her visit.

A Stranger You See Me

What I hold inside
from my face is hidden.
I smile and laugh,
yet the pain inside, too long has burned.
Anger intense, grips me, with two fists clenched.

My faults and insecurities, guards indomitable,
forever prisoners to their watch.
A stranger you see me, in light as good.
Who are you? And from what view do you peer?

Your words so kind, God's love universal,
so foreign and sincere, I timidly accept.
Your earnestness bombards, and the light
filters in; the guards they falter.
Captive an eternity, I struggle to take hold.
Don't let me go, an escape I'll attempt,
a change I'll make.

Over the course of his sentence, Joe's correspondence had disturbed the faithful Hazel. His letters had taken on such a note of distress and self-doubt. *How,* she pondered, *could someone so filled with the wisdom and doctrines of the Church have become so weak and spiritually needy in his faith?* First, he had informed her no longer to address him as Father, and then he had written of his refusal of early parole, and later he had confessed he was no longer attending prison mass. The totality of these letters had finally prompted her to action. She had decided she would make a visit to enlighten Father Deeny and help him see he was trudging down an errant path. She would bolster this poor soul; the devil would not take this good man from the flock of the Church. She had timed her visit for a few short months before his release. She knew his self-doubt couldn't go on. He was a priest and, as far as their parish was concerned, a good one.

Her visit had taken Joe by total surprise. Although, upon his arrival at the prison, he had given permission for any of his parishioners to see him, none had bothered, and he had expected none ever would. Nor had Hazel mentioned in her letters she was coming. So when the guard had come to get him and informed him he had a visitor, he had just assumed it was legal counsel with communication about his upcoming release. Had he known it was Hazel, he might not have agreed to meet with her, especially if he could have foreseen the course their conversation would take. It was one thing to let legal spout encouragement about his future, but to say no to well-intentioned but wrong-headed advice offered by a caring person was harder.

Joe might have guessed why Hazel had come if he had thought a little more carefully about who it was he had been writing to and what they had been writing about. In his letters, he had written freely, almost too freely. He had truly let go of the "Father Deeny" image and written as a man to a friend, a peer. In this manner, he had let his thoughts flow more openly, not thinking how he was affecting the spiritual core of someone who looked to him for spiritual guidance. He had only wanted to understand a little better what had just happened himself, not inflict more pain on the good people he had been taught to look after. How could he have avoided wrongdoing? He had only wanted to do the right thing. He was so tired of failing at doing what he felt was right.

Hazel had been shocked when the guard had escorted Father Deeny into the visitation room. Where she had held in her mind all this time the image of the powerful priest who had left St. Mary's parish, she now saw before her just the remnants of that vibrant man. He looked so aged and worn. The once tall, broad presence of dignity now seemed terribly humbled and weighted and old for his years, his hair tinged with premature white. Hazel knew he was only nearing fifty; but today he looked so worn. All his earlier stature of character was gone; he was but a shadow of the priest she had known. She had quickly risen and reached for his hands as if to guide an ailing friend to the nearest seat.

"Father Deeny," she had began, "what on earth...?"

Joe had gently interrupted her, "Hazel, please." He had taken her outstretched hands and let her guide him to the chair next to the small table in the tidy little room. "Hazel, what are you doing here? Why? And, please, it's Joe, not Father Deeny, not anymore." He had cringed as he had said it; it had been his first physical effort of standing for what he now knew among those with whom he had been. He had not been able to help the feeling of shrinking inside, for he was still young in his newborn knowledge.

Hazel had responded to Father Deeny's physical change, unaware of its connection to his startling spiritual transformation. While the man she had known had been an imposing and commanding figure of Church authority, this new presence appeared broken and humbled. And although that state exactly prepared Joe for openness of spirit and his rebirth, it would have an entirely different effect upon his dear friend. The sight of that retiring figure had moved her to motherly compassion.

MATTHEW 21:42-44 Jesus said to them, "Have you never read in the Scripture: 'The stone the builders rejected has become the capstone; the Lord has done this, and it is marvelous in our eyes'? Therefore I tell you that the kingdom of God will be taken away from you and given to a people who will produce its fruit. He who falls on this stone will be broken to pieces, but he on whom it falls will be crushed."

"Nonsense, Father," she had insisted, and Joe again had cringed inwardly, not unnoticeable to Hazel who had searched his face, trying to understand. *Why am I here?* she had wondered in the presence of such a broken man. And then she had realized her mission. *This is exactly why. No more 'Father Deeny.'* She softly admonished, "How can you even say such a thing? We—the Church—we all need you. You can't throw away or stop who you are. Whatever could have you think such nonsense? You've done your penance. We forgive you; you must forgive yourself. I am here to help." With the kindly patience of a grandparent speaking to a wayward toddler, she had waited for him to explain.

Upon entering the room, Joe had been equally astonished to see Hazel. He hadn't been up to visitors and most especially not those with misplaced help and compassion. He had sagged visibly at what he knew her visit would bring. Only recently had he come to know and accept the truth, and this had been after years of seeking. He had finally seen. His eyes had been opened. Yet, he hadn't felt ready, strong enough, to defend his recent spiritual decisions. He still had been examining his new vision of life and hadn't known if he was up to explaining, especially to someone who had been as ingrained as he. The thought of the number years he had taken to reach this point had made him sigh heavily. In that brief visit, he couldn't have expected Hazel to see a truth so foreign to what she had experienced. How could he have helped her understand? He certainly hadn't wanted to inflict anymore pain on that dear lady. Nor could he have turned away from her, so he had gone forward into the room, his person void of anything but doubt and whirling thoughts. What on earth would he say? And here the Lord had stepped in as he had foretold.

> ROMANS 8:26-27 In the same way, the Spirit helps us in our weakness. We do not know what we ought to pray for, but the Spirit himself intercedes for us with groans that words cannot express. And he who searches our hearts knows the mind of the Spirit, because the Spirit intercedes for the saints in accordance with God's will.

She had been so kind and undeserving of his failing person. How could he have helped her to let him go? She had not changed from that evening of the fateful turn of events, a breath of life and goodness. How could he have warded off what she had brought—his old beliefs wrapped in kindness, care, and community love? She could never have understood, and why should he have had to be the one to make her? His thoughts had brought his words forth with such inner anguish, and he had seen Hazel fight back tears of compassion as she, too, had struggled for words and strength to bring him back into the fold of her professed faith in Catholicism.

He had taken her outstretched hands as if to help her understand what he had been about to unload and share with someone as kindly, good-hearted, and well-intentioned as she. In a painfully exhausted voice he had begun, "Hazel, you're wrong." Joe had thought back over the years of their shared correspondence, trying to remember when his tone had changed. How could he have helped Hazel to understand that he wasn't leaving God and all that God offered? He was departing from the instruction of man-crafted doctrines. His own struggle to understand what he had then accepted with what he had been raised to believe had caused him much grief, but try as he might, the two concepts could not righteously be merged. He had come to a fork in the road, and he had made, what he had believed to be, the true and righteous choice. How could he have imparted that to this dear friend without having alienated her friendship, hurt her, and made her think him entirely mad? He had known it couldn't have been done; so he had proceeded with great difficulty, praying for words from another Source.

We are never truly alone in life, but when we most feel abandoned, the grace from God intercedes. It is at those times when we turn humbly and receptively to God without human interference that we can truly hear the Spirit of God. Unbeknownst to Joe, life and circumstances beyond his knowledge and understanding had been at work, molding him into who God had planned him to be from the very beginning. Joe spoke with God's guidance.

"Hazel, these past few months have been such a battle." All that he had felt came rushing back, and the surge of emotion had caused his eyes to tear. He had struggled and taken a deep breath to regain his composure lest he seem mentally unstable. He had continued, with quiet strength. "These years have been my purgatory, not a confinement imposed by others, but my own self-willed purgatory, my opportunity to make amends, in some small way. Yet, the whole time I did my deserved penance, I felt no reprieve. All that loomed before me was time, and my companion was overwhelming guilt and wretchedness for the wrong I had done. I prayed for forgiveness. I forced solitude upon myself even when I was with others, so I could do my penance as it should be done, with whole-hearted repentance. I was, and am, so sorry for the pain I caused those families and the loss the world will never know because those two young lives were taken before they were fully lived." His emotions had caught up with him, and the intensity of his hopelessness at his inability to receive forgiveness and make right his wrongdoing had overcome him. Sobs of anguish had escaped. But just as quickly, Joe had regained his composure at the remembrance that he did have forgiveness, and that was what he had to help Hazel see.

Hazel, upon having heard and seen Joe's anguish, had not been able to stop the silent tears that had rolled down her age-worn face. *Why didn't I come sooner?* she had lamented. *The parish should have sent someone every day to help this man.* Yes, she had seen, then, he wasn't "Father Joe" the strong religious leader but a man like every other in need of human assistance.

She had interrupted Joe, "We failed you as a community and as a parish, Father." With understanding, she had softly continued, "We should have come to your side in these your darkest hours. We didn't, but we will seek forgiveness and do our penance. Don't you see? Purgatory is just what you said, a time for reflection, a time away from all life to know the depth of our sins. From what you have just said, it worked as we are taught. This was just a test. Don't you see? One for you, and now I see one for us, your parish. We sinned, but won't you please let us help you now? We failed you. I know this now, and I am deeply sorry; and when I report back, the entire parish will be equally filled with remorse over our failing. You simply must forgive us this sin and let us make amends. You simply cannot walk away from the Church because we left you astray. Please, our parish needs you."

Joe had released Hazel's hands in mild astonishment and sat up with renewed strength. "No, Hazel, you and the others did no wrong. Yes, I agree it was a test, but even more, it was a revelation of what I came to see and accept as the truth. Being here, imposing punishment and penance upon myself, only helped me to see the glaring truth. There can be no end to purgatory if you believe that you have to suffer there to achieve forgiveness for your sins. It's just not possible to make sufficient amends. Eternity isn't long enough. This time here, this alone, made me see I could no longer accept the teachings I was taught. Purgatory, it's…," and Joe had struggled to find the right word, "it would have to be endless punishment and suffering. My time here has been a blessing. I now see."

Forgetting the discomfort of familiarity, Hazel had simply stated, "Well, of course, Joe. Purgatory and punishment are not supposed to be easy. How else would one be repentant if the time spent in repentance was bearable?" Barely taking time to draw a breath, she had continued, "Let me set this straight. What you are saying is because you have been here and suffered, you no longer accept purgatory?

What then of forgiveness for our sinfulness if we don't do penance in purgatory upon death? Are you saying you believe we mustn't suffer for our wrongdoings? Are you implying we don't have to be forgiven, we don't have to do penance? Joe, surely you must agree no one is good enough to go straight to heaven?" She had finally taken a deep exasperated breath as she had searched his face for sanity.

"No, Hazel, listen." Joe had tried again.

"Let me finish, Joe," Hazel had sternly interrupted. "Don't you see what has happened? You have been tested; there you are right. But because the penance was painful and had no end in sight, you decided not only can you not do it, but you are going to throw away all you have been taught and known as righteousness your whole life. You say there is no feeling of forgiveness and no end to the sentence. Again, Joe, you may well be right. But let me ask you, do you really think God will accept people who have sinned even more grievously than you into heaven when they have the ugliness of guilt upon them?" With barely a pause, she had continued with righteous indignation. "If what you say is true, that you felt this overwhelming wretchedness and lack of forgiveness for the wrongs you did, how can such a soul possibly be received into heaven with this weight of blemish on it?"

"There you have it!" Joe had rejoiced for she had just voiced what Joe had come to know, what he had tried to tell her. In amongst her ranting, she had spoken the wholeness of the truth. He had said almost joyously, "We can never do enough penance; there will never be enough Hail Marys or Our Fathers prayed, never enough time spent in someplace carved out for soul-searching, for the sins of the lives we live. Not for the smallest of sin—and scripture says even thinking the thought is horrible in its ugliness to the perfection of God—can we ever do enough. You are indeed right. How can such a soul ever be received into heaven, into God's perfect love? It can't, not by anything humanly done or offered. Don't you see? Only God, in the perfect sacrifice He chose, His own Son who was blameless, could cleanse us from the ugliness of the sins of our humanity. Jesus Christ took our punishment, and only Jesus Christ dying for us could free us from our sins, from the smallest to the largest. All sin is an abomination to God. To truly be forgiven, a person must first accept Jesus Christ as the Son of the God of Abraham, the God of Isaac, and the God of

Jacob, and then this person must believe and accept that Jesus Christ's death on the cross is God's sacrifice to the world for the forgiveness for its sins. There is no need for anything more—no penance, no time in prayer—just humble acknowledgment of the wrongdoing, the asking of forgiveness of the Lord Jesus Christ, and the willingness to sin no more and accept the gift of forgiveness offered by the sacrificial death of the Lord Jesus Christ, God's only Son." He had prayed her eyes would be opened to the truth she herself had just spoken.

"What?' Hazel had asked in surprise. "You are in agreement: We must make amends and be purified from sin before we enter into heaven. Then why are you leaving your position?"

All of a sudden, Joe had realized she was blinded to the truth. She could not understand the wisdom in her own words. He had tried again. "No, listen, Hazel. You said, 'How can such a blemished soul be received into heaven? God wouldn't allow it.' That is what I agree with. But what I also have come to see is that there is nothing we or anyone can do to remove that sin. There is no amount of prayers that can be said, and there will never be enough time in all of eternity to earn forgiveness." The overwhelming feeling of this statement had again brought Joe back to the weakness of who he was, a broken man, a humble sinner, a soul in need of forgiveness that he could never attain by himself. His voice had broken, but he had continued and repeated the simple truth yet again. "I have come to see the only hope for forgiveness is through our Lord and Savior Jesus Christ. Jesus Christ is the only way I can ever receive forgiveness for what I have done and anything I will ever do." Stating those words out loud had brought forth a steadiness in Joe, reflecting the firm conviction of his new-found belief, and looking directly at Hazel, he had sought a hint of understanding.

"Well, Joe," Hazel had spoken as if Joe were a little slow, "that's exactly what the Church teaches, what you yourself have spoken of over the years from the pulpit. Why stop preaching what we both accept?"

"Listen to what I am saying differently, from what you—what we—were taught, Hazel." Joe had disagreed softly lest he make greater the barrier between them. Her depth of blindness was almost overwhelming, yet he had remembered the years of his own struggle to see, and he had made another attempt to show Hazel the way and the truth. "Listen carefully to what I am saying. When a person accepts Jesus Christ's death on the cross as forgiveness, one receives total forgiveness. There is no need to do a litany of prayers or any amount of time set aside in purgatory to be made clean from the ugliness of sin. In the Lord Jesus Christ, forgiveness is complete; there are no Hail Marys or Our Fathers that need to be recited. When you confess to Jesus Christ you are a sinner and you bring your sins to Him with true repentance in your soul for your transgressions, Jesus Christ accepts your sins and the punishment for those sins committed. Jesus Christ willingly accepts death on the cross for us. He shouldered the weight and ugliness of sinful humanity. Yes, Jesus Christ took our place and did our punishment because He loves us, and He was the only sacrifice that was perfect and could make all things right between God and humanity. Through the perfect sacrifice of God's only Son, Jesus Christ, the wrongfulness of mankind's sin is made right by the grace of God. Jesus Christ did our penance and our time of purification when he willingly hung on the cross and accepted our death. Sitting here in prison, I came to understand that that is purgatory—a seemingly unending and agonizing period of time, void of love and light. I came to see we humans, of ourselves, can never and will never achieve perfection; we could never do enough to earn forgiveness. I came to see because we couldn't earn forgiveness, purgatory could never end. It's like a shadow of hell. Forgiveness is a gift from God through his only Son the Lord Jesus Christ." Joe had taken a slow deep breath, silently praying that Hazel would see the truth of the Lord Jesus Christ's sacrifice being offered.

Hazel had tiredly and sadly shaken her head. She had been taught as a child that desperation is the devil's greatest tool, and here this poor man had been abandoned by his parish into this hell and had fallen into Satan's grasp. His frantic need for the cleansing of his sins had him reaching for the devil's compromise. She had had to make him see the wrongness of his decision. This poor wretched soul, crying out for help, had responded to the devil. The tempter had stood up and said, "Here, it's easy," and Joe had accepted. "Oh, Joe, if what you say is true, that we are forgiven for all our sins, why would anyone be good? If they know they are forgiven for doing wrong and don't have to do anything in recompense, why do what is right?"

"Dear Hazel," Joe had countered her honest question, "why wouldn't I do the one thing Jesus Christ asks of those who come to him for forgiveness: 'To love each other as Jesus Christ loves me'? Jesus loves me so much he took my punishment for all the wrong I have done. Why won't I love others in return? Because of Jesus Christ, I am a new person. Because of His willingness to die for me through His blood, I am now 'born again.' I am not just a man, but I am also a child of God. This knowledge, that I am free from unending death and I am loved so deeply, fills me with joy and happiness. How can I not do my best to love others as he has loved me? He has saved my life, literally, for all eternity."

"Joe, it's just not that simple." Hazel had shaken her head. How could she get through to him? How could she make him see his very salvation was at stake? The poor, poor man. Gone was the imposing figure, who had stood at the pulpit and preached the liturgy and led the congregation in the centuries-old rituals of mass. All that was left was this broken, misguided shell of a man.

"No, Hazel, it *is* that simple; it's just not easy. Not in this world." And here Joe in his youthful state of being born again had sighed. His life was just starting, and he had felt overwhelmed and in need of strength and direction. With the realization that he had failed his dear friend of old, he had drooped in sorrow.

Hazel had seen the sigh and had misread it as a last cry for help. She had reached out as best she could, "Well, if you aren't attending mass, what are you doing for religious services now?" Inside she had cringed. Heaven forbid he be snagged up by some Bible-thumping born-again crowd. What was this world coming to?

The question had been innocent enough and yet the one question Joe had found no answer for. He had simply and honestly stated, "I'm not."

"Oh, Joe, I'm sorry." Hazel's heartfelt compassion had been genuine, and Joe had understood.

His decision to accept true forgiveness as stated through Christ and Christ alone had forced him to leave the faith of his whole past life. Thought of what lay ahead had weighed heavily. Yet he would not deny the truth of forgiveness, and he had pushed away the sorrow for what was perceived to have been lost.

Ironically, he remembered most of their conversation, but he couldn't recall their parting words. He never had another letter from Hazel. Her visit was the reason he did not return to the community from which he had come. He had made a choice, and he was sticking with the truth he had come to see.

Yet, a little over two years from that conversation, he still struggled to belong.

He had finished his breakfast in his musings, and still mentally distant, he rose to put his few dishes in the sink.

No roadside signs designate the number of days until one's time is at its end. How well Joe knew this truth. He had done his time in prison, but to him his true confinement had just begun: the remainder of his life on earth. What was he to do with the unknown number of days ahead?

Life's Captivity

We were once upon a time
babes in the bosom of
God's most ultimate love,
cradled in the Garden of Eden.

Then we disobeyed and ate
from the tree of knowledge,
coming to know the secrets
of good and evil too complex
for our human minds to comprehend.

Our own limiting humanity now
holds us captive to our
quest for understanding of
knowledge only God can understand.

PSALM 139: 13-16 For you created my inmost being; you knit me together in my mother's womb. I praise you because I am fearfully and wonderfully made; your works are wonderful, I know that full well. My frame was not hidden from you when I was made in the secret place. When I was woven together in the depths of the earth, your eyes saw my unformed body. All the days ordained for me were written in your book before one of them came to be.

If only he knew how many more days until he could go home, surely his time would be more bearable. Or more, he wished he knew what he should be doing with the remaining days. Shaking his head to try and rid himself of his troubling thoughts, he turned off the coffee maker, grabbed his lunch, and headed out the door to start his workday.

Joe had yet to learn the need for daily spiritual nourishment, for praying and reading the Word of God, to be able to continue in the way of the Lord.

The sun broke the horizon, giving way to the beauty and joy of another spring morning. Though Joe doubted and pondered, wondering at the enormity of life and unconsciously attempting to cover himself with knowledge his humanity was comfortable with, God knew Joe's future. The old Joe, stuck in habits like a needle in a scratch on an old record, had fallen into a misery that shrouded his soul. But God's beauty of dawn, creation revealing itself anew in spring, life arising from winter's deep sleep, woke his soul. In delight, it responded at the bursting sunrise and the serenading of songbirds, and Joe's features lightened as he absorbed the beauty created by God. He relaxed his mind, and the thoughts swirled away, the smothering fog lifted, and the joy of life seeped in. His wonderment and awe of the One who created all before him filled his being.

Joe's spiritual growth would continue on God's timeline, silent and unseen to Joe.

Chapter Four

Michael

On the outskirts of Cornell, Michael and his young family arose to the same spring day with equal appreciation for the unfolding beauty of the morning masterpiece. Michael, ever the man of habits, woke first. He relished coming fully awake with ease to look over to his sleeping wife. Married almost eight years, thirty-year-old Michael still marveled at how his life had unfolded, and he smiled in gratitude for all the blessings bestowed upon him.

Though not a morning person, his sleepy-eyed wife, Claire, was a joy to him every morning. Her sunny disposition and carefree attitude and strawberry-blond, blue-eyed good looks always made him thankful he had married the willowy young girl who had been introduced to him eight short years ago. He shook his head and sent a *Thank you, God* skyward. The muffled sounds of his two little girls reached him as they, like him, got up early each day.

As Michael watched Claire slowly come to life, he thought back on how life had turned so unexpectedly joyous. It had caught him completely off-guard.

He had had no plans other than to return home to the family he had run from. What he would do when he arrived had never entered his mind. He knew only to go home.

His dear mother had quickly realized her returning son had no plans beyond fulfilling her wish to return home. With all Michael's free time, they were soon stepping on each others toes. Not but two weeks after his arrival, the wise Mrs. Calhoun had gently handed Michael the employment section of the morning paper as he had relaxed with a last cup of coffee.

With a sheepish grin, Michael had blushed and confronted his mother about her boldness. "Are you tired of me already, dear Mother?" he had asked with the best wounded look he could produce.

"Michael, put the sad face away." She had refused to let him derail her. "You know how happy I am to have you home, but if you plan to stay, then it's time you did something a little more permanent than vacation." She had smiled as she had finished her pronouncement, squeezing his shoulder as she had wiped the table in front of him with her dishcloth.

"We both know idleness doesn't suit our family, and what better place to look for something to do than right there in the paper."

"Well then," Michael had said agreeably, "let's see what we have. Hmm." He had furrowed his brow to study the small print of ads. "Oh here's one, 'part-time clown.'" And he had smiled and ducked as his mother had swiped at his head.

"Seriously, Michael," she had begun, but Michael had interrupted.

"I know, Mom. You're right. I don't know why I didn't think about a job until now." Michael grinned at his mom. "It *is* getting a little slow around here."

Not one to miss an opportunity to drive her point home, Mrs. Calhoun had added, "The Calhouns have never been slackers."

Seeing his mother wasn't going to rise to the bait, Michael had given the paper some serious attention and noticed how his dear mother had helpfully circled some of the ads.

Michael smiled, thinking how it was one of those very ads that had eventually brought him to Claire. Life, what an enigma.

The job he had taken had led down a road of happiness he had thought would never return.

He had taken a job as a mechanic at an auto shop in the small college town of Cornell, about an hour and a half from New Haven. His mother had made the pitch that it was an ideal location for a single young person—plenty of night life.

Michael was a hard, conscientious worker, and the young man recently discharged from the army had impressed the owner. Two months after he had been employed and settled in his new apartment, the owner had introduced Michael to his daughter Claire. The rest was history.

He and Claire had dated almost a year and then married. Claire's dad had given the young couple a home on the edge of town as a wedding gift. Claire was their only remaining child, after the tragic loss of her brother, Jacob, to a brain aneurysm at the age of fourteen. The suddenness of his death had drawn them ever closer to their only daughter.

Claire was so different from Michael—so carefree and full of hope. And she had such a zest for living despite having lost Jacob when she was just eight. She and her brother had been so close; yet her belief that he was truly with her had allowed her to accept his sudden physical absence from her life. She really believed he was not gone. Her absolute faith had totally amazed Michael and had challenged everything his religion had taught him. That anyone could immediately go to heaven upon death was unheard of, and here she was so sure and steadfast in what she had shared with him. He had so wanted the comfort of what she had. This unfulfilled need in Michael had drawn him to her. In time, he had known he wanted to spend the rest of his life with someone who possessed such a profound comfort in living life one day at a time, enjoying all life had to offer. Her whole family possessed this faith, one steeped in a loving, forgiving, and saving God. Their simple belief astonished Michael.

Claire's family had been given a bitter pill to swallow with the loss of a young son and brother, so like what Michael had run from, and yet they had no bitterness or fear. Michael had come to see through her family's example that life was to be lived, not run from. They had presented a new way of looking at the world and a new way of behaving in it. Michael, weary of his own view, had accepted theirs. He was tired of all his circular thoughts that led nowhere but into sadness. He had grabbed their views and gone forward, no questions asked. And his life had blossomed.

His thoughts were stopped when six-year-old Sarah ran into her mommy and daddy's room shortly followed by the slower and unsteady three-year-old Ruthie. Narrowly missing the doorframe, Ruthie stumbled into the room, colliding into Sarah's backside, who could barely contain her excitement. "I saw a robin, Mommy! It was on my window. Can I wear shorts today?" She steadied Ruthie with a protective hand, who echoed and nodded, "On the window, tweet, tweet, tweet," mimicking bird noises for emphasis as she wobbled around, trying to be a bird.

The little girls presented such a contrast. Sarah, a little tall for her age, had very blond hair and the big, blue eyes and slight build of her mother. She had an ethereal appearance, like a little fairy princess. People often stopped in the street when they saw the youngster for she was breathtaking. Their reaction made Claire more protective of little Ruthie who was chubby and cuddly. And no matter the amount of brushing, her curly, brown hair always looked unkempt and wild. She had her daddy's deep brown eyes, but she had been born with one eye crossed. After corrective surgery, she had been given glasses to help with her poor vision. The same people who would gush over Sarah completely overlooked little Ruthie. Sarah must have sensed her mother's hurt at the slight toward Ruthie, for she would always pull Ruthie forward and proudly introduce her as her little sister and state her age, whereupon Ruthie would beam and extend her little hand as Sarah had taught her, and she would say "Hello" in just the right pitch. Sarah would smile back at her pupil with praise at a job well done.

Sarah's personality was precise and neat, always one to do as she was told, where little Ruthie even at the tender age of three could be stubborn in her independence and fearless in her curiosity, more in need of watchfulness.

Claire now peered from under the blankets and slowly rose, sleepily smiling at the two little tousle-haired girls before her. She forgot how she hated to get up so early and tossed the blankets back over Michael as she stretched long and slow to focus on the business of waking up. "Look, Michael," she chided, "two little girlie birdies woke us up." Ruthie and Sarah both giggled at their mommy's description of them, and Sarah again inquired about wearing shorts while Ruthie resumed the tweeting noises and wobbly motions, adding some flapping of her arms. Her comical display lured Claire up from the warmth of the bed, and she took both little girls by the hand, and the three of them headed out of the bedroom a short ways down the upstairs hall of the old farmhouse to the bedroom the two little girls shared.

As they headed down the hall, Michael listened with pleasure to the sounds of his girls starting their day. He felt so very blessed.

"Yes, Sarah, you and Ruthie may wear shorts today, but you'll need a sweater to take with you to school. You shouldn't need it for recess." *It should be warm enough*, she said more to herself than the two little ones. Meanwhile, Sarah pulled out purple shorts and a mismatched sleeveless top as Claire searched for something for Ruthie.

Ruthie, as she undressed, stated, "Jesus lub me, Mommy," with a confident tone of one imparting great wisdom.

"Yes, Ruthie, Jesus lub you," Claire repeated into the drawer while extracting shorts that were either too big or too small. With her spring-cleaning just begun, things were in a bit of disarray.

"Jesus lub you, Mommy," Ruthie intoned in the same manner.

"Yes, Ruthie, Jesus lub me, too," Claire again repeated as she headed to the closet thinking, *There must be something tucked away on the top shelf labeled 'spring clothes.'*

"Jesus lub Sarah, Mommy." Ruthie continued her little litany.

Sarah giggled at this and replied before Claire could respond, "Ruthie, Jesus LOVES! LOVES!" She enunciated in little Ruthie's face, "Jesus LOVES everybody, you little silly." She patted Ruthie's head and rolled her eyes in older-sister exasperation. Turning to her mother, she said helpfully, "Mommy, Ruthie can wear my shorts."

Ruthie now emphatically stated, "Mommy, Jesus lub, LUB," looking in Sarah's direction, aiming to please her teacher, "Jesus LUB little silly, too."

Claire gave up the search for something more fitting and acknowl-edged, "Yes, Ruthie, Jesus LUB little silly, too. Thank you, Sarah. We'll let Ruthie try a pair of your shorts and a top. It's okay if they're a little big for now. We'll look for something better later." She proceeded to help Ruthie who was struggling to undress.

Michael had dressed in his mechanics uniform and was down-stairs, making the morning brew. With the coffee set to perk, he retrieved the morning paper and opened the window over the kitchen sink. Outside, close to eight a.m., the sky displayed a masterpiece of colors, its beauty confirming that there is no greater artist than God. Yes, how truly blessed he was.

After lunch, Claire settled Ruthie down for her afternoon quiet time. Rarely did she nap anymore. Claire switched on the VCR and put in an old *Sesame Street* tape for Ruthie to watch as she lay on the couch. She removed Ruthie's little glasses, as she did everyday, hop-ing it would encourage her to sleep. Claire gave her little sweetie a generous hug, enjoying the feel of Ruthie's smallness and innocence of one so young. She felt such joy being a mother, caring for Ruthie and Sarah. Yes, she admitted to herself, it could be exhausting, but at times like these, the quieter ones, she cherished the overwhelming feeling of love.

"When this is over, we'll go outside and work in the yard a bit, okay, Ruthie?" Claire gave her another quick little hug and a kiss on the forehead. Before she could escape to clean up in the kitchen, Ruthie wrapped her arms around her mother's neck and hugged her fiercely back, saying, "Jesus lub us, Mommy," and planted a kiss on her cheek. "Yes, dear, Jesus lub us, and I love you!" She returned the hug, breathing in her sweetness and unhooked Ruthie's little arms. She kissed her again, and with a light touch to her cheek, she walked into the adjoining kitchen to attend to the dishes.

Absorbed in *Sesame Street*, Ruthie hummed along with the "C" is for "cookie" with Cookie Monster. Unable to see clearly without glasses, she had learned to be content listening to her favorite song. She lay on the couch, hearing the comforting sounds coming from the kitchen. The abrupt ring of the telephone startled Ruthie, and she sat up and peered in the general direction of the kitchen to see the shadow of her mother cross the floor. Hearing her mother answer the phone, Ruthie got off the couch and went to the toy cupboard. All was in disarray, another result of Claire's unfinished spring cleaning. Ruthie began to pull things from the shelves, and a stray marble rolled from under a stack of puzzles. Popping what looked like a blue gumball into her mouth, she ran back to her spot on the couch, hurtling herself face first with all the force a three-year-old could muster onto the cushions. It was enough: The jarring motion sent the marble into her windpipe where it lodged, slowing and silently choking her as she lay face down, looking for all the world as if she had rolled over in her sleep.

Upon finishing her phone call, Claire hung up the receiver and peeked quietly in on Ruthie. *How wonderful for both of us*, Claire thought, glad for her little one's rest and happy to have a moment to work uninterrupted. She turned back to the kitchen to restart the cleanup from lunch and breakfast. Twenty quiet minutes passed, and the phone rang again. With a sigh and a quick peek in on Ruthie, undisturbed by a second phone call, Claire answered the phone to hear her mother. Checking the time and seeing she still had one and a half hours until they would have to pick Sarah up from kindergarten, she went to the far corner of the kitchen where she could quietly talk with her mother and not wake Ruthie.

After a full half-hour without a peep from Ruthie, Claire brought her conversation with her mother to a close. "Okay, Mom, we'll see you this weekend. I love you, too. Bye."

Checking the clock, Claire saw they still had time to go outside and enjoy the fresh air. She walked with a little more purpose into the living room to slowly rouse her sleeping little girl.

"Hey, little sleepy." Claire reached out to the still figure on the couch. As she touched Ruthie's shoulder, a sense of alarm coursed through her body. With panic in her motions, she grabbed her daughter full force and turned her face-up, revealing what her instincts had already concluded. Holding the dark blue little girl in one arm, she frantically ran into the kitchen and seized the phone, dialing 911, all the while tears streaming down her face.

"Hello, 911. What's your emergency?" calmly asked the attendant.

"My little girl's not breathing!" Claire shrieked in panic back into the phone. Not realizing she had pronounced the inevitable, she tried to revive Ruthie, sitting her up and patting her back.

"Ma'am, is she sick? What happened?" the operator inquired.

Through frantic tears and vain attempts to revive Ruthie, Claire managed to get out, "She was sleeping on the couch. She's blue. She's not breathing. Oh God, no, please no," she cried over and over as she struggled to help her daughter.

"Ma'am, someone will be right there. Keep trying to get her airway open. Ma'am, don't stop trying. Help is coming. Ma'am...," the operator proceeded to instruct Claire after hearing Claire's continued frantic pleas for help.

The scream of the ambulance siren going past Michael's place of work didn't happen often. But when he and his coworkers did hear one go by, all in the shop would pause a moment and send a quiet prayer heavenward for whoever was in need of the speeding services. A little over an hour later the shop phone rang, and an employee in the office called Michael to take line four. Despite the lapse in time, Michael couldn't help connecting the earlier emergency with the call. An unnerving feeling formed in the pit of his stomach as he approached the phone. "Hello," he answered a little gruffly, as if his tone could stave off anything undesirable that could come across the wire.

"Mr. Calhoun?"

"Yes, this is he."

"This is Mrs. Mable at the school."

"Hey, Mrs. Mable, you caught me off-guard. What can I do for you?" The friendly voice of the elementary school secretary had disarmed him, and his whole body relaxed inwardly.

"It seems your wife may be running a little late. Sarah is here, and she said her mommy hasn't come yet. I know it's not that late, but Sarah seems truly upset. We tried the house, and the line was busy. We don't normally call so soon, as there are still children being picked up, but as I said, she's extremely upset. Do you think you can come and get Sarah, or maybe just talk to her, and let her know Mommy's on the way?"

"Sure, Mrs. Mable," Michael stated, still thankful the call was nothing more.

Mrs. Mable handed Sarah the phone, and she clutched the handset, sniffling and sub-subbing from too many tears. "Daddy?" she hiccupped into the phone through still flowing tears.

"Hey, little sweetie, are you making mountains out of mole hills?" he tried lamely to calm Sarah. "Momma's just a little late."

"No, Daddy. Ruthie's gone, and Mommy's not here." She wept into the phone.

This simple statement followed by heart-wrenching tears sent chills down Michael's spine. It was all he could do not to scream into the phone "No!" or hurl it from him as if it were some poisonous viper.

Mrs. Mable, sitting next to where Sarah stood, clutching the phone, felt a similar inner fright. With tears in her own eyes from such a precious little one's obvious distress, she took the phone. With great strength to hide the alarm in her own voice, she said, "Michael, why don't you run home and check on Claire, and we'll keep Sarah here until you come?" In the background, Michael heard Sarah crying "No, I want my daddy."

This plea brought tears to his own eyes, which he fought to control. "I'll be right there to get Sarah." He hung up the phone and told the now quiet shop he needed to go.

Unaware of what was happening but feeling the alarm of their coworker, the others in the shop responded, "Sure, Mike. We got you covered. Be safe, and call us."

Trying to drive safely and yet quickly, Michael headed to the school. He remembered noticing the ambulance quietly returning in the direction from which it had come. He sent up another prayer, this time with a little more urgency, and concentrated on getting to the very upset Sarah, all the while hoping to greet Claire and Ruthie there when he arrived.

Pulling into the school parking lot and not seeing his wife's Honda, Michael rushed from his car, not bothering to shut the door, and headed to the office. Trying to calm himself, he stopped at the threshold and, with great determination, slowly and quietly opened the door. "Hey, little one, what's with all the tears?"

Upon seeing her daddy, Sarah threw herself into his arms, and as Michael crouched to collect her, she managed to get out, "Ruthie's gone. She's gone," as she collapsed into his comforting form, her anguish too much for her to bear.

Dabbing at her eyes over Sarah's great distress, Mrs. Mable shrugged her shoulders, unable to understand the reason for the girl's upset. She was such a kind little girl, always so polite and not one to make a scene. What could have set her to such a state of fear for her mother and her sister?

Michael gazed across the top of his daughter's head with such a look of alarmed puzzlement, silently inquiring an explanation from Mrs. Mable.

Mrs. Mable filled in what little she knew. "I really don't know what happened, Michael. Right when the kindergartners reached the front door and Sarah didn't see your wife, she just broke down. Her teacher physically carried her here, as she had to see to the other children. We did try to console her, and we've been trying to reach your wife, but the line is still busy. We just couldn't calm her." She ended with a quiet look of empathy, wishing she could be of more help.

Rising with Sarah, Michael replied, "Thank you, Mrs. Mable. I'll take her home." He tried to smile. "And I'm sure we'll find Ruthie and Mommy in the back yard." He held Sarah close and added for Mrs. Mable's comfort as much as his own, "She's probably just worn out." With a deep breath to steady himself, he added, "It was the first real warm day of spring, and she did wake up pretty excited."

"You know you're probably right. When they're little like that, they don't know when too much is too much. Do call and let us know, won't you?" she implored.

"Yes, I will, and thank you for calling me." Michael said, appreciative for the care given his spent little one, and left the office.

After buckling Sarah's inert form in the back seat, Michael took a deep breath to steady himself before starting the car and heading home. Sarah remained silent and withdrawn, her tears still creeping down her cheeks, but she took comfort in her daddy's presence.

The sight of Sarah's distress had frightened Michael horribly, and he had to work hard not to turn the car into a vehicle for escape. But escape to where and from what? He still didn't know what on earth was going on. Sarah's anguished state had almost sent him into near hysteria himself. She normally wasn't one to make such a scene.

Gazing back at her, he didn't want to ask her anything for fear of what she might reveal, and from her still flowing tears, he knew it wouldn't be good. Upset with himself for feeling so cowardly, he took some small comfort in the knowledge that Claire would more than likely be home to unravel whatever had so traumatized six-year-old Sarah. This was definitely her department. Then the thought hit him full force. It was Claire's absence that had sent Sarah into her heart-wrenching grief. He fought the wave of fear rising in the pit of his stomach and concentrated on getting home safely.

Pulling into the driveway, he noticed nothing unusual and gave a little sigh of relief. As he put the car in park and got out to help Sarah from the car, he heard the door to the house open. Glancing from his task, he saw their elderly neighbor, Selma, step out to greet them. It gave him pause, for her face was anything but normal. She had obviously been crying, and Michael's feeling of relief vanished. For a moment he thought about getting back in the car and racing away. *Yes, escape. Escape from whatever might hurt,* he thought. But then, *No!* He was done with running away. He continued watching Selma, all the while not wanting to know why she, instead of his wife, was coming from his house and why she looked so upset. He quickly felt overcome with anger and wanted to shout at her to go away, and almost instantaneously he was sick with fear. As if in a horrible nightmare, he slowly lifted Sarah from the seat and held her close. She buried her head in his shoulder and let loose a fresh river of silent tears. With much effort he felt himself moving slowly forward to the now frozen figure on the porch. He felt a hundred years old. Why did his feet have to keep going toward the unwelcome unknown?

Selma, a small, frail-looking widow of seventy-two, had known the Calhouns since they had moved into the house next door. When the ambulance had come to a screeching halt in front of her neighbor's house, she had immediately dropped what she had been doing and gone outside to see whatever could be the matter. The scene she had witnessed had been more than she could bear. The Calhouns were such a nice young couple with two of the sweetest little girls. The sight of the paramedics leaving the house with a sheet over a small figure on a gurney had nearly brought her to her knees. As a frantic Claire had emerged with them, she had caught sight of Selma and had stopped the paramedics long enough to fall into Selma's arms. With a tear-filled plea, she had asked Selma to please tell Michael to get Sarah; she had to go with Ruthie. Selma had only nodded to the dear mother lost in unacknowledged grief over what appeared to be the death of her little one. What had happened remained unspoken.

Michael's halted approach to the house with a weeping Sarah nestled at his shoulder had led Selma to believe he had heard the worst. Thinking someone else had been able to reach Michael because he had Sarah, Selma let her tears fall and could only get out, "Michael, I am so sorry."

"What Selma? What happened?" Michael questioned. Confusion more than fear held sway over Michael. What did everyone else know that he did not? And why was everyone so upset? Everything looked okay. What could possibly be wrong?

"Oh, I thought…, I mean…." Selma, at a loss for words and not knowing what he did or didn't know, simply stated, "I don't know exactly, but I think Ruthie is gone."

"Gone? What do you mean, gone? Sarah keeps saying that, too. Where is she, and where is Claire?" Michael wondered, *Has Ruthie wandered off and gotten lost? Is Claire out looking for her?* He asked, "Is Ruthie lost?"

"Oh, Michael, I'm so, so sorry…, I mean…," and she swallowed the words. She could hardly bring herself to state the sad truth of someone so young. The words just wouldn't come. Ruthie definitely wasn't lost. If only…. Finally she managed to get out, "I think she's passed." Selma looked at him with the hope that he had understood for she just couldn't bring herself to say the truth any clearer. The family had become like her own, Ruthie like her own granddaughter, and she couldn't believe the little girl was gone. She had been such a little sweetie, so full of love.

"What!" Michael almost screamed and fought the wave of nausea that filled him. Anger quickly replaced it, but Sarah's racking sobs broke into his rage and reminded him to be calm. Desperately fighting for control, he asked with quiet intensity, "What happened?"

"I don't know, Michael. I don't know. I am so sorry. I only know the ambulance came, and they took Ruthie out on a stretcher." She quietly added to make sure he understood what she couldn't say outright,

"She was completely covered, Michael. Claire told me to ask you to get Sarah and to tell you she was with Ruthie. I saw you had Sarah, so I thought you knew. I am so sorry."

"Where is Ruthie?" Michael inquired again, absorbing only parts of Selma's story. *How could Ruthie be gone if Claire was with her?* Then the words he had blocked out, "She was completely covered," hit him, and the reality of the situation left him weak. Selma caught Sarah from his arms as he sank onto the porch, overcome with understanding. "No! No! NO!" He shouted his angry words heavenward. Forgetting for a moment about sheltering Sarah from his own grief, he let the tears flow freely. "Not my little girl. Oh, God, no. Please, no! Not little Ruthie. Oh, God." He looked to Selma, anger, sadness, disbelief all mixed in one simple question and asked, "What happened?"

Selma could only shake her head as she cradled the now quietly sobbing Sarah, subdued by the fear of her daddy's tears.

Michael rose and reached for Sarah, and she settled back into her daddy's arms, no longer crying but motionless. Drained and exhausted from the ordeal, she had only sadness as her companion now.

The jarring ring of the phone from inside the house startled all three occupants of the porch. Michael turned with Sarah in his arms to go inside to answer. Selma, reluctant to enter into such sadness, nonetheless slowly followed, hoping to give assistance in any way possible.

Five days later, Michael floated through an equally surreal scene. Around him stood most of his life—his wife and remaining daughter, his mother and most of his siblings and their families, his wife's family, the people they knew in the community. Great numbers had poured out at the tragic loss of such a little one. As he stood at the graveside, the reading of the religious passage dropped to the background as he thought about life, the enormity of it and the smallness of it. How quickly it could all change. His thoughts circled and entangled and tightened within, giving him such agony that he clenched his jaw. *Oh, to lose someone so dear and sweet.* He could barely handle the thought, never to see his precious girl again, alive and loving. He drew in a deep ragged breath, *WHERE is my little girl? Yes, MY little girl.* The profoundness of the question swayed him for a brief moment, and Claire's dad reached out to steady him.

Michael had drawn close to Claire's dad, letting him fill the gap left by his own father's death so early in his life, and today Michael drew on his father-in-law for strength. He pushed his tangled thoughts far away to spare him his own sanity and focused on the words of the reverend. "Little Ruthie is in the arms of her Lord and Savior, Jesus Christ, this very moment," he reassured them. *Yes, that's right.* Thank God, he had caught those saving words. His dear little Ruthie was with her Jesus. Claire's family had known this truth, and the reverend was there reminding them where Ruthie was. Michael looked to those about him, drawing on their presence to calm the storm that had threatened to break within just moments before.

He was now ever so thankful he had come to accept the view and truths of his wife's faith and the knowledge that upon death a believer went to heaven. How comforting he found them. And to think he had almost been snared in the teachings of his former religion! A loved one was not lost in the unknown of purgatory as the faith of his youth had taught. The thought of sweet little Ruthie sitting somewhere all alone, suffering punishment just for living all of three years. *What sins could a three-year-old possibly be guilty of?* He had to stop himself and remove such a horrible thought. His little Ruthie was with her Jesus, but still, he felt a small sadness. He loved Ruthie, and, oh God, he hadn't been ready to let her go, not yet. Though he had been reassured with the reminder of where his little girl was, his own sense of loss overwhelmed him. He quietly prayed, *Please, God, please. Can't this just be a nightmare that I will awaken from?* He had not even dared to look at Claire, who he knew fought her own battle over the loss of innocent love.

"Mommy?" Sarah, sitting as close to her mommy as the seat belt would allow, softly questioned on the ride back to the church hall for the meal the community had put together for the mourners.

"Yes, Sarah, what darling?" Claire asked in response to Sarah's query.

With a deep, shaky breath and obvious effort to control tears not far from the surface, Sarah breathed quietly into the interior of the car and said, "Jesus lub us." Reliving and sharing Ruthie's words from her last morning sent the tears cascading down Sarah's face as she looked for her mother's reassurance that in spite of all the sadness they were still loved by Jesus.

Fresh tears falling from her own eyes, Claire smiled weakly at Sarah's imitation of Ruthie's last pronouncements. She hugged Sarah tightly and replied, "Yes, Jesus lub us very much." Sarah sucked in a big breath and exhaled with slow relief.

"Mommy?"

"Yes, Sarah?"

A little more hesitantly, Sarah stated simply and clearly, "Ruthie says, 'Jesus lub the babies, too.'"

Puzzled but too emotionally drained to think about such an odd statement, Claire simply replied, "Yes, sweetie," and she pulled Sarah close for a hug. "Jesus loves all the babies." She momentarily wondered what babies Ruthie could have referred to. And, with a little sense of alarm, she realized that Sarah seemed to have heard from Ruthie. But with a small sigh, she recognized she had neither the energy nor the mental acuity to correctly address the issue and left the issue unspoken.

She did make a mental note to keep a close watch on Sarah. She had to make sure she would be okay. The thought of Sarah's loss of her little sister sent renewed tears down her face. *Life is so unfair,* surfaced and was replaced with the frustrating, *Why, God*? But "Why?" didn't matter; it wouldn't bring Ruthie back. Like Michael, Claire, too, quietly wished this could just be a dream, a terrible nightmare. *Please, I just wish this wasn't real.* Her tearful plea went silently heavenward and joined the hundreds more she had sent since the moment she had discovered Ruthie's still body on the couch. *Where had that marble come from?* She racked her brain. She had never let marbles in the house, for that very reason. They looked too much like gumballs. *How had poor little Ruthie found one? Oh, dear Lord, how? Where had that darn thing come from?* If only she had finished cleaning and rearranging that stupid toy shelf. Maybe she would have found the marble before Ruthie. *Oh, God,* she was so tired of thinking. She just wanted her life back, her old life, not this one filled with tears and grief and loss. *Oh God, oh God, oh God, help me through this.* This anguished plea sank her into the cushion of the car seat and released a fresh wave of tears and sorrow as she held her remaining little one close. Sarah snuggled closer, and her own tears abated. She seemed resigned to the comfort her mother offered to her statement of Jesus' continued love for them and the babies Ruthie told her of.

A week later, Claire heard Sarah softly call from the living room where she was quietly playing, "Mommy?"

"Yes, Sarah," Claire answered as she walked into the much too orderly living room. Since the funeral she had kept an extra ear for Sarah. She had seemed deeply troubled by the loss of her sister. The quiet and order gave her such a twinge of sadness, yet she had to mask it for Sarah's sake. Life had to move on.

"What's a catlik?"

Thinking Sarah was asking a joke, Claire searched with pretended concentration and with a small smile suggested, "I don't know honey, something a cat licks?"

Looking extremely puzzled, Sarah stated, "Well that's just silly. Daddy can't be a catlik."

"Whoa, wait a minute. What are we talking about? I thought you were asking a riddle, honey," Claire replied in a more serious tone.

All matter-of-fact-like, Sarah continued, "At Ruthie's good-bye, a lady said they needed to pray for Daddy to be a catlick again." She then became small as her words tumbled forth, "Mommy, what's a purda-tory? And is Ruthie there? Didn't the lady know Ruthie loves Jesus? Why doesn't the lady want Ruthie to be with Jesus?" As her questions spilled out, Sarah's eyes filled with tears. Then, as she remembered, she softly said, "Ruthie really loves Jesus."

"Oh, sweetheart." Claire gathered Sarah into her arms and settled her into her lap as she took a spot on the couch. "You want to know what a *Catholic* is." And she enunciated the "th" in the word.

"Yes, Mommy, a catlik, like the lady said."

Claire sighed and kissed the top of Sarah's head, wishing grown-ups would be more careful of what they said at such times. How was she to explain, and why? Sarah was only six. What did it matter to a six-year-old? She sighed. *Where to begin?*

"Let's talk about Ruthie's good-bye, huh?" Claire suggested softly into Sarah's hair as she cradled her for comfort. It had been so hard the week of the funeral, and the pediatrician had recommended letting Sarah be their guide in dealing with the death of her little sister.

Sarah pulled away and with a small sigh looked up at her mother. "Okay, Mommy. It was a big good-bye," she suggested with a small smile.

"Yes, it certainly was, honey," Claire quietly agreed.

"I miss Ruthie, Mommy." Sarah, feeling her sorrow, swallowed her tears.

"Me, too, honey." Claire fought not to cry. Trying not to give in to their combined sorrow, Claire quietly began, "Let's see. What's a Catholic?" She smiled as an idea came to her. You know, Sarah, how your cousins have Bernard, and he's a hunting dog, right?"

Sarah nodded in understanding.

"Okay. And Mrs. Selma next door has Pepper, and he's a little Scottie, right?"

"Yes." Sarah smiled. She loved animals.

"So you see, Bernard and Pepper are both dogs, but they are different, right?"

"Yes, Mommy." And she giggled a little for Bernard and Pepper were two entirely different animals, both which she adored.

"Well, to make it simple, Catholics and everyone in our church all believe in Jesus, but Catholics believe in Him just a bit differently than the people we go to church with. Does that make sense?" She looked at Sarah and was pleased as she nodded her understanding.

"So why do they want Daddy to be a catlike? I love Bernard *and* Pepper." Sarah was puzzled.

Claire took a deep breath. "Well, honey, Daddy used to be a Catholic, but now Daddy is 'born again' in Christ. The people he knows who are Catholics feel he should come back to them, and be what he was."

"Is Daddy different, Mommy?" Sarah was getting confused.

"No, sweetie. Well, yes, he is but in a very good way." Claire's brows knit as she mentally searched how to make the explanation clearer for Sarah. "The difference is in how people believe, mostly in how they get forgiveness and when they get to be with Jesus. Let me see, how to explain." She pondered a moment more, trying to figure out how to make this clear to someone so young. "Okay, let's see. Think about when you do something wrong or you hurt someone."

"Yes."

"Well, you tell the person you hurt you are sorry you hurt them or that you did wrong. Then that person forgives you, and you try not to hurt them again or do the same wrong thing again. Do you agree?"

Sarah hung her head and replied quietly, "Yes, but sometimes...," and she hesitated. "Sometimes, I'm not sorry, Mommy," and she looked up into her mommy's eyes with pain. "Am I bad then?"

"Oh, sweetie, you aren't bad; but it's not right to hurt someone, even if someone hurts you. When you hurt someone, you should be sorry, okay?"

"I'll try, Mommy," Sarah said on a hopeful note.

"Okay." And she gave Sarah a little squeeze. "So, Catholics believe they need to tell a priest what they did wrong so they can be forgiven for hurting someone or doing something wrong." She looked at Sarah with hope for understanding.

"Mommy?"

"Yes, dear."

"Why does the lady want Daddy to be Catholic again?" Sarah implored with a quiet tone of seriousness, and she continued most sadly, "Will Daddy leave us?"

Pulling Sarah close once more, Claire reassured her, "Oh no, sweet darling, Daddy will stay with us always."

Sarah sighed into her mother, relaxing for a moment, seeming to be content.

Claire silently rested her head on the top of Sarah's and pondered how to answer the why of her question.

Then Sarah suddenly and abruptly sat up. With a small breath of excitement, she pushed off her mother's lap, took hold of one hand to pull her into a standing position, and said, "Mommy, come with me."

Relieved at not having to come up with an answer to Sarah's "Why," Claire followed her daughter up the stairs and into her bedroom to the small vanity she and Ruthie once shared. Sarah's eyes shone with excitement as she pulled open a drawer and took out a little box Claire had given her for special things.

Not quite sure what had transpired or if Sarah had understood the explanation of Catholics, Claire looked at her daughter with mixed concern. Seeing Sarah's interest in showing her the treasure box, she decided her answer must have resolved her quandary well enough. She stepped forward to examine what Sarah was so excited about.

"Look, Mommy." Sarah opened the little box and pulled out a string of colorful glass beads. "A man at Ruthie's good-bye gave me these pretty beads. He told me if I prayed to Mary, Ruthie would get out of purdatory and no more bad things would happen to us. Aren't the beads pretty? Who's Mary? What's purdatory? I asked Mary to take the bad things away, but what bad things? Ruthie wasn't bad, not always, and I'm bad, too, sometimes. Am I going to go away, too? Where is Ruthie?" The questions had come out in a rush, and upon their release, Sarah started to cry in great sobs. Her head sank low, and the beads hung from her little hand. Her excitement had vaporized, replaced by confusion as she cried in anguish and sorrow.

Claire, shocked at the rapid transformation and the revelation, gathered Sarah to her and settled her upon her lap on the floor. *So much for Sarah understanding.* Her attempt on the couch had been a dismal failure. And now she also had to explain "where" Ruthie was. How could she do this? Claire held Sarah close as she cried and placed a gentle kiss upon her head. Her own tears start to fall as she reflected. *Grownups! God, why does life have to be so hard? Oh God, please, help me."* Claire silently prayed for the right words to help her answer all of Sarah's questions.

Sarah's tears began to lessen while Claire asked for guidance. As Sarah's weeping drew to a close, she began with a slow deep breath, "Okay, one question at a time." Sarah nodded at her mother and looked into her face with hope.

"First, I love you so very much, and you and Ruthie were not—are not—bad. Even when I scolded you or Ruthie, you weren't bad. You just made mistakes."

Sarah took a little breath at this, relaxing some.

Claire continued, "You needed to know you made a mistake so you could learn to do the right thing. Sometimes Mommy talked loudly." To that, Sarah nodded vigorously, and Claire smiled. "Mommy talked real loud because, even though you and Ruthie were listening to Mommy, you weren't hearing. It's like when you are playing in your room and you need me; you holler so I will hear. Well sometimes when Mommy was trying to help you do the right thing after you had made a mistake, it was like you and Ruthie weren't in the same room with me. Sometimes making mistakes seems fun, and you want to continue to have fun and not do what is right, so you don't want to listen. But you and Ruthie are not bad, okay?"

"Okay, Mommy, we just didn't hear." Sarah seemed content and a little less sad, knowing she was not bad and Ruthie hadn't been bad either.

Mulling over which question to tackle next, Claire decided, "Oh yes, the beads. They are very pretty, very sparkly."

To this Sarah brightened and smiled considerably in agreement, holding them aloft as they both admired them. "I like them."

"Me, too. They are pretty. Now, let's see. Hmm," she pondered, "Oh yes. Mary was Jesus' mother. You know this?"

"Of course, Mommy, that's silly." She looked at her mother, rolling her eyes. At the mention of Jesus she remembered how much Ruthie loved Jesus, and she shared her thought with her mother, "Ruthie loved Jesus." And she smiled.

"Yes," she agreed with a shared smile, "Ruthie did indeed love Jesus very much." The thought almost brought Claire to tears. She pushed past them to answer the next question.

"You know Ruthie is with Jesus." She searched Sarah's face for belief and continued as Sarah remained silent. "When Ruthie left us, she went to Jesus because she loved Jesus and Jesus loved her."

Sarah nodded in serious agreement as she repeated, "Jesus loved Ruthie." Then with some confusion she asked, "Did Jesus take Ruthie to purdatory?"

Claire sadly shook her head. "No, sweetie, Jesus took Ruthie to heaven to be with him. Ruthie is in heaven with Jesus." She ended with a happy note, "Okay?"

"Why did the lady say Ruthie was in purdatory and needed to get out?" Sarah felt a little angry with the lady for having told her a lie.

Claire shrank in weariness, took a slow breath, and searched for inspiration. She continued, "Remember how I said Catholics are different in forgiveness?"

Sarah looked confused.

Claire reminded her gently, "Bernard and Pepper?"

Sarah smiled sheepishly and nodded, "Oh, silly me. I remember."

"Well," Claire continued, "that's another difference. Catholics believe when they die they go to a place called 'purgatory' so they can be forgiven completely and then, after a time or after many prayers with the beads, they go to heaven, too."

"They pray with the beads?" Sarah asked in astonishment. "But they are so pretty," she exclaimed, as if pretty and prayers just didn't mix. Then she added with much relief, "I'm glad Ruthie got to go to heaven with Jesus."

"Me, too," Claire agreed, keeping quiet about Sarah's comment about the beads. She just didn't feel she could truly explain the need for extra prayers to a six-year-old or why Catholics believe people go to a place called purgatory when they die to be made pure and clean or how they must do a certain amount of penance for full forgiveness, in case they had a sinful thought immediately before death or if they hadn't been able to go to confession to be forgiven for sins before they died or how asking Jesus' mother for help will get them out of purgatory quickly and the beads are to help them pray. She silently prayed that Sarah would be content with her answers. She tried to be as honest and straightforward as she knew how so as not to confuse Sarah further.

"Ruthie must be very happy to be with Jesus and not at purgatory. But, Mommy…." Sarah's voice cracked and her tears welled up. "I miss Ruthie. Does she miss me?" Sarah cried again, and Claire joined in, unable to control her own grief at the ache for her child.

Through her own tears Claire managed, "Ruthie is happy, and I miss her so very much, but Ruthie is still with us," she softly comforted into Sarah's hair. "She's not really gone, honey, so she doesn't miss us."

Upon hearing these words, Sarah stopped crying, pulled back from her mother, and looked at Claire as if she had suddenly proclaimed Ruthie right there in the room with them. "What? She's not gone?" She forcibly removed herself from her mother's lap and stood up, facing her mother, placing her hands on her hips, and with total disbelief and shock, as if a cruel joke had been revealed, demanded, "Well, where is she?"

Poor Sarah was so confused. She hadn't seen Ruthie since the morning of her death, but she had heard her speaking to her in the car ride home from the funeral. Was she still around? And the burial hadn't made any sense to her either—everyone kept calling it a "good-bye. Why were they saying "good-bye"? Where had Ruthie gone? And now what was her mom saying? Had Ruthie never even left?

"And why has she been hiding? I've missed her, Mommy." And the tears started down her cheeks.

Claire realized her mistake, and she visibly sagged into herself at the thought of resolving one more misunderstanding. "Oh, dear Sarah. Come here and sit with me. Let Mommy explain." She waited for Sarah to come to her, which she did with great drama. But she sat across from her mother to keep an eye on the situation, for clearly, something wasn't right, and through her tears she kept glancing about, looking to see if Ruthie would make an appearance.

"Okay," Claire said as she took both Sarah's hands in hers for reassurance that she spoke the truth and to capture her gaze. "Now listen very carefully. Even though we can't see Ruthie or hug her or hear her, she is not gone."

"Mommy!" Sarah interrupted in exasperation and tried to get up.

"No, wait." Claire stilled the struggling little fairy form. "Listen to me, honey. Ruthie is with us forever because she loves us. It's kind of like the wind. Some days you feel the wind, and other days you don't. Ruthie will always be with us because she loves us so very much. We miss her because we can't see her, hug her, or hear her. But because she is with Jesus, who is always with us, she is always with us, too, and that's why she doesn't miss us."

Sarah seemed a little less perturbed, but now grew a little concerned. "Will she tell on me?"

This question relieved Claire, and she smiled at the all too normal honesty. "Oh honey, Ruthie wouldn't tell on you."

Sarah gave a big sigh.

"Besides," Claire added, "Ruthie doesn't need to tell on you, because you," and she lovingly poked Sarah in the shoulder, "accept Jesus as God's Son."

At this Sarah nodded, "Yes, Mommy, I know, and I love Jesus, too."

"Well, remember when you do this, God gives Himself to you in the Holy Spirit. The Holy Spirit helps your conscience tell on you. When you do something wrong and you know it's wrong, you feel bad."

A little brightness came to Sarah, and she nodded with deeper understanding, murmuring quietly, "That's why my tummy hurts sometimes."

Claire smiled lightly and continued, "That little tummy hurt is your conscience. Ruthie isn't telling on you, but she will be glad you are going to do the right thing."

"One day will I be with Jesus, too?" Sarah asked with a hopeful look.

Claire nodded, "One day we all will be with Jesus, honey, but we don't get to pick the day, and we can't go unless Jesus calls us, okay?"

"Will I hear Him, Mommy?"

"Oh, yes, dear; we all hear Him when it's time."

"Is that why Ruthie went?" And her eyes brightened. "Did Jesus call Ruthie?"

Trying to control her sadness, for she wished Ruthie was not gone and didn't want to upset Sarah again, Claire said, "Yes, yes, Sarah, I guess Jesus called Ruthie, and she went to be with Him." Her eyes had a far-away, contemplative look. *Could it really be that simple?* she wondered, lost for a moment in thought.

"Can I wear my pretty beads?" Sarah asked, getting up, ready to resume playing.

Claire mentally shook herself at Sarah's question and got up from the floor. "How about we hang them up," she asked as she went to the vanity, "right here as a reminder of Ruthie's good-bye? And I'll let you have some of mine to wear."

Sarah hesitated for a moment, and then she agreed, "Okay, they are kind of special." She twirled the beads for a moment between her fingers and removed them from around her neck. Together they hung up the rosary and walked to Claire's room to pick out some of her jewelry. Claire sighed and admitted to herself that for the first time she felt better than she had since Ruthie's accident. Maybe the worst was over, and they could all start to heal. *Please, dear Lord please, no more pain; at least not for a while.*

Chapter Five

Catherine and Hazel

*M*ichael sat comfortably in the porch swing with his mother, who shared the opposite end. It was a warm spring Saturday, and he and the children had decided to give Claire the day to herself. With the ever-worldly help of eight-going-on-forty-year-old Sarah, he had loaded up the year-old twins, Luke and Paul, and gone to visit his mother. She lived just over an hour and half from Michael's home, and the drive had been pleasant and filled with the scenes of unfolding spring. Sarah was her usual chatty little self, and Michael could not help smiling inwardly at what a little mother she was, always watchful of her brothers and extremely gentle when they would misbehave. They followed her everywhere. For someone still so young, she could talk and act so old. Sarah sat with the boys under the shade of the century-old elm in the sand box he had built last summer, entertaining her brothers.

"Michael," his mother quietly asked as she watched the children play, "would you consider staying a little later today and attending mass with me?"

"Mom," Michael looked across at his mother with a puzzled countenance, as he continued with gentleness, "what brings this on? You know I haven't been to mass since Claire and I married. You've been so understanding, not to ask that of me. Why all of a sudden do you want me to go to mass today?"

"It was such a blessed surprise that you and the children came to see me, that you came today of all days. Well, I just saw it as a sign, and I took a chance." She looked at him with a mother's look of "Please consider my request."

"What is so special about today that it's a 'sign'?" Michael joked to try to lighten what seemed to be a conversation heading into deeper waters.

"This evening's mass is being offered for Ruthie," his mother said in earnestness.

Michael, fully realizing the implications of what his mother had said, looked at her with complete astonishment and disbelief. He tried to control his emotions. "Mom, please, not this." He lowered his head.

His mother only silently nodded, her look one of desperation, and she whispered, "For Ruthie, son."

Michael worked to control his anger and looked up into his mother's eyes. "You can't honestly mean to tell me that you believe little Ruthie, dear sweet, 'Jesus lub me' Ruthie, is any place but in heaven." His look quietly dared his mother to say she believed otherwise.

"Michael," his mother pleaded, "it's not my teaching; it's the Church's, and you can't just throw away centuries of church teaching."

Michael bit back his response, respectfully letting his mother finish.

"Consider, please, what I'm really asking. This is for Ruthie's sake, Michael, that she may be released from purgatory," she continued somewhat breathlessly as she could see he was not pleased. And before he could stop her, she added, "How can you not? You're her father." Upon completion of her charge, she dropped her gaze to her lap to soften what she knew were harsh words.

Michael, not wanting to insult his mother or dishonor her in any way, searched for the right words to help her see why he couldn't honor her request. He tried for the simplicity of the whole idea of punishment for atonement. "Mom, Ruthie didn't even know how to recite a Hail Mary, much less say an Our Father. How can you really accept that a three–year-old would go to purgatory?"

"All the more reason why *we* need to say prayers. And the mass is such a great help to one such as Ruthie."

Michael tried again. "Mom, you said it's not your teaching but the Church's. Why do you accept this teaching? Do you believe it?"

As she noticed his look had taken on the hardness of rebellion, Catherine felt compelled to explain and try to draw him back to her faith—and what once was his faith. "Yes, Michael, I do believe in purgatory. How can I not? How can *you* not? It's what has been disseminated over the years and is known as truth and imparted to us by those in positions of God's grace, the leaders of God's flock, to help those of us who aren't as learned in the ways of theology. Michael, the Church's leaders just don't make this stuff up."

"It's Ruthie, Mom!" Michael was at a loss for a way to reason with her. He wondered how his mother could ask this of him, and he gazed upon his three children, sure of their innocence of life and sin.

Seeing Michael's pain, she tried again. "Don't look at it in that light, Michael. We all fall short of the grace of God. Even babies lost at birth don't get to go to heaven."

"But, Mom, you know how Ruthie was." Michael started to lose his patience. "She loved Jesus; she sang about Jesus all day, almost everyday." His memories of Ruthie's little mispronounced litany brought a smile to his face and tears to his heart. How could his mother not see her genuine, simple love for Jesus? "There were days she just wouldn't stop."

The memory of Ruthie's salvation the year before her death came flooding back to Michael. Ruthie was about to turn two, and that year Ruthie's birthday fell on Easter Sunday. She seemed to know the importance of the day, possibly thanks to Sarah. She was just five and had been attending Bible pre-school on Sunday mornings. Sarah had felt very grown-up and was doing her best as the older sister to educate little Ruthie with the knowledge she was privileged to receive. He could still see them on Sundays after quiet time, Sarah sharing what she had learned with Ruthie.

"No, Ruthie," Sarah would admonish earnestly to her little sister, "you must sit down to color your picture." She would then smile and placate sweetly, "How can you color anything if you keep running around?"

Ruthie's response would be, "Jesus lub me, Jesus lub me."

"Of course, Jesus lovvvves you," the ever-patient Sarah would enunciate. She was pleased Ruthie had learned the words to the song she had been taught, the real meaning of Easter. "But we must do our work, and coloring looks nicer if we sit while we color."

Ruthie would stop suddenly, look sorrowfully at her teacher, and reply with a big sigh, "Okay, I'll sit wif you." She would walk slowly back to her little chair, slump over the sheet on which Sarah had drawn a picture for Ruthie to color, and with the utmost of exhaustion at the task before her, begin to color. After two swipes of her crayon she would look up suddenly with a huge smile on her face and question Sarah, "My color is nice?"

Sarah would get off her stool and come around to Ruthie's side of the table, lean over and take some time to examine Ruthie's two attempts to color the hand drawn picture, and reply with kind authority, "Why, yes, Ruthie, your work is much improved."

If Ruthie's smile was great, Sarah's compliment would make it even more so. Ruthie would then sing quietly, "Jesus lub me," and Sarah would join in, in an effort to take her beyond the first line of the song. They were quite the pair, and his heart ached at the memory of Ruthie's second birthday.

Easter Sunday and Ruthie's birthday dawned with a beautiful sunrise. Ruthie was in high spirits with her "Jesus lub me," and they barely made it to Sunday service in time. They never did figure out how, but Ruthie had somehow slipped from Claire's watchful eye during the service and made her way to where the pastor was baptizing those who had come forth to receive the Lord Jesus Christ as their personal savior. Her absence was made known to them by the quiet laughter of the congregation at the little one who had stepped forward and made her presence known with a loud "Jesus lub me!" When the pastor nodded but didn't speak directly to her, she tried ever more forcefully and took hold of the end of his jacket, giving it a tug, and repeated with singsong sincerity, "Jesus lub me, Jesus lub me."

Claire had tried to be stealthy in the retrieval of her little one, and when she had managed to make her way to the scene and scooped up Ruthie, Ruthie had let out a wail and proclaimed with outstretched arms to the pastor who had stopped the baptismal, "Jesus lub me! Jesus lub me!"

They say when allowed in, God works mysteries untold; and that day the pastor allowed God free reign of who he was. The pastor stepped forward to Ruthie's little outstretched arms and, amid her tears and "Jesus lub me," lifted her from Claire and proceeded to baptize her with the other souls in search of forgiveness. Claire stood quietly as Ruthie's tears dried up instantaneously, and a smile of pure joy filled her little countenance. She was saved. Her little face beamed with salvation, and she was received, dripping wet, into Claire's waiting arms with a quieter but still insistent and, if possible, even more joyful, "Jesus lub me."

What happened next was almost unheard of: More than half those attending for the first time came forward to receive salvation, many with tearful emotions and words of thanksgiving.

MATTHEW 19:13-14 Then little children were brought to Jesus for him to place his hands on them and pray for them. But the disciples rebuked those who brought them. Jesus said, "Let the little children come to me, and do not hinder them, for the kingdom of heaven belongs to such as these."

Michael didn't know how he had forgotten that incident, but reliving it brought him profound peace. He made a mental note to remind Claire of Ruthie's second birthday, as she had seemed so detached these last few days. Who was he kidding? She hadn't seemed herself in so long.

With that retrieved memory, he shook his head. To think that Ruthie was anywhere but with Jesus was preposterous, and he searched his mother's face for understanding. With great difficulty he held back his anger that a religious institution would teach such an absurdity. "Mom, I can't even accept the teaching of purgatory. No, I won't choose purgatory for myself, and I certainly won't choose it for someone I love so dearly, someone as innocent as Ruthie." He shook his head and continued, "I can't even begin to imagine how many Hail Marys and Our Fathers I would be sentenced to. It would become meaningless, to pray over and over the same litany of prayers for an endless number of days or months, probably decades in my case." And he weakly smiled at his mother, hoping she would see understanding at what she professed to be sound doctrine.

She ignored his ill attempt at humor and stated, "It's not about our love or goodness, or even innocence, Michael. Surely you remember that." She shook her head and berated herself for not having enrolled Michael in the Catholic school. Then he wouldn't have strayed so very far from his upbringing. Why did the Catholic school have to be so expensive? Then again, she should have made the sacrifice. Under the weight of her own guilt, she sagged visibly.

She thought of Michael's older brother Jerome, second in age to Joseph, who also had fallen from the flock after having served in Vietnam. Yet, she mused, Jerome had attended the parochial school. She shook the thought from her head. When she had learned of Jerome's refusal to attend mass, she had consulted a close friend of Patrick's who was a bishop. When Catherine had told him of Jerome's struggle, the bishop had taken Jerome aside, out of loyalty to his friendship with Patrick, and had counseled Jerome personally.

Jerome had confided to his mother somewhat cynically that he had been given absolution for his actions during his entire tour, upon completion of a penance assigned by the bishop. But he would not give his mother the details. Jerome had returned to mass but only on the holy days. He had assured his mother he had not left the Church, and he was definitely not joining another.

Why had Michael left the flock? Surely Jerome had suffered more. To the ever-faithful Catherine the only reasonable answer came back to Michael's lack of a proper Catholic schooling. She had failed him herself. Jerome had even married a nice girl from the parish, and his wife and four children attended regularly without Jerome. Her thoughts ran on. Her bishop friend had since passed, and she didn't know who to turn to. *Where is help when it is most needed, oh dear Lord?* How long would Michael stray? Didn't he realize he himself was in mortal danger? After the tragic loss of Ruthie, she was so sure he would realize his mistake and return to the Church of his upbringing. She hadn't approached him and felt it best to wait for the right time. She certainly didn't want to drive him farther away. She had been so blessedly surprised when he had showed up today of all days. She loved him so and only wanted eternal salvation for him. What mother wouldn't? *Oh dear, dear Lord, forgive me.* She must remember to confess her newly revealed failure in her weekly confession. How she had failed in her most important role as a parent.

Well, she would not give up, not on little Ruthie. The poor little dear. She needed prayers, and the more the better. She would not let her little granddaughter spend any more time in purgatory than needed. One more time, she would try with her son. She reasoned this time, "Michael, you know we are all born with the original sin of Adam upon us, and this is why no one but martyrs go directly to heaven."

The peace in knowing Ruthie's salvation overcame his anger, and Michael softened his tone, "Aw, Mother, I know that's what I was taught, but I won't believe it for my little Ruthie. She loved Jesus, and yes, I know it sounds silly, but I know even at two she had accepted Jesus Christ into her little life. Mom, I no longer believe or accept what I grew up with. I've come to know and to believe that when a person accepts the Lord Jesus Christ into his life, he accepts Jesus Christ's death on the cross as forgiveness for his sins, all of his sins." He paused to search his mother's face. "I believe these people, including Ruthie and me, really do go to heaven when we die."

His mother sighed in weariness.

Michael continued, "Mom that's what Jesus Christ died for, so we could go to heaven. Really, Mom, think of it. If God's own Son's death isn't good enough to get us into heaven, how many prayers or how much time for punishment is needed? If it's all about time and prayers and punishment for wrongdoings, why did Jesus die? There simply is no other way," Michael finished, not wanting to wound or worry his mother, hoping she would accept that Ruthie had no need of prayers because she was in heaven right now.

"Michael, please, this is nonsense. Ruthie needs your help. You simply must." His mother reached for his hand as she begged in her urgency, tears in her eyes.

Refusing to give in to his mother's tears, he gently held her hand. "Now, Mom, don't cry. I promise you Ruthie is in heaven. I know she is with her Lord and Savior Jesus Christ right now. She is not condemned to an eon of punishment." He tried one more time to help her see the truth. "You said no one is good enough to go to heaven. Well then, who decides how many masses or prayers must be said, huh? Is there a guide book—you know, ten Hail Marys for lying, twenty years and daily rosaries for underreporting income taxes?" He joked lightly at the thought.

"Michael," his mother lightly slapped his hand, "you mustn't; this is not a joke. I won't bother you anymore, but I will continue to pray for Ruthie and pay to have masses said for her. I will also continue to pray for you," and she glared at his lack of respect for his upbringing, "and for Claire and the children, too. It's not right they don't know the Church, Michael; it's not right. You are failing your religion."

"I love you, Mom. Just remember our family has God and His Son Jesus Christ in our lives. We just don't have Catholic doctrine. We'll be okay," Michael offered softly in hopes of ending the conversation. It had been a long time since his mother had taken him to task for leaving the Church, and today certainly caught him off-guard, but he would not give in. He couldn't begin to imagine Ruthie in purgatory. No way.

Realizing they were at a stand-off, his mother changed the subject, not wanting the visit to end. "The boys are sure growing. Is Claire doing better?"

✳

Later in the fading spring evening, Catherine Calhoun walked quietly by herself. It was early to be leaving for the five o'clock mass, but after Michael and the children had left, she did not want to be alone in the house with her thoughts. The church was a good mile from her home, and she would take her time and enjoy God's created beauty. Breathing deeply and delighting in the freshness of the season, she started a rosary. After sixty years, some habits began themselves. Her rosary beads were in her purse, but she didn't need them to pray. She absently wondered how many rosaries had she said over the years. *Goodness what a thought.* She didn't know exactly when in her life she had become such a pray-warrior.

Her thoughts turned to Michael. She must renew her prayer efforts on his behalf. How he could so mock what he had been taught—and she cherished so dearly. Her thoughts wandered on. She truly loved God, and what better way to love than to pray? Walking alone had always seemed, to her, the best time to pray.

As a young girl, she had prayed for friends and family members in need, and she always prayed the most often for those who had died, for they needed prayers to get into heaven. How many rosaries she had recited for those in purgatory, she had lost count of; it didn't matter; she said them anyway. It was God's business to keep track of her prayers; hers was just to pray. The older she got the more she felt the need to pray. The rosary became her source of comfort, a true friend.

She had learned during her early married years to keep track of the Hail Marys on her hands and used facial parts to keep count of the mysteries. The work in the garden those hot summers seemed to fly by when she was preoccupied with saying a rosary. It kept her mind busy as her hands did their manual task before them. There was always someone to pray for. She loved getting lost in the recitation of the simple yet beautiful words of the prayers learned in childhood. The words brought her tranquility and inner peace; she felt almost transcended from all that came to trouble her. Reciting the prayers also made her feel useful, helping someone get to heaven. And maybe when it was her turn—she couldn't help the thought because she had so selflessly prayed for others—someone would pray for her.

But today she couldn't stay focused on her prayerful meditation; thoughts of Michael and their conversation intruded. How could Michael reject the power of the Church's centuries-old prayers? His words had hurt her so deeply. He had been so callous with his remarks. Surely, he didn't really mean the holy words of praise had no effect. What sacrilege he spoke! Her heart felt so heavy at what she felt he had lost. Such depressing reflections were too much for such a beautiful day, and she, with great will, stopped her thoughts from wandering back to the day's surprise visit and made an effort to refocus on the words of the Hail Mary. Her prayers soon brought the peace she had been seeking, and she was transported back to another time, a time of understanding and shared love, when her Patrick was still with her.

She had always loved saying the rosary. Catherine had been taught that to pray the rosary was to draw nearer to Jesus through his beloved mother; to love Mary was to love Jesus. God had found favor in her and blessed her above all women. The Virgin Mary was pure and obedient, full of grace and goodness. Every little Catholic girl at some time wished to be as good as the young Mary—pure, innocent, and obedient. When Catherine was confirmed she took the confirmation name Mary. Mary would be her guide, the one she could call on for special spiritual help, who would help her in times of spiritual need. She could look to the Virgin for guidance and help, and to take her name as her own was something the young Catherine took very seriously. How could Michael have missed out on the depth of love she herself had felt and experienced? Where did she go wrong?

She had always loved her faith and the Church, but upon confirmation and the taking of the name of Mary, she felt she had chosen a special path for herself to serve God. As Catherine continued to grow into a young woman, she grew to love going to daily mass, but the services leading up to and including Easter were her favorite. The high holy days, fasting and repentance, the veneration of the cross, the ritual of the masses all made the religion and its teachings so sacred, real, and alive. She felt removed from the world as it was. The Church was her place to feel close to God, to have refuge from the hardness and unfairness of the world. When Catherine prayed her rosary, she felt one with the Blessed Virgin. She smiled at remembering how she had even contemplated becoming a nun. She so loved the solitude and sanctuary of the quiet dark of the church and the peaceful life of prayer. She smiled again when she thought how God had showed her the path he had chosen for her instead.

She had met Patrick, of all places, saying the rosary at her house. She was young, barely fifteen when his repeated appearances at their house for the rosary intrigued her enough to ask her mother why the young man kept coming. "Catherine, where are you when we pray? It is his family we are saying the rosary for. You really must be more attentive," her mother had scolded her softly. She felt embarrassed to have been discovered inattentive during the rosary, but she was also pleased the young man felt comfortable in his religion to be seen praying. Her mother's prayer group said the rosary for Patrick's family for the entire month, and she remembered he didn't miss a day.

Patrick had started courting her after his family's troubles passed. She came to love the young farmer, three years older than she, for his shared love for the Blessed Virgin. All their early years of marriage when they were spent from working the land, they would lie in their bed, too hot to move, and Patrick would reach for her hand and begin a rosary. It brought quiet and peace to their tired bodies and took their minds off the stifling heat of the room as they lay in the dark, waiting for the cool evening breeze to bring relief. She never took stock of whether their prayers were answered. She just relished the shared intimacy of prayer. Praying together brought her so much closer to Patrick—and both of them to God. Oh, how she missed Patrick! He had been her life. She loved his love for God and his sharing it with her. His passing would have killed her but for the rosary. She kept his rosary beads with her everyday that first year, and prayed almost nonstop. It was their special connection. Her bittersweet memories gave way to thoughts about how, if only Patrick were alive, her life would be so different. And maybe Michael's, too. How sad she suddenly felt. Young Michael had no lost love for his faith, the faith of his father.

Yet she prayed with confidence to Mother Mary to intervene, to go to the Heavenly Father on Michael's behalf. She wouldn't, couldn't lose hope on Michael and his young family, for his return to the Church. His unexpected visit on this day of all days was the answer she had sought. That she had had seemingly unanswered prayers made no difference in her belief in their importance. She asked, but God knew best. Not getting the answer she wanted wouldn't stop her from praying or send her from her religious upbringing. How had Michael, her own flesh and blood, left that which was so near and dear to her? How he could reject the Church, she just could not grasp. His fall was beyond her understanding. She sighed. *What is it with today's world? Everyone wants immediate answers and expects rewards. No one believes in sacrifice or hard work for anything. What is the world coming to?*

Despite her efforts with the rosary, the day's conversation continued to intrude, and as it came back, she struggled with Michael's argument. *Where had Michael received the idea that all could go directly to heaven upon death?* He had told her when he had married Claire that he had started reading the Bible and was going to a Bible-study group. Surely he did not think he could understand the holy words without assistance. Reading the scriptures without the guidance of those who had studied many years and learned how to interpret their messages correctly only led to error. She read medical books but that didn't make her qualified to diagnose diseases or remedies. She shook her head. Religious instruction was best left to religious scholars, those who had become learned in the ways of the Church.

And look where his unguided readings had led! Poor Michael, thinking he could go directly to heaven upon death just because Jesus had died on the cross. To think a person went straight to heaven, sinners that we are—what lunacy. The chance for repentance was a must; it was what purgatory was for. People without proper education in the Church's teachings could easily be misled when reading on their own. The doctrine of the Catholic Church was born of men who received inspiration from God and learned the true meaning of the biblical texts. The Word of God held more than the words so plainly written; clarification and interpretation came only with extended study by those close to the Word and familiar with the Church's teachings. The Bible was not a book to be read without the doctrines of the faith. Look at what had happened, how Claire's poor family had come to misinterpret it and now her Michael, too. "Oh dear Mother Mary," she sighed quietly for solace.

Dear little Ruthie in need of prayers and her own father thinking she had been immediately received by our Lord. What sorrow in such misguided thinking. That poor little sweet soul, to suffer needlessly at her father's error. We all need absolution. Everyone should have the chance for forgiveness, to reflect and be lifted from their guilt once they see their wrongness of life. Goodness, all fall short of the glory of God. She mused, *Even Mother Theresa wasn't assured of straight acceptance into heaven upon her death, unless she had received last rites.* For only through receiving the last rites could a person possibly go right to heaven with no time spent in purgatory. To think, her own son had made a joke about who decided the length of time or the number of prayers needed for release from purgatory. Surely he knew God was the final judge, not man. Where had she gone wrong? She was worn out from her thoughts.

"Hello, Catherine. How are you this fine evening?" The friendly words broke into her contemplation.

Focusing on the warmth of the greeting, Catherine responded, "Why, Hazel, it is so good to see you." The two women shared an embrace and entered the cool, semi-dark interior of the church.

Both women had arrived early, seeking the solace and solitude of the church for matters too big for their souls to bear. With almost thirty minutes until mass would start, the two women who had known each other their whole lives but were never close, stepped into a pew a short distance from the altar. They knelt, made a sign of the cross, and almost simultaneously sighed, releasing the weight of their troubles into the quiet.

The church was almost as old as the town. It had been built a mere five years into the town's existence, constructed of the same rough brownstone of the much smaller VFW building that sat across from the courthouse. Though the outside gave the impression of sturdiness with its rustic simplicity, the inside of the church imparted inspiration in its stained glass windows. Fifteen scenes from the mysteries of the rosary were depicted, five on each side and the final five in the windows in the forefront, bringing natural light from the setting sun onto the altar and giving the surreal sense that God was indeed truly present, saying the mass Himself. The floor in the sanctuary and around the altar was marble and continued into the center and side aisles, with oak flooring beneath the pews. The pews were handmade of the same solid oak and polished by the cleaning staff twice weekly. The small children loved the soft curving, sleigh style of the seats and often slid when attempting to sit on the glossy surface. The little church was lovingly cared for, and over time each nook had been adorned with the highest quality marble statues purchased from abroad.

Entering St. Mary's transported one to another realm and allowed the troubles of the world to fall off weary shoulders. The silence was deep, serenity surrounding those who sat in contemplation. The reverence and love given the little house of God comforted the most despondent of parishioners who entered through the massive, hundred-year-old, ten-foot doors.

As each woman finished her silent prayers, she made the sign of the cross and settled back to relax into the solidity of the pew, the atmosphere of holiness relieving and removing the heaviness of life's burdens.

Hazel reflected on the sadness that had taken over her brother's once happy family. She was always considered a member until Jenny decided to live a life of her own choosing. Dear Mother Mary, should she have risked Jenny's anger and told her niece of her misgivings of the path she was contemplating? Why hadn't she stopped her? If only she had known how terribly bad things would turn out. She would do anything now to do it over. But life didn't allow do-overs.

Hazel's thoughts rolled on. Where was her Jenny now? Did she still have her baby? Goodness, the thought hit her, she wouldn't be a baby anymore. How old would her little girl be now—eleven, twelve? How was Jennifer doing? Was Jennifer in need?

Her old anger surfaced. How could her own brother have done such a terrible thing, his own child and his only one at that? Why hadn't Mae done something to stop Shaun's actions? Jennifer was her daughter, too. That's ridiculous. Poor Mae, she could do nothing where Shaun was concerned. Hazel knew that better than anyone, the poor dear; that she was still with him was a miracle. Yet in the time since Jenny had been disowned, her name had never been mentioned, not even from Mae. It broke Hazel's heart. All pictures had been taken down, and her room was emptied, and all the items donated to charity. Hazel was grief-stricken. The harshness of her brother's actions still tore at her heart. She sighed deeply. All those years gone by, and in moments of quiet, thoughts of Jenny would still have the same effect on her.

With deep sorrow, she recalled the events that had led up to Jennifer's and her last communication. When Jennifer had called home and Shaun had found out she was pregnant, he had cruelly disowned her on the phone, forbidding any contact with her by anyone in the household. His murderous look had given no room for negotiation. Yet Hazel, being his senior and having nursed Jennifer from birth, had done what she knew in her heart was right. She had written Jennifer a long heartfelt letter explaining as best she could her father's actions. She had put the letter in the mail, feeling Shaun would never know. Ah, life; one wonders at the turns it takes.

The letter had come back "return to sender, address unknown." Poor Hazel. In her state of anxiety to send quick comfort to Jennifer, she had transposed the numbers of the zip code when she had addressed the envelope. As life would have it, Shaun had retrieved the mail the day the letter had come back, something he rarely did. But Mae had taken Hazel to a doctor's appointment, and they were gone for the greater part of the day. Hazel shook her head at the outcome of her attempt to send love and comfort to Jennifer, help that never made it. A storm had greeted the two upon their return, and Hazel hoped never to witness such a scene again.

✦╞═╪═╡✦

As they had entered the house in the early evening, they had been drawn like moths to the light of the kitchen on that dark fall day.

"How about a cup of tea, Hazel?" Mae had asked over her shoulder after shedding their coats and putting their purses in the hall closet.

"That sounds nice, especially now with these new hearing aids," she had chuckled at her lame joke.

"Oh, Hazel, that was bad," Mae had returned. The two had grown closer since Jennifer had left. Mae had always looked up to Hazel as an older sister from the moment Hazel had moved in with her and Shaun. She had been so good to her and Jennifer.

As they had entered the kitchen, they both had stopped, for sitting there in heavy silence was Shaun. It wasn't normal for him just to sit there, and his menacing countenance had alarmed them both. They immediately grasped hands. What could have caused his stony silence?

Hazel, a little behind Mae, had taken another step up and then spotted her envelope on the table, solitary and severe in its accusations. *Oh no, Jenny's letter.* She had visibly shrunk.

Mae, feeling Hazel weaken next to her and spotting an envelope on the table, had taken Hazel by the shoulders and helped her to the nearest chair, her concern visible. "What? What is it? Hazel, dear, are you okay? Shaun?" She had looked with worry and concern to her husband, but only silent, seething anger had greeted her. His silence was deafening.

Shaun, holding back as a tempest before the outpouring, had slowly pushed back his chair and waited for Mae to seat Hazel before confronting her with her betrayal. After she had assisted Hazel and had taken the chair next to her, pulling it close, he had reached toward the offending letter and slid it angrily toward them. "Hazel, do you want to explain this?" he had spit out with controlled anger.

Hazel had flushed with embarrassment. She was a good woman, honest, never having done a sly thing in her life. Knowing what she had done was right yet also expressly forbidden, she had briefly felt shamed. She had also wondered for a quick moment how he had gotten the letter meant for Jenny. As the letter had slid across to them, Mae had gasped in shock and dismay. Hazel had cringed in self-reproach, the red marking on the address label glaring in its error. How had she not made sure of the address? Her anger at herself had flared, and then at the whole situation, it had flamed up in self-defense. Her eyes had ignited, and she had taken the challenge thrown at her by her younger brother. What had she to lose now? *Nothing*, her heart had answered.

"I shouldn't have to explain anything, Shaun. Jenny is my niece, and I have every right to write to her. What you've done is wrong," she had stated clearly and with conviction and power. "She needs us," she had motioned to all of them seated, "and our love and support, and I can't abide by what you've asked." She had challenged him to say she was wrong in her pronouncement.

Shaun, having had the better part of the day to seethe and mentally play out his course of action, had kept his emotions in check; he would not be undermined by anyone. This was his home, and his rules would be followed by everyone in his care. "You are wrong, Hazel," he had pronounced with control and bitten his words out slowly, one angry syllable at a time. "If that is truly how you feel and this is what you are going to do, you can go." He had motioned to the hall they'd just come down.

Mae had gasped, "Shaun, surely, no. You can't mean it?" She had implored him, coming closer to defying him than she ever had in their marriage.

Hazel was speechless. She had looked to Shaun with shock and hurt. In confusion, she had asked, "You are asking me to leave?" She had said it quietly, looking for the brother she had helped out so many years before. Where had he gone, and who was this irrational madman who had taken his place?

With a hardness that had been cultivating since Jenny had left, Shaun had nodded his intent and replied coldly, "If you will not honor my wishes, I won't have you under my roof."

Mae had pleaded with sorrow, "Shaun, no…."

But he had cut her off with a look of intense hate and challenged her with, "Did I not say there would be no communication and you would honor me in my wishes?"

Mae had dropped her eyes with shame. He was her husband. She had never been a confrontational person, and all her life, being the fourth of seven children, she had done as she had been told and been respectful of those above her. She had known nothing else. She had squeezed Hazel's hand in sorrow and sympathy.

Hazel, refusing to be brow-beaten and knowing she had done right, had asked of the challenge thrown before her, "You would have me leave now?"

Shaun having had the time to think things through had been prepared. "No." And he had smiled as if she had been a wayward child. "As long as you promise to make no further attempts to contact...," and he had stopped, for he had not said Jennifer's name since the phone call. For but a moment his pain had been visible on his face, for Jennifer had come to mind, and he had waged a battle to remove his love for her from his heart. But she had defied him, and his wrath at her actions had overwhelmed his anguish. He had continued with full strength, "As long as you abide by my wishes, you may stay until you have made other arrangements. But you will leave." He had made his final pronouncement and gotten up and left.

Both women had sat in silence. Hazel, realizing she had gone too far, could hardly fathom what had transpired. How had she been so careless with the address? All in an attempt to help someone they all loved. It was crazy, utter madness.

Mae, sitting next to her, had started to cry silently. She had leaned in to hug Hazel. What on earth had happened to her life? Where would Hazel go and what would she do? had been foremost in her mind.

⊹══•══⊹

Hazel sighed deeply, and Mrs. Calhoun, seated now next to her and hearing her, reached out and squeezed her hand in comfort.

The kindness of the gesture brought Hazel from her reflections and a small tear rolled down her cheek as she nodded a thank-you to her long-time acquaintance.

"After mass, let's have a cup of tea at my house," Catherine whispered quietly to Hazel.

Still trying to regain her composure, Hazel only nodded yes, and managed, "That would be so nice."

An hour later, the two women breathed deeply of the cool evening air as they exited the church and make the slow walk to Catherine's house.

"That was a lovely mass," Hazel offered to Catherine. "A good turnout for little Ruthie."

"Yes," Catherine agreed, a little despondently, her thoughts going back to her dashed joy earlier in the afternoon, "and Father's homily was so appropriate. We all do fall short of God's perfection." Her thoughts on Michael's comments plagued her again. How could he be so sacrilegious? His flippancy made her ill. What was wrong with today's young people? It was her turn now to sigh deeply.

Picking up on Catherine's sadness, but misinterpreting her reasons, Hazel offered, "Ruthie was such a sweet child. Her time in purgatory will be short; she will surely be with the heavenly Father soon enough. I include her in my prayers often." She took Catherine's hand in a gentle reassuring squeeze of returned comfort.

Not wanting to share Michael's disrespectful ideas of the Church's teachings, Catherine accepted Hazel's comfort with squared shoulders and renewed strength at the mention of Ruthie being often included in her prayers. "Thank you so very much, Hazel. It means so much to me. She was a very special little girl," Catherine replied and then inquired, "If you could do me a favor…."

"Why yes, Catherine, what?" Hazel responded.

"Could you please, now and then, pray for Michael and his family to return to the Church? It would mean so much to me. But more important, Michael is headed in the wrong direction and taking his little family with him."

"Most certainly. In fact, I will start a weekly rosary for them. Now if I could ask a favor in return?" Hazel queried.

"Well, of course."

"You remember my niece, Jennifer?"

Catherine nodded.

"I haven't heard from her in, oh…," she hesitated as she tried to remember the date of her only phone call to Jennifer. If only Jennifer hadn't hung up so quickly. And why did she never take another phone call? Hazel was left with such an ache in her heart. Giving up on the exactness of the time, she continued, "Well it's been a good number of years, since…, you know." Hazel hesitated to go further.

Catherine politely squeezed her hand. "Yes, I recall." And she nodded to spare Hazel from further discussing Jennifer's act of indiscretion."

"Can you please include her in your prayers? I just wish I knew if she was okay," said Hazel, also ending on a sad note.

With hope in the rosaries Hazel would say for Michael and his family and the full faith in the power of prayer, Catherine joyfully returned the kindness. "Hazel, I will gladly say a rosary for Jenny's spiritual well-being."

"Oh, what a blessing we entered mass together this beautiful day," Hazel rejoined, comforted and uplifted by Catherine's obvious joy. "That cup of tea is looking so much fuller." Hazel smiled her happiness of Catherine's generous offer.

"Here we are. Watch your step; I may have missed a toy or two. Michael and the children were here this afternoon," she warned Hazel as they started up the porch to enter her home.

"How nice. Did you have a good visit?" Hazel politely inquired, not knowing this was the source of Catherine's despondency.

Focusing on the offer of a rosary for Michael's return to the faith, Catherine held the door for Hazel and decided to talk only about the joy of Michael's surprise visit. Mary would intercede for Michael and his family, as she, too, is a mother. She would rest on the thought that all would work out. "Yes, it was a lovely visit. The children are growing so fast." As they removed their light sweaters, for the house was warm, Catherine offered, "May I take your sweater?"

"I think I'll just hold it. I may take a chill in a moment or two. You know how it is." She warmly smiled to Catherine.

"Yes, I have two or three sweaters positioned around the house for that very reason." She gestured to one neatly folded over one of the kitchen chairs as she led Hazel into the dimly lit interior of her home. She reached for the light switch and proclaimed, "Let there be light!" as she flipped the switch.

"You've a lovely home, Catherine," Hazel said as she settled into one of the chairs around the little table in the kitchen.

"Thank you. Even though it's been years now, with Michael gone, the place seems a little empty now and then. How are you settling into your new home?" she politely asked Hazel.

"New!" Hazel said with a little laugh. "It's hard to believe I've been living there almost thirteen years, and it still seems 'new.'"

After having lived in a home for over twenty-odd years, Hazel considered anything less to be new. She had lived on her family's farm the first twenty-seven years of her life before she moved to the next county to teach in a one-room school. There she had met and married her husband. And after his death and her niece's birth, she had moved in with her brother, staying for almost twenty years. That had ended the day she woke up to the reality she was no longer welcomed. She had decided then and there to move out and get a place of her own as quickly as circumstances would allow.

"I like it well enough; though it was a little hard at first. The difficult part is making it seem like a home, with no one there to share it with, though Mae is good to come by now and then. But it's so hard to feel useful," she ended quietly.

"Tell me about it," Catherine agreed as she set the kettle on to boil. "When Michael left, it was all I could do not to go stir-crazy. I always thought I had enough to do, too, but," she settled into the chair across from Hazel, "it's different, coming home to an empty house and not having anyone to care for on a daily basis. I really miss it."

"Yes, I think that is what made moving into a place by myself so hard. I truly missed doing for others, people I cared for deeply and who cared for me in return." Hazel reflected for the first time on the truth of resettling into a life on her own. It had taken the better part of a year to find a house to buy, and that almost proved her undoing. She was sixty-two years old and had been living under someone's care most of her life. Her savings were adequate for someone with no expenses, but to provide for a roof for herself on her meager income had been tough her first five years. She had no worldly goods, save for the bedroom set she had kept from her marriage and the clothes she had acquired. All she and her husband had owned had been sold, for she hadn't needed anything when she moved into Shaun's home, and money from the sales helped relieve the medical bills of her husband's illness. She had been in a fix when Shaun had thought to throw her out, and he knew it. Yet she being of the same stock would not be bossed by her youngest sibling, and resiliently she had moved out. She had survived. The first thing she had done from her new home was contact Jennifer, and the call hadn't gone as planned. Life was a creature with its own plans, she remembered, and her spirit sagged.

"It's really sad when you realize you're not needed, after having taken such detailed care of people for twenty-four hours a day, seven days a week, three hundred sixty-five days a year for eighteen-plus years," Catherine admitted. "Even as they seek their independence, they're still yours to care for. Until they leave the nest, you feel responsible and inexplicably bound. Then they leave, and the tie is broken. The largeness of freedom is so unexpected. There is so much time, and it's all yours. You're faced with the expanse of 'Now what?'"

Hazel nodded in understanding. She added in reflection, "I hadn't felt that way since before I had married, and to feel it now, when life was so far gone.... I didn't have my youth, and I just couldn't imagine what I could possibly do to be of use." Her voice broke as she recalled her first feelings of despair when she departed Jenny's parents' home.

The tea kettle whistled, and Catherine rose to pour the water. "Would you like a piece of coffeecake to go with your tea? I made it fresh yesterday."

"Yes, that sounds delicious." As Catherine moved about getting the coffeecake, Hazel shared her difficulty for the first time. She so appreciated finally talking with someone who really understood her struggles. "You know I was truly scared. I realized I had no job skills other than to care for people and, of course, my teaching experience. Yet how could I get a job doing either when I was too close to retirement age? Plus," and she swallowed her pride and added ever so quietly, "I wanted to be cared for, again, too." She missed her close relationship with Jenny so very much. The love they had was so very special.

Setting the plates with the coffeecake on the table and returning with the tea, Catherine sat and reached for Hazel's hand. "I know. To be needed and loved, to know you are special to someone, too."

They cautiously sipped their tea after blowing to cool it.

"When Michael first left, I tried to keep busy with my gardening and volunteering at the church. It helped, but I felt something was missing."

"I started a little garden, too, and got more involved with the seniors' activities in the community, but," and she carefully added, "I missed the zest of youth."

"I know," Catherine agreed with a smile. "When I first found out we were pregnant with Michael and I was so far past having babies, I thought, 'How will we ever raise another at our age?' Then when Patrick passed, Michael gave me life. He was so young I forgot I was supposed to be getting older." She smiled to herself at the memory and added, "I still don't feel old per se, I just feel...well...I don't rightly know how to describe it."

"I felt that way with Jenny, too. She was such a dear, and she shared so much with me. I felt ageless. I felt included and hopeful about life. I felt like I was still living, and now, well...."

Catherine nodded her understanding of Hazel's half-finished sentence. "Yes, I think that is what it is. Being around the younger generation helps us feel alive and a part of the hope of tomorrow, and we forget our loss of usefulness. Michael would come home so full of energy, and he would fall into a chair with such vigor. I always felt he gave me his energy and removed some of my tiredness of living." Then she added with a smile, "You know I even miss listening to his favorite radio station." She looked to Hazel as if she has spoken insanity.

"Oh, you are so right!" Hazel added with a gleeful note. "That music—it was so bad, but some of Jenny's songs, well, I rather enjoyed them." She continued in Catherine's joy, "There was one group Jenny really liked, something called 'Queen,' I think." Her brow knitted as she tried to recall. "She would blast the radio and just enjoy. I do miss that." She reached out and softly touched Catherine's relaxed forearm. "Jenny would always take the time to share the names of her favorite groups, and she would even 'make' me listen to a new song she really liked. She would always say, 'Aunt Hazel, you just have to hear this.'"

"Oh, I know. Michael liked something called 'Supertramp,'" and she rolled her eyes at the absurdity and continued with melancholy, "I did like a couple of their songs, but you know, he also liked my songs, too. It was such a nice exchange. He would come home from some evening event, and I would be listening to my 'oldies' station, and he would sit with me and ask who was singing. Once in awhile, he would even ask if I could get a tape for him."

"The same with Jenny. She thought my little 45s were cute. She had her favorites of mine, too. I sure do miss the sharing, but I can't make myself listen to her station." Hazel softened. "It just doesn't seem right anymore."

"I know. I've tried, too, but my interpreter is missing," she joked with a sad smile.

Hazel sipped her drink. "This tea is so good."

"It's a new flavor. They've mixed chamomile and allspice. It's got a bit of a bite, but I enjoy it. Helps clear my sinuses."

"I started volunteering at the local schools for tutoring a few years ago. I finally worked up the courage to approach the principal. Even at my age, he was very receptive." Hazel shared her relief. "I thought it would help fill the emptiness. I sure enjoy being with the children."

Catherine looked up from her cup and smiled. "I never thought of tutoring school children." Her mind started churning. "I do help with adult illiteracy at the public library. Do you think I could tutor, too?"

"I was fearful at first, but the principal assured me they're always looking for help. You should consider it. Some of those children…it breaks my heart." Her gaze reached out to Catherine. "They seem just to want someone to listen to them, to give them some one–on–one attention. Some parents are so busy, and then the family situations of some…it's so tragic," she said, shaking her head.

"I know," Catherine agreed. "They just can't seem to catch a break." And she recalled some of the young adults, new on the road to life, for whom she helped improve reading and writing skills.

"They seem to struggle so hard. I often wish there was more I could do to help." Hazel thought of some of the children she assisted who came from broken homes. "I honestly don't think children mind so much doing without things, but it's the time spent with a loving adult they crave, someone to make them feel special and loved. Just like what I miss now that Jenny's gone." She swallowed her sadness.

"Yes, I, too, miss that sharing with Michael, about the little day-to-day things he would tell me about school, his friends, and his different activities. I miss feeling a part of life. If only there was something we could do." She rested her chin in her hands and gazed into the distance in thought.

Hazel quietly sat across from her, enjoying the coffeecake Catherine had offered. "Catherine, this cake is so moist; may I have the recipe?"

"I'm glad you like it, and of course. I'll write it out for you now." She got up, searched for a pen, and selected the card from her recipe box. Making herself comfortable again, she began to copy the recipe. "You know, that is the other thing I truly miss—cooking and baking for someone other than myself."

Hazel nodded her assent. "It's much harder to cook for one. I didn't realize it all the years I spent with Shaun and Mae. And you know, I think it's more than just trying to come up with something to make for myself. I think it's making something for someone because you know they are really going to enjoy it and they need it."

"I think you've hit the nail on the head. There were days when Michael would come home with a couple of friends, and—you know teenagers—it's as if they haven't had a meal in days." She smiled at the thought of the quantity of food her son and his friends would consume. "Just to make them a bite to eat was such a treat for them—and for me."

"Yes, Jenny often baked treats for her classmates because she enjoyed sharing and she loved to bake. I would help her out with the frosting or preparing different ingredients, as she loved to bake from scratch. Whatever she took to school was always appreciated. Once she left, well, there was no reason to bake. The fun seemed to disappear with her." Hazel's voice trailed off.

"You want to hear something crazy?" Hazel quickly recovered with a hint of spirit as she caught Catherine's eye.

"What?" Catherine asked, taking a moment from her writing to look at Hazel.

"Okay. It's…well…my house is only blocks from the junior high school, and I've often wondered, as I've watched the students leave for home and lunch during the day, what if I offered sandwiches and a place to relax where they could spend a moment or two relating their day to someone my age?" She looked to Catherine, hoping her idea didn't really sound so crazy and maybe even met with approval.

"That's a splendid idea. I actually wondered the same thing when Michael first left home as I watched children go home to empty houses and I sat by myself in my own empty house." Catherine added, "But I must admit I also wondered if they would come and would it be okay and would I have to have a license or something. I chickened out, but I still think about it, plus I'm way out here close to the edge of town. Then, too, there's my age, and it's not decreasing." She concluded with a small smile on her defeated note.

Hazel reached out to pat Catherine's hand. "I have often thought because I don't have much yard I shouldn't make an offer. Kids need room, and I must admit I've wondered about the legality of my giving kids a sandwich without having to be a business. Some of the children I tutor just seem so in need of someone to listen to them. I think they would come, but I'm more afraid of not having enough of me for so many of them." She laughed gently at her fear of too many kids coming where Catherine was afraid no one would show up. She didn't address the issue of age—both ladies were over seventy—but what is age when the heart and mind are strong and determined?

Buoyed by Hazel's thought of too many kids, Catherine offered, "What if we worked together?"

Hazel lighted on Catherine's infectious glimmer of possibility and voiced her enthusiasm, "Could we? Do you really think we could?" Happiness filled her at the thought of truly being helpful and useful once again.

Catherine added with spirit, "What have we got to loose? What is the worst that can possibly happen?"

Hazel strengthened up. "Okay. Well, one, the kids may not come, and we would have sandwiches we would need to do something with." She grinned broadly at the idea of having trouble getting rid of food. "And two, somebody might say we can't because of some zoning law or something. We might get a ticket or a fine."

"I agree. Those are the two worst things that come to mind. Now, can we deal with those two scenarios?" She looked to Hazel as if she'd asked if she can sit in a chair without assistance.

Hazel responded with a small smile at the recognition of the absurdity of their fears. "It does sound petty when one says it out loud, being afraid to offer help or kindness." She looked sheepish for a moment.

"Oh no, I believe our fears are justified. I just don't think we should give in. We both believe there is a need, granted for a few, but everyone matters. And I think if you're willing to risk the two worst things happening, well, so am I. We'll just do it together." Catherine smiled conspiratorially at Hazel.

Hazel reached across to Catherine with an outstretched hand. "Partners in giving kids a sandwich or an after-school snack and someone to talk to, what do you say?"

"Oh, I think it's so wonderful, something to be excited about." And Catherine gave Hazel's hand a firm shake.

Once again Catherine's contagious excitement infused Hazel, who added, "You just never know how this might blossom, and it's such a wonderful second chance for us, too."

Chapter Six

Jennifer

ennifer glanced in the rear view mirror to give her appearance a quick once-over as Michael's garage came into view. She tried to calm the butterflies in her stomach at the excitement of seeing him. She pushed aside the little voice telling her what she was doing was wrong. She had been in and out of several such relationships in the past five years, and she still had to fight down the feelings of wrongdoing. Her argument remained the same: If these men weren't with her, they'd be with someone else; so why not her? She had needs, too. Feeling more secure in her choice, she refocused on her destination and smiled at the thought of meeting Michael.

Jennifer's fall from grace had been brutal. She bore little resemblance to the brave young woman who had led another to freedom from the agony and stresses of the world so many years previous in the bank robbery.

MATTHEW 13:3-9, 18-23 Then he told them many things in parables, saying: "A farmer went out to sow his seed. As he was scattering the seed, some fell along the path, and the birds came and ate it up. Some fell on rocky places, where it did not have much soil. It sprang up quickly, because the soil was shallow. But when the sun came up, the plants were scorched, and they withered because they had no root. Other seed fell among thorns, which grew up and choked the plants. Still other seed fell on good soil, where it produced a crop—a hundred, sixty or thirty times what was sown. He who has ears, let him hear."

"Listen then to what the parable of the sower means: When anyone hears the message about the kingdom and does not understand it, the evil one comes and snatches away what was sown in his heart. This is the seed sown along the path. The one who received the seed that fell on rocky places is the man who hears the word and at once receives it with joy. But since he has no root, he lasts only a short time. When trouble or persecution comes because of the word, he quickly falls away. The one who received the seed that fell among the thorns is the man who hears the word, but the worries of this life and the deceitfulness of wealth choke it, making it unfruitful. But the one who received the seed that fell on good soil is the man who hears the word and understands it. He produces a crop, yielding a hundred, sixty or thirty times what was sown."

Her modeling career in California had started out slowly. Jennifer was young and ignorant of the ways and workings of the world of fashion, and she was a country girl suddenly thrust into the big city. Still, she had been warmly welcomed by the agency's manager and the girls in the closely monitored boarding house they resided in. Elise, or Elli, as the older woman preferred, the house monitor, had taken the young Jennifer under her wing. It was Elise's job to make sure the new girls learned the ropes of how the modeling industry worked and to try and steer them clear of the pitfalls of the life they had chosen.

Jennifer remembered Elli's welcoming statement. "Don't worry, little farm girl; we will have you fitting in with all the others in no time. You just wait and see. Leave it to me, and no one other than you and I will know you are from the land of bumpkins."

Elli herself had been in the modeling business for the past twenty-some years. At forty-six she was old in the modeling world but young in her outlook on life. She loved showing the young girls the ropes of the trade. She did have to admit that the young girls coming into the business in the past few years carried an air of insolence and self-importance normally associated with girls who had become top models. Where did they get this attitude of—what? She couldn't quite put a finger on it... they seemed to expect—demand, even—everything, attention, money, expensive gifts, as if life owed them whatever they wanted.

But this girl was different. She seemed eager to please. Yet Elli detected a note of independence and strong-willed nonconformity. She had tried to be welcoming, but her words to the young Jennifer had been met with a look of resistance.

Elli sighed. Maybe it was time for her to leave this avenue of modeling and open the dress shop she had dreamed of managing. She mentally took stock of herself. She was still attractive with only a few strands of white that her profession demanded be masked. Her figure was flawless, as she had chosen the single life over that of motherhood, and her face fairly free of the lines from sun, age, and stress. Her job of being in charge of the newly recruited models was loosing its appeal. The new girls just didn't want guidance. Lately they seemed to reject outright any offer of experienced help. They came in and felt they knew everything and could do a better job of running their own careers. *Ah youth, poor misguided youth.* She felt Jennifer, whose eyes showed the intensity of independence, would have a tough time if she couldn't learn to follow the rules in the game of life, especially in this industry. Yes, Elli had learned that, to survive and succeed, one had to join the crowd and abide by the rules; the loner who tried to go it alone always crashed and burned.

Jennifer nodded in respect to Elli's offered kindness, but she assured herself she would not become like the other girls. Elli had been correct in what she had seen in Jennifer's youthful face, only she wasn't privy to the reason for Jennifer's self-willed determination to remain the "country bumpkin."

Jennifer's last scene at home had been vicious. Her father's words had been cruel. The final argument she had had with her parents before she left home had almost devastated her and shadowed her every action; she could never erase the memory. She had known her father would be upset she was embarking on such an "empty" career path; but she was unprepared for his complete disgust and revulsion.

The exchange had been her father's last-ditch effort to stop her, and he had made sure she knew exactly how he felt. She cringed as the scene played back in her mind.

Her packed suitcases had sat in the living room by the couch, and she had come down the stairs for one last home-cooked breakfast. Her mother had made her favorites, bacon and French toast with the thought a new model probably wouldn't be eating much of either, especially accompanied by generous portions of melted butter and syrup. They had all risen early as she had an early flight out to California. As she descended the last steps, her dad had greeted her at the landing.

"So you are going through with it?" His tone had been brisk and demanding. "Are you determined to become one of those people?" He had continued, speaking the words slowly and deliberately, "Another empty shell of a human, concerned only with outward appearances and drawn into the sinful world of drink, drugs, and sex?" He had shaken his head as if to push away the horrible prediction and painfully continued, "You will, Jennifer; I promise you." He had known his words had hurt; he had seen the pain on his beautiful, young daughter, his only child. His own heart had been breaking, but he had had to stop her from proceeding down this horrible road she seemed hellbent on going down.

His next words had been so out of character for the young woman he and Mae had raised that he had had to force them from within. Looking to the kitchen before uttering them, at the risk of opening up old wounds, he had spoken, "If you end up pregnant…." The cruel words hung in the air, and Jennifer's shocked look had burned into his heart. Yet he had continued; she had to know what would happen if she would not heed his advice. "Then you will be alone.

I mean it, Jennifer. You will have only yourself to blame." At her continued silence, his anger had returned, and his next words had been even more devastating. "I am telling you now: Do not come looking to us for help or sympathy. You are throwing away all you have worked for, all we have given you, all we have raised you to be for—what?—money and adventure?"

Jennifer had just stood, listening to her father. If only he had believed in her. She had had no words to make him understand how she had felt. She hadn't seen her future as he had. She had tried to explain to him her need to see the world and experience life. The deaths of Glen and David had shocked her to her very core. She hadn't really known the two boys, but they had been her age, young, and their lives had been taken in a flash. What had they done? Where had they gone? What had they seen beyond the close confines of their community? They had hardly lived. It had frightened her to think that she would be like them if her life ended today. What would she have lived for? She hadn't wanted to die having experienced so little. She had felt she had to go out in the world, take some risks, and see life. College hadn't seemed to offer as much freedom as modeling. She hadn't wanted to sit in a classroom anymore and study subjects that held no meaning for her. She had wanted to live *her* life. Why couldn't her dad have seen that? Aunt Hazel had told her not to let her dad's words hurt her, but his statements that morning had pierced her. Had he really thought she would do the things he was implying? Had he no faith in her? After all those years, had he not known her? She had been stunned at his blindness.

Jennifer's lack of reaction to his final plea for what he felt was her very life, had brought forth his final pronouncement. He had said most simply and quietly with words of deep disappointment in her choice, the words burning into her heart, "You disgust me." They had been said with such force and so harshly she still felt the pain he had intended. He had warned her: You choose this path, and you are choosing immorality. She had vowed then, to herself, to show her dad she was stronger than he knew. She would prove him wrong. She would be somebody and not give in to the temptations offered by a lifestyle of falseness.

In the end the lovingly made breakfast had gone uneaten. Jennifer had lost her appetite. Her father hadn't given any good-bye, other than his words of hurt and pain. She had ached for one last hug but had had to settle for quietly whispering "I love you" as he turned and walked back into the recesses of the house, not bothering to walk her to the car.

Mae, Hazel, and Jennifer had silently loaded her suitcases into the trunk, gotten into the car, and left for the airport. Jennifer hadn't even glanced back as they had left the only home she had ever known. Her mother had quietly squeezed her hand and said, "Give your dad some time, honey; he'll come around."

"Didn't you hear what he said to me, Mom?" Jennifer had cried in her grief.

"Jennifer, he was just upset. He is your father, after all, and he is afraid for you." Her mother had tried to reassure her.

Jennifer had shaken her head. "No, Mom, he was mad. I can't believe he really thinks I would do—be that way." She had continued in a torrent, "I've never even had a date, and he has me sleeping around." Her tears had flowed unabated.

Aunt Hazel, sitting in the back, had been quiet in her anger. She had heard every word yet had said nothing in Jennifer's defense. She had fought the urge to march into the living room and let her brother have a piece of her mind. She had felt he had been out of line in some of the insults he had hurled at Jennifer. It had taken years for her to gain the self-control necessary to stay out of his discipline of Jennifer, and she had been glad she had overcome the need to jump in and intervene when she thought Shaun was out of control. Part of their arrangement had been that she wouldn't interfere in the raising of Jennifer if she were to stay with her brother, and she had abided by his wishes. That morning, though, he had been lucky; his anger had been just too much. She had wanted to hurt him as she had known he had hurt Jennifer. She had been so angry, but she had not wanted Jennifer's last moments to be all anger. She had held her tongue.

"He doesn't trust me at all. I feel so sick. What did I do that he thinks I would do those things?" Jennifer had twisted the tissues in her hands in agony, crying in her frustration.

Her mom had given no insight to her father's anger. She had known that revealing the reason behind it would not have made his words any more forgivable. She had only responded, "You didn't do anything, honey. Trust me." She had taken one hand from the wheel to gently cup Jennifer's chin and had brought her gaze to her own for a moment of strength. Jennifer had read something in her mother's eyes that indicated more lay behind her father's words, but no explanation followed. Instead, her mom had sighed with deep sorrow. But for her—or for her dad—she knew not.

The remainder of the ride to the airport had been quiet and filled with Jennifer's silent tears. As they had drawn nearer to the airport, Jennifer had managed to dry her eyes and take a deep breath. "Mom, please, just drop me off." She had fought off the tears that had threatened to spill forth. "I don't want to cry in the airport and have people stare, okay?"

Knowing the morning had been a nightmare, Mae had said with uncharacteristic determination, "No, Jennifer, you need us to see you off. People always cry at airports. You're leaving us. Jennifer, please."

From the backseat, Hazel had reached forward. "Jenny, listen to your mother. Let us come in with you and wait with you until your plane departs. It's really okay to cry. We won't be seeing you again until the holidays. Please. We will miss you, dear."

Knowing what had been their foremost concern, Jennifer had bitterly come back with, "That's not what we're crying about, though; is it?" The ugliness of her father's words had hung over them like a death shroud. "I can't go like this!" She had waved her hands at her face. "I'm a mess. I just need to go, okay?" She, too, had pleaded for understanding, trying hard not to give in to the tears.

Hazel had reached for Mae's arm from the back seat. "It's okay, Mae. Let her go. She'll be fine." She had given reassurance as she had searched Jennifer's face for a sign she would, indeed, be all right. Her brother's words had been so cruel to his only child. She had prayed so hard he wouldn't do this morning what he had done. It had been no way to turn a child out into the world. Granted, she had had no children of her own, but she had known in her heart it couldn't be good to part on such harsh terms when a person was embarking on such a treacherous path as Jennifer had chosen. Jennifer had needed to know her parents, most especially her dad, had faith in her as a person to do the right thing. She was such a good girl. Why had he done what he had? She had been so angry with him. Yet she had refused to let Jennifer know. She hadn't needed the knowledge there would be residual anger among those she loved upon her departure.

Jennifer had put on her best smile. "Thank you, Aunt Hazel. I love you both." She had given her mother a hug in the front seat. "I love you, Mom, and I'm so sorry. I didn't mean to make Dad so mad."

"Jennifer." Her mother had held her as closely as she could. "I love you, too, so very, very much dear, and it's okay. You just be careful out there." She had squeezed Jennifer hard. "We ALL love you, honey."

Jennifer had turned into the back seat and hugged Aunt Hazel as fiercely as possible. She then had quickly gotten out before she could break down completely. She hadn't wanted to start her new life as an emotional wreck. She was excited, she had reminded herself. Taking a deep breath, she had gone to the trunk to remove her bags. An airport skycap had assisted her immediately, and her life of independence had started. She had waved a brave good-bye and turned to enter the airport terminal.

She hadn't meant to show defiance towards Elli's offered advice, but her resolve to show her father she was better than he had pronounced her to be influenced her every action. She just wouldn't lose sight of one of her main goals, to prove her father wrong.

Over time, Elli was right in her assessment of Jennifer. In her efforts to be the daughter her family had raised, she alienated herself from the other models. They had been warm and welcoming at first, but as time passed, Jennifer's insistence at living a "wholesome life" had rubbed girls she boarded with the wrong way.

Kim had been her roommate from the first day. She was fresh out of high school also and from the state of Washington. Of Asian-American Indian descent with jet black hair and the most beautiful, big almond eyes, she was tall and thin and carried herself with an air of self-assurance, thanks to her upbringing in the city. Their first weekend, she had asked Jennifer to join her and a couple of the others to go see the sights. Elli had said they were allowed to go out and had told them of their curfew. The girls had tried to assure her they weren't going out to break any rules; they just wanted to live and enjoy the life they had embarked upon—the very reasons Jennifer had left home in the first place. But in her quest to prove her father wrong, she had unknowingly lost all sight of her goal.

"Hey, Jen, come with us. We're going to catch a show and go check out a couple bars." They had been all excited to see if the nightlife was what everyone had warned them it would be.

"No," Jennifer had offered, remembering her dad's words, "I think I'll stay here and do a little laundry and get to bed early."

"Come on, Jen, please. It'll be fun."

Chloe, another model had tried to encourage her to come. "We'll be careful." She had sensed Jennifer seemed a little hesitant in her new surroundings of freedom, and as if to show understanding without revealing to the others Jennifer's fears, she added, "You can make sure WE don't drink too much." And she had smiled in an effort to put Jennifer at ease.

"Thanks, but really, not this time." She had faked a yawn. "I'm pretty tired; maybe next time," Jennifer had responded, hoping they wouldn't think too harshly of her.

In the end, they had left, and Jennifer had done her laundry and cleaned her room and finally gone to bed, alone. She had been proud of herself for resisting temptation, but she had wondered all the while what the others were doing.

The next morning she had listened to their tales of the night before and was simultaneously glad and sad she hadn't gone. She had felt terribly left out when she had nothing to add to the conversations. She listened with interest and tried to seem supportive and compassionate to the girls that had had too much to drink for the first time in their young lives. In the end she had felt it had been a small price to pay to show her dad she was stronger than he had thought.

The girls she worked and lived with had soon stopped trying to include her. Each time they had extended an invitation, she had had a ready excuse. Kim and Becca, who were new to the modeling business, had still been nice to Jen, but behind her back they had become very resentful of her pristine living. Chloe, who had already been modeling a year, had been trying to be supportive of something she felt was not

Jen's doing. But resentment crept in toward Jen who was always fresh and ready to start a shoot when the others had days when they were tired from staying up late or haggard-looking from drinking one too many shots or red-eyed from crying over the loss of attention from one young man or another whom they had become attracted to.

In an effort to try and stay connected, Jennifer had offered her advice on dealing with their broken hearts and tiredness. But her help had only come across as judgmental and pompous. One Saturday Chloe had come in at two a.m., threatening to take her life because life sucked, wasn't fair, and wasn't worth living. Her insight had come to her after she had seen the young man she was sure she was in love with making out with another model. Jennifer had offered her compassion and understanding, truly trying to console her.

"Chloe," she had softly and innocently begun, "don't you know these guys are only out to 'get a piece'? You shouldn't give them your heart in the process." Her efforts had failed dismally.

"That's not true, Jen," Chloe had argued in her boyfriend's defense. "With me, he was different. Ian told me he had never met anyone like me, and he wanted to take me home to meet his family for Thanksgiving. Of all the guys I've known," and she had smiled a little sheepishly, "I mean guys don't say that and not mean it." She had continued sobbing into her shirt sleeve.

Jennifer had felt awful. She had really liked Chloe, the only one who had seemed to understand without being told all the details why she did not hang out with them. Chloe had come to her aid and offered her an alibi—you don't have to drink; you can drive if you come with us. Chloe hadn't continued to pester her to join them. And Chloe had always woken her up when they returned to share the evening's events. Without being too obvious, Chloe had made her feel as if she belonged. Of all the girls she had met modeling, Chloe had been unbelievably nice and truly beautiful, a rare combination in their profession.

Ian probably had spoken the truth when he had said he had never met anyone like her. Chloe was of West Indian and African American descent, and she was absolutely stunning. She was tall with a light brown coloring and naturally curly, golden hair giving way to a white ancestor somewhere in her genetics. Her physical beauty was regal, yet her face was her most stunning feature. She had large, light blue eyes, an aquiline nose, and the most perfectly arched lips any woman would love to apply lipstick to. Jennifer had been there when Ian had caught sight of Chloe. She had always had fun watching guys' reactions to the tall, athletic, young woman. They would stop in mid-sentence and just stare. God definitely had made Chloe a work of art. Every now and then, one of these young men would literally drop his jaw upon seeing Chloe, and Ian had been one of them.

Most of the models had loved Chloe for she never let her beauty affect her. What had annoyed them was her nonstop desire to find a young man to love. Eventually some of the girls avoided Chloe for that very reason. She was always seeking out the opposite sex. Her overwhelming neediness seemed to repel anyone who had the courage to approach the young beauty to ask her out. Ironically, as beautiful as she was, she seemed to latch on to whoever offered her the slightest interest. She could have had anyone, and she took whoever and settled for whatever was offered, whether they were legitimately interested in her affections or not. She had her heart broken more than anyone. It had started to annoy the others that she let these guys drive her life. She never seemed to see through their charades.

Jennifer had only been trying to offer a little insight to steer Chloe from Ian and any future young men who would soon take his place.

"How would you know anything about guys?" Chloe had forced out angrily. "You don't even go out. Have you ever even been in love, Miss High-and-mighty?"

Jennifer had blushed in admitted embarrassment. Trying to disregard Chloe's brutal words, she had blurted out without thinking, "But you have, and look how many times you get dumped. These guys say they love you, but all they want is a girl just to sleep with a couple of times and dump her. It's the industry we're in, Chloe. It's not us." She had tried to soften her words and not make it seem as if Chloe was putting out regularly for words of love.

"I hate you, Jennifer!" Chloe had said with such swift anger Jennifer had been surprised. No one there had called her Jennifer. "All these months you sit in this dorm acting like a cloistered nun. How can you even offer advice on life when you've never gotten out to see what life is? I know people like you, goody two-shoes. You sit on the bank of the river watching others have fun, afraid something might happen, and the minute it does to someone living life, you say, 'See? I told you so.' Well, you can't hide from life forever, Jennifer. It'll get you in the end. I've seen it happen to others like you, and then I'll be the one going 'Now what?' And there won't be anyone there to help you because you have no one."

This time Chloe's hurtful words couldn't be ignored. Jennifer had slumped at the words hurled in anger. She had really liked Chloe and had been surprised Chloe thought she judged her or the others for that matter. She had come to like all the girls she had started modeling with. Did they all hate her and see her as judgmental? She had just wanted to show her dad he was wrong about her. She had reminded herself Chloe was a little drunk, felt hurt by Jennifer's attempts at consolation, and still nursed her pain from Ian. Ian had been especially spiteful.

Ian had been a hunk; all the girls had agreed on that from day one. He had had a reputation, and they had been warned by Elli to avoid him. Ian himself had secretly hoped Chloe would come to him. He had been pretty full of himself and knew his appeal to the opposite sex, but Chloe had listened to Elli and hadn't chased after him. Elli had rarely interfered in the girl's love lives. She had fully believed matters of the heart were illogical to begin with and therefore no reasoning could apply. However, she had felt it was her duty to warn the girls of danger, and Ian was only out for himself and dangerous to her young impressionable charges. So Chloe had stayed away from Ian.

When Ian had had to approach her, he was angry. Girls chased him; he was not used to chasing them. His only consolation to his pride had been that he knew he would make her see he was the one who was to be pursued. He would use her and leave her, and she would know who had the power. He was the man, yeah, he was the stud, and he would have any and all the girls. He truly was everything Elli had said he was, yet he had turned on his charm and offered affection to Chloe who swallowed his attention like the needy person she was.

Jennifer's heartfelt words of advice had fallen upon a Chloe she did not know just as Elli's words had fallen upon a Jennifer Elli did not know. Words of helpfulness cannot penetrate what over time has become a mechanism of protection, hiding our true self from the world. Our coverings of automatic reactions to hurtful words and actions from the past also keep us unaware of the power of those who had interacted with us on a daily basis. We now do and say according to the grooves that have been worn into our psyche, failing to address inner feelings and emotions. If we could see and were made to see, if life were so simple and held no emotional challenges, would we be as we are? Would we walk the paths of pain to come through with lessons learned and personality strengthened?

Chloe, as beautiful as she appeared, had been left bereft of love at a tender age. Her equally beautiful mother had borne her into a marriage with a proud, young, ebony African American. At birth, Chloe's light skin color and fair eyes had raised some doubt as to Ben's paternity of the little girl. A few years after her birth, when her fair hair and eyes had persisted, the man was sure his wife had stepped out on him. The addition of two younger brothers as deeply dark skinned as their father, a few years later, only seemed to solidify the proof of his wife's indiscretion.

Her mother had pleaded with Chloe's father to believe in her fidelity. She had reminded him her own family had served in the big house of a plantation during their years of slavery. Ben had scoffed at the very idea of ancestry. He had reasoned too many years had passed for something to show up now. If he only could have looked back in time, he would have been ashamed of the blame he was trying to shoulder on his young wife. It was his dad's great-great-grandmother who had been viciously raped at a young age.

She, too, had been a real beauty, as Chloe was now: slender and athletic with the darkest of ebony skin. Regal in bearing, Esther had stood tall and straight, even in her youthfulness. Though Esther's mother had worried her young daughter's beauty would draw unwanted attention, she hadn't discouraged her from her proud carriage. She had taken pleasure in her daughter's great appearance and the reaction Esther had received when she had walked into a room or across the grounds of the plantation.

The plantation overseer had been a hard man with a deeply dark look on life and a love of drink from his fair Irish heritage. His temper had been as wild as his fiery red hair and blazed as did his vivid blue eyes when he felt the need to put slaves in their place. He not only had worked his field-hands mercilessly; he also had abused them at his discretion. Breaking their spirit, he had maintained, made them more manageable and productive in the life God had given them. Pride was not a trait to be tolerated in the slave, and Ben's great-great-grandmother's self-assured way about her walk inevitably caught the overseer's eye. He had seen only a slave in need of adjusting, and he, the overseer, had done his job to try and break the young girl's spirit.

Ben's ancestor had been the product of rape, but his great-great-grandmother's pride hadn't been broken, just buried. No one but Esther's mother had known of the brutal rape, and no evidence of the paternity had showed in Esther's young daughter. The secret had remained, for Esther had loved her child and protected her, never telling her daughter of her parentage or the brutality of her conception.

The same could not be said of Chloe's own father. Chloe's father hadn't been physically abusive; he just hadn't allowed himself to love Chloe as he had loved her two younger brothers who he knew were truly his own flesh and blood. His differential treatment had not been lost on the little girl growing up as she had witnessed his favoritism towards her brothers. The depth of the void of love denied had grown within the little girl, and despite her mother's affections, the emptiness had become an ache that had demanded filling. She would quietly watch as her father showered her brothers with hugs and attention. At times she would catch him looking at her with such regret, and she had misinterpreted his gaze to imply there was something wrong with her and thus he could not love her.

How tragic that the wicked actions of generations past can filter down into the future to rear their ugliness and spew hatred onto unsuspecting victims such as the innocent young Chloe. The true irony is that the instruments of destruction are the very emotions and feelings that are unique only to the human animal. How tragic, too, that Chloe's own father had held her skin color against her, as in the past his own skin color had been the reason his ancestors had been treated as less than deserving of human compassion. Again, the tools of wickedness were the emotions, the withholding of love and acceptance of the worth of the human individual. Chloe, as she had grown up, had sought to fill the void of paternal love in anyone of the opposite sex who she had thought offered love. Had she known this? No, she had been but a child, and human children innately seek love from their caregivers. But when that love is denied, they search everywhere and desperately grasp at any substitute they can find.

Had Jennifer known Chloe's past when she had offered what she had thought was caring and compassionate help to her friend? No. She had unknowingly shot an arrow of hurt and judgment that Chloe threw back to Jennifer, doubling the pain. And so they had worked, feelings and emotions, to became vehicles high-jacked by wickedness. In time, Chloe's words had proved true, when life had caught Jennifer and changed her forever.

Jennifer's isolation from the other girls had escalated when an odd job had sent her soaring to the top where she herself had been swept off her feet by a young man. She had prided herself on being so strong in her upbringing all the previous months. But when the trap had been set, she had walked in and had failed to see she had fallen victim to the very thing she had taken so much personal pride in, moral self-control. She had, time and again, warned her roommates and modeling friends they were silly to fall for the obvious false flatter of the young men they all worked with in "the business." Jennifer had worked so hard to keep her distance of all the young men associated with the looks-oriented business. When she had finally fallen, the others had been less than supportive to the one they silently felt had finally gotten what she had deserved, a helping of real life.

Her refusal to partake of the life she had so sought had left her innocent Midwestern farm-girl looks intact. She had maintained her freshness, for she never looked tired, and she still possessed the air of naïveté of someone who had lived a sheltered life. Jobs others felt should have been theirs had gone to her. She had unknowingly gained a reputation and set herself apart in ways dangerous to the profession she had chosen. As with most people who try to live outside the world, its tendrils filter in and coil about to snare and entrap without warning, until the victim is fully bound, helpless to do anything but recover from the fall. And so it had been for Jennifer.

A challenge is often more attractive than a certain success. It was this hidden threat for which Jennifer had been unprepared. She had unknowingly set herself up as something to be conquered and brought off her high horse of morality. To her back, some had referred to her as "that little bitch." Jennifer's steadfastness in her morals had rubbed quite a few of the other models, males and females alike, the wrong way. Who had she thought she was? They all had done things they were truly uncomfortable with, but it went with the job, or so they were told. Now here she had come, refusing to do exactly as everyone before her and then winning shoots that should have been earned over time and with the mistakes they had made. Jennifer had made unseen enemies without intending to, only trying to show her dad she wouldn't be like those he feared she would become.

Jennifer's trip home that first Christmas had left her wondering about all she had been brought up to know. Home had changed, or at least it had seemed so different. Her small family hadn't been the same. She had failed to see it was she who had changed and not her family. They were stunned at the young lady who had surprised them with her unexpected trip home, without any assistance from anyone. Who was this independent young person who hadn't needed so much as a stamp from those who had provided for her every need until her sudden and unhappy departure five months ago? The Christmas trip she had anticipated was miserable. She had so wanted her dad to see she hadn't become what he had feared. She was who he had raised her to be, and he had every reason to be proud of her.

Her choice to isolate herself at work had left her feeling homesick as the holidays had approached. She had survived the loneliness of Thanksgiving but feared facing Christmas alone. She had written home weekly and treasured the letters from Aunt Hazel. They had kept her focused on her goal: to prove her father wrong. So when Aunt Hazel had written she should come home for Christmas, Jennifer had called the very next morning when she knew her parents wouldn't be home.

"Aunt Hazel," Jennifer had laughed into the phone, "yes, it's Jennifer." Her eyes had misted and her throat constricted at the sound of the voice so loved. "I'm coming home. Okay, just don't tell Mom and Dad. I want to surprise them."

"Jennifer, it's so good to hear you. Oh little darling, yes, do come home. I won't tell your folks. But hon, I don't think it's a good idea not to tell them." She knew her brother and his wife were not preparing for the holidays. With Jennifer's absence, they had decided there was no need to go to all the trouble of Christmas. If Mae knew Jennifer was coming home, she would want to decorate. But a promise is a promise. Hazel hadn't wanted to set her brother off on one of his tirades either. She had decided Jennifer's disappointment would be easier to deal with than her brother's days-on-end cynicism of the evil turn the world had taken, how youth were being bombarded by emptiness and self-indulgence. The first few months after Jennifer's departure had almost been hell. If it hadn't been nearing the end of summer with all the work on the farm, she would have felt the need to seek new living arrangements. Shaun had been almost impossible, actually blaming his sister for Jennifer's decision to model. In turn, she had given him the silent treatment for a whole week for thinking she approved of her niece's career; she had even refused to be in the same room with him. Oh it had been awful, no, miserable.

"Aunt Hazel?" Jennifer had questioned into the silence of the receiver.

"Yes, dear," Hazel had replied, trying to remove the doubt from her response.

"I want to make it my gift to them. Won't it be the best?" Jennifer had been filled with happiness at the thought of pleasing her parents.

Hazel had agreed to keep silent again, cringing inwardly, thinking back to the last time she had kept silent at Jennifer's request. She had also vowed to be as surprised as Jennifer's parents when Jennifer showed up unannounced.

Surprises have a way of sometimes capturing the innovator as much as the intended recipient. And so it was for Jennifer. She had showed up only three days before Christmas. Aunt Hazel had known she was coming but had not known the day she would arrive. Hazel had tried to get this information from Jennifer, but Jennifer had assured her that her not knowing would help her to play the part of being surprised. Jennifer's excitement at coming home was infectious, and Hazel had reluctantly agreed.

Jennifer couldn't have picked a worse day to arrive home unexpectedly. The three had not intended to celebrate, and the house gave no indication of the approaching holiday. In fact, Jennifer's dad had decided to redo the downstairs bathroom. He had warned the women they wouldn't have water for the day, and after having torn out the old fixtures, he had departed for the hardware store to buy new ones. Mae had left that morning to lend a helping hand to a neighbor who had taken sick after the birth of her fourth child. And Hazel had gone along with Mae, figuring Jennifer would not arrive before the supper hour. Heaven knew Mae would need assistance helping with three toddlers, a new baby, and a sick mother at Christmas time. And she certainly did not want to be in the house during the reworking of the bathroom either. Projects like that always became more than what they started out to be. She would go where she would be useful.

Walking into an empty house devoid of any celebration and welcoming love had affected Jennifer in such a way she had been unprepared to deal with. She had been totally shocked. Where was the Christmas tree? Where were all the decorations? Where was her family? How could they not celebrate? Something had to be wrong. It was Christmas. She had felt panicked. She hadn't talked to Aunt Hazel since their phone call. Had something happened? She only had five days to spend with them. A day before she flew home she had been offered a commercial shoot for the celebration of the New Year, and she had had to be back sooner than she had wanted. But she had felt a few days with her family were better than not coming at all. She had wanted to be home. Now that she had arrived home and found them absent, she had felt fear. She had forced herself to take a deep breath and started looking for clues as to their whereabouts. She had quickly spotted the state of disrepair in the downstairs bathroom and had concluded her dad had probably made a trip to the hardware store.

Where had her mom and Aunt Hazel gone? And what was she to do? She had debated driving to the hardware store but thought better of it when the idea had come to decorate the house. It had made her feel happy, and she had pushed aside the unpleasant thoughts that had greeted her when she had first walked into the home of her youth.

She had carried her bag to her bedroom and changed out of her carefully selected outfit. She had dressed to impress, but she could put it back on later for supper to show her dad how decent and modestly she chose to dress. Putting on an old pair of favorite sweats and t-shirt, she had made her way to the attic to haul out the decorations and the artificial tree from her childhood. She had refused to be beaten down and had pushed aside intruding thoughts about the emptiness of the house, the absence of any holiday spirit, and the possibility she'd made a terrible mistake in coming. Intent on capturing the sense of family togetherness she had so terribly missed, she had, instead, concentrated only on the feeling of being home, drawing strength from all of its happy memories.

She had had no idea she would feel as she did. It almost made her wonder at her sudden departure from such a place of love. She had quickly halted those thoughts, too. She had refused to give up her pursuit of life for the feel of comfort and love.

Jennifer had managed to drag everything safely downstairs and had the tree assembled when her dad had walked into the front room. She had been surrounded by the strings of Christmas lights and had to gingerly get up to avoid crushing them, but as soon as she was fully upright she had thrown herself into her dad's arms, forgetting all the hurt of the words he had said when she had left. She had only wanted to feel the love she had been showered with all the years previous to her departure. Her dad had meant the world to her. He had been her protector, she had been his little girl, and she had always felt loved and special to him. It was this she had come home to regain—and what Chloe had grown up without and would ache for and seek in others.

Shaun, upon driving up to the house after his trip to the hardware store, had been perturbed with himself. Had he left lights on in the house? He knew he was getting older, but darn, he couldn't be that forgetful. He had taken his purchases from the truck and made his way up the steps to the front door. The sound of Christmas tunes had met him, and he had wondered, *What on earth?* He knew Mae and Hazel had gone to help the neighbor. Who the heck had entered in his house? He had stomped his feet loudly to warn whoever it was. Times were changing, and crooks had more nerve until they were confronted. It was the holiday season, and people often stole out of desperation. He hadn't wanted to tangle with a desperate person. He had wanted to give them a chance to get out. He had taken great pains to open the front door slowly and even went so far as to holler into the interior, "I'm back."

Carefully stepping through the door and, with a deep breath, standing to his full height, he had been shocked into awed silence. It had not been the intruder he had expected. Instead of the ramshackle mess of burglary, he had been assaulted with the love he had turned off and turned his back on. Before words could form, the little girl he had so loved all her life had made her way out of the mess of Christmas she had been swallowed in and jumped at him with the exuberance and joy of her youth. As a young child trusts her father to catch her as she jumps into waiting arms, Jennifer had anticipated the same. She had expected nothing less than the returned joy and expressed love from all the years of her growing up.

Hurt, disappointment, expectations not met—these have a way of cloaking and hardening even the softest of hearts. Hearts that shun shows of emotion and give cautiously to love are the ones often coated so thoroughly and most rapidly when life turns sour. Shaun had stood, and the arms that should have lovingly encased his only child had hung limp at his sides. Fear had kept him captive. Why was she home? Was she home for good? Had something happened? He was a man of few words, relying on Mae for most of the news on Jennifer. Even throughout her childhood, Shaun had not been a confidant, but he had loved Jennifer as he had been taught. He had provided and protected. In time he had been softened enough to read with her, and they had had favorite stories. They had sat together now and then and enjoyed a few television shows when farm work had permitted. Their relationship had been special. He had thought she had respected his word and authority. She had been a perfect daughter, questioning nothing, always obeying. She had been beautiful and a delight to raise. The day she had broken the news about her decision to leave had almost killed him. He had almost wanted to kill Hazel. If only he had known what Jennifer had been up to, he had felt he could have prevented what she had set out to do. To be told what she was going to do, what she had already done, and that the matter was final had been an assault and disrespectful to who he had been all her life. Had all those years meant nothing?

When the arms of her father had not enclosed and embraced, Jennifer had stepped back and looked up at the face that had always reflected approval and pride. Her father's look of shock and perplexity had made her heart sink, and her joy had melted away in confusion. Wasn't he happy to see her?

"Dad," she had ventured, "I'm home."

"Hmm." Shaun had cleared his throat. "I see." In the back of his mind, the questions swirled: *Why? How long? Is everything okay?* They had kept him where he was, and any joy he may have felt he had withheld.

Hiding her own crushing hurt, Jennifer had stood with her arms at her side and then had turned to the Christmas mess to give herself a moment to figure out the failure of her surprise. Having drawn on her reasons for coming home, she had made her voice strong and sure. Her father's reaction now had made her feel little and crushed. Where was her daddy that had loved her? She had just wanted to cry. She was home; where was he?

"I was able to get a few days' break before my next job, and I thought I would spend the time with you. I wanted to surprise everyone," she had ended on a hopeful note.

Gathering his manners and subsequently hiding behind them, Shaun had made polite talk. "Well, a surprise it is." He had moved into the house and closed the door to shut out the chill, but the cold of his heart had stayed with him. Hurt in the past had taught him to be guarded with his affections. He had felt strange guarding himself from his only child; yet survival of the heart is innate and what one does in one's youth is often carried through into adulthood. Shaun's method of protection from emotional hurt had always been to push away from it. The deeper the hurt, the farther Shaun would distance himself and the colder the appearance of care or concern. He knew no other way to cope.

Jennifer knew nothing of this aspect of her father; he had never allowed her to see his vulnerable side. She hadn't known Shaun the person, only Shaun her daddy, who had always loved her until, in his eyes, she had done something wrong, and her heart had sunk.

Jennifer had felt as if her dad was treating her like a guest and not his daughter. She had been confused and had no idea how to respond. "I'm putting up the tree," she had said in an attempt, again, to draw him back into her love. "Want to help?"

"I see," he had commented and then added, "I can't. I'm kind of in the middle of redoing the bathroom."

"Oh, yeah. I saw that. How's it going?" Jennifer had grasped at straws, making small-talk to keep her father engaged. She hadn't wanted such awkwardness or feelings of not belonging—certainly not in her own home. She had come home to be with those who she knew loved her and made her feel welcomed, not alienated and isolated as most of her new "friends" had made her feel. She had wanted her family and, most important, her dad, the man she had grown up with, the one who had showered her with love and approval. Surely now that she had come home he was happy. Or…? Her heart had slowly crumbled, though she had tried as best she could to hold it together. She had fought so hard all these past months to hold to what she was, for her dad, and now this. She had never experienced personal rejection. She had grown up with love—and, yes, discipline—but never this cold indifference, not from those closest to her. His reaction had caught her unprepared and was most crushing. She sagged beneath the weight of what had gone wrong with her surprise.

Struggling to resist her offered affection, Shaun had moved into the house with his purchases and said, "I've only got today to finish it as the weather should be better tomorrow, and there's always plenty to do outside."

Acting on his cue, Jennifer had replied as if all had been normal, "Huh, Dad, where are Mom and Aunt Hazel?" Try as she might for control of her emotions, at the mentioning of Aunt Hazel and her mom, Jennifer's voice had cracked just enough to reveal her hurt and disappointment at her dad's seemingly uncaring reaction to her surprise visit home.

Hearing the hurt in her voice and hardening his heart to her pain, Shaun had reached into the past and retrieved his old anger. "You mean to tell me they didn't know you were coming?" The hint of accusation had not been lost on Jennifer.

Realizing the past was in the present and huge in its ugliness, Jennifer had quietly said, "I wanted to surprise everyone."

Giving in totally to his past hurt, Shaun had released the stain. "So you're really not in trouble?"

The realization of what her father had hinted at had stunned Jennifer: She had come home only because she was "in trouble." The words, however subtle, had cut deeply.

Seeing the withered look of hurt and shock, Shaun had pressed the issue, hoping finally to get through to his daughter that she had made a big mistake and needed to amend her ways. "I told you if you get pregnant, you are on your own, and I meant it. So if you're in trouble you might as well go back upstairs, get your things and leave. I'll not have dishonor in my home, and I won't argue it with your mother or my meddling sister. This is still *my* home. So I am warning you, if you are in trouble, you better leave before your mother and aunt get back. I won't 'discuss' the issue with anyone." He had purposefully ended on a harsh note, subconsciously wanting to wound as he had been wounded. She had disappointed him deeply, making plans—and foolish ones at that—without talking it over with him. He was her father. Hadn't he always done his best for her? For this most important part of her life, she had done whatever had struck her fancy at the moment. He had had to make her see she would be throwing their love away permanently if she continued on her chosen path. It had hurt him to withhold his love—she was his only child and he loved her dearly—but the life she was choosing was a big mistake. She had better see now than after it was too late how painful life would be without love.

Is there no end to his cruelty? Jennifer had wondered, incredulously. *Surely he doesn't mean what he implied!* She wasn't about to get pregnant. How could he stop loving her? He was her father. Love wasn't like that, was it—to be turned on or off at whim, conditional on doing this or that? Not wanting to continue the conversation, Jennifer had replied, "I'll let you get back to the bathroom, and I'll get back to the tree."

She had turned back into the living room and with much less enthusiasm had picked up the lights she had joyously abandoned moments before. She had sat amid them, tears finally blurring her vision as she had wondered at everything, feeling tired of life and all it had turned out to be. Dashed expectations, delusions of dreams, withheld love—the utter disappointments had made her want to sink into the floor and weep.

Then from somewhere deep within, a quiet resolve had emerged. Inherited traits, strands of ancestors reaching out from the past in the continuity of life, she had decided she would not give in. She had sat up straighter. She would make her father see he was wrong. Anger had set in, replacing her weariness, over his insinuation that she might have been pregnant, and so soon after having left home. She was stronger than he knew. She had wiped away any trace of tears and with determination told herself she would have her Christmas and her family. She would pretend her dad hadn't said the hurtful words. Mom and Aunt Hazel would surely be home soon, and things would be as they should. Feeling a little better, she had gotten up and found an old Christmas album and put on the tune "I'll Be Home for Christmas" to help restore cheer to her assaulted spirit.

Several hours later, Jennifer had finished her decorating, and when her father had announced that there was once again water to the house, Jennifer, tired of waiting and not knowing when her mom and Aunt Hazel would arrive home, had turned off the Christmas tunes and dragged herself upstairs to shower. She had not wanted to chance another conversation alone with her father.

Aunt Hazel and Mae had been surprised when they had arrived home around eight thirty that evening. When they had turned on the entry light to hang their coats in the hall closet, they had noticed the house was filled with Christmas. Unaware Jennifer was home, both ladies had been further shocked to see that not only was the tree up and decorated but all the assorted decorations were neatly displayed too. What could have turned Shaun from his earlier decision not to celebrate the "holiday of consumerism"? Ever since Jennifer had left, what little joy he had, had disappeared. Their discovery had filled them with excitement. Maybe he had had a change of heart, a Christmas miracle.

Hazel had played along as best she could, for she knew Jennifer was home. Had her brother helped her in all this? Surely he must have; she couldn't have done all this alone. Their little family was going to be okay. She was so happy.

"Shaun?" Mae had questioned into the interior of the still house. "Shaun?"

"I'm here, in the kitchen," had come the reply from the recesses of the house.

The ladies had finished taking off their coats and hung them in the closet, walking back to the sound of his voice. "The tree looks lovely. I'm so glad you had a change of heart." Mae's happiness had been genuine, and she had gone to her husband with eyes alit, arms outstretched to enfold him into her pleasure.

For a second time in a matter of hours, Shaun had held his chosen course of control and guarded aloofness. He had carefully forced out, "I did not put that thing up, and if I was a real bastard and had had the time, I would have taken the damn thing down."

His angry words had shocked both his wife and his sister. Mae's outstretched arms had instantly dropped to her side and her face had turned white with dismay. She had been deeply puzzled and unsure how to respond. *What on earth? Who?* She had sat down.

Hazel, knowing, had cringed quietly inside. *Oh no. Poor Jennifer.* And she, too, had sat down, silent, as Mae had struggled to comprehend.

Into this scene, Jennifer had made her appearance. She had been in the shower when her mother and Hazel had arrived home and had not heard their greeting or her father's stony response. As she had made her way to the kitchen to grab a bite to eat, she had attempted to reach out to her dad in normalness. "Dad, I'm gonna make a sandwich. Do you want anything?" she had asked into the silence of the house, not knowing where her father was. Receiving no response she had made her way into the kitchen.

Surprises, ah, they can sometimes take on a life of their own. We all love them when they are joyous in nature and even take pleasure in them when they are comically frightful, but Jennifer's intended surprise had continued to evoke anything but a positive response.

The contrast of the darkness of the living room and connecting hallway with the light of the kitchen, into which she had entered, had temporarily blinded Jennifer's eyes. There it was, but a moment. If only moments could suspend time—to give us the chance to take in events about to unfold, to think upon decisions about to be made, to prevent changes too hastily embraced—perhaps we would not stray from the intended path. But the surprise of such moments without time to think often forces individuals into situations they would not otherwise willingly enter. Only in retrospect and reflection do they see beyond their scars and pain that the path gave them a greater wisdom and was a worthy journey. They say, *I wouldn't have chosen this walk, but in the end, the forced path was the better one. I've survived. I'm a better person for it. I am indeed thankful.* They would never wish such occurrences on someone they love, but life is indeed full of just such walks and revelations, paths chosen because of emotions uncontrolled in situations of surprise not intended.

Time had not suspended for Jennifer, and she had quickly adjusted to the light. The first face her eyes had met was dear Aunt Hazel. The events of the afternoon and the heartache and loneliness of the past months had come to an ugly head, and instead of surprise and joy all round, Jennifer had burst into tears and dived like a little child into her aunt's loving lap.

"Goodness, Jennifer," Hazel had exclaimed, remembering to be surprised, "What on earth? Was it you who put the tree up? Oh, honey." She had wrapped Jennifer in a loving embrace. "I can't believe you're here. What's with all the tears?" She had refused to acknowledge the cold comment from Shaun moments earlier. Surely he hadn't welcomed Jennifer's trip home with the response he had offered to her and Mae. Had he not seen that Jennifer was making an attempt to please him? Her anger had risen, and she had fought it valiantly. She would not ruin Jennifer's trip home. She had pushed Jennifer from her gently to look into her tear-streaked face. "Let me get a good look at you. Why look, Mae. It is our little Jenny." She had wiped a tear from the face she had known from birth and kissed her cheek. "How long are you going to be home?"

Jennifer had sucked in a deep breath, inhaling Aunt Hazel's presence, surprised, too, at her outburst of tears. Where on earth had that come from? She had felt the comfort of the hug and drawn on the love offered for strength. "I took a late flight last night so I could get home early, so I could…," she had struggled, "to surprise you, everyone." She had ended softly, her eyes shifting down. "I'm so happy to be home." She had taken a deep breath, smiled, and gotten up to go to her mom. "I've missed you all so much. Did you see the tree?" She hadn't wanted to relive the afternoon and had tried to bring joy into the room.

"Jennifer." Her mom had wrapped her into a loving embrace. "The tree is lovely. We haven't seen all your handiwork, but it was so nice to come home to the holiday spirit." Her words and look had gone toward her husband across the room, who was leaning against the counter, carefully watching for signs that they had known Jennifer was coming home. He would not be tricked in his home.

His wife's look had angered him, and his words had come out bitterly. "Yes, Jennifer, how long are you home for?" He had known the question was loaded, and he hadn't cared. He would not accept the decision Jennifer had made, the life she had chosen. What the devil! If she had loved and missed them this much, why on earth had she left them? His anger from the past spring had risen fresh and stronger as it had silently grown over the summer. Hurt is an ugliness that can take on a consuming life of its own, and Shaun's had been growing to monstrous proportions. He had wanted only goodness for his daughter. What she had chosen was evil. This was not the life he had envisioned for her—thousands of miles away, living among strangers in a world filled with falsehood and wickedness. His eyes had grown dark with hatred over the life she had chosen. She had turned her back on the goodness she had been raised to know. To come back here with tears and "I miss you" reeked of the falseness he had feared she would embrace. His anger and bitterness over the situation had made him feel sick. He had shoved his weight from the counter and forced out, "I'm going to bed. Goodnight." He had departed from the kitchen, leaving them with a withering look of anger and disgust, not waiting to hear Jennifer's response to his question.

Upstairs in the bedroom he shared with his wife, Shaun had stood silently, overcome with anger as he had gazed out the window into the darkness beyond. Where had he gone wrong as a father? Over the years, he had done his best to make up for his past mistake. Why hadn't his efforts been rewarded? What more had he to do?

He had been young and on his way to adventure when, on the encouragement of a buddy, he had stopped back in his hometown for one last farewell. He remembered the trip home well and had thought of it often. What would have been? Could have been? He had felt so old at the recollection though he was just over forty.

Upon his discharge from the army, he and a buddy had planned on going north to Alaska, the last of the frontiers. Shaun had been excited and eager to be on his own with no one to tell him what to do, when or how. Freedom, at last and into a vast expanse of unknown.

Earl, his army buddy from Tennessee, had visited Alaska as a child and had family there that would put them up for a couple of days until they decided which direction to head into in the unsettled land. On their way north from Earl's home, Earl had suggested they stop by Shaun's home so he could say a final farewell to his folks. "Family is most important" was always Earl's motto, and Shaun had become like a brother to him during their two-year hitch.

They had planned only to stop at the farm and say good-bye, but Earl was so taken by Shaun's family he had urged him to stay a few more days. Their Monday stop had turned into a farewell town party that Friday. Shaun had drunk too much and danced a few too many with the local beauty, Mae O'Flynn. But how could he have resisted? She had been tall and slight, shy and engaging at the same time, with the most lovely blond hair and green eyes, not common among the dark-haired Irish community.

As he recalled, she was slow to take to him, but after a few dances her shyness had faded with the fun of the evening. He remembered how at the last dance's end he had offered to walk her home. She had protested and told him, no, she would catch up with her brothers a few paces ahead. Shaun had stubbornly insisted it was his duty, as he had delayed her departing with her brothers because she had had the last dance with him. God, how he regretted that now.

The evening had been a summer's dream, a full moon and a slight breeze. He had felt alive and ready to take on the world. Walking Mae home, they had shared their dreams. Shy at first, she had finally told him she had hoped to go off to business school the next year after graduation and then on to the big city to see what life was all about.

He had loved her spirit and in a slip of the tongue told her he loved her, leaving out that it was her spirit he loved. What had only meant to be a walk home turned into a night of passion upon which the young Mae became pregnant. He still could feel the anger when she had informed him.

Fate, at best, is imagined, although circumstances so profound can make one think all is predetermined. For probably at the very moment Mae had conceived, Earl had been hit by a local farmer on his way home from the same dance. Had they stuck with their original plans, Shaun and Earl would have been long gone and probably in Alaska.

Instead, Earl was in the nearest hospital with a compound fracture of both his femurs. In the few short months Earl took to recover sufficiently under the careful watch of Shaun's family, Shaun had learned he was to be a father.

Shaun had done the right thing and married Mae five days after she had told him. He couldn't disgrace her or her family, his father had told him. Earl had stood up as his best man and then left for Alaska without Shaun. His departure had been the saddest day in Shaun's life. His freedom had disappeared with Earl's departure, and he would have to settle into the life of his father and his father's father. He had felt so weighted with disappointment and trapped by lack of choices. He hadn't wanted the life he had grown up with.

Life can be a cruel trickster, never letting on the twists and turns in the paths ahead. Hardly three weeks later, Mae had lost their child in a miscarriage. Shaun had been so angry. Why had he married her so quickly? As beautiful and interesting as she was, he hadn't wanted to settle down. He hadn't wanted responsibility and work. He hadn't wanted a child. He had only wanted the adventure and excitement of the Alaskan unknown. When she had lost the baby, he had felt again it was punishment for his selfish feelings. With the loss of the child, he had briefly contemplated leaving her. The thought had been so spontaneous and brought him such exalted happiness he had instantly crushed it. He had known if he were to leave her now, his actions would surely bring more than shame; he had known it to be wrong. So he had guiltily stayed.

Mae had been devastated. She, too, felt the miscarriage had been punishment for the wrong they had done. They had been brought up to know sex was for marriage, and they had sinned. But her sin was greater than that. She had never been one to act spontaneously; she had always listened to her parents and older siblings, relying on their wisdom to guide her decisions. Deep in her heart she had wanted desperately to find out what it would be like to try something on her own, without a plan or the protection of others. But her silly thoughts had shamed her. She was ever so thankful the only one who ever knew her desire to see the world was Shaun, and look where her loose lips had gotten her. For such foolishness, she deserved punishment, but to lose her baby…. It hurt her so. The baby had done no wrong; she was the sinner. Oh God, she would make up for her sinful ways and be the perfect wife, submissive and yielding, never questioning. So Mae had chosen her road and never looked to dream again.

Their community, sensing perhaps that the couple had suffered enough for their wrongdoing, had protected them. Their secret had remained hidden, not even spoken in whispers. And as Mae had invested her kindness in good works for neighbors and their church and Shaun had labored to be the upstanding man he wanted all to believe he was, memory of their youthful indulgence had gradually faded.

But such forgetfulness had eluded Shaun. He hadn't confided in Mae, but he had thought in marrying her he would be forgiven. But the loss of their little child had him thinking he had to do more to receive forgiveness; he had vowed to be better. He had buried his anger and resentment of having to give up his plans of adventure and thrown all his efforts and energy into farming until he was too tired to think of dreams lost.

His efforts had been rewarded for Mae had conceived again soon after their loss. The fact he had almost lost Mae during the birth of Jennifer had further terrified him of even sinful thinking. He had known that her brush with death and the subsequent and painful truth that there would be no more children had been punishment for his contemplating leaving her after the loss of their first child. This had cemented Shaun's resolve to abide by his upbringing and avoid all occasion and thought of sin. Maybe he hadn't loved Mae as she professed to love him, but he would be the best husband and father he could, and life would be good to him and those in his care. That was the lesson the young Shaun had derived from his losses—of freedom, of a child, of the chance for more children.

The years had proven his reasoning until the past spring when his daughter had chosen to throw away her life. What had he done to deserve such ingratitude?

Shaun could not see that his daughter had inherited his sense of adventure and sought the feeling of freedom. In the darkness of his ignorance, in their unlit bedroom, he had stood, silently seething, aching for the freedom he had sacrificed so very long ago. He had worked so hard to do the right thing, and now she had thrown everything he had sacrificed away, as if his sacrifice was of no importance, wasted. The anger he thought he had buried so many years ago engulfed him.

Jennifer would never know the reason for her parents' hasty wedding or her mother's miscarriage. Mae and Shaun had thought it in their daughter's best interest to withhold those very personal facts and only tell her theirs was a love meant to be.

Downstairs Aunt Hazel, Mae, and Jennifer had looked at each other in shocked silence. Another moment had passed, each not knowing what to say. Finally Jennifer had breathed into the heaviness, "I get five days, and today is my first day. I have to fly back to do a shoot for a New Year's Eve promotional commercial."

Her words had hung in the quiet of the kitchen and had been answered only by the ticking of the clock. Her mom's silence and Aunt Hazel's look of continued shock had alarmed her. Shaun's words and actions had deeply upset both, and speechlessness had tightened around them. But they had reacted only to part of the picture. Jennifer had indicated nothing to them of her dad's unpleasant reaction to her arrival home or her resolve to beat it back. She had mistaken disapproval from them, as well, not realizing those who loved her unconditionally had been struggling with the ugliness of what should have been a joyous surprise. Her error of perception had brought feelings of shame. What she had been so proud of now sounded hollow and lacking in importance. Fly back to do a commercial—it echoed such emptiness even to her. She had drooped inwardly, but from somewhere deep within, she had resolved to grab at the happiness she had come home for. She had not wanted to let go of the love she knew was here. "I came downstairs to get a bite to eat. Does anyone want a sandwich?" Her words had been weak, but they had broken the hold of shared shock.

Pushing aside the elephant of anger and hurt left in the kitchen by the departing Shaun, Mae and Hazel had resolved to enjoy their time with Jennifer, however brief it might be. Both had chorused in, "A sandwich would be nice, dear." In unison they had risen to make noise about the sandwiches, and the elephant had faded and then disappeared altogether as they had made small talk about their afternoon's whereabouts and the true sadness of the plight of the young family they had spent the day helping, especially occurring over the Christmas holidays. In that, they all allowed themselves feelings of sadness and reflection.

All three had left Jennifer's life and Shaun's response to her trip home untouched. Jennifer had decided not to talk about herself if it would only bring pain and anger among those she loved. She had purposefully directed the conversion away from her life. She had come home to absorb home, and. she would fill herself with home. The sadness in having to hold back had infected her soul with doubt and a seed of despair.

Later alone in her bedroom, Jennifer had pulled forth her disappointment to examine it and understand. What had happened? What had gone wrong? She had wanted her family to see she was still their Jennifer. She had done well, and she had wanted them to be proud of her. She hadn't taken to drinking, drugs, or sex as her father had predicted. She had still gone to mass, and she didn't think she was any different from who she had been when she had left the end of the summer. She was still obeying and doing what she had been brought up to do. She had written them weekly. Why had her dad still been so angry? She had told him she was glad to be home, that she had wanted to come home, and that she had missed them all so much. What puzzled her had been that those words, instead of making him happy, had seemed to anger him to a degree she had never known or seen in her dad. What had happened to her family? Even Mom and Aunt Hazel seemed a little subdued. She had sighed deeply, trying hard not to give in to the tears that were threatening below the surface. She had lain back on the bed of her childhood and in the semi-dark room wondered at her life. The tears silently and slowly had made their way free and slid down her cheek. What was she going to do? She had been so sad. Where was her dad's love? Why had he despised her? Oh God. And she had cried.

Mae had knocked quietly on Jennifer's closed bedroom door. "Jennifer?" she had softly questioned into the quiet dark. "May I come in?"

Drying her tears and taking a slow deep breath, Jennifer had replied, "Yes."

"Honey," Mae had said as she had opened the bedroom door slowly, not surprised to hear tears, and she had gone to Jennifer's bedside. She had been so angry at Shaun she could have beaten him. To have hurt Jennifer to this degree. She had known Jennifer and Shaun's relationship was so precious to them both. Damn! She had been angry, but now she must set anger aside. "Honey, I'm so sorry Dad is being so…, well, mean. He's just, well, he is so unhappy about what you are doing. He is afraid for you." She had ended with a touch of sadness, as she had reached out to stroke her daughter's cheek in comfort.

"But Mom, I'm not doing anything wrong. I'm actually doing everything right, so right everyone hates me." And she couldn't stop the tears from reappearing. She had cried quietly.

"We know, sweetie, but don't you see? If these people aren't nice to you and you aren't happy, why are you staying and still doing what you have chosen to do?"

"I just want you to see that I am still me. I'm still what you raised me to be." She hadn't answered the "why?" The question had thrown her. She had been puzzled by it and thought momentarily on it. Why was she so unhappy? Then she had pushed it aside. She had come home to prove to her family that she had succeeded in not being what they had thought she would be. Couldn't they see that? What she had done had cost her dearly: She had no friends. Her family's lack of acceptance and approval had angered her—and surprised her. She loved her mom, and her mom hadn't deserved her anger. She had been very supportive all these months. Yet her mother's lack of understanding, in why she was doing what she was, made her angry.

Seeing the mix of emotions parade across Jennifer's still innocent face, Mae had withdrawn. She had not wanted to push Jennifer farther from the love of home. "I know you are you. Goodness! I just don't see…." And she had trailed off, not knowing how to explain her father's fears without causing a scene. Instead, she had leaned over and given her a hug, holding her a little longer. "I love you so much, Jennifer. Just don't ever forget that, okay?" Her own eyes had teared up just a bit, for she hadn't seen a way to help Jennifer understand the depth of their love and their concern. Not knowing all that had transpired during her absence that day, Mae had decided to leave the matter alone. "Let's all get a good night's sleep, and tomorrow will be better." With that she had brushed the tears from Jennifer's face, her love for Jennifer almost overwhelming her. If only she could make things right. She had sighed softly and given her cheek a kiss and then risen and turned out the light to leave. "Good night. I love you, Jennifer."

"Good night, Mom. I love you, too," Jennifer had said to the closing door. Lying in the quiet dark of her room after her mother had left, Jennifer couldn't help but think back into the early evening. Aunt Hazel's quiet had bothered Jenny more than anything. Why hadn't she said something to her dad?

The question had finally forced her to get out of bed and see her aunt, as she had done so many times when she was growing up. Her aunt's room had been dark, but that had never stopped Jennifer in her youth. She had spoken quietly into the darkness, "Aunt Hazel?" Silence. She had tried again, "Aunt Hazel?" Still she had met only silence. This had never happened to her. After two more attempts, she had quietly closed the door and gone back up to her own room.

Meanwhile, Aunt Hazel had slept soundly, if somewhat restlessly. Hearing aids removed, she had heard nothing to disturb her slumber.

The ugliness of the afternoon and the weight of the evening had filled the darkness of Jennifer's room. The most distressing thought haunted her: What had happened to her family and her home and the life she knew? She had only left home; she hadn't left the world. Why was everything and everyone suddenly so foreign? When she had finally realized she honestly couldn't wait to leave, she had felt sick. She had shoved the thought away and fallen fitfully asleep.

The next day Jennifer had felt uncomfortable. It seemed everyone had been watching her, to see what she was going to do next. She was still Jenny. Couldn't they see? The feeling of being scrutinized had persisted throughout the remainder of her short stay. She wouldn't concede to come back home, and she couldn't talk about what she was doing or why. She had felt so miserable.

Over the next few days what Jennifer had revealed to her family and had failed to see in herself was the transformation of her person since she had left. She had exuded independence and confidence. Even when her heart was breaking from the weight of hurt, she had managed to hold it together. She was strong, and strength can sometimes be unappealing in a woman, and even less appealing in a young woman. These new traits had cloaked her in a way her supportive family had been uncertain how to interpret. She was not the little girl who had left home. They had been unsure how to deal with this unfamiliar new Jennifer. Where had their "Jenny" gone? Who was this self-assured, strong, young woman from the West Coast?

Even dear Aunt Hazel had been a little taken aback by Jenny's strength of character. She still loved her niece dearly, but she had seemed a little less soft and more like her father, all take-charge and in control, not even coming to her for advice or comfort. So Hazel had resigned herself to the thought that everyone grows up and loses the wonder and innocence of youth. But still, why her dear little Jenny? She was so much like Shaun now. Hazel had shuddered. Maybe that was what Shaun had been so angry about. Maybe he knew Jennifer better than either she or Mae. She hadn't wanted Jennifer to be like Shaun, all tough and self-assured. He had no softness to him. With Shaun, it was all "yes or no," no room for "maybe." In men that hardness was okay, but not in Jennifer; she was supposed to be soft and a woman, not a man. *Oh, dear Lord, please let Jennifer see she needs to stay home and not return to where she had come from, please.* She had wanted the old Jennifer back. This one seemed too hard. As the days had quickly passed, she hadn't meant to pull away from Jennifer, and she hadn't realized she had, but she hadn't felt the warmth and closeness of the relationship they had shared before Jennifer had left.

Time, there is either too much or never enough of it when love and relationships are in peril. In the Ryan family, there wasn't time enough for the hurt born and the anger spawned to beat the one back and put an end to the other. Feelings were raw, and all involved were not used to these two. Their family had known love and approval, harmony and acceptance. The time to resolve what had transpired over the past months had been spent, and now hurt, anger, and disappointment remained. Evermore sad, there was not a one of them willing to walk into the trench of communication and with words reveal the cause of the hurt that had spawned the anger and disappointment. And so, the once loving family crumbled into separate pieces.

When it had come time to leave, Jennifer had hugged her mother, cried on Aunt Hazel's shoulder, and told her dad from across the room she would continue to be good. She had gotten on the plane thinking it would be a long time before she would go home again. She had felt lost and all alone, more lonely than she had ever felt before.

Alone

Alone, I feel so utterly alone,
not in the sense of loneness.
Loneness is good, in independence.
Aloneness is emptiness and aching.

Aloneness is as vast as the endless ocean,
when one is surrounded by water
but yet cannot drink.
People are everywhere,
but they are not you, and I feel so
utterly alone.

My mind, it drifts
from thought to thought.
There is no will to snag it fast;
for emptiness and aching hold me captive.

She had worked so hard to be the daughter they had raised. She had gone home to show them she was still herself, and they had treated her like a stranger. Why? What had she done? How had she failed to show them she was doing all they had raised her to be? Why hadn't they loved her anymore? She hadn't done anything wrong. Such troubling thoughts were her companions on her flight back to California.

Her first spring after her Christmas trip home had left her with such feelings of hurt and sadness. It had lent an air of poignant melancholy to her looks, which made her whimsical and youthful. This had opened a door to another commercial spot highly envied by the more senior models. When Jennifer had been awarded the contract, it had further fueled the angry talk about her.

The day of the commercial, Jennifer woke up feeling unusually bereft and empty. She had arrived looking youthful, fresh and tragically innocent beyond comparison in a land of superficial glamour. Still fairly naïve of video, film, and television production, Jennifer's honest questions, revealing her ignorance and her lack of fear to ask "stupid" questions, had breathed fresh air to the supporting crew and, especially, one of the assistant directors in charge. He had been so taken with her genuine independence of character he had told her dinner was his treat. In a take-charge kind of way, he had informed her he would be at her dressing room after the session to pick her up. Not having had anyone do anything for her in so long and tired of having no friends to care for her in such a basic human way, Jennifer, to her own surprise, had agreed without hesitation or thought.

Caught unaware, Jennifer had had the most wonderful night of her life. The life she had sought to live and left home to find had finally and tragically, as Chloe had predicted, found Jennifer. She couldn't remember when she had had so much fun or been so happy and care-free. The weight of trying to please her father she had buried deep within, or so she had thought.

Jennifer had come home from her night out a changed person. Chloe had been the first to notice, and though she guessed at Jen's reason for her new lease on life, she had plied her with questions.

"I didn't think you ever slept past noon," Chloe had greeted Jen as she had come into the shared living area the next day. She had managed to hide her own disappointment at losing the job Jen had received over her and had been genuinely curious about what she was sure was Jen's first real love interest. "What kept you out till all hours?" As much as she had wanted Jen to hurt as she herself had been hurt before the holidays, she had fought back her vicious feelings. If her assumptions of Jen were true, she had figured Jen's pain would be all too real of its own accord soon enough.

Wanting desperately for Chloe's friendship and approval, Jennifer had smiled and shared with abandon, finally feeling she belonged. Jennifer had really admired Chloe, and after her wonderful evening, the world hadn't looked so lonely; life had taken a turn for the better.

Maybe she and Chloe could be friends, too. With youthful, girlish enthusiasm, she had revealed her evening with Brian. That he was ten years older had sent both of them into squeals.

Chloe had held back her thoughts to warn Jen of her own advice offered so recently—to beware of the worldly wise and those having grown up in the business. Sensing Chloe's reservations, Jennifer had admitted, "I know. But Brian"—the smile that had lit her face as she had said his name had made Chloe cringe—"and I talked frankly about all the ins and outs and the ugliness associated with what we both do." She had reached for Chloe's hand and squeezed it as she had added, "Chloe, he is so gorgeous." Her eyes had shone with adoration.

Chloe had realized Jen had been hit hard, and she sadly knew what a player Brian was, as she had worked with him before. He hadn't personally taken an interest in her, but he had done so in many others. Knowing how Jen felt, she had seen no sense throwing back her own advice. Chloe had known Jen wouldn't believe her, just as she herself hadn't believed Jen earlier. Why did the male's constant pursuit of sex have to parade in the smooth seductive veil of love? A sadness for all women so caught had suddenly weighed her down. She had known Jen was in for trouble.

"Chloe, what's wrong?" Jennifer had seen her friend's spirit suddenly droop, and she had become concerned.

"It's nothing, Jen." Chloe had realized Jen would have to learn this lesson without her help. She had only hoped someone so naïve of relationships wouldn't take it too hard.

Jennifer had continued, her eyes colored with love, "Chloe, he is so understanding and sympathetic to my isolation."

At this Chloe had raised her eyes. "Isolation? What do you mean?"

Jennifer had taken a deep breath before continuing, "I told Brian how when I left home my dad pretty much told me I was going to become another empty person, living a life of falsehood, and how he was so angry." The memory of pain had cast a shadow of hurt across Jennifer's fine features. "I told him how my dad said I would start drinking and partying and how…." Here Jennifer had fought back the words of her father's greeting at Christmastime. "He even implied I would end up pregnant." She had raised her gaze to meet Chloe's, her face aflame with embarrassment.

"Oh, Jen, I'm so sorry. I just knew there was something wrong when you wouldn't come out with us to have fun, but I had no idea it was as bad as that. I'm so sorry. Most of the girls thought you were stuck up, that you thought you were better than we are. I tried to tell them it was more than that, but that is awful." She had gone to Jen and given her a hug.

Jennifer had returned the hug, and leaning back from Chloe, her eyes bright, she had continued, "Brian was so sweet. Oh, Chloe, I feel so blessed. He really understood."

Chloe had cringed inwardly over Jen's having revealed so much to such a player. The poor dear had struggled alone, and now she had picked—no, life had brought—the wrong person into Jen's life to teach her the mean lessons of love in disguise. Poor Jen. She had unknowingly given Brian everything he would need to have his way with her.

"What is it, Chloe?" Jennifer had asked. "You look positively sick."

"I do feel a little ill," and Chloe really had felt so. Jen was in for such heartache. Knowing there was nothing she could say, she had abandoned Jen to her joy. "I think I got up too early. I may go lie down a little while more. I'm excited and happy for you. Just promise me you'll be careful, okay?" She had looked at Jen in earnest. In her heart, she still couldn't believe Jen had told Brian so much. She had practically announced to him, "I'm a virgin, and I'm all yours." Still, she knew the futility of warning someone head-over-heels in love. As much as she had wanted not to hear any more of Jen's perfect night, she had encouraged her to continue. "So how did this Cinderella-night end?"

Jennifer had taken a deep breath and continued, telling Chloe how Brian had been a perfect gentleman. She hadn't registered Chloe's warning to be careful and went on with her dreamy memory of the preceding evening, "He walked me to the door, gave me a tender kiss upon my cheek, and said ever so softly, 'I'll see you tomorrow, and keep your weekend open.'" Her face had positively glowed with happiness.

Chloe had had her ill feelings of the moment before return. Poor Jen. Men were pigs. Jen had been right. It had been a first for Chloe to be on the observing end of someone being…what? Duped? Yes, that fit: duped. For Brian was surely just going to use Jen, and he was duping her big time.

Jennifer had told Chloe, "I went to sleep peacefully for the first time since I got back from my Christmas trip home. It was so nice just to sleep for a change."

Not knowing what else to do, Chloe had gotten up from her chair and given Jen another hug. "I'm happy for you. Remember, though, be careful," she had repeated to Jen. Her words had surprised her; she hadn't meant to say that, but Jen's vulnerability had been so evident, and she had felt the innate need to offer protection in some form.

Jennifer, not knowing Chloe's reason for her warning, had dismissed it as she had welcomed Chloe's hug in friendship. She had remained blissfully happy. Her life was suddenly looking up. Things were going to be great.

The days had turned into weeks and the weeks into months. Jennifer had never felt so alive and free of the weight of decisions. She had been having FUN and loving every minute of it. Brian had been the true gentleman. She had been sure her family would have approved of her spending time with a motivated, career-minded individual. In time, he had shared with her some of his not-so-stellar past but had assured her their friendship was a friendship he truly valued and he would never do anything to pressure her into being something or someone she wasn't comfortable with.

Love withheld and approval not found will send the one in need to any source seeming to satisfy. Jennifer, when she had stepped into independence, had lost both love and approval from her dad. Now what she had perceived as love and approval in Brian was life about to teach her the exact opposite.

Busy living the side of life she had only heard of, Jennifer had forgotten her words of wisdom offered to her working companions. She had thrilled at experiencing such a forbidden world she had previously only heard existed, and she sadly trusted the very thing she had once warned against. Brian had been true to his word and hadn't pressured her to drink or try the drugs that freely flowed at the parties they occasioned. He hadn't judged her for not joining in, so she had trusted more, preparing herself for her subsequent downfall.

They had been an item for about five months when, after one particularly glamorous party where Jen had been too much the center of attention, Brian had become possessive and more passionate in his feelings for Jen. Caught off-guard and riding on a wave of adulation and feeling secure in her trust of Brian, Jennifer had succumbed to his newly revealed feelings of love and his suggestion of being a permanent couple.

She had awoken the next day with a tinge of guilt and embarrassment about her actions after the party when they had arrived back at Brian's apartment. As she had sat up in the bed Brian had vacated to make her breakfast, she had relaxed some and wrestled with the thought she had made the age-old mistake so many before her had made. This was different, she had reasoned. It wasn't as if she had just met Brian. The thought of pregnancy she had brushed off with the rationale few people get pregnant the very first time. She had reassured herself there wouldn't be a next-time anytime soon either. She hadn't been sure how she would tell Brian, but she had known she wouldn't make last night a habit without being married. It wasn't who she was. She hadn't even wanted to think of what she had done the night before. Her actions of the previous evening had brought thoughts to mind she hadn't been able to deal with right then.

The sounds of Brian approaching had made her duck under the sheets. She couldn't help who she was. This had been so new to her. She had peeked out as she had heard his footsteps. His total nude appearance had sent the sheet back over her head.

"Hey, lover, how about some sustenance?" he had smiled wickedly to the form under the sheet as he had entered the bedroom.

At his suggestive words the thoughts of the previous evening had brought embarrassed laughter from beneath the sheet. His choice of words should have sent the alarm bells ringing, but she had been truly naïve. She had really believed their relationship was different. Yet, there it was in all its ugliness. The sex trap had been set, layered in love and approval so thick Jennifer had stepped in and become a willing victim.

+≡≡+

As she approached Michael's garage, Jennifer still felt the hurt in remembering how she had plummeted so far and without any seeming effort to stop the fall. The embarrassment of her naïveté was almost too much. It had been over ten years, and she still felt shame. How had she survived? Survive she did, but at a cost.

After their "first," things had changed subtly, but quickly, and not for the better. The movie Brian had been interning on had been cancelled. He had been offered another movie project, and as a relatively unknown director, he had had to go where the jobs dictated. It had been their first separation. In the short time they had been together, Jennifer had blossomed in her belief of Brian's true love and affection for her. She had missed him deeply, and when he had left, she had felt guilty she had failed to return his deeply voiced feelings of love. She had held back out of fear. She had loved her family, and they had stopped loving her. Now that Brian had gone, she had wished she had told him how much he meant to her, that she loved him in return.

In the early weeks after Brian's departure, they had called one another frequently. Jennifer had been touched by the flowers and little cards that had come regularly in the mail. The few friends they had made as a couple had kept her free time busy, but time with them had not been the same. As the weeks had passed by, Jennifer had realized she really did love Brian, and finally she had worked up the courage to tell him.

She would never forget the phone call and the feeling of his response. The memory still caused her such embarrassed agony. If only she had told him of her love before he had left. Their breakup had been all her fault; he had left her because he hadn't known she loved him as she believed he loved her.

She had had a great day of shoots and was relaxing after going on a long run to gather her courage to tell Brian of her true feelings later that night. She had been looking forward to telling her parents of what she was sure would be good news after she and Brian had talked. She had known he loved her so much; she had felt so blessed. Wrapping herself in a fluffy towel to recline on her window-seat, she had made her phone call and waited for Brian to answer. They had always called each other at a set time to assure the other was available. She had been surprised when an unfamiliar male voice had answered Brian's phone.

"Brian's," a voice had answered into the receiver. The loud music in the background had caught her off-guard. Brian hadn't said anything about a party, or he wouldn't have scheduled the call.

"Hello, is Brian there?" Jennifer had questioned.

"Hey, Brian, some chick's calling for you" had been hollered into the background.

After several moments, he had finally come to the phone. "Brian here."

"Hi, Brian. It's me, Jen," she had spoken, trying not to be upset that he hadn't remembered their arranged phone call.

"Oh hey, Jen. Man, I can't believe I forgot our call. I'm sorry," he had answered with sincerity.

"It sounds like you're having a blast. What's the celebration?" Jennifer had done her best to be upbeat, but it had hurt when Brian had admitted he had forgotten they were to share a phone call. He did love her, didn't he? had risen from her subconscious.

Brian had responded, "It's so hard to hear you. We're having an impromptu party. It was a rough day with some major glitches, but yours truly saved the day with ingenuity and charm so we wrapped it up a little early and are relaxing." He had smiled to himself at his success and continued. "Plus, due to my innovative way of saving the day, they offered me the position of first assistant director on their next movie that everyone is saying is sure to be the biggest release of the year, possibly even a Grammy-award nominee."

He had lost Jennifer's interest when he had said the words "impromptu party" and the mentioned offer of another job away from her. She had done her best at pretending shared happiness for him and had forced some measure of excitement into her voice. Then she had remembered what she was going to tell him.

"Hey, Jen, are you still there? Hello?" he had asked into the phone loudly after a few moments of silence on her end.

"I'm still here, Brian," she had replied, taking a deep breath, and mentally tried to push away the fear at what she was attempting to do. Her voice had become quiet at her hesitancy.

"Are you okay? What is it?" He, too, had been trying to be the friend he felt he was, yet he really just wanted to get back to the partying. He had been so filled with the realization his dream career was unfolding that very moment.

"Brian, I love you," she had finally blurted out, and then her heart had cringed, and her face had displayed the great emotion of fear for having let go so wantonly of her deepest feelings.

"Oh," he had returned softly and quietly from the other end and followed with, "I love you, too." His stomach had sunk as he had leaned into the wall next to the phone, his dream suddenly dispersing with the utterance. His thoughts had raced. A few weeks ago, he would have loved to have heard those very words from Jen, but now…. God, he had been so thankful she hadn't made those tender replies back then. He had distanced himself slowly when she had showed her hesitancy.

At the time he had gone out on a limb. He had never felt for anyone as he had for Jen. That night at the party when everyone was swooning over her, he had felt so alive and happy that she was his. He had wanted to have those feelings forever. He had told her so and had let Jen know of his love for her. Then when she had hesitated and hadn't even reciprocated his vulnerability, he had felt the fool. Was she, too, like all the others—just out to see how far she could go, how successful she could be no matter whom she had to sleep with? Why was she now saying she loved him? Had she somehow heard how well he was doing? Was that all she was after? Their separation had hardened him, and after today, well, now he knew he had to end it. They weren't meant to be; his career was his life. Jen was great and yeah, different, and he truly had thought he loved her. He had never felt about anyone as he had felt for Jen, but after today…. He had been wrong; he knew where his true love lay. He had never felt so alive with all that he could do. He wasn't going to give that up, and he had determined he was going after it, without her or anyone else. He needed freedom. He had to tell her.

In Brian's silence, Jennifer talked. She hadn't known what had overtaken her, but she had blurted out all her dreams and a myriad of feelings for him. "I'm just so sorry I didn't tell you before you left, but," and she had taken a deep breath, "you know, with all that happened with my dad, well, I guess I was just a little afraid." Without giving Brian a chance to respond, she had quickly continued. "I really do love you, and I know we can have a great life together. I can model anywhere and be with you wherever you are. These past months have been the best in my life. I've never felt so alive and free, and it's all because you love me." She had paused a mere moment to take a breath and had exhaled, "Brian we can travel and see the world together." She had done it. She had finally professed her love. She had been proud she hadn't faltered.

The silence on the other side had been deafening. She, then, was the one who had thought they had been disconnected.

When Brian had finally responded, his words had broken her heart. "Jen, I can't, not now. This is too big. I'll always love you, really. You're a truly great person, but this, this directing, is what I've always wanted. I didn't know that before, but being away, well, I've had some time to think seriously. I'm just not ready for what you're talking about. It's been wonderful, but I need the space to be really creatively free, to do this directing with all I am. I just want to do something greater than be with someone." And he had finished, truly finished, with, "I'm really sorry, but this is good-bye." He had hung up without even letting her respond. He hadn't wanted to chance giving in. What was love against a dream career? He had put the receiver back on the phone and gone back to his party. He had needed a drink.

Jennifer had been numbed to the point of speechlessness. Brian had hung up on her love. He had dumped her right after she had poured out her heart to him. She had felt so humiliated. She remembered hanging up to the dial tone and wondering how this could have happened in the few short weeks he had been gone. What had she failed to do? Why had he stopped loving her? How could he? Love wasn't a switch you turned on or off, was it? Had he even loved her at all? Had she been the fool? Maybe she had love wrong. She had felt sick. She had gone to bed, refusing to think she had been fooled just as so many before her. The thoughts that had chased themselves around her subconscious throughout the night had left her waking up in a daze.

Jennifer had told no one of her and Brian's breakup. She had thought of going to Chloe for comfort but remembered her own advice to Chloe the previous year. Yes, she, Jennifer, had deserved what she'd gotten. What had happened had been her own doing, and she would deal with it on her own.

But the news with a life of its own had spread quickly, only with an added torture—Brian, the latest hot director, had a new love in his life. A tabloid released several weeks later with photos of a much talked-about after-shoot party had made Jennifer's humiliation unbearable. Cops had been called to break up a fight, and the front page had featured a picture of Brian and, on his arm, an inebriated young lady half-exposed from a night of wild adulterous lust. The article had rumored the new starlet and Brian were living together, and there was talk of marriage between the two.

All Jennifer's coworkers, who had been waiting for just such an event to happen to "Miss High-and-mighty," had actually taken pity on her. The Brian they knew finally had shown his true colors. And therein lay Jennifer's deepest loss. That was not the Brian she had known. He had been good and kind to her, had treated her respectfully, and had truly loved her. She had brought out the best in him—a side hidden from all of the others—and in failing to realize in time her effect on him and her love for him, she had sent him back to his old self. The loss was twofold: She had let slip a man who truly loved her, and he fallen back into his lesser self. She hurt, but she hadn't reacted as so many others had in similar situations.

Even Chloe had been surprised when Jen hadn't come to her for comfort and advice. She had tried to reach out to Jen, but her attempts had been rebuffed. A few days after the story had broken, Chloe had knocked on Jen's door. "Jen, can I come in?" Chloe had truly thought they were becoming friends, and for a change she was happy.

Jen's response had been quietly muffled. "I don't care."

Chloe had slowly opened the door to the darkened room. "Hey, are you okay? You sick or something?" Chloe had had a hunch when Jen's conversation in the several weeks hadn't mentioned Brian once that there was trouble in Jen's paradise. "You want to talk?"

"No" had come from beneath Jen's pillow, quietly yet firmly, almost bitterly.

"Hey, it can't be that bad. Remember who you're talking to," Chloe had joked, surprised at her poke at herself.

Again a single harsh "No" had come from beneath the pillows. "Please, Chloe, just leave me alone. I don't want anything or anyone. Just go." Jennifer had hated herself and everyone. She had learned, finally: Trust and love only led to pain and embarrassment. She was through with them and people.

Chloe had left with feelings hurt and regret about her own goodness offered. She had almost started to feel true friendship for Jen, but she had reasoned, friends are there for one another in good times and bad. If Jen couldn't be human and share her bad times along with the good, then who needed her? No one was perfect, and no one had a perfect life. She would see just how lonely life could really be, and she would have no one to blame but herself.

Jennifer had kept her true feelings close to her and continued her work. She hadn't even cared when Chloe had offered her sympathy. She had been too angry at herself. How could she have been such a fool? She had warned Chloe of the very thing she had become victim to. She couldn't even bear to face Chloe. She had been such a hypocrite.

In her self-flagellation, poor Jennifer couldn't see she was only being human, making mistakes all too common.

As days had turned into weeks, she had seemed to lose weight. When the flu she had been fighting persisted, she had kept even more to herself. She would not let her father's prediction come true. And her worry had only made her more ill.

The truth can be painful, as it was for Jennifer. "If only" kept coming to mind. She had fought the truth with all her might but that hadn't stopped it. She had realized she had made a mistake, a big mistake, but a mistake all the same. She had told herself over and over she wasn't what her father had said she would be. She wouldn't be; one mistake did not make the person. Her life wasn't over; it had hardly begun. She had vowed she'd never be deceived again. Her anger at her own foolish trust had become bitter as she had admitted what was the truth: She had done what her father had predicted.

Silently and alone, she had suffered humiliation and defeat and held those two little pills of poison close to her heart. In time her embarrassment had magnified as her mistake had become known to so many she had counseled against doing the very thing she had allowed herself to become victim to; only she had been caught as the others had not. They would look at her in passing, saying nothing as she had made it obvious through her rejection of Chloe's friendship she didn't want anyone or anything. Chloe may have been needy and easily deceived, but she was well liked, and Jennifer's selfish rudeness to help offered circulated faster than the news of her pregnancy; she had again isolated herself.

Chloe, knowing the others were giving Jen a wide berth on her account, had made one last attempt. "Jen, you don't have to do this. There are things you can do," she had offered, and in a moment of unselfish compassion shared, "I know, I've been there."

Jennifer, lost in her own fog of agony, had alienated Chloe completely. With the harsh look of shock she could not hide and words of equal brutality, she had said, "What? I couldn't do that. It's murder."

Chloe had reddened in embarrassment. She had never told anyone what she had revealed to Jen. Jen's reaction had angered her, but she had kept quiet and left Jen to her choice of self-persecution. It had been Chloe's last attempt at friendship with anyone, and it had hurt. Jen had seemed so different from all the others. Why couldn't she see Chloe was trying to help? Would she never connect with anyone, male or female? Chloe couldn't help but wonder what was wrong with her. Why couldn't she have a close friend like all the others? She had tried so hard with Jen, all for nothing.

Jennifer would not unburden herself to anyone. Not even Elli could get her to open up and talk about what had happened. Jennifer owned her mistake, and she would suffer the consequences alone. She had known she couldn't go home. Her father would only be there to make sure she had absorbed his predicted judgment of the life she had chosen. Besides, she hadn't wanted to go home to the nothingness she had left. She had never felt so alone and almost forsaken. God, how had her life turned so quickly?

Her efforts to prove her father wrong had alienated her from her coworkers, and her own harsh words to Chloe had left her without any friends. The friends she had thought she had with Brian had left when Brian had broken off his relationship with her. Jennifer had been alone, and pregnant. The humiliation had been two-fold. She had finally admitted she was everything her father had said she would be.

The thought, *No, I'm not*, had been buried, for she knew even though she had only made a mistake—well, more than one mistake—she could not forgive what she had done. Self-forgiveness was not to be had. She hadn't even wanted to think of telling her family. She had no idea what to do and no one to turn to. How would she model? What would she do with the baby, her baby? Oh God, what a mess. Where could she go for help?

When she felt she could no longer keep her pregnancy a secret, she had finally gone to Elli for help.

"Well, I'm only sorry you waited so long to come to me. I've known for some time, Jen," she had admonished her. "You are not the first this kind of thing has happened to. If you had come to me sooner you would have had more options." Elli had tried to be kind, but she, too, was still a little hurt by Jen's refusal for comfort and help in the beginning. Jen had been almost ruthless to poor Chloe. All the girls had come to Elli for comfort, and Chloe had been especially dear to her. Jen's treatment of her had angered her. What Elli hadn't been able to figure out was why Jen had felt it necessary to keep herself so isolated and go everything alone. After the Christmas break, Elli had thought Jen had finally seen her coworkers weren't the heinous people she had conjured them up to be. Jen's relationship with Brian, though Elli would have warned her to be careful, had seemed to be just what she had needed. The other girls and even some of the male models had been so offended by Jen's need to be perfect, Elli had worried they would have to let her go. Despite her hesitancy in approving Jen's relationship with Brian, she had felt it would help her see life a little more realistically and lend her a little more compassion to those she worked with. When she had suspected the relationship had soured, she had ventured motherly comfort. All the girls had welcomed Elli's non-judgmental comfort after their many relationships had failed. Jen's rejection had surprised and hurt Elli. She hadn't been able to understand Jen's need for self-isolation. But being there for the girls had been her job, so she had put her own feelings aside and offered Jen a ray of hope.

"There is a job you could do. The girl who works in scheduling and helps order the clothes for the shoots just had twins and is taking a few months off. I think you would work well there." She hadn't disliked Jen, and she truly hoped maybe Jen would open up to the other girls.

"Oh, Elli, thank you so much." The news of continued employment had been such a light of hope Jen had almost cried. "I was so afraid I would have to go home in shame. I promise I will work hard."

"I know you'll work hard, Jen. Just know you aren't alone. Don't make it so hard on yourself," Elli had offered with a deep look of motherly concern. "You will have to move out of the residence, for it's only for the models. I'm sorry." She had added quickly when she had seen alarm register on Jen's youthful face, "It's policy; that's all." She had squeezed her arm to reassure her it had nothing to do with her condition. "I'll talk to management and see if they won't give you a little time so you can find a place."

This time Jen had cried and, through muffled tears, again thanked Elli. Having a job had been foremost in her mind; she hadn't even contemplated needing a new a place to live. There was so much she was still unaware of in the game called life. She had been so relieved to have a job and an extension of a place to stay that she hadn't noticed Elli's offer of friendship. Through her tears, Jennifer had quietly resolved she would make it.

Jennifer had worked hard and learned the details of her new job. She had been adventurous enough to learn the duties of her supervisor. Over time with the compassionate guidance of this wonderful woman, Jennifer had even started back to night school to give herself more opportunities for future employment.

She couldn't keep her pregnancy a secret from her family forever. The thought of not ever telling them had never occurred to her. She had never kept anything from them, except her application to model, and look what keeping that secret had done. No, she argued with herself, it was best to be honest and come clean. They loved her, and they would be there for her; they were her family.

The day she had told her family was the last day she had spoken to them. She had called them on a Sunday as she had from time to time. To her disappointment, her dad had answered the phone. The holidays were fast approaching, and she had felt especially vulnerable. Her heart had sunk at the sound of her dad's voice. "Hi, Dad. It's me, Jennifer." She had tried to sound normal, but for some reason her tears had started immediately.

Forgetting his anger and hearing her tears, Shaun had let down his protective guard. This was his little girl, and she was hurt. "Jennifer, what is it? Are you hurt? Did something happen? What's wrong?" His concern had been true.

Disarmed by care that had been withheld since her torturous departures after graduation and Christmas, Jen had unburdened herself with abandon. She had her dad back. *Oh thank God.* "Oh Daddy, I am so sorry," she had cried into the phone.

Her tears and terms of love almost had had her dad crawling through the phone to offer her protection; she needed him. "What is it, Jennifer? Who hurt you? What happened?" Shaun had needed to know. Mae and Aunt Hazel had soon gathered nearby, trying to listen, the ring of the phone having summoned them from their locations in the house to see who had called. Shaun's sudden show of compassion and hearing "Jennifer" had them at his elbow in shared distress. Had something happened to their Jennifer?

Without a thought for tact, just reveling in her dad's return to care, Jennifer had let go without inhibition. This was her dad who *did* love her. He *would* be there for her. "I'm in trouble, Dad." She had had a hard time saying the word "pregnant." She realized she had yet even to say the word to herself. The word now scared her: pregnant. Saying it would have made it real. But she *was* pregnant. She had cried uncontrollably for the first time since her breakup. She had cried about the breakup, the return of her dad's care, her fear of what she had done. She had cried because she could; she was loved again.

"Jennifer!" her dad had commanded into the phone, "Jennifer, take a deep breath."

Her dad's deep voice of concern blaring from the phone had caught her, and she had stilled her tears and taken a slow deep breath as he had told her.

Hearing her take a shaky deep breath, Shaun had started over. "Okay, now honey, what is wrong? What happened? For me to help you, you have to talk to me. Then you can cry, okay?"

Still shy of the word "pregnant" and all it connoted, Jennifer had blurted out, "I'm 'in the family way.'" It was the way her family had always spoken of those who were pregnant. It seemed more genteel in the company of mixed generations.

When Shaun had lost his grip on the phone and gone white, Mae and Aunt Hazel had turned to each other in fear. Aunt Hazel immediately had started Hail Marys for she knew something terrible had happened.

With a quiet rage Jennifer hadn't picked up on, Shaun, with iron control, had spoken, "What happened?"

Her tears falling, Jennifer had offered only, "I thought he loved me Dad, but I was wrong. I am so sorry."

The words coming from the phone had stabbed Shaun's very core. She had done it. She had become exactly what he had said she would be. At her admittance, his heart had resumed its old guard. The wall of protection had risen once more, his care had fled and his love extinguished in disappointment.

Hazel, standing with quiet recitations of Hail Marys, had noted the change in Shaun's demeanor. Having grown up with her sometimes stubborn, hard-hearted brother, she had recognized the combative stance and had moved toward him to take the phone. Something wasn't right.

As she had attempted to take the phone from him, Shaun had elbowed his sister aside. With quiet rage, he had carefully enunciated into the phone, "I should have known. You are no longer my daughter. You were warned and still you chose to disobey. I will not raise a bastard. My home will not be further dishonored. You will not call here, you will not write, and you will have no more contact with anyone in this household. I told you not to come to me when this happened, and I meant it." With those words he had hung up. His hand still on the phone, his face presenting pure rage, he had defied Hazel or Mae to try to call her back. He had looked menacingly at both and spit out, "She is gone. The little whore is pregnant. The matter is done. She is not welcome here. She rejected who we raised her to be so she can be what she is. This is *my* home, and you will not communicate with her; you will honor me that much." Her disobedience, her rejection of the life he had raised her to know, her decision and now her downfall had blackened Shaun's countenance to such hatred Hazel and Mae felt no choice but to abide by his ill-gotten command.

Jennifer on the other end had been stricken. What had happened? She had held the receiver out and looked at it as a foreign object. The love she had felt had disappeared, and the harsh words coming from the phone had her wondering if she hadn't somehow been inadvertently connected to a madman. The shock had halted her tears, and she had stood in frozen disbelief. Her father had disowned her. Could he really do that? How? She had put the receiver back in the cradle and then picked up the phone and redialed. There must have been a mistake. Her dad loved her. She had heard the love in his voice just moments ago. The phone had rung and rung. No answer. She had tried three more times and then had hung up, and the tears had never returned.

The call home had been the end of her old life forever. Or so it had seemed.

She had then done the next best thing. She had sat down and written a heartfelt letter. In it she had apologized to her father. To protect the family from embarrassment, she had assured him she would not come home until after the birth. She had even told him she was planning on giving the baby up for adoption to a good Catholic family. She had written she was no longer doing the modeling but was doing scheduling and ordering work, and she would be fine. She had informed him she was being responsible and trying to fix her mess. To show him of her efforts to be what he had raised her to be, she had detailed her search for a place to live, the possible purchase of a car, and insurance for both. She had thought for sure he would see she was living up to his expectations, even considering night school after the baby was born. She couldn't help but ask if they would please call her so she could talk with her mom and or Aunt Hazel. She had assured him she would not further shame the family, and she would do her very best to make him proud of her.

Her letter had come back unopened. Her spirits had drooped. She had known her father would be displeased, but the complete rejection had cut her deeply. The thought of her father not loving her had left her anguished, but she had never voiced her mortal hurt. When the letter had come back unopened, she had called home only to find the phone number had been changed and unlisted. Her shock and hurt deepened. What had troubled her more than anything were her mother's and Aunt Hazel's failures to write to her. They had had her address, and knowing she couldn't communicate with them, she couldn't understand why they hadn't written to her. She had thirsted for their words of love and comfort and understanding that she had only made a mistake and they still loved her.

Jennifer had valiantly tried to do the right thing to make up for her transgression, but to no avail.

What is so tragic in all human cases of wrongs done one to another is that hurt felt by the victim can never be truly weighed or understood by the perpetrator. This is especially true when the harm that is unintentional for its victim is often the closest and most intimate to the perpetrator. And in most cases, the perpetrator can do nothing to correct the actual or perceived wrong. Often times when this fact is unveiled to the person trying to make amends, his life forks to take either an ugly and mean turn or one of humility under the true power of creation and humanity. Most lives spend time on both paths as they make their way more and more often along the more rewarding one, that toward the truth and the only way: total and utter humility to what we are as a creation, in total and desperate need of the indwelling presence of the One who formed us in the palm of His hand for His design and His purpose.

The many returned letters to Jennifer's family finally had hit her, and she had given up in defeat. What good was doing the right thing? It certainly hadn't helped her. She had decided to follow her own path since her family didn't care. When the baby had been born, she had made the decision to keep her. No one had loved her then, but she would love her baby as she had been loved back when…and she had stopped the inevitable train wreck of thoughts. She would keep her baby and love it as she wished she had been loved, with no conditions of right or wrong. There had been no sense in trying to do what was right according to her upbringing; it had only made her life miserable.

And in the process, Jennifer had unknowingly stumbled down the road to truth.

She had finally confided in her supervisor, Caroline. This wonderful woman, who had joyously taken her under her wing, had become a friend. She would help her through her pregnancy and become her only sense of family. She was never critical, and she had never pried into Jennifer's situation. She was always supportive and helpful. It had been so nice not to be judged by another. It was through Caroline Jennifer had come to the feet of the Lord Jesus Christ and accepted forgiveness for her mistakes and the loss of those she so loved. Bereft of family and having no friends, overcome with the burden and weight of guilt over the path of life she had chosen, when the salvation of the Lord Jesus Christ was shown and offered, Jennifer had clung like a drowning victim.

Salvation had come when Jennifer had felt she had no one and nothing but regrets. When she had reached out for help to those she had thought loved her, she had been rejected, admonished, judged unforgivable. And charities she had approached had looked upon her youthful beauty and self-assuredness and seen a chance to put the wayward girl in her place. Life was hard, unfair, and just because she was pretty she wasn't going to get any special treatment. In fact, many times those who were in charge of the assistance had made remarks that she'd gotten what she had deserved. And Jennifer's vulnerability had absorbed their harsh criticism as truths. She was nothing, and she had no one. Her pain had been great, and her despair that she would never have anything or anyone had been overwhelming.

The day of salvation had come when an exhausted Jennifer had spent her lunch hour searching for another place to live after the baby was born. She had come back tired and weepy. She didn't have a car, and the small savings she had was too meager to secure a loan for one and cover the amount needed for getting a one-room furnished apartment. She had been so tired of going it alone.

Fighting back tears, Jennifer had sat at her desk and swallowed hard.

Caroline had seen the young figure walk in the reception area of the agency she had once modeled for and fall into her chair. She had watched as the expectant girl of barely twenty had sat with weary resolve and swallowed hard. She had known Jennifer was trying. She had been pleasantly surprised when Jennifer had learned her new assistant scheduler job with eagerness and happiness. Caroline had expected attitude and sullenness. When she had found out the reason for Jennifer's demotion, she had been quietly saddened, but she had not judged. She hadn't known all the circumstances of what had transpired; she had felt only sorrow, for Jennifer's road was going to be tough.

As the months had passed, Jennifer had showed initiative to learn more, and she had begun to be more open about what had happened and to share with Caroline how she intended to take care of things. Caroline had encouraged her when she had mentioned she was giving the baby up for adoption. And when she had then decided to keep her baby, she had been understanding and had even told her she would help her with enrolling in night school. *The poor girl*, Caroline had thought, *needs someone to help her.* Her supervisor had noticed that Jennifer was always by herself. She didn't go out and never received personal phone calls or told of outings with friends. Caroline had offered what help she could in putting her in touch with different agencies but had not been overly surprised when Jennifer had come back without assistance. It had always saddened Caroline when people who claimed to serve the down-trodden only helped those *they* deemed deserving of the help their positions offered.

It had been a hard week for Jennifer. Caroline had known she had been looking for a place to stay and that she had kept coming up empty-handed. She had been further burdened by her lack of transportation. Today she had seemed so bereft that Caroline, who normally didn't intrude, had gone to her.

"Hey, Jennifer, how did it go?"

Not wanting to take any more from Caroline who had been so generous, Jennifer had taken a deep shaky breath, but try as she might, she had only squeaked out, "Not so good." And her tears had slipped down her cheeks.

The motherly instinct in Caroline had brought her to Jennifer's side with a hug. She couldn't bear to see her so tried and so alone. "What is it, Jennifer?"

"I'm sorry, Caroline. I'm just so tired. I can't do this anymore. I don't know what to do or where to go or anything. My life is such a mess, and I can't fix it or get any help or anything. I don't know what I'm going to do. I can't find a place to live that's within walking distance. I can't afford a car. And even if I could, I can't afford the insurance. And I've got to think about child care, I just feel like quitting, and," she had taken a shaky, deep breath, "I don't even know if I can quit 'cause what am I quitting? Life? How can I quit life? Oh God, I've done so wrong. And I'm trying, but nothing's working." And she had given in to her loneliness and her pain and her frustration, and as her troubles had tumbled out so had her tears flowed.

Caroline had felt her loneliness, and at the outpouring of Jennifer's troubles, she, too, had experienced the pangs of anxiety. "It's going to be okay," she had reassured the young form crying into her shoulder. "Sure you made a mistake, but it's just one mistake, and is a baby really a mistake?" She had pulled back from Jennifer and forced her to look her in the eye. "Let me help you. Together we'll figure things out. And remember, you're never alone; nobody is, ever." She had made sure to emphasize her words as she had steadily looked into Jennifer's worry-filled countenance.

"Yes, I am." Jennifer had insisted as she had pulled out of Caroline's arms. "My family won't talk to me or even take my letters. They hate me." And through her tears, she had whispered out, "I can't take your help. You've done so much already, and I'm so grateful. Thank you for this great job and your kindness." Jennifer started to cry again softly.

"Well, Jennifer, you need my help, and as for the job, somebody had to have it. Why not you? You're doing great so you're helping me, too. As for your family, I'm sorry." And she had squeezed her hands. "Sometimes we have to be separated from those we love to come to know who loves us more than life. Who really and unconditionally loves us? Never forget God is always there for you, always. Sometimes when the world gets in the way, we forget God's importance. Sometimes when we make mistakes and those we love most and our society toss us out as unlovable and unforgivable, we fall into time by ourselves. When we reach that point, God is waiting for us to see and to come to him. For He and He alone showed us He loves us more than life here. It is He who really loves us, who is always quietly there waiting for us to acknowledge His great love for us."

Jennifer had sat silently as Caroline had continued.

"It's sad when circumstances in life—often tragic—send us to the complete and forgiving love of God, but there it is. I guess it is only in true need that most of us ever find God's great love for us." Caroline had ended on a sigh.

"What do you mean? I've always known God, and I know God is with me, but I'm still alone here, and I need help. There is no one to help me who loves me." Jennifer had spoken quietly as she had calmed, having released the pent-up anguish from the months past and voiced her fears for her immediate future.

"Honey, your family loves you," Caroline had insisted hearing that Jennifer had labored under such misplaced anger from her family. "I will help you. Maybe I'm not the one you want to help you, but I am here. I believe you know God, but maybe it's His forgiveness you should really come to know. You need to ask for *His* forgiveness." She had gently stated, "It seems your family hasn't forgiven you, and maybe in some small way, you're being so hard on yourself as some sort of self-punishment."

Jennifer had looked up guiltily, a flash of anger on her young face, but the futility of the days of searching and uncertainty had beaten her down. She had resisted no more.

Caroline had gone further. "It seems you won't even allow yourself to accept any help from those who do care for you. You feel you don't deserve help because those you've asked have told you 'no,' and they themselves have passed their ugly judgments upon you which you have decided to accept." Caroline's voice had strengthened, and her tone had become a little firmer.

Jennifer's posture had wilted under Caroline's intensity.

Seeing Jennifer shrink into herself, Caroline had quieted for a moment. The intensity of her passionate discourse over Jennifer's situation had taken even her aback. She had done her best to stay out of Jennifer's business, but sitting and watching this young girl struggle to be perfect in an imperfect world, she had had enough. Jennifer had to stop her self-persecution. Realizing her own words were causing more pain, she had offered more kindly, "Self-punishment is not going to correct what you did. It honestly won't, and it never does."

Jennifer had started to cry again. "Then I will never get my family's love back," she had stated emphatically and with sadness overwhelming her. "I really miss them, and I need them."

"Let me tell you something, hon, and bear with me; this is not easy." She had taken Jennifer's hand as she had continued speaking. "Your family, well, the power within your family"—for she had known it was Jennifer's father who had forbidden her to have any contact with them and they had complied—"withdrew their love because you did some things that displeased them. You have been isolated and without their love for a few months. It's horrible not to have heard from them and not know if everything is okay with those you love. There's a lesson here. We all make mistakes, and the best we can do is to learn from them. As much as you yearn and want for the return of your family's love, imagine an eternity without love."

Jennifer's eyes had opened in startled shock. "What do you mean— never to have their love again?"

"Here's the lesson. When we sin, we risk spending eternity without God's love, and the love we feel and need from our family is just a sliver of the love God has for us."

"To never have the love of those I love ever again. God loves me more than I love?" Jennifer's thoughts had swirled. "I'm so sorry for not doing what I was told. I want my family's love back. I don't want to be alone. I need their love. What can I do?" Jennifer had been truly puzzled and had started to feel fear at the thought of never feeling her family's love. She had even thought of just going home and showing up on their doorstep, but then ugliness had crept in. What if she did go home and her dad refused her entrance? His rejection on the phone had been most painful. The thought of being rejected in person, turned away, and not allowed into her own home to see her mom, dad, and dear Aunt Hazel, to be pushed away had been too much; she didn't think she could do it. So she had remained in California, trying to make amends on her own, once again trying to be the perfect daughter to show her dad she was worthy of his love.

Seeing her abject fear, Caroline had been brutally honest. "Nothing. Truthfully, there is not one thing you can do, nothing, except be truly sorry." Caroline had smiled softly for she had seen Jennifer was right where she needed to be. She had continued, "I know you're sorry, but you need to tell the Lord Jesus Christ you are sorry. Only He can forgive you, and only He can make the wrong right. Only Jesus can give forgiveness, and you must accept forgiveness and give Him the burden of guilt and self-punishment you are carrying with you. Jesus Christ hung on that cross for what you did wrong. He did that for you; He is your forgiveness; He made things right long ago. All you have to do is tell Him of your sins and of your sorrow for all the pain you've caused and allow Him in your life to be your savior."

"There is no other way to be forgiven?" she had implored, thinking of her attempt at confession when she had found she was pregnant. She had tried to confess, but she had been too ashamed to speak the words to the priest. She couldn't receive the forgiveness from the priest, as she had been brought up to know, for she couldn't bring herself to confess. She had so wanted and needed forgiveness. She had continued, "I don't have a choice then do I? I mean, what else is there?" She had looked to Caroline for help, barely understanding the fullness of Caroline's words. She had been so tired of carrying around guilt and doing what she felt was right to earn back love from those who once had loved her.

"No, Jennifer, you do have a choice. No one is going to force you to Jesus," she had stated, unaware of Jennifer's religious background. "And I do agree, what else is there? Without Jesus Christ in my life, I have found there is nothing, nothing worth living for. This world is hard and will never truly satisfy the human soul. It will disappoint you every time, and as you know, even those we love dearly will hurt and abandon us from time to time. With Jesus Christ, I have found I have His unconditional love, and the world and all it is, is not so dark. It is for this I am so thankful and happy."

"I don't want to be alone, and I am so tired of being guilty." She had finally confessed to Caroline her need to have people in her life. "I am so ashamed." She had dropped her head in humility. "I can't get forgiveness any other way." She had known she couldn't make herself go to the confessional again, "And I am so very, very sorry. What do I do?" Jennifer had been puzzled. "How—whom do I confess to?"

"All you have to do is tell Jesus Christ you are sorry and you need and want Him in your life to be your lord and savior. You don't want to go it alone."

Jennifer, truly exhausted, had taken a slow deep breath and, with sudden realization at what she was doing and who she was forgiving in asking for true forgiveness, had started to cry again, for her heart had been full and aching. "I really am so very sorry for all the pain I have caused those I love and those I work with, and I am sorry for the mess I've made and for screwing up my life because I sinned, I gave in to temptation." She had cried in shame and sorrow. "I feel so wretched, and I am so sorry. Please forgive me." Her words had faltered. *Who will forgive me?* she had wondered, looking slightly confused. And then she had understood, and she had continued in a humble whisper, "Lord Jesus Christ, please forgive me. I need you." As she had shed her tears she had felt a release of the guilt she had carried for her misdeed and the path of life she had chosen against her father's wishes. She had felt free as forgiveness for wrongdoing had washed away her self-loathing. She had then seen that she wasn't unlovable or unforgivable. She had just been a sinner in need of salvation, like so many others, and like the others she had desperately let go of her guilt and joyfully accepted forgiveness and life.

Caroline could see the pain leave Jennifer's face, and she had added, "The road ahead isn't easy, Jennifer, but you must know you will not be alone, ever. In accepting forgiveness and telling Jesus Christ you want Him in your life, you are now 'born again' a child of God." She had swiveled her desk chair and opened a drawer to extract her Bible. She had turned to John 3:1-21 and proceeded to read to Jennifer the truth she had just spoken to her:

JOHN 3:1-21 Now there was a man of the Pharisees name Nicodemus, a member of the Jewish ruling council. He came to Jesus at night and said, "Rabbi, we know you are a teacher who has come from God. For no one could perform the miraculous signs you are doing if God were not with him."

In reply Jesus declared, "I tell you the truth, no one can see the kingdom of God unless he is born again."

"How can a man be born when he is old?" Nicodemus asked. "Surely he cannot enter a second time into his mother's womb to be born!"

Jesus answered, "I tell you the truth, no one can enter the kingdom of God unless he is born of water and the Spirit. Flesh gives birth to flesh, but the Spirit gives birth to spirit. You should not be surprised at my saying, 'You must be born again.' The wind blows wherever it pleases. You hear its sound, but you cannot tell where it comes from or where it is going. So it is with everyone born of the Spirit."

"How can this be?" Nicodemus asked.

"You are Israel's teacher," said Jesus, "and do you not understand these things? I tell you the truth, we speak of what we know, and we testify to what we have seen, but still you people do not accept our testimony. I have spoken to you of earthly things and you do not believe; how then will you believe if I speak of heavenly things? No one has ever gone into heaven except the one who came from heaven— the Son of Man. Just as Moses lifted up the snake in the desert, so the Son of Man must be lifted up, that everyone who believes in him may have eternal life."

For God so loved the world that he gave his one and only Son, that whoever believes in him shall not perish but have eternal life. For God did not send his Son into the world to condemn the world, but to save the world through him. Whoever believes in him is not condemned, but whoever does not believe stands condemned already because he has not believed in the name of God's one and only Son. This is the verdict: Light has come into the world, but men loved darkness instead of light because their deeds were evil. Everyone who does evil hates the light, and will not come into the light for fear that his deeds will be exposed. But whoever lives by the truth comes into the light, so that it may be seen plainly that what he has done has been done through God.

When she had finished reading, Caroline had closed her Bible, and taking Jennifer's hands and looking at her, she had continued, "Listen. When we accept Jesus Christ as God's Son and His death on the cross as forgiveness for our sins, we are blessed to receive the gift of the Holy Spirit, God's very presence within us. He now is our new master, and we must let Jesus be our good shepherd, following Him wherever He leads us, even if we do not see or understand. We must hold tight to this knowledge when the world tries to grab us from His loving grasp." She had not been so sure Jennifer had fully grasped what she had just accomplished.

Jennifer had been filled with such exquisite peace for the first time in so very long that she hadn't caught the fullness of Caroline's statement. The knowledge of the perfect eternal love of the God of Abraham, the God of Isaac, and the God of Jacob through His only Son the Lord Jesus Christ was the gift she had said yes to, but had she fully understood this? Forgiveness for all she was—a failure to everyone whom she knew and loved and to herself—had been her objective. This she had felt. Was she again loveable? That was tied to the forgiveness, for forgiveness was given out of God's great love for us in His only Son the Lord Jesus Christ. These were the gifts Caroline had prayed Jennifer understood Jesus Christ offered.

In her joy Jennifer had felt hope. She had confessed her wrongdoings to the Lord Jesus Christ and accepted his death on the cross as payment for her transgressions. She had understood she could live her life a new person with Jesus Christ as her way, her shepherd. She could have a new beginning. She had looked to Caroline with happiness and had given her a big hug. "Thank you, Caroline. I will be forever grateful."

Caroline had returned the hug, "The thanks isn't mine; it's Jesus'. Now, go rinse your tears in the bathroom, and we'll make a plan for finding you a place to live, okay?"

Jennifer had embraced the new sense of freedom from guilt and condemnation. The happiness of the gift of love, being loved without having to earn love, hadn't impacted her as deeply, for the oppression from guilt had been far more relevant to her situation.

Jennifer had accepted Caroline's help and guidance. Her life hadn't been easy, but she hadn't been alone anymore. It was so nice finally to feel a sense of belonging. Caroline's family and church community had openly accepted Jennifer. She once again had a feeling of hope.

So many moments in life are reactions, and it was a reaction that had made Jennifer change her mind and decide to keep her baby. Her family had rejected her, and she had decided she just couldn't, with a clear conscience, give up her child. Where she had planned to give up the baby to please her father, she had then kept the baby for herself. Reactions are often times the fork in the road and a course of life forever altered. Jennifer, in keeping the little girl she named Hazel, had made her own road a little harder, and life's struggles and the pull of the world had become ever stronger. The unfairness and injustice that had come in dealing with caring and providing for another brought a little cynicism and anger to a once carefree and adventure-seeking soul. This was the Jennifer that some years later would walk into a bank and witness to another about God's never-ending grace.

Although she had seen and accepted God's grace in her life, she had then rethought all that had happened at the bank and found it terrifying. She had let fear of what could happen to her—or worse, to her daughter—slide insidiously into her life. God's presence slowly fell from the position of master to that of observer, and Jennifer was not even conscious of her participation in the demotion. Fear is an efficient enabler of sin.

With fear ruling her heart, six years after her daughter had been born and only a few short months after the incident at the bank, Jennifer had decided to leave California and move back to the area where she had grown up. To leave Caroline and the new life she had been living had not been easy. The more she had grown to love those she was with, the more she had missed those she had grown up with.

Memories are the substance of who we are, and there are times when they can be most detrimental to the human condition. What was cannot be regained in its original form, yet memories, like deceiving temptresses, can taunt and deceive one into thinking just that— that we can recreate what is now gone. But they are mere tools of this world, causing mental anguish and unrest and sending the soul to search for something that once was and can never be had or regained as it was remembered to be. Memories are rarely if ever accurate but rosy illusions of reality and too often lead humanity to err in the most tragic events in trying to recapture an essence of what once was. Even if one goes back to the same situation or person, they are not the same. What was is not what is; time marches on, and life changes all people and places. Change is the nature of the beast called life, and a beast it is without God at the helm. Many lives have been destroyed by those errantly seeking to regain the illusion of what one remembers.

They gain only pain and sorrow when the reality of the world shines into the dream and presents them with the truth: the loss of what was sought; we can not recapture the past.

Jennifer had been wrestling with the thought of moving back to the Midwest for a short time, and she had not credited the robbery with the final push for her decision to make the leap. She had not realized how much the fear born of the bank robbery had affected her. She had thought she had handled the situation well. The police had questioned her extensively and had offered her counseling. Jennifer had assured everyone she was fine; she had no need for counseling, or more important, to her a single mother, no time or money to spend in counseling. She had not known she had buried the sheer terror of the sound of the first round of gunfire under the great joy she had witnessed when Ken, the robber, had received salvation. As the days had passed and living life had continued, the intense fear of loss of her own life and what it would mean to her only child had crept in to her subconscious and filled her with restlessness. Questions she had thought she had all but left behind her so many years ago when she had first left home had come flooding back, fueled by the fear she had buried. *There had to be more to life* had screamed at her from the deepest recesses of her subconscious mind.

Caroline had sensed the change in Jennifer and had tried to get her to address all that had gone on during the bank robbery. "Jennifer," she had begun again as she had numerous times before when Jennifer had had a particularly distracted day, "please, let's get Hazel and go to the park and just talk. Something's bothering you." She had looked pleadingly to Jennifer.

"I would, Caroline, but I don't really know what." Jennifer had been honest; she really had not remembered much of anything that had happened. She had tried to be helpful, but for some reason she could only remember the very beginning of the robbery, the first sounds of gunfire, the feel of the hardness of the floor, and praying for help. The rest of her memory of the bank incident had been the salvation of one of the men who had tried to rob the bank. It did bother her that she had remembered the intensity of the fear and could still, at times, feel its grip. The fear was as profound as the peace that had come with praying as she had lain on the hard floor of the bank. She had told the police of her conversation with the robber, and she could even still feel the joy when Ken had accepted Jesus Christ as his savior. The relief of leaving the bank was the last thing she had remembered, other than telling Ken she would pray for him, and that she had done daily. "I don't know what else to tell other than…," and she had trailed off, wondering at what she was feeling inside. The old restlessness of her youth had awakened, and she had wondered at her life and felt dissatisfied. "I think maybe I need a change," she had offered with the hope of Caroline's understanding.

"Yes, I think a change is good." Caroline had smiled, thinking Jennifer was looking for a new job, which she herself had encouraged. She had known Jennifer had been raising little Hazel virtually alone and working while going to night school. She had hoped Jennifer would find better employment. "And I'll do everything I can. I know a couple of people who would be willing to write you letters of recommendation," Caroline had assured her. "You're organized and diligent, and you have a good sense for trends in fashion; your choices have been right on the market lately."

"Thank you, Caroline. You've been a wonderful and supportive teacher. Still, it's the same career path," Jennifer had sighed. Their industry wasn't geared toward developing long-term relationships; most lasted only as long as the job.

She had known Jennifer was feeling lonely. Many times, they had both discussed the peril of their line of work. Caroline had tried over the past couple years to hook Jennifer up, to the amusement of both. But Jennifer just hadn't been ready to trust. And quite a few men who, upon finding out she was a single mom, had assumed she was an easy one-night stand. Their assumption had hurt and only made Jennifer less willing to date. "Maybe we can find a job in promotions or retail," Caroline had suggested, not fully understanding what change Jennifer had hinted at.

"I don't really know what I want to do. I keep praying for guidance, but I don't feel any sense of what to do. I just feel like I need to go." Jennifer had looked quietly at Caroline, hoping her words hadn't wounded her only friend and at the same time imploring her for understanding. She had wanted to tell Caroline of the safety she had felt growing up, but Caroline had come to know the circumstances of her departure, and Jennifer didn't want to address her old fear of being alone without family. Caroline and her family had become her family. She hadn't wanted to seem ungrateful for all they had done the past six years. She knew she couldn't go back home, for where was home?

Jennifer had told herself she wasn't going to recapture what she had left. But she wanted her daughter to grow up as she had, free from fear, in a small rural community where everyone knew everyone and looked out for each other. Even with the help from Caroline, she had had a hard time raising Hazel alone. The daycare system was a nightmare, and she had constantly worried that some form of harm would come to her little Hazel. She hadn't even wanted to think of all the child-care providers she had been through with working and trying to go to night school. She hadn't wanted to try and explain that longing to Caroline; she had only wanted to leave.

No, she really just wanted to run—run away. From what? The thought had caught her, and she had felt guilty. She had tried to quell the feeling inside, but the door had been cracked, and what had come rushing out was frightening. Life was passing her by, and she had nothing but a six-year-old daughter to show for all she had tried to…what? What had she tried to do? This question had puzzled her even more, and she had quickly ended her thoughts. No, she really just wanted the good wholesome living she had grown up with for her daughter. Thoughts of desires for herself sneaking in had been pure nonsense. That was it. She had made her decision. She would move back to the Midwest. She would not move home, to face possible rejection, but close enough to feel as if she were home. She had pushed aside her fears and guilty thoughts. She wouldn't tell her family. They would never know. She hadn't spoken to them in years, and she had known they didn't care. They would never know. Those few thoughts brought back the disappointing call from her most beloved Aunt Hazel seven months after she had had little Hazel.

Her day had started early for little Hazel had had an ear infection and had been up most of the night. Her only reprieve had been that it was Sunday and she did not have to go to work and leave her sick child at daycare. That thought had brought another agony to her:

She had so needed someone to be there for her. She had pushed the thought from her mind as she had rocked and Hazel had cried. Without any effort, Jennifer herself had been in tears. She had known she needed to take Hazel to the doctor, but emergency-room calls were so expensive; yet to wait until tomorrow to try and see her regular doctor would have meant missing a day of work and she would still have had to pay for daycare even though Hazel wouldn't be there. She was trying so hard. *Why did it have to be so impossible?* had screamed to her consciousness, and Jennifer's tears had fallen. Her crying and misery had been interrupted by the ring of the phone. She had gently gotten up to answer the phone, lifting Hazel to her shoulder.

"Hello," she had answered, having no idea who would call her on a Sunday, and so early.

"Jennifer?"

"This is Jennifer. May I ask who is calling?" she had politely inquired.

"Oh, Jennifer, it's Aunt Hazel. How are you, darling?" The love in Aunt Hazel's voice had not been lost on Jennifer.

"Oh, my God, Aunt Hazel, how did you find me? I'm fine." Her tears had quickly disappeared, and she had been filled with the joy of returned family love. "How are you? How are Mom and Dad?" She had been so overcome with shock.

"I'm fine, We're all doing well." Aunt Hazel had decided Jennifer didn't need to know the details of the situation, at least not immediately. There would be plenty of time to inform her. "Tell me how you are, Jennifer. It's been too long."

"I'm really doing quite well." She had shifted the now content Hazel and pulled the rocker next to the phone. "I have a job scheduling photo shoots, and I'm learning the purchasing and retail end of fashion." She had so wanted to impress her aunt that she had gushed on without a breath. "I'm also going to night school to get my business degree. I just started this fall, but I'm going to do it." She had ended on a firm and proud note.

"Jennifer, I am so proud of you. And, hon, what of the baby? Did you find a good home for it?" She had quietly hoped Jennifer hadn't done the unimaginable. Where she lived, it was heard to be quite common.

"It's a little girl. I named her Hazel, after you, and she was born April 6, and yes, she has a good home, because I kept her." Her joy had projected across the line to Aunt Hazel.

Without thinking, Hazel had released, "Oh, Jennifer, no, you didn't!" She had not been able to keep her disappointment from her voice. Jennifer had been on her mind so much, and she had agonized so, praying nonstop the past year as she had made her move out of her brother's home. Aunt Hazel had forgotten she had never spoken her true feelings to Jennifer in the past, but with Jennifer's absence over two years ago she had slipped for the first time in their relationship. And one small slip had led to a cascade. "Jennifer, that baby needs a mother and a father. What do you do with her when you are gone all day and night?" Her questions had come as bullets, unintentionally but nevertheless wounding an already overwhelmed Jennifer. Hazel's concern for both Jennifer and the baby had taken precedence over any consideration for how Jennifer would receive her words.

The shock of Aunt Hazel's disappointment in Jennifer's accomplishments had hit her hard. She had been dumbfounded and at a loss for words. With equal lack of thought, she had responded with a little resentment, "No one could love little Hazel more than I do. And I've made some really wonderful friends." The memory of how helpful Caroline had been had come vibrantly to life, and the love the woman and her family had offered had pushed Jennifer's negativity aside. She had tried to change the mood of the conversation and convey her joy to Aunt Hazel. She had been so happy to hear her voice. She had plunged forward. "Oh, Aunt Hazel, I met the most wonderful person: Caroline, my supervisor. She's been there for me and helped me find, well, everything, a place to live, a car, and someone to care for little Hazel when I'm busy. She's been a godsend. You would like her." She had taken a breath to let her aunt absorb her reassurance that all was truly well with her.

"Have you had the little one baptized?" Aunt Hazel had been still in shock. How could Jennifer have kept the baby? What was wrong with her? And who was this woman who had allowed such a decision—or hadn't encouraged the right thing where the child was concerned? To raise a child alone in today's world. *Oh Jennifer, first one*

*mistake and now another that involves another's life and one so inno-
cent and undeserving of the hardships that lie ahead.*

Jennifer had taken a slow and quiet breath. This would not be easy
for Aunt Hazel, and she didn't feel like getting into it. All of a sudden she had felt old and tired. She had been up all night with a sick
baby, and now she had had to battle questions from one who she had
thought was on her side. She had been so happy to hear from home,
but the answer to that last question would destroy everything. She had
had no choice but to give the truth; she could not lie. "Aunt Hazel, I
don't go to church anymore, well not…," and she had struggled for it
seemed suddenly cruel to say such a thing to someone she loved so
dearly. "I go to Caroline's church."

"Caroline's church?" Aunt Hazel had been puzzled. "She
isn't Catholic?"

"No, Aunt Hazel, the Church refused to help me when I needed…
when I…no one would help me, they just…," and her voice had fallen
off at the memory of the disapproving and reproachful looks she had
received when she had gone to the local churches for assistance. She
had felt for sure they would be glad she was doing the right thing in not
having an abortion, but there had been so much pressure put on her to
give her baby up she had felt their disappointment return in her aunt's
accusing questions. "Caroline was there for me; she helped me to see I
wasn't…," and quietly in the voice of the young girl who had left home
and been disowned she had whispered, "bad and unforgivable."

"Jennifer, what nonsense are you talking? Of course, you are not
bad, and everything can be forgiven through confession, as you well
know, dear. What is going on?" Aunt Hazel had been alarmed. What
had happened to Jennifer in the months they had had no contact
with her?

"Nothing is going on. I've just seen the truth, and," she had taken
a deep breath and stated, "I've been saved." Upon saying the words she
had felt stronger.

"Saved, from what? Goodness Jennifer, are you sure you're okay?
Some new mothers suffer depression problems. Are you depressed,
dear?" Aunt Hazel's tone had been as clipped as her understanding.
"Jennifer, hon," she had tried on a more grown-up note, "you need
to get to mass, and go to confession, and dear, I bet you can still give

your little girl a good home with two loving parents. She's not that old. There are lots of people who want a baby, at any age. If you're suffering depression, giving up the child will help. You'll recover quicker with no one to care for other than yourself." She had ended with a strong voice to encourage Jennifer's understanding of the sensibility of her words.

Aunt Hazel's words had wounded Jennifer deeply, and the infant in her arms, feeling her mother's unsettled state, had instinctively whimpered. Jennifer, slowly and haltingly, with much effort and remembered love, had spoken more calmly than she had felt into the receiver, "Aunt Hazel, I need to go; little Hazel needs a bottle." It had been a small lie, but Jennifer had been unable to take any more of the conversation. The hurt and sense of betrayal she had felt at Aunt Hazel's heartless and self-righteous words had been too much. She had ended with more cheer than she had felt, "I love you, and I'll write. Good-bye." She had hung up with no real intent to send any letters home. With her dad in charge, she knew they would only be returned unopened. And with her abrupt termination of the call, she never learned that her aunt had moved—and her one chance to maintain ties to home had been severed.

Her disappointment and the lack of approval in a conversation with one she had thought had supported her had weighed heavily on Jennifer. When had Aunt Hazel become so like her father? Thoughts of what could be happening at home had filled her heart.

⊹══⚬══⊹

With that memory of her last contact with home, Jennifer had known she wasn't going home to live with her family. She was going to the general area for a simpler way of life.

The world, how sneaky in its stealth, had slipped back into the life of the born again to steal away the stewardship of the true Master. Jennifer's course had been set and altered, and she herself had been unaware of the change and would be as her life unraveled once again.

Caroline, watching the play of emotions dance across Jennifer's expressive face, finally had grasped what Jennifer had hedged at. "Wait, you don't want to stay here. Oh, Jennifer, are you sure?" Surprise and concern had filled her. It had only been four—no, almost five—months since the hostage situation. She had felt sure the bank incident had been the reason Jennifer was struggling.

Jennifer had seen Caroline's concern but with sorrow and determination had silently nodded her head yes.

Again, Caroline had mentally struggled to find a way to get Jennifer to examine all that had happened that day in the bank. "Are you sure you want to leave here?" And she had made a sweeping motion to encompass Jennifer's life. "It seems so drastic." She had remembered Jennifer's loneliness before Hazel had been born. Where would she go? The bank robbery had to be the reason Jennifer had wanted to leave. She had felt fear for her new friend and tried to reason. "Jennifer, do you really…you want to move? I know you wanted a change, but moving, I mean, that just seems…I don't know, more like running away than change."

Incredibly, Caroline had hit the nail on the head to Jennifer's own disturbing subconscious thoughts. Just as surprising, her suggestion hadn't set off alarm bells and indicated the amazing power the world had already usurped from the true Master of Jennifer's life.

"No, Caroline, I'm not running away. I just want to feel…," and she had taken a big breath, "I don't know…freedom, space. I guess you can't take the country out of a person." She had joked in hopes of relieving Caroline's concern. Then in subconscious error, she had added, "Besides, Jesus is in control," when it was Jennifer who had taken the helm of her life and was making all the decisions.

"Oh, Jennifer, I know. It just seems so impulsive. You will call me, please, for anything?" She had added with a touch of sadness, "Remember, if it doesn't work out, you always have a job here, and we—we are family, okay?"

Jennifer had hugged Caroline for her understanding. "Thank you so much. I don't know what I would have done without you." She had been so filled with excitement at the prospect of starting out for something new and unknown.

Once again with Caroline's help, Jennifer had found a job in a specialty dress shop in Cornell, a small Midwestern college town just outside a large metropolitan city. The small store provided high fashion for clientele who occasioned the city society yet wanted a more country environment in which to raise their families, exactly what Jennifer had been looking for. She would be taking the job of assistant sales director.

Jennifer had gone ahead with her plans, determined once again to be the best. To do what she wanted from now on, she had felt confident she could do whatever she set her mind to. It was her life. She could start over and have the life she had wanted, the life she had dreamed of. She would be in charge; she would show "them." She had never felt so alive. She would forget what had happened and what others had said or thought about her. She was her own person. She would be everything she had set out to be when she first had left home so many years ago. *This is my life*, she had told herself.

She had loved her new position in the small high-end fashion shop and had kept busy in making the little dress shop the best in the sales district. Jennifer had continued to raise her daughter alone.

Meanwhile her life in the spirit, through neglect, had unwound, slowly and steadily to barely a single tiny flame, present but unseen, flickering, waiting until the time would be right to be reignited, when Jennifer would be ready to turn from the world and recommit to the truth. And so, the world would have its way with Jennifer.

Jennifer had made good on her ambitions. With what she had learned in the more sophisticated environment in California and her natural fashion sense, she had soon been put in charge of sales. This promotion had included business trips to the fashion reviews she once modeled in to view the new styles. As Jennifer had focused on doing her job, traveling and putting in long hours, plus doing her best to raise Hazel, she had lost sight of her true goal. And the world and its needs and wants insidiously became the master of her life. This new master grew, and without the continued nurturing, help, and comfort that she had known with Caroline and fellow believers, those small seeds of self-doubt, humiliation, and lack of self-worth had awakened from dormancy to grow and strangle the light of love freely given from above. Jennifer had been driven by the need to prove she was worthy of…

Jennifer halted her thoughts as she stopped the car. A new one replaced those just fleeing: Michael is married. Her mind successfully challenged that: His marriage wasn't her problem. That done, and other similar thoughts were rejected and pushed out, too.

There had been other men her first few years in Cornell, too, who had been married. If the married men didn't care, why should she? If there was something wrong with what she was doing with these men, shouldn't they be the ones to discourage the meetings? She was tired of being the one who was always responsible for keeping others in line. Was it too much to ask for a little human love, to connect with someone? She was just thirty-two, with a twelve-going-on-thirty-year-old daughter, and she smiled at the thought of little Hazel. Jennifer was lonely. The need to have another physical being love her had slowly transformed Jennifer into someone unrecognizable in the young woman who had fallen in desperation at the feet of the Lord Jesus Christ a few short years before.

In the beginning, Jennifer had rationalized her actions with the thought there was certainly no harm in meeting someone and just spending time together. She could see no wrong with talking and drawing comfort and strength from some intangible connection she felt with these men. Yet they failed to satisfy; her male friendships remained transitory, always ending after a few sexual encounters. Despite her history, she was blinded to the stark truth she had tried to impart to Chloe so many, many years before. She wouldn't acknowledge that now, here she was, as Chloe had been back then. She wanted friendship, and she had come to use the male desire for sex to her advantage. She had unknowingly learned to play the game, only on her terms. Jennifer stopped caring if those she spent time with were married. She had decided after the first few mistaken relationships to live for the moment. This transformed woman was a long way from the young lady who had bravely shown light into the lost soul of another. She shrugged these thoughts from her mind. Her life in California had never existed. To her, nothing good had come from her time in California, aside from her daughter. She quickly stopped these nagging thoughts.

Jennifer so looked forward to her time with Michael. The times they had spent with each other gave her such feelings of being alive.

She hadn't felt this way since, well, since Brian. This self-realization alone should have blasted off the warning whistle that she was traveling down a dangerous path. Yet Jennifer had wandered so far from the truth on her own path that she didn't even recognize it when she herself shined the light upon it.

She kept telling herself that she and Michael hadn't done anything morally wrong. There was no sex involved—yet—just time and phone calls interspersed with a few spicy emails; she blushed at the thought. There was certainly no harm in friendship. She pushed away the thought that Michael's wife, Claire, knew nothing of their friendship. Michael told her Claire wouldn't understand. He had said his wife had some self-confidence issues resulting from the loss of their youngest daughter a little over a year ago. To tell Claire he had a female friend would only cause further harm; she was still trying to deal with the loss.

Michael also felt their friendship was special. He had told Jennifer she was so much easier to talk with. She listened and understood him, where Claire questioned and became needy. Michael admitted to Jennifer of the shared chemistry between them, which made him feel so happy and free from life's struggles. He said he hadn't felt this young since before he had met Claire. He did admit he was extremely drawn to Jennifer in a physical way. She was very attractive. He assured her, he was for the most part happily married, and he would not act on his desires. His morality had made her angry. She had subconsciously decided at his declaration of fidelity to show him he was no better than those she had befriended before him. He had even gone so far as to write one time in their often-exchanged emails if he were single it would be an entirely different story.

In a short time, Jennifer, though she knew Michael was no different from the others, had let herself fall in love with him. She would catch herself daydreaming from time to time if something ever happened to Claire, she and Michael would have a wonderful life. It was at these times she had to remind herself such love was deceitful. She forced herself to remember all her past encounters which were harsh lessons. She didn't believe in human love. These painful mementos of past liaisons always brought her rosy thoughts to a screeching halt. She forced herself to live for what she could get now, not the future.

She quietly tolerated Michael's spoken words of his deep love for his wife, and she kept his confidences of how he wished Claire would be a little less emotional. Michael confided in her how Claire's emotional outbreaks were getting worse, and they wore him down and made him tired. About all this, Jennifer couldn't care less, but she listened for she knew his wife didn't. As she got out of the car, Jennifer pushed all these thoughts away. She knew Michael appreciated—no, needed—her light view of the world. How far had Jennifer fallen, she was totally unaware; the world held her so tightly in its dark, loveless, self-serving grip. Jennifer would never tell Michael how much she had come to know of human relationships. Thank God for her self-control. She put a smile on her face at the sight of Michael.

"Hello, Jennifer." Michael greeted her with a smile and a happiness he felt from seeing only her. In a few short months, they had become such good friends, and he needed to feel good, especially after last night. The boys had been up most of the night, and he was exhausted with dealing with them and Claire's sensitivity. God, Jennifer smelled good and looked great. What a beautiful woman! He was certainly lucky to have a friend like her.

Jennifer gave him a small hug and delighted in his maleness. She knew he would take her scent with him through the rest of the day as a reminder of their time together. His fellow mechanics were off for lunch, and she sat with him in his little manager office, enjoying the privacy. She shrugged out of her lightweight jacket, knowing as she did he watched her every move and appreciatively eyed her still attractive figure. The fact they hadn't really done anything physically intimate made the sexual magnetism between them so much more powerful and exciting. They had kissed a couple of times, but they hardly counted. Heaven only knows she would have given in if he had only said the word. He had always managed to pull himself back. What will power. Though, it only made her more determined to be even more appealing.

Today she wore an unusually form-fitting top with a revealing neckline along with one of the shorter skirts that had just come into style. She had decided to be a tad bit risqué and neglected to wear hose or even panties. She felt delightfully naughty, and her thoughts of her secret gave her a little more spark than usual.

Michael picked up on it immediately. "You look ravishing today, quite an outfit." He gave a low whistle. "You're like a ray of light." His smile was so genuinely happy and appreciative.

She was glad she had decided to be naughty. She dismissed the feeling of guilt in so deliberately tempting someone who had declared his love and fidelity to another.

The irony of her subconscious attempts to bring Michael off his moral high horse of "I love my wife; we're just friends" was lost on Jennifer. As she had fallen, so she became the instrument of another's fall.

She sat down in her usual spot and again toyed with him by sitting in a very unladylike manner. She knew she was being more than a little raunchy, and she blushed.

Intently watching Jennifer cross to sit in the chair across from him, Michael admired her beauty and sexuality. He wished for a mere moment he was single and could give her pleasure as he knew he could. This thought he had had on more than one occasion, and today the wickedness of his lust awoke with more power than he realized. They had talked of sex, and he knew her experiences had never been very satisfying for her. His early days in the army had given Michael his share of experience. He was assured by more than one of those past partners he was good in bed. Every woman should experience the joy of great sex, and he wished he could help Jennifer feel such pleasure. He also knew he shouldn't think such thoughts. But the more powerful picture in his mind of his showing her how good sex could be pushed away the admonishments from his conscience. His ego had won.

"You are an evil temptress today, aren't you?" he said with a wicked smile, acknowledging her obvious attempt to seduce him.

She laughed and was even more brazen with her posture in the chair.

Michael, being only human, got up and went to her with intense desire in his eyes.

Her breath caught in her throat. A small "Oh God" escaped from her lips as he kissed her deeply into the chair and slid his hand up her thigh under her skirt to introduce her to the sexual pleasure she had lacked. It was all she could do to breathe. She had never felt such pleasure. What must have been minutes seemed like a lifetime. Still in the arms of sexual ecstasy, Jennifer trembled in the greater satisfaction of knowing he had succumbed. The mighty had fallen.

Michael, not understanding the true source of her pleasure, was happy to have shown her how a woman can feel. His own desire and excitement was obvious.

Jennifer noticed and beckoned him closer to her. She had never known such pleasure for herself, but she had her own reputation for making a man or two extremely happy.

In a short time, it was Michael who was spent. He smiled broadly and luxuriated in having such a friend so willing to reciprocate. He told himself how truly lucky he was as he tried to convince himself what had just happened wasn't wrong. They didn't have sex; they just gave each other pleasure, like scratching an itch, no harm done.

Jennifer rose, rearranging her skirt and keeping her emotions in check, and said to Michael, "You are really an artist. Your wife is one blessed woman. I hope she knows how lucky she is."

"She does, believe me, she does," Michael said with a knowing smile. "You are one beautiful woman, Jennifer. Call me later, or email me, my extra-special friend," he added with a disarming smile.

Jennifer further straightened her outfit and gave Michael a gentle hug, drawing strength from his maleness. She planted a light kiss on his cheek, saying, "I've some things to do this evening, but I'll be in touch." She kept her tone light, knowing how much he hated his wife's constant neediness. And she purposefully made herself unavailable to keep Michael wanting her. She had learned to play the game. If she couldn't have him full-time, she'd have him on her terms. Ha! Hadn't she just proved her power today? What a rush. She had *won*! This one had taken her a little longer than the others, but so what? She had WON! Knowing she had conquered such a forbidden fruit, Jennifer slowly lifted her skirt as she left to give Michael a good view of her firm, round, creamy white ass, a vision of things to come for her and for him. She walked from the garage on cloud nine. *Life is good*, she mused.

Michael, watching the departing Jennifer, grinned at her brazen behavior and felt the happiness leave him as he reached for the phone to call home and see how things were going. *If only I could feel like this at home and about Claire*, he sighed. He did love her, just differently, oh so differently. The phone rang once, and Claire answered.

"Hello."

"Hello, sweetheart, how's it going?" He knew when he left that morning things were rough. He and Claire had had words, and he now felt remorseful. "How are the boys?"

"They just went down for a nap, and I was actually able to get a little housework done." She, too, felt bad about their harsh words and tried to make up for it. She offered, "Are you ready for tonight," Claire said with an unmistakable smile in her voice, "you sexy guy?"

Michael, pleasantly surprised, answered in kind, "For you, anytime."

"You are so bad," Claire responded, continuing the banter. "You sound tired. Is everything okay?" Claire questioned, concern in her voice.

"After last night, it's a wonder either one of us is still on our feet." He tried to make light of their long night. He added, "It's just been a busy morning." Thinking of Claire's efforts to smooth over the morning, he added, "I'm looking forward to you tonight." Michael smiled at the thought of making his wife happy.

"I'll be ready. I love you. Call me later." Claire smiled her good-bye, none the wiser about Michael's noontime activities.

"I love you, too. Bye." Michael hung up the phone. He marveled at how, whenever he had sexual thoughts of Jennifer or they had actually shared a kiss, his wife always brought sex into his conversations with her. It was almost as if she somehow knew he was being less than honest with her. He knew she had no knowledge of his "friendship," but her reaction unnerved him some. Here today again, it was a little uncanny after his episode with Jennifer that Claire was thinking of sex with him. He felt a small twinge of guilt but brushed it aside, knowing he would please his wife as much as he had pleased Jennifer. There was no real harm done. He told himself he truly did love Claire, or he would have already left her before Jennifer. He couldn't see himself leaving Claire, and at the same time he was so very, very happy and grateful to have Jennifer in his life. He refused to give the situation any more thought and set about the business of running the shop for the afternoon hours.

Chapter Seven

Claire

With the children out the door to school and the fall morning stretching out before her, Claire felt the need to escape. Distraught over imagined betrayal—by the boys' teacher, her mother, and yes, even her husband—that no one understood, Claire headed outside for a walk to clear her head of thoughts she knew bordered on insanity. *It doesn't matter*, she told herself. It may indeed be her time of the month, but she still had thoughts and they mattered. *Oh God! Life sucks*, she cried, her anguish straining from inside. It was all she could do to walk. In moments, the sounds of nature crept into her consciousness, and the crazy ideas lost their cruel grip on her tormented mind. Walking, more at peace but still feeling life was unfair and meaningless, Claire began to cry.

Why is life so hard, and so very lonely? When did life get so heavy? She had always felt joy, even when her older brother had died. Their relationship had been so special, but she hadn't felt this profound sense of loss and loneliness. She had been only eight, but she remembered she hadn't felt sad.

They had been outside playing their own version of touch football. He was six years her senior, and she loved him dearly. He had been so cute. All her friends had constantly told her so and confided they had serious crushes on him. She had felt so honored to be his little sister. She had worn her love for him on her sleeve. Jacob had equally adored Claire. Her love for him had been so obvious he had had no choice.

Jacob had just snatched the football from her and run off to the far side of the yard. She remembered him tripping in the fading fall evening. She had lain in the grass and rolled over to see him run into the beauty of the blazing sunset, seeming to disappear in a brilliant blaze. It had been the most beautiful sight. She had finally gotten to her feet to run over to him, and to her surprise, he was still lying on the ground as if asleep.

"Jacob," she had called as she had neared him. When he had failed to answer, she had run and tackled into him as she had done a million times previous. But this time there had been no response. The ball had rolled slowly from his prone arms. She, too, had rolled off him and shaken him. "Come on, Jacob!" she remembered pleading. When he had refused to move she had run to get their mom.

"Mommy, Jacob won't get up," she had breathlessly told her mother.

"What on earth, Claire? Jacob's outside; he's not sleeping," her mother had dismissed the girl's urgency as she was busy preparing supper.

"I know, Mommy, but he won't get up." Claire had started to cry. She couldn't remember why, but the tears had spilled. She didn't remember feeling sad, but for some reason, telling her mommy Jacob wouldn't wake up had made her feel sad for her mommy.

Finally realizing Claire was telling her something was wrong, her mother had run from the house to see what on earth had happened. Claire never had felt sad about Jacob's death. Her only memory was the brilliance of the light as Jacob had run with the football. She could still recall the beauty of the moment.

So when did this sadness set in—and so heavily? she wondered as she continued pondering over her life.

Meeting Michael had seemed like a dream come true. Then when the children came, she couldn't believe she had been so blessed, until…and her crying resumed.

Now, and she drew in a deep breath with the thought, there were times when she just wanted to quit, to step out of life, but not really. She loved the children, and they needed her. She loved Michael, and she knew he was true to her no matter how upset she made him. Her mother, well, you're not supposed to always get along with moms. She gave a little smile at this personal reprieve from guilt, but the overwhelming sadness that had sent her out of the house returned with its relentless, overshadowing darkness.

The Tears They Come

The tears, they come
and I don't know why.
They come from deep,
deep, down inside.
My soul, it bleeds;
my heart, it hurts.
The tears, they fall
and I don't know why.

They rise to fall,
from time to time
a mournful, heartfelt song.
A scene, whose emotion
touches deep inside.
The tears, they fall
and I don't know why.

Years of soulful silence
put them there
to pool and build.
And now with time,
the tears burst forth,
and I don't know why.

Sitting in the shade of the huge old maple, listening to the morning birds, Joe rested a spell after walking a bit. Formerly, Joe had walked back and forth to his work, his reason for existence, with no pleasure. But now he walked with wholehearted enjoyment. He allowed himself the pleasure of seeing what maybe could have been. Passages from the Old Testament came to him, "Adam and Eve walked in the garden with God" and "Enoch walked with God," and he rolled them around, thinking how wonderful for them to have walked with the One who created such utter beauty.

This morning he didn't have to go to work, but being a man of habit he rose at his regular time and went for a walk. The morning hours were so fresh and full of life. The fall air had a distinct fullness and maturity of scent. The twittering birds' darting back and forth along the blacktopped road was such a delight. They were so delicate and brilliantly colored. He felt very blessed to be able to have the time to absorb such beauty. Taking a moment from his walk, as he did not have a destination or appointed time, he sat to enjoy the serenity of the unfolding morning, to be awed by what God had created. All that he felt inside, the awe of the Creator, he offered to God.

As always, when Joe took pleasure in the beauty of nature, his old friend came to sit with him in thought. *What is it all for?* The old question, such a burr, and he sighed tiredly. It used to trouble him, but now he credited the constant questing with drawing him closer to God's Word. His thoughts started to turn.

He had accepted the Lord Jesus Christ as his savior years back, right before his release from prison. He felt he had grown closer to

God in his search for answers. But after getting out, he no longer felt comfortable in the Catholic upbringing of his youth. He just could not mesh the doctrines of Catholicism with the truths revealed in his everyday reading of the Word of God. He now read with eyes unveiled, and the Words of God were the Words of a Master. He had come to treasure the Bible as the wondrous work and gift from God it was.

He had tried different times over the years attending other churches. The people he met were always warm and welcoming. Yet the church proceedings didn't compare to the beauty, ceremony, and ritual inherent in the religion he had been born into and devoutly loved for almost a half of a century. He had felt foreign and out of place attending other houses of worship. Eventually, he gave up "trying out" other churches, deciding to leave his spiritual growth and guidance up to the last high priest, the Lord Jesus Christ.

HEBREWS 7:20-28 And it was not without an oath! Others became priests without any oath, but he became a priest with an oath when God said to him: "The Lord has sworn and will not change his mind: 'You are a priest forever.'" Because of this oath, Jesus has become the guarantee of a better covenant.

Now there have been many of those priests, since death prevented them from continuing in office; but because Jesus lives forever, he has a permanent priesthood. Therefore he is able to save completely those who come to God through him, because he always lives to intercede for them.

Such a high priest meets our need—one who is holy, blameless, pure, set apart from sinners, exalted above the heavens. Unlike the other high priests, he does not need to offer sacrifices day after day, first for his own sins, and then for the sins of the people. He sacrificed for their sins once for all when he offered himself. For the law appoints as high priests men who are weak; but the oath, which came after the law, appointed the Son, who has been made perfect forever.

At first, those feelings of no place to go had weighed heavily on his newborn soul. But he could not, no, he would not go back; he would not forsake the truth he had found. Forgiveness was a gift, and eternal love and life were not earned by attending mass or receiving sacraments or saying litanies of prayers to people the church had given the status of sainthood. In the absence of organized religion, he had made the decision to live each day trusting in God, letting God be his guide.

Joe may have thought he studied alone. But a child of God is never alone. Such imagined moments of aloneness often more fully reveal God's presence for then the soul seeks and accepts more willingly that which created it. Joe felt if God wanted him to attend a certain house of worship, He would let him know. Until then, he would read his Bible daily and let the Holy Spirit be his teacher. As the New Testament promises:

> 1 JOHN 2:27 As for you, the anointing you received from him remains in you, and you do not need anyone to teach you. But as his anointing teaches you about all things and as that anointing is real, not counterfeit—just as it has taught you, remain in him.

At first, Joe missed the habit of scheduled fellowship with others who shared his love for the Lord Jesus Christ. He knew that support from others traveling the same spiritual path is vital to growth in God, but God lovingly brought people into his life, providing for this need. Joe was surprised that, with God in control, the fellowship He provided sent him deep into the scriptures in search of truth and understanding. People who seemed to have a deep love for the Lord Jesus Christ seemed to appear naturally most every day of his new life. Through them, he had come to experience the most wonderful sharing of God's Word and the Lord's love. Invariably, wherever he went, with whomever he met, conversations would turn to the Lord and his soul would be fed. Scripture passages were shared, and the Spirit of the Living God of Abraham, the God of Isaac, and the God of Jacob grew within Joe. Despite his upbringing, studies in the seminary, and practice as a priest in the Catholic Church, he reasoned the Son of God had no denomination, so he would forsake man's splintering of the fellowship of believers into organized, religious classifications until God let him know otherwise.

Grace is a precious gift from God, and with it, Joe relearned God's Word and came to love and marvel at the revealed beauty and knowledge of the Bible. He knew of the promise of heaven and the truth in the human limitations of this physical life.

But his old friend, even after nine years of seeing the truth, still hounded his subconscious. There surely had to be a reason for this earthly existence. The question would rise to mental observation, prodding him with the insignificance and smallness of humanity. Why was this always his reflection? Was it a reminder, a demander of humbleness before the greatness of infinite existence? He believed with his whole heart in the realness of the One True Living God of Abraham, the God of Isaac, and the God of Jacob. Yet this question still came to taunt him. Maybe his intellect brought the question as a friendly reminder of man's true intellectual insignificance and limited capability of understanding, of man's original sin of trying to become like God in eating of the Tree of Knowledge.

Joe pondered on and past this thought. We are born, most of us alone, one at a time; and the majority of us die alone, one at a time. Our lives are gone, and after decades of our passing, who remembers us? Who is still alive that knew us, our dreams, thoughts, hopes, and desires, all that made us the unique individual God created us to be? Who really has touched the person that has, with the passage of time, become just another face in a picture on a wall?

A Picture on the Wall

A picture on the wall,
a face within a frame,
a name passed down,
these living memories are no more.

A life once lived,
passions, feelings,

dreams, and fears.
No more these emotions
from a picture on the wall.

Endless pictures handed down,
tales of lives told,
voices passing on lives,
lives leaving life,
entering pictures on the wall.

This question, so simple, yet so enormous troubled him. He thought of all the people he had known over the years. He was almost fifty-eight, and he reached back to the earliest he could remember. He wondered, did any of the people who had walked through the years with him wonder of *him*, how *he* was, or what had become of *him*? Did they have fond memories of him? Had he even made a memory in anyone? Why was this so important to him? Why did he care that people remembered? Why did he have this constant yearning that no one's life should be made insignificant? Ah, Lord, there had to be a reason for this recurring circular questing.

Into this depth of mental wandering, God presented Joe with the work of salvation, and being open to receive God's intention, he accepted.

Joe sensed the heaviness of heart in the young woman walking his way on the path. Unwilling to give up his spot on the bench and not wanting to end his enjoyment of the morning, he stayed quietly put and watched her approach. *Maybe she won't even see me*, he thought, *and she'll continue on her way*. He would let happen what would happen.

Claire continued on, letting the tears flow and, through blurred eyes, saw a bench ahead. The morning was cool and the light breeze refreshing. To sit but a moment and pray would do her good, maybe let these feelings of doubt and sadness seep out of her. Realizing her nose was running, she took her eyes from her way and busied herself searching for a tissue from her sweater pocket. The bench now at her side, she sank into the wooden back and let loose a river of tears, unaware of the bench's other occupant.

As he watched the visibly upset young woman approach him, Joe rethought his decision to remain seated. When she nearly fell sobbing into the bench, Joe realized she hadn't even seen him, or surely, she never would have fallen apart so vulnerably in front of a total stranger. He feared moving or even acknowledging his presence, knowing nothing of her. Silently, he remained, praying somewhat guiltily that she would leave as inattentively as she had come and spare both of them what was sure to be an embarrassing situation. It is said in the New Testament:

> ROMANS 8:26-27 In the same way, the Spirit helps us in our weakness. We do not know what we ought to pray for, but the Spirit himself intercedes for us with groans that words cannot express. And he who searches our hearts knows the mind of the Spirit, because the Spirit intercedes for the saints in accordance with God's will.

Claire's truly distraught soul sent up such a silent inward plea that God, hearing, placed Joe where he could be of use to Him.

Joe sat silently, and Claire wept loudly. Each prayed a silent prayer in quiet desperation, Claire for relief from her private distress and Joe for rescue from a most uncomfortable predicament. In time, Claire quieted down, and Joe, still shaken at such show of emotion, relaxed and drew a quiet breath when he felt the young woman at his side no longer hovered at the brink of self-destruction.

As Claire unwound, she let weariness enfold her, taking the void of the released anguish. More at peace yet still greatly sorrowed, she dried her now quietly falling tears and glanced about. Somewhat startled, she realized someone had come to sit beside her. Not knowing he had witnessed her meltdown, she politely said, "Hi," and moved over some to give him more room.

Trying hard not to smile, Joe realized she didn't know he had been there all along and replied, "Thank you." Silently he thanked God for her lack of awareness. *Dodged a bullet that time. Thank you, God.*

Attempting to lighten the young lady's mood, Joe offered, "Sure is a beautiful morning."

"Yes." Claire swallowed, her tears starting to freshly roll down her face. "Oh dear, I'm so sorry," she squeezed out, trying not to lose total control in front of a complete stranger. Making light, Claire said, "I seem to have a leak." Her nervous laughter mingled with muffled sobs and controlled attempts to breathe through the onslaught of renewed anguish rising within. "Goodness," she added.

"It's all right; we all have those days," Joe stated, trying not to appear too interested in case she wanted—*Please, God, yes, please*—to leave. He did care but was reluctant to delve into what might be a very troubled life. He wished only for the solitude he had been enjoying.

Her strength almost spent in attempted self-control, Claire got out weakly, "It's not fair, the beauty of the day when I'm so miserable."

With no chance she'd just be on her way, Joe resigned himself to offer what little comfort he could. He patted her arm lightly as if she were a little child and told her, "It's God's way of comforting us. When a little child is hurt, his mom pulls him into her arms for a hug or a kiss of comfort. The injury may remain, but her care and concern overwhelm it, and it seemingly disappears. We may be in despair, but God surrounds us with the beauty of His creation, and we let it remind us of Him and stir hope within."

Briefly distracted by the stranger's quiet words, Claire felt a calm enter her, and she took a slow, deep breath.

"Yes," she exhaled, more relaxed and less upset. "You're right; it is so beautiful. It's too bad we women have to be so emotional," she offered in explanation for her behavior, trying to reassure the stranger she wasn't a total basket case.

Joe smiled at her and said, "Crying is just the way the heart washes the clutter from the soul. Sometimes it takes a downpour." He was glad to see she attempted a smile at his weak humor.

Claire with a lighter tone, said, "I like that, clutter from the soul," and she nodded quietly in agreement, thinking that his words truly reflected all she had been thinking. Then her mood started to darken. She shook her head, trying to hold on to the fast-fleeing calm.

Joe could see the tears build and sent a frantic prayer heavenward. *Oh God, what can I do?* All he wanted to do was leave—and quickly.

Before he could find any words to comfort her or, better, encourage her on her way, she forced out, "My little girl died." Her sobbing was most loud now and alarming, pushed from some place deep inside, and new tears poured forth unrestrained.

"I'm so sorry," Joe quietly responded.

"I feel so guilty. I just can't forgive myself for not being there, for not being more careful. I'm her mom; I should have been there. I miss her so much. She was so little and so sweet. She needed me, and I failed her." Claire's words flowed as freely as her tears, releasing all the pain she had locked so carefully away.

Joe, once startled, now felt deeply the young woman's pain and, with a look inward, marveled at God's great wisdom. He sat speechless at the plan of the Creator. *Who would have thought?*

"It's okay, let it out, and then let it go," Joe encouraged. He now felt no need to flee. When the sobbing finally quieted, Joe started to speak.

"I know. I had that same guilt." The feelings came rushing back, and now it was Joe who choked back shared emotions. He knew the pain she felt, so raw and engulfing it left room for nothing else. With great strength to keep from weeping at her pain, Joe continued, "It is good to speak the words of pain. Address them and then release them; there's nothing else to do with them. You must accept forgiveness for what you feel you did or did not do. There is no other action to be had but death. Forgiveness is a gift and a great one at that. It can't be earned or bought; it is only given. All we need do is accept it, freely, no strings attached. No one—not giver or receiver—looks back at the pain; both must go forward, brand new in the gift of forgiveness. Remember what the Bible says:

PSALM 103:11-12 For as high as the heavens are above the earth, so great is his love for those who fear him; as far as the east is from the west, so far has he removed our transgressions from us.

"Sometimes the hardest person to forgive is ourselves. But no matter how very hard, we must forgive—or we die, slowly, painfully. We also hurt others we love unintentionally when we let guilt be our new master. He is there night and day, chipping away, destroying us as we slowly reflect the internal destruction of ourselves on those around us. Bad within reflects bad without. In one way or another, guilt will have his way; through either sickness or action he will triumph. Guilt is heavy, ugly, and it grows monstrously as it consumes. It can be destroyed only by forgiveness."

Claire looked in awe at this man's intense pronunciation of the despicable yet powerful force of guilt. She'd given wrapt attention, and she understood. How many years had it been since Ruthie had died? Six?—No, seven. All these years, she had thought she had forgiven herself, but here today she had blurted out the painful truth. She had voiced what had been eating her up inside. She hadn't protected her child then, and she couldn't protect the ones she still had from all the disappointments, hurts, and unfairness in life.

To forgive herself would be so freeing. Just the thought of letting go comforted her. She was so tired of holding on to what had happened, trying to make up for what she felt she had done wrong. Could she really just say she was sorry and be free of the pain and keep only her sweet memories of Ruthie? Her tears fell quietly. Was it really so simple?

Almost as if reading her thoughts, Joe interjected, "Yes, it is that simple."

Surprised, she blushed at her doubts somehow revealed. Again, and this time out loud, she asked like a hopeful child, "Really?" And she so wanted his pronunciations to be true.

"Yes, it is. Give your burden to Jesus so you can do the work God has before you to do more freely. Do you have more children?"

"Yes, we have three more."

"They need you, *all* of you, well and free of such a weighty burden."

With fear mingled with much hope, Claire quietly said, "I am sorry, dear Jesus, for failing to protect Ruthie, and I accept forgiveness for myself." Her tears flowed freer, washing away years of guilt. "And I am sorry for not being there for you, Ruthie." Her voice broke. "Dear sweet little Ruthie, I love you so very much, and I miss you oh so much. I am so very sorry, honey." Through the free-falling tears, she took a labored breath and, looking out at the beauty of the morning, clearly stated, "I thank you, Jesus." Then she repeated more convincingly, "I accept forgiveness." She rolled the thought of self-forgiveness around and felt the release from guilt. She stated as a fact, to reassure herself, "I am forgiven."

"Yes, you are because Jesus forgives. What He does, we do. He forgives others as do we forgive them. And as we forgive others, so do we forgive ourselves. If you can forgive others, you must forgive yourself."

"You are right, we are taught that." Feeling better and then again not really feeling anything for the first time in a long time, Claire turned to the stranger and said, "Thank you so very much for being here today. I don't know what I would have done."

"You are very welcome, and it's okay. I am truly glad I was here." Joe basked in the appreciation of how he, of all people, who truly knew the depth of her pain, was there to guide her in one of the greatest gifts: forgiveness. *What a master planner God is.* How blessed he felt to have God in control of his life.

"I must be on my way." Joe rose to go. "Do remember, no strings attached," Joe admonished lest she fall back into the quagmire of guilt she had struggled free from just moments before.

"Oh yes, yes; only forward for me." She sighed. "Guilt is too heavy." And she added, "Again, thank you." She shook his hand and, on impulse, shared a hug. Both voiced a "God bless you," and Joe wandered off on his way. Claire sat for a moment more, amazed at what had just transpired and feeling new in spirit.

As he continued on his way, Joe's thoughts traveled back to his own struggle for forgiveness and how the feelings of peace he had now had eluded him for so long. He shook his head at the remembrance, for it had truly been a fierce battle. Had he known the struggle to survive and overcome going into the ordeal, would he have stepped forward? He did not envy the young lady's place in the days, weeks, and years ahead. He was very thankful to have come through just such agony himself. He would definitely keep her in his prayers. She would need them to come out and remain in the light. Again the recollection of his own struggle to accept salvation and peace came to mind.

The evil trickery of this world takes many forms and is often unrecognizable to the person struggling. When Joe first accepted salvation, he remembered being assaulted shortly after with the question, "What of all those in the faith he had grown up with?" If what he had just accepted was true, what of them? This horrific judgmental thought had halted the train of salvation and nearly sent it to derailment. Only the grace of God stepping in had kept Joe's eyes on the Lord Jesus Christ with the gentle murmurings of the Spirit. God had admonished Joe: Man was not to judge, only to see the truth and accept it; let God do God's job; Joe was just a child, born again in Jesus Christ. He would have hope in God for those in his past who had not seen the whole truth of the cross and of salvation. This soft whispering of Spirit allowed Joe to continue his yes to salvation.

Evil does not stop at one attempt. It assaults daily and uses humanity and intellect at every turn. The world was not done with Joe. Its next assault screamed even louder and most viciously, "What of those *you, the priest*, led astray when they came to you for forgiveness?" For he knew now that forgiveness can only be given by Jesus Christ; no amount of penance can earn it. All the penance he had dispensed to parishioners seeking forgiveness over the years weighed heavily upon his shoulders. The burden of guilt and his own acknowledgement of this charge of wrongdoing had sent Joe to his knees. He had done this. This was a truth the whisperings of the Spirit would not quiet. Joe had to admit he had done wrong, and he wept bitterly for being so terribly sinful. The loving kindness of the Spirit had assured Joe that he had only been doing what he had learned to do in believed righteousness at the time, and he had done so devoutly and in good faith of service to God. The Spirit of God revealed to Joe that he was not the first servant of God who had erred so wrongly. What of the apostle Paul, who, as Saul, had crucified the early Christians until God Himself had showed Paul the way? This startling truth had sealed Joe's salvation. He had thanked God with humble tears and wept at the forgiveness offered and the graciousness of a God so loving.

As Joe continued his morning walk, thoughts of the difficulties Claire would surely encounter—that we all deal with as we both hold onto the light of salvation and listen to the world telling us to doubt God's gift to us—would not be released. He had walked a similar path, and he could not stop the mental trip into his pain-filled past.

Chapter Eight

Joe

U pon entering the correction facility so many years ago, Joe had resolved just to exist. He didn't care, wouldn't care, and couldn't care. Caring had proved to be too costly.

Behind These Walls

Behind these walls I sit, untouched and uncaring.
For behind these walls there's safety;
Love can hurt
And caring cause grief.

Happiness is elusive and not long lasting.
Behind these walls all is in control.
Alone there are no complications,
No other's feelings to consider.

So it's behind these walls I hide,

*And ride life out with feelings numbed
Untouched and untouchable.*

He could not accept what had happened or how his life had changed so dramatically. He was solely responsible for loss of life, two young lives barely lived. He refused to acknowledge any fault on the part of the young boys, Glen and David. He knew more than anyone the full story. He would never forget that last night those two boys had spent in the rectory. He should have reported them, or at least called their parents. They would have been hauled home, possibly beaten for doing something bordering on sacrilegious; but they definitely would have been grounded—and kept home. Their families were staunch Catholics, and what they had done was disrespectful to the faith. They would not have been out driving, and he would never have run them off the road. *Oh God*, he had internally wailed over and over. Why hadn't he done the right thing and called their parents? They were so young, so full of potential. What had he stolen from the world? What children would they have had? These questions only compounded his guilt.

Why had he tried to be nice and attempt conspiratorial friendship? The one time he had given way just to be friendly, even human, had gone sour. He was tired of being someone everyone held at respectful, almost inhuman, distance. He was a priest, he wanted to scream, not a God. He had reasoned it was his own selfish need for friendship that had cost those two young men their lives. He could list the many sins he had committed that night, and they overwhelmed him; he had so gravely erred. Forgiveness was a mountain with no peak, forever unattainable. He could never be forgiven. Those poor parents. The utter agony he witnessed of having to bury their young sons. It was burned into his soul. He could hardly face them and couldn't look into their sorrow-filled eyes and say how sorry he was. Sorry wouldn't do for the taking of a life.

Joe had accepted the manslaughter charge and his punishment, ten years. There had been no trial. He felt he deserved more time than ten years. His whole life would not be enough. Penance, there was not enough penance in the entire world. He thought even if he prayed for an eternity, it wouldn't change any of the pain or sorrow he had selfishly inflicted on those undeserving families. It was this cloud that surrounded Joe and went before him as he entered his new home for possibly the next ten years.

As in any small community, especially a closed one, talk spread. Curiosity, then genuine pity, and finally true concern spread among the prison population for the preacher, as he was dubbed, until Joe put an immediate and abrupt end to the title as he defrocked himself.

The prison population could not understand how such a one who was supposed to spread the Word of God could be so dejected and in such bleak despair. All were concerned lest he die from self-will. The guards and prison staff had never witnessed such a united care and concern for anyone. All respected his request to be called Joe. No one harmed him. Few interrupted his need for self-isolation. The atmosphere in the prison seemed to be quieter and more controlled with the arrival of the new inmate. His self-punishment seemed respected and accepted, though no one understood. All came to know of the circumstances of his incarceration and felt he should forgive himself. Most became more reflective of their own sentences, and less fighting and fewer infractions ensued among those doing time while Joe was incarcerated. Most felt it truly was a very misfortunate accident. Some had carefully and respectfully approached Joe with questions, and in the pretense of advice, they carefully constructed ways to help him see the error of his way.

Carlos, a young Hispanic man in his mid twenties, had attempted to draw Joe out, and the last occasion was Joe's most despairing.

Carlos had come up to Joe in the prison yard one afternoon. "Hey, Father, you got a minute?"

Joe, seeing no way to avoid him, unwillingly but politely had responded, "Sure."

Carlos had made a show of firmly planting his feet, adding emphasis to his words. "You know, Father, you just got to keep going to confession, doing the prayers and the mass, you know. You can't just quit; you're a priest, man. If you quit, what does that say for me? I'm, like, so much worse. If you can't be forgiven, how can I?" he had implored, hoping for a resolution for the tortured man before him.

Joe had tiredly risen, for Carlos had come to him before, put his hand on Carlos' shoulder, and with the weight of layered guilt, responded, "Don't you see, Carlos? Because I am a priest, I should have known better. It has to be worse for me. I had more responsibility as a servant of God, and I took two lives. Two lives God created for his purposes, purposes that will never be realized because of what I did."

"But it was an accident, Father," Carlos had put forth.

"Carlos, please, you don't know. I can't explain. No." Joe had stopped and then looked him fully in the face and continued. "I'm sorry. I can't give you what you seek, reassurance of forgiveness. And I can no longer serve. I am truly sorry." With that, Joe had turned and walked away, his thoughts roiling. He could no longer be a priest because of his own lack of…what…faith? The realization had caught him, and he had sagged. He was hurting others, and his burden of guilt grew. Would this punishment never end?

He had been a priest; his punishment for error had to be worse. How could any amount of rosaries or even prayers forgive taking two innocent youthful lives? The world didn't hold enough prayers or time to say them.

In the end, most of the prisoners came to accept what Joe had chosen. They remained concerned and respectful but knew a hardened man when they encountered one and left him to himself. Joe adapted to his new life well. He shut life out and fed the body that carried his weighted soul. There was nothing left to live for, not here, and he knew from his religious upbringing his eternity would be long spent in purgatory. He had no hope, no forgiveness. He lived, but he didn't.

This existence went on for eight of his ten-year sentence. During this time Joe slowly reflected on every aspect of his life, forcing himself to recall detail down to smells, feelings, and ideas from the carefree childhood years through his dream-wielding teens into the reality of young adulthood. It was a long mental walk that left him questioning everything he had come to accept about who he had grown to be and what he had matured to believe in.

He looked over so many aspects from so many different angles but came to no answers. He could find no comfort or relief from the new restless yearning seeping into his very being. He had no idea what he was yearning for, but for the first time in his memory, he felt totally empty. This feeling startled him at first and then scared him. If everything he had been and now was were for nothing, what meaning did life hold? He had to be wrong. Life wasn't emptiness. There was too much to a life and all too many who had lived. Life was not for nothing. He would not accept this rational.

Before We Were

From where did we come
before we were?
The mind and thought not existing
is impossible to comprehend.
And then the thought is born,
if we knew not before we were,
will we know not when we cease to be;
and if so, is this the promised eternity?

He started over. He looked at and examined his life, and the people who had come and gone before him. They were all regular people, no one anyone outside of a small circle would ever know. There were none who had made any claim to fame. Everyone he had ever known was just ordinary. They were regular people who grew up and accomplished what most of their peers did. They attained the appropriate level of education for their era, fell in love, dreamed of a better life, had a family, struggled, and left this world. They had hardly made a mark to show for their existence other than a descendant or two, or more for those who followed the faith, and a face in a photo album. Every life was basically the same, different only in the small details. Why should the knowledge of anonymity of the individual who had lived leave such a feeling of emptiness?

It was to this searing question God introduced Ken into Joe's life.

Chapter Nine

Ken

*K*en had been incarcerated at a medium security federal prison for only a year of his thirty-year sentence when, due to budget constraints, he was moved to a distant facility in another state to complete his sentence.

His life had changed the day of the horribly failed bank heist, and Ken had accepted his sentence without question or hesitation. He lived his life now as a passenger who viewed each day as a new journey. Even in prison, he never took the monotonous days for granted. Life was full of surprises, and he recognized and appreciated all that came his way. Those he was with were the greatest of treasures. While he knew some were hardened criminals, he couldn't overlook the fact that God had created every one of them, and within each lived a soul thirsting for the light. He knew how his own hopelessness and despair had led him to his crime—and to the light—and he came to learn the stories that had brought his fellow inmates where they were now.

One young gang member told of trying to save his younger brother who had excelled in school but had been lured by the excitement of gang membership. He knew the path too well and had wanted better for his little brother. As he had tried to retrieve the thirteen-year-old from one such meeting, a fight had broken out, and he had accidentally shot and killed his own brother. Ken met him during Bible study and made a connection in tragedy shared. The youth gave Ken a glimpse into a life he would never have been privileged to see, and an understanding awoke in him. All people struggle, and the struggles, though unique to the area and the individual, have a common thread—the need to be connected to someone or something bigger than the self, whether through the love of those we feel closest to or membership in a group that fully accepts us. Together Ken and the young man reveled in the love of God.

Another, an older man, had seemed successful in life with a business, love of family, and all that most people dream of. But his accountant had discovered the truth, that he had maintained appearances through embezzling, and in an attempt to keep all secret, he had put a hit out on the employee. In time this older man, too, saw his need for more was just an escape. In greater discussions with those who had had nothing, he had asked himself, How much was he after? How much had he needed? And what was he really seeking? When he happened upon the answers, his transformation was miraculous.

He would never forget how the momentous change in his own life had occurred. He knew not everyone was as blessed as he was, but he was glad he had been hit by the train of salvation. Ken had been blessed not only to have been hit full on but also to have been open to receive. Oh how thankful he was. The hymn "Amazing Grace" had real meaning to him. It brought tears to his eyes every time he heard it. He had been blind, oh so very blind and wretched. How was it he had come to be open to receive? He didn't honestly know but was truly thankful he had said yes to the Lord Jesus Christ coming into his life and being in charge.

Yes, Lord, he was truly blessed and thankful everyday that his eyes had been opened and his heart softened so when the train of salvation plowed into his desperate soul, he saw and said yes. *Thank you, thank you, thank you, God.* Ken had days he felt he could never praise God enough; he was so filled with thanks, happiness, and joy for Jesus Christ's reconciling his relationship with the God of Abraham, the God of Isaac, and the God of Jacob. He would be forever thankful for that miracle.

His own transformation, from wretchedness to saved, gave him great understanding and much sorrow for those he now spent his days with. So many were so lost. Life in this world was so dark and seemingly hopeless with no light in sight, and the prison environment terribly compounded the darkness. He felt such pity. He knew his fellow prisoners could be freed and saved. They could be made brand new in the precious sacrificial blood of the Lord and Savior Jesus Christ. They could be filled with the joy and hope of an eternal life of love, knowing they were saved, forgiven. He prayed daily for all and knew even if they said yes, their journey was only just beginning. What a journey.

Ken knew salvation was a gift, and the walk with the Lord was not promised to be easy, yet it was a new lease on life. And God did promise and give help in the presence of the Holy Spirit to whoever believed. The power of the Most High God never ceased to amaze him. Wonder and joy at God's great plan and His will was never far from Ken's thoughts.

That day in the bank was burned into his memory like a brand. The young girl, hope flickering within and unknowingly on a mission for Christ, had boldly offered him the way out.

Everything had gone so horribly wrong, in the worldly sense, that day at the bank. Bruce, his friend, at the time, had assured him it would be a simple matter. He had also assured Ken this was going to be the start of a new beginning for them. It would be easy. Hitting the bank in the middle of the week on an early morning with only an elderly guard would get them in and out in no time. It would be like taking candy from a baby. Bruce had said he had been watching the bank, that there were never more than one or two customers and usually only one teller and a loan officer.

Bruce's idea had been the spark Ken had needed. His life had become so mundane and meaningless nothing mattered anymore; he had nothing to live for, so he had agreed. His wife had run off, she had grown tired of trying to make a life in their small one-room apartment. His son was staying with her unforgiving parents, and the custody situation seemed hopelessly lost to him. Her parents had taken him aside after one court hearing and viciously told him he had taken their daughter from them and they would do everything in their power to make sure he never saw his son again. They had made good on their words. When he had gone to plead for guardianship, the courts had said he was unfit because of his record—only one previous arrest for possession, and it had been proven the drugs weren't even his.

At the time of that arrest, Ken had been taking Bruce to his place of work. The police officer had pulled them over for a broken tail light. The pot the officer had spotted had been set in the center console by Bruce, but it was Ken's car. The officer honed in on it immediately, and the rest was history. He had a criminal record.

His life had been one wrong step after another, all spiraling downhill. He had loved his young wife, Rachael, so dearly. She was petite and darkly, wildly beautiful in an exotic way, favoring the Italian heritage of her father over her mother's Irish background. The oldest of four daughters, she was the apple of her daddy's eye. Rachel had found favor with her father because he, too, had loved her spirited nature.

But that same wild spirit had also cut her off from him. Ken had fallen for her in the eighth grade, and they had become high school sweethearts with such youthful dreams and ambitions. Her unexpected pregnancy the start of their senior year and her parents' violent anger and rejection of not only Ken also but Rachel had set the chain of events in motion. Amid accusations and verbal abuse, they had thrown their daughter out of their home. They would not have her bring shame to the family business, nor would they allow her to sully her three younger sisters with her wild and willful ways. Against their sound advice, she had dated this young man, and now she saw why they had been against her friendship with him. Their words of wisdom had gone unheeded, and she was paying the price. Her beloved daddy had harshly told her she had literally made her bed; she would have to lie in it.

Ken's own family had not been surprised, but they were not supportive either. He was not his father's son. His mother had become pregnant at the tender age of fifteen and a single mother at sixteen. Her young lover had abandoned her, and she had been forced to start her life alone. Ken had been a beautiful baby and a joy, always happy. His mother loved him deeply and showered him with love and affection. She had no lack of sitters for the jovial little fellow at the small diner where she had found a job waiting tables. It was a family-run business, and it had a small room off the back where daily patrons would take turns entertaining the toddler while she worked.

Her simple but joyous life had changed when she met the man who would become Ken's stepfather—and so did Ken's. His stepfather was a construction worker whose education had come from living life and surviving. He had fallen in love with the strong and independent young mother but did not take to what he perceived as a very spoiled momma's boy who seemed to be the center of her world. He was quite a bit older and widowed for nearly five years with four grown sons of his own. He knew how a boy should be raised. He had swept Ken's young mother off her feet, marrying her after four short months and then had set out to show her life was not about joy or love. Ken was not mistreated, but his coddling and tender treatment by his mother was discouraged. He must grow to be a man and learn from his mistakes. His mother must refrain from hugging him every time he fell or did something she felt was wonderful. He also led her to believe Ken must learn without her constant guidance. His new stepfather had felt if Ken couldn't make it on his own wits, he wasn't man enough to be in the world, and the world needed men, not sensitive girly boys. With four grown sons, Ken's mother had felt his stepfather must know what was right, and she had forever changed her relationship with her son to one of withdrawal and distance.

Ken was intelligent enough to realize his situation, and he had survived. The hunger for love and intimacy was too strong to beat down. When the circumstances presented themselves in his first love, Rachel, he had poured out his soul to her and fallen deeply in love. So when Rachel's family abandoned her, he did what he had felt was right. He had no guidance, but by his stepfather's own example, he would sink or swim. Ken and Rachael, feeling they had no other choice, had run off and gotten married. They were determined to prove both sets of parents wrong.

Ken had faced a world different from the one his stepfather had grown up in, where a man could make a go of it without much education and support a family. Without a high school diploma, Ken could find only jobs with low pay and hardly enough to support one let alone three. Their struggle became too much. His spirited little beauty of modest means had grown weary of the drudgery of motherhood and a life of responsibility she hadn't been fully prepared to take on and wasn't mature enough to accept. Their son, Anthony, or Tony as they called him, had not been an easy baby. He had suffered bouts of colic and been sick several times his first year to the point Ken had had to miss work to give Rachel some needed relief.

The demands of little Tony and Ken's missed work had left them in need of opportunities both had taken for granted when living under their parents' care—the time for themselves, the time to spend with people their own age, the chance to have fun catching a show, or hanging out at the local eateries sharing dreams of their futures. Rachel was a social person, and she had begun to feel old and worn. She had wanted more in her life than childcare; she had felt she was too young to be her parents. To taste again what she had left, she had started going out at night when Ken would arrive home from his minimum-wage job at a local factory.

Ken had let her go; he had thought maybe she just needed to see she wasn't really missing anything, and he had encouraged her. He had loved her so very much and had only wanted to help. But he had made an immature and horrible costly mistake. How very misguided his help had been.

Rachel had started coming home later and later. When he had asked her, out of concern for her, to please try to be back home by two a.m., she had reacted as if he was stealing her very life. Their relationship had spiraled quickly downward: She simply stopped coming home.

The first incident had worried him, and he was sure Rachael had met with harm. She was so young looking and still so beautiful. He just knew in his heart, she wouldn't desert him and their little boy. When she had staggered home around eight a.m. the next day, he had become afraid. Where had she been? He had also missed a day of work, and they couldn't afford reduced paychecks. He had brought this to her attention, hoping to shed some light into her irresponsible actions. They had had one of what would be the beginning of many screaming matches. He recalled their first fight and could still feel a knot start to tighten in his stomach at the words they had exchanged.

He had gone into their small bedroom with Tony with the best of intentions. He looked so much like Rachel with dark curly hair and big brown eyes. "Hey sleepy girl," he had said, gently sitting on the edge of the bed and leaning over to kiss Rachel awake, "we're so glad you're home." He had deliberately started out on a positive note so she would know he loved her.

"Ken, leave me alone. I'm tired," she had pleaded from the bed.

"Rachel, I'm sorry you're tired, but I need you to get up so I can go to work." He had spoken quietly and with some firmness. Tony had struggled to climb onto Rachel, and Ken had released him from his lap. "Momma," he had gurgled and crawled over her.

"Ken, please, get him off me." She had gently shoved Tony away from her face. "I need fifteen more minutes, that's all."

"Momma," Tony had repeated and crawled back to give his mommy a kiss.

"Ken, *please!*" she had quietly yet angrily forced out, "give me a couple more minutes."

He had taken Tony and risen from the bed, saying, "Okay, but I really need to get going, hon."

"Let's go get some lunch and have a nap, big guy," he had said to Tony as he squirmed to get back to his mommy on the bed.

He had given her more than fifteen minutes. After he had left their bedroom he had called in to work for a second day in a row and explained his wife was sick and he wouldn't be in at all this day either. His supervisor had told him thanks for calling, but he needed to check into childcare if he wanted to keep his job. Ken had fed Tony, put him down for his nap, and gone back in to rouse his hung-over wife.

"Rachel, honey," he had implored to the still sleeping figure on the bed as he had opened the curtains to let the afternoon sun in, "I took the rest of the day off, but we need to talk."

"KEN! Fifteen more minutes is all I want," she had hissed at him.

"It's been an hour, Rachel; it's one o'clock," he had quietly stated as he had sat down next to her.

"What! Oh God," she had moaned from under the sheets, shielding her eyes from the daylight streaming in the window.

"Sweetheart, where have you been? I was so worried about you when you didn't come home yesterday. I even called the police and reported you missing. Why didn't you call?" He had tried to keep calm, but he was afraid of not knowing what was happening to his wife, their relationship, their life.

"God, Ken, lighten up. I'm here." And she had groaned as she had sat up to face him. "Will you please pull the curtains? It's too bright. Where's Tony?" she had asked as she had pushed her dark hair from her worn and tired face.

"I put him down for his nap. We need to talk," Ken had implored softly. "Rachel this can't go on; it's going to ruin us."

"Ruin us," she had snorted out. "Ken, look around. What's to ruin? This is hell. My God, we've got nothing to ruin." And she had rolled back down and over as if to escape what surrounded her.

The pain of her words had brought tears to Ken's eyes. How could she say they had nothing? What of Tony? What of their life? He had taken a slow breath, and belying his pain, he had calmly said, "We have each other and Tony," and added with hope, "we're just getting started; things will get better."

His words had brought her back to a full sitting position, the blankets falling and fully revealing her physical beauty.

His breath had caught in his throat. She was so beautiful, all he had wanted to do was take her in his arms and make her his.

The desire in his eyes had reminded her of the power of her youth and beauty. She wasn't meant to be trapped in what their life had become. Her own eyes had taken on a hard light.

"No, Ken, you're wrong. Things will not get better. I've been stuck here for over a year." Her voice had started to rise, and Ken had reminded her that Tony was sleeping. This small act had sparked her anger. "No, I will not *ssshh*. I am tired of living my life for someone else. What about me? What about what I want? Ken, I'm too young to be tied to…," and searching for words she didn't have, she had made a sweeping arc to the entire room and settled on, "THIS, this nothing! There is no hope here. I want to live, not exist. I don't want to be old and just get by. God, I am so sick of getting by." She had spit out the words and thrown off the covers to get out of bed.

Her full nude figure had almost undone Ken. He hadn't had her for days. Her beauty was stunning, even after having had Tony. He had thought her even more beautiful then—her hips had flared ever so slightly to make her small waist appear even smaller and her breasts had become even more supple. "Oh God," had escaped his lips, and he had forced himself to focus, to save his family. He had turned his head and spoken his words to the light streaming in the window, "But you love Tony. And what about our plans?"

She had surprised him by coming to stand directly in front of him. Taking his chin so she had his full attention, with a firmness she was unaware of and a hardness to her dark eyes, she had acknowledged, "I do love Tony. I just don't love this…this life. I need…," and she had released his chin and turned to the window, "I need freedom." She had said that with conviction and then had added with scorn, "Love! What is love?" The edge of anger had returned to her voice. "I've known and seen love, Ken. Let me fill you in. It's weak and fleeting. Love is conditional, and God, it hurts. I know, Ken, it never lasts. Never!"

She had finished her pronouncement, knowing the past few months of partying had opened her eyes and hardened her heart. She unknowingly had wanted Ken to see as she had seen. She had wanted him to share in the ugliness of life as she had come to see it. The thoughts of what she had been doing the past months almost made her physically ill. The men she had been with, the things she had done—she had pushed these thoughts away, thinking, *God I need a drink.*

She had needed to be with those who were looking for the same things she was. She had gravitated toward others who also found the constant day-to-day struggle to survive tedious but sought to replace it with they knew not what. Disillusioned married men, who could barely keep their families going and had become distanced from their wives, sought solace in youthful girls such as Rachel, plying her with compliments and drinks for favors and understanding they no longer received at home. Other men were wealthy and just wanted someone young and pretty to decorate their arm. In return, she'd receive their affection and expensive trinkets. They craved the admiration of youth to confirm their self-deceptions, pretending they still held youthfulness in themselves. These were the messages she had been inundated with the past few months.

Rachel had concluded that love and dreams were not to be trusted. She would not be as the women all these other men had left at home. Ken may love her now, but she knew he would one day become like these men, and she would not give the best years of her life to a fruit-less struggle of service to others for love and a promise of dreams that were never fulfilled. She had come to believe life was crap, and she would get as much out of it for herself as she could because in the end no one would take care of her but her, no matter how much someone said he loved her. Love only brought disappointment and pain.

Turning his gaze from the light-infused silhouette before him, Ken had tried again. "What if I sign on to the night shift and can be with you during the day? We can do things together like we used to. Or you can even go to school. I can look into financial aid." His attempts at fixing their problems, keeping her happy, going forward with hope, had been met with an anger that had shocked him.

Screaming, "*No!*" she had slapped him. "I will not be pulled. No! I will not be sucked into a fantasy life that never materializes!" She had grabbed her own hair in suffused anger as if to wrench the words he had released into the room and replace them with her own feelings. She wanted him to feel her despair and hate at what their life had become and what she saw as never-ending. She wanted to hurt him as she had felt hurt by what life had dished out. "I will not sit here and let life pass me by," she had screamed. "I am too young. God! I'm only twenty—*twenty!* And all this…," she had moved her hands up and down her body, "all this is not going to waste." In a final effort to break through his rosy view and hope of a wonderful future she had gone to her nightstand. "Here," she had opened the bottom and pulled forth her treasure of gifts. "When will you ever give me *this*?" She had thrown the jeweled bracelets and diamond earrings into his lap, angry at his lack of understanding. "I am going to live! I don't care what you do, but don't try and stop me!" With that she had turned away and rushed into their small bathroom slamming the door on Ken and any words he may have wanted to add.

The sting of the slap, the slam of the door, and the jeweled pieces flung at him had left him speechless. The sound of Tony's wails from the room next door had finally propelled him off the bed. Her words had left him hurt and stunned. Where did all the jewelry come from? Had she stolen it? He couldn't bear the idea she had given pleasure for it, not his Rachael. He would rather she be a thief than…. He couldn't proceed. She was his. Even in her anger, she was a vision of utter beauty.

He had touched his burning cheek and replayed her cruel words. He was at a loss of what to do, how to fix what had become a nightmare. He had left the room.

She had emerged shortly later and told him she was going out and it was none of his business where. When he had asked when she would be home, she had only snorted, turned, and walked out.

From there, their relationship had soured completely. She would refuse to listen to reason and avoided all attempts to talk. Ken had struggled to care for Tony and still desperately tried somehow to reach out to Rachel. The burden had been great, and he was only one person. The fights would start with the slam of their bedroom door when she woke up and then she would leave as soon as she had showered and cleaned up. Nothing was ever resolved.

He had managed to find daycare for Tony, but in time he couldn't afford that. Rachel had stopped coming home except to sneak in and take the little money he soon learned to try and hide from her. Their fights rose to a new level of accusations and physical abuse by Rachel as she had trashed the place searching for money, money he knew they couldn't afford for her to spend on frivolities. Their frightened neighbors had reported the young family to Social Services, and Tony had been removed and given to her parents.

The loss of Tony had been devastating. He had ached so over the loss of his son. Without his son and only a ghost of a wife, Ken soon found he had no will or reason to go to his mundane job, so he stopped working. Upon the loss of his job, he lost his lease to "their" apartment. He scoffed at the word, "their." When "their" had evaporated, so had his life. Everything that had meant anything to him was gone. The life he and Rachel had once dreamed of had turned into a hellish nightmare with no solution. Ken had become homeless and hopeless, filled with despair and nowhere to turn for help. His own mother had stood by her husband, who had told Ken that to marry the girl would only add to his first mistake of getting her pregnant. If he went through with his plans to marry her, then he was man enough to be on his own.

When it seemed he had been at the end, he had run into Bruce, a friend of sorts who had some knowledge of living on the edge. Bruce had been in trouble all his young life. He was a couple years older than

Ken and street-wise in the ways of small-time dope and petty crime. He had offered Ken a place to lay his head and promised to help him find Rachel, who had seemed to have disappeared into the nightlife after Ken had lost his job and had no more money for her to come and take.

Ken had welcomed Bruce's help. He had felt if he could just spend some time with Rachel on her terms, they could start over. He was hoping, through his friend's contacts, he could find her. What else was he to do? He still loved her. He reasoned they could get Tony back after they got back on their feet. He was sure he could make her see reason once he had nothing else but Rachel to focus on.

He had soon learned the truth about his old high school acquaintance. Bruce had just been looking for someone to help advance his own chosen path. Bruce's lifestyle hadn't been enough, and he was stepping into the world of drug running and trying to set up his own operation of sorts. Money had always been Bruce's goal. He now needed more than what pick-pocketing and the small change from snatch-and-grab street crime could bring in. His plans literally frightened Ken. Yet, he had nowhere else to turn. He had needed to find Rachel. He had stayed with Bruce, and he had slowly been sucked into the shadowy life of crime.

He wouldn't have recognized himself in the two years since he had slid into the other side. He had no steady job, no responsibility, and no hope. He had even given up looking for Rachel and forced himself to stop caring about future custody of Tony. He had simply stopped living. Ken had been existing, just following, and he hadn't even known why, and even sadder, he hadn't cared.

When Bruce had suggested robbing the bank, Ken had clutched at the promise of a new beginning where maybe he could break out of the misery that had become his existence, and he had agreed to participate. He had had a bad feeling about the whole thing, but what else was he to do? He had had no other choice. He had had nothing to lose. Everything he had he had already lost.

This was when God had stepped in, and Ken, knowing this now, sent up a small litany of thanks.

How life had turned, Ken marveled. There was that young woman God had placed in the bank that early morning so many years back. She had so shocked him with her words of hope, her idea of the way out, almost two years ago. It still made him laugh in nervous disbelief she had had the nerve to speak up with words so insane.

He knew, now, her assistance had come from God. No person could act in a manner as she so willingly had without Him. He remembered vividly thinking when she had offered a way out that she had meant another physical way out the bank. His soul, on the other hand, had heard and knew she was offering a way out of his desperate hopelessness. The small light of her salvation had shined out into the darkness that had enveloped him. It had glimmered so that he had incredulously listened to her offer.

He had let the other hostages go, keeping her. In the end, this act had spared his physical life here and led to his eternal salvation in the hereafter. He had allowed that small glimmer of light into the wasted desert that had become his soul. The rest was the grace of God's salvation. Oh, what a miracle was wrought that day in the bank. The words she had so softly dared to offer had penetrated the shell of hopelessness encasing his soul. The words they had shared during his greatest hour of despair had cracked the shell. The caring human he had once been realized he didn't have to accept the situation he was in. Yes, he knew his life had been a mess of seemingly endless mistakes. He admitted he had made some very bad choices, but it could all be changed if…if he would just believe and accept the struggle to change that lay ahead.

Like a drowning man, he had said yes while inside he had screamed it. He was so very tired of living a life of nothing. He knew there could be more; there had to be. He really did want life to be more. Oh God, how he had wanted life to be more than it was revealing itself to be, wants that could never be realized.

Through the tears, she had convinced him to accept his earthly punishment and know that he was not alone. His life would be forever different with his acceptance of the Lord Jesus Christ into his life. She had assured him his life would not be easy.

JOHN 15:18-20 "If the world hates you, keep in mind that it hated me first. If you belonged to the world, it would love you as its own. As it is, you do not belong to the world, but I have chosen you out of the world. That is why the world hates you. Remember the words I spoke to you: 'No servant is greater than his master.' If they persecuted me, they will persecute you also. If they obeyed my teaching, they will obey yours also."

This incredible woman had also shared the promise Jesus Christ gave to those who accepted salvation and forgiveness through him. She had told him he would never be alone in his struggle to follow Jesus Christ, to give his life to God. The Holy Spirit would come to him, she had told him, and be present in him to change and use him for service to God, to be what God had created him to be. He would now be a servant for the Lord Jesus Christ for the greater glory of the one true living God. He would no longer serve the world but the Lord Jesus Christ, the Son of the living God.

JOHN 15:26-27 "When the Counselor comes, whom I will send to you from the Father, the Spirit of truth who goes out from the Father, he will testify about me. And you also must testify, for you have been with me from the beginning."

After this revelation and his acceptance of salvation, they had approached the bank doors together so he could turn himself over to the officers waiting outside the bank. Ken remembered the world had made a last ditch attempt to pull him back: Fear had caught him, and he had hesitated. God knew and had sent that miracle of a young lady simply to take hold of his hand. That one small gesture of human concern had been enough to propel him into the unknown, his very personal, truly faith-filled walk with God. And what a walk it was turning out to be.

The minute they had exited the bank, the officers had had him on the ground. With only moments left, she had managed to tell him, before she was hustled away, to have faith and trust in God's promises in Jesus Christ. He had vowed to himself to be as brave as he personally knew she had been.

✳

The past two years had not been easy. His new faith was tested and tried, questioned and taunted. In the environment he had been placed, he was mocked relentlessly. Salvation was looked at as an easy way to parole. Ken had remained steadfast in his beliefs. He would not forget the only other option to not believing and accepting salvation.

The other option would be forever burned into his memory, the utter sense of despair, no meaning, nothing to live life for. He would not forget the true emptiness of this world without Christ in his life. The endless wanting and the glaring injustices were pains he never wanted to suffer alone. Ken joined the prison's Bible study group, and his joy at salvation and the gift he had received lifted him up in his moments of despair at where he was. He often contemplated, once knowing Christ, how anyone could ever choose to remain on such a road or go back to the world, rejecting Christ. With his conviction, his faith blossomed, and the Holy Spirit grew within. Not all in the group shared his conviction; some attended only to receive an early release. Dariel, a young man in for possession, dealing, and second-degree manslaughter, would often laugh at Ken's eagerness to learn more and ask so many questions.

"Ya gonna get outta here an' be one a those TV reverend crooks? 'Look at me! I was a bank robber, but I been saved. Yessir. Jeeezus done saved me, and he can save you, too. Just send me yo money, and Jeeezus gonna save you too.'" Dariel would taunt and elaborate the "Jesus."

The leader of the group, Ray, would only shake his head and look at Ken reassuringly to continue his questions. "Dariel, you don't have to be here." Ray would offer him the chance to leave the group.

"Ya'll're too much fun. Plus ya jus' never know; maybe I be saved yet, huh, Ken?"

Ken could only feel sorrow for Dariel. He sat in and got credit for attending, but at the moment he was blind. Maybe one day, as he suggested, he too would see. One could only hope.

He remembered how he had once been among those who had scoffed at people who, when asked what their favorite book was, had responded, "The Bible." He used to think this was some major brown-nosing. Having accepted salvation and seen the light, now the Bible was his favorite book. He understood. The Bible had truly come to life for him. Ken had come to see it was God's encrypted code for those of us here to serve him in a world where we don't belong so we could be of full service to His Son, the Lord Jesus Christ. He loved his Bible. It spoke to him in different ways every time he read it. When he reread the same passage, it was as if he was reading the words for the first time. Ken knew not everyone who read the Bible saw the light within, and Dariel and others ridiculed him for believing it was God's Word. Yet he also knew they were still blinded and their hearts not ready to see and accept.

Ken saw how God presented His Word to others in odd ways, not always directly or through the Bible. He recalled watching the movie *The Never-Ending Story* with, oddly enough, Bruce. They had been killing time, and Bruce had popped in the video. At the time Ken thought it was quite a scary video for little kids, but now looking back, he saw that it was designed to teach kids to believe. When the characters in the story stopped believing, everything was lost to the "nothing." In the end when everything was almost gone because all had stopped believing, the main character had been told just to say the name, the one name that mattered. And in the final moment, the main character shouted the name, and a tiny light came into the enveloping darkness of the "nothing" to overcome the emptiness. That one spark brought further belief that restored the whole of the community and the world of the characters. The more they believed in the name spoken, the more that came into being. Ken now saw that this was parallel to the Bible.

This revelation—that God could work so incredulously in all walks of life—humbled Ken, and he gave himself fully to God's service. The more Ken said yes to God, the more he was used as a servant of salvation, the Lord Jesus Christ. He did have days of sorrow. There were also days of such great joy, hope, and peace and the ultimate comfort of knowing this life wasn't the real life. His days here were only temporary, the length of which were determined by the loving God that had created him.

It was the knowledge that one day, a day of God's choosing, he, Ken, would be going home to God's perfect love that filled him with joy. His time here would be done, just like his time in prison. We are all captive here in this life for only a short time in the all of eternity. He knew he would get to go home to the perfect love of his Creator. To know this gave him peace and happiness, and it sustained him in trying times.

In the two years he spent incarcerated, he was never more shocked than when he found himself thinking he was making progress, feeling he was gaining wisdom and understanding of the Lord, only to be gently reminded how small he was. Life wasn't about him; it was about God. In these moments, he would find himself back to square one, a small child seeing the error of his understanding, and feeling the awe and the greatness, once again, marveling at the depth of the Almighty.

ISAIAH 55:8-9 "For my thoughts are not your thoughts, neither are your ways my ways," declares the Lord. "As the heavens are higher than the earth, so are my ways higher than your ways and my thoughts than your thoughts."

He had come to find this passage so very, very true, and it gave him comfort in God's great power and omnipotence. It humbled him and gave him the sense of security to know he could call this One True God, the God of Abraham, the God of Isaac, and the God of Jacob, his God. To belong to this Supreme Being, to be in a relationship and worship One so great, he was truly a blessed man.

He saw a new meaning to the words "Give us today our daily bread." His soul needed the Word of God to grow in the ways of God. He did not have to understand how the Spirit of God within him grew. He did not understand fully how our physical bodies grew from eating food, yet he ate. Likewise, he did not know how his soul flourished from devouring the nurturing words of the Creator in the Bible, but it did so he read.

He came to know the importance of starting his day with a prayer to keep him in the ways of the Lord and to end his day the same way. He now felt the agony the Lord surely must have felt at leaving the apostles here without him. Ken knew he would be lost without the nourishment of the Word. There were days when he would be over-excited in his enthusiasm for Christ. He would have to remember that he needed to slow down and let the Lord do the work. Instead of running ahead and shining the light of salvation into the blinding dark, he needed to let the spirit go where God commanded, not where he, Ken, wanted it. He knew why the Holy Spirit had to come. Jesus had promised a helper would be here. Through this Helper, more and greater would be done in the very name of the Lord Jesus Christ by those who believed and accepted, for the greater glory of the One who is, was, and always will be.

> JOHN 14:11-17 "Believe me when I say that I am in the Father and the Father is in me; or at least believe on the evidence of the miracles themselves. I tell you the truth, anyone who has faith in me will do what I have been doing. He will do even greater things than these, because I am going to the Father. And I will do whatever you ask in my name, so that the Son may bring glory to the Father. You may ask me for anything in my name, and I will do it. If you love me, you will obey what I command. And I will ask the Father, and he will give you another Counselor to be with you forever—the Spirit of truth. The world cannot accept him, because it neither sees him nor knows him. But you know him, for he lives with you and will be in you."

It became a comfort to Ken. To those who accepted the Lord Jesus Christ as the only son of the living God, the Holy Spirit—God himself—would be given as a helper. If they truly believed and accepted the death and precious sacrificial blood of the Lamb of God, the Lord Jesus Christ, as forgiveness for all their sins, they would be born again children of God.

God's very presence, in the form of the Holy Spirit, would come and reside in them just as the Lord Jesus Christ said, "I am in the Father, and the Father is in me, and, we are one." Ken tried to explain to some who came to him for understanding that to pray in Jesus' name was the password of sorts that gives us access to God, just as someone must have a password to use a computer. Yet God in his great wisdom knew there would be instances of abuse, so He also states over and over again that He knows the desires of our hearts. Unlike a computer where passwords can be stolen, giving unauthorized access, when one prays in Jesus' name, God searches the heart of the implorer—Is this a follower of the Lord Jesus Christ, a server for the Lord, seeking to serve God's will for the glory of the Almighty God? It is the only way to the Father, through the Son, and the Holy Spirit serves the will of the Almighty, answering prayers according to His will and in His ways. No one can deceive the Almighty.

MATTHEW 9:35-38 Jesus went through all the towns and villages, teaching in their synagogues, preaching the good news of the kingdom and healing every disease and sickness. When he saw the crowds, he had compassion on them, because they were harassed and helpless, like sheep without a shepherd. Then he said to his disciples, "The harvest is plentiful but the workers are few. Ask the Lord of the harvest, therefore, to send out workers into his harvest field."

Sadly, Ken came to know the hard part of accepting God in his life was giving total control to God. At times he caused himself much sadness and stress when he tried to force the love of Christ on an individual who wasn't ready to receive. He found he was more at peace when he allowed God to use him for what He had designed him to do for His greater glory. He tried to be like a small child who is well cared for and doesn't worry about tomorrow or what will happen. He reminded himself how children trust in loving parents to provide for all their needs and take care of all the details of the day just as it is with God if we believe and accept his love as little children. God's Word tells us, with God in us and in control of our life, no eternal harm will ever befall us. God does not and cannot fail.

MATTHEW 18:2-4 He called a little child and had him stand among them. And he said: "I tell you the truth, unless you change and become like little children, you will never enter the kingdom of heaven. Therefore, whoever humbles himself like this child is the greatest in the kingdom of heaven."

Ken understood this, and the shackles of the earth fell from him. Free of worldly worries, he was so joyously grateful. Although he stumbled from time to time when the darkness of this world closed in, he always had the Word of God and the guidance of the Holy Spirit to bring him back.

Ken had come to the full realization that this world was not the world God had made for us. The world we reside in was not where God first put Adam and Eve. Fallen humanity, through its actions, has molded this world with a limited understanding of knowledge, wrongly and disobediently taken in that bite of fruit from the Tree of the Knowledge of Good and Evil. Through Adam and Eve, we were sentenced to a life of captivity and now choose our master. Will we serve the world, or will we serve God through Jesus Christ? Either we live with Him and His love eternally if we have seen and accepted The Way, or we live eternally in darkness, despair, suffering, and agony without His love. The choice is ours. This world is but a taste of eternity for God's love is here through His Son as are the horrors and agonies of eternity without God in the injustices of what humanity can and does allow to be done to each other through self-serving power and greed.

Ken had come to see earthly existence as a prison sentence of sorts and eternal life as the end of captivity. He felt once a person had accepted salvation, the life of captivity here was more bearable, only a short sentence compared to everlasting oneness with God.

Knowing this world with all its injustice and unfairness was not permanent gave Ken such liberation. Through this understanding, he saw God's work in nature and the innocence of youth; he learned to enjoy the small things and refused to be spiritually overwhelmed by the power the elite of this world thought they had. For there was nothing between himself and God but himself, and he could more easily give over the nothing he knew himself to be to the One who values him the most, the One who created him for the glory of the Creator. In humbly doing so, he who was nothing now became one with the Creator, and he glorified the Creator in all he has now become as the Creator resided anew in him in the Holy Spirit.

But Ken's path didn't follow a straight line; it had twists and turns. Sometimes he forgot who he had put in charge of his life. He would make decisions based on his human needs, living by his own guidance. But he would recover, and these falls only helped draw him closer to his Lord. He realized he needed Jesus Christ, not man, to lead his life in the paths of the righteousness of God.

People and situations still angered him at times, and he felt great sorrow for suffering and injustice. These feelings made him wonder at the great loving kindness of the One who created all and gave His only Son to them, for the very same who would reject Him so vehemently. God was surely unimaginable and incomprehensible to the puny human mind.

He felt great sorrow for the many who deluded themselves with their own imagined greatness. *To him who has everything, he has nothing,* he often thought. For all he has can be lost, and upon physical death, he who thought he was, is nothing for all eternity; he holds nothing but the agony of knowing he never came to accept the truth and know the Son, the Savior. Those who grasped worldly pleasures had the greater struggle in letting go of the world's dark and deadly charms and finding peace in God.

Ken was ever mindful that he was only an instrument of the One who had made him. And he derived great happiness serving One so powerful and omnipotent as the One true Living God. To be one with the Most High God through His only Son gave life its meaning and made it interesting. For Ken had come to know that it was not his strength that defeated the temptations of this world, it was not his strength that gave him the courage to start each morning on bended knee in prayer, and it was definitely not his strength that set him forth every day with peace; it was the strength of the Spirit of God within him. To this power, Ken willingly gave himself over each and every day, reminding himself he was but a witness to the victor within, the risen Lord Jesus Christ. He saw the revelations of each new day and wondered how God would use him—and if he would even be aware of God's will working through his human form.

The new Ken had accepted God's Word like a drowning man desperate for salvation. He gave himself passionately to whatever work the Lord Jesus Christ had chosen for him. This was the Ken that Joe met during his prison sentence.

Chapter Ten

Joe

That morning in July started as all others, mundane. Yet one small incident would trigger an avalanche of changes inside Joe, erupting into the beginning of a new life, a scraping away of a lifetime of well-intended and devoutly believed but wholly misguided rituals of love for God.

Joe went about his janitorial chores, cleaning the showers and shared living areas. All inmates took jobs in preparation for their reintroduction into society, and Joe had chosen maintenance and janitorial service for his training, shunning his education and showing no interest in associating with people. His work suited him fine—cleaning public filth, a perfect punishment if he ever reentered life. He would deny himself all pleasure.

Joe started his day checking the stools and sinks for objects jammed into them. It surprised him to find nothing as, invariably, an upset inmate usually took this avenue to vent frustration. His next surprise came from the closet that held the mops and buckets. He stopped short when the sound of soft whistling from the closet's interior came to his attention. "Amazing Grace"? Who could be in the closet—and singing that? And who was usurping his position? This was his assignment and a solitary one; he wanted no help.

Before he could enter the wash closet, out a man came, who looked to be close to thirty-odd years. Something different about the man snagged Joe's dying interest in human life. The man himself seemed disinterested in all but what he was doing. Even more, the man seemed so at peace. He showed no tension and no wariness. Prison made everyone alert all the time of all around them. Joe had been warned upon entering never to let down his guard, and his constant awareness became second nature, just as it did for his fellow inmates. Such watchfulness was part of prison survival; it helped to avoid skirmishes, minor as well as dangerous, that were a part of incarcerated life. In all his time in prison, he hadn't witnessed such an event but he had not discarded the advice offered.

This man emanated such lack of concern that it caused innate worry to resurface from deep within Joe. The man looked Joe squarely in the eye and offered Joe a polite, "Pardon me; I've a floor to mop." With that, the man continued slowly moving the wheeled bucket in the direction of the faucet to fill it with water. The seemingly open innocence made Joe wonder if the man was a little deficient in his mental facilities. If this was the case, he could truly be in danger here. His concern deepened, and he turned to educate the newcomer on the perils of his way. Not having spoken to anyone without first addressing them, Joe fell back into his long-forgotten, polite ways.

"Excuse me, sir." Joe reached out to halt the man. "Are you new here?"

Ken had started his day like all others since he had received salvation. He would roll out of his prison bed and fall upon bended knee in reverence to the One True Living God and quietly speak the words of the Lord's Prayer and the 23rd Psalm. These gave him moral strength to get through another day of captivity in his earthly sentence and reminded him to see the little blessings and subtle pleasures in the day ahead. The Heavenly Father's gifts were numerous if one only believed. God was everywhere, and His love often showed in the most insignificant daily occurrences. Awareness of God's presence made Ken's time on earth, in any given situation, even within prison walls, a blessing.

Ken, especially, leaned on the messages of the prayers to shore him up against the constantly blaring television, inescapable in his current environment. He could change the channel, but the impact remained the same: Programming promoting the emptiness of the world, news displaying the cruelty of the human situation, and advertisements pushing empty wares bombarded his soul. Power and greed gave a false promise of happiness, and he knew that this world could never offer enough to fill his—or anyone's—aching void for the love of the heavenly Father.

ECCLESIASTES 1:2-11 "Meaningless! Meaningless!" says the Teacher.

"Utterly meaningless! Everything is meaningless."

What does man gain from all his labor at which he toils under the sun?

Generations come and generations go, but the earth remains forever.

The sun rises and the sun sets, and hurries back to where it rises.

The wind blows to the south and turns to the north; round and round it goes, ever returning on its course.

All streams flow into the sea, yet the sea is never full.

To the place the streams come from, there they return again.

All things are wearisome, more than one can say.

The eye never has enough of seeing, nor the ear its fill of hearing.

What has been will be again, what has been done will be done again; there is nothing new under the sun.

Is there anything of which one can say, "Look! This is something new"?

It was here already, long ago; it was here before our time.

There is no remembrance of men of old, and even those who are yet to come will not be remembered by those who follow.

Everything is nothing; we live, we die, mused Ken. All around him he saw many who understood this stark reality but hid from it in addictions to drugs, alcohol, sex, money, and power. They saw but part of the picture, the emptiness of this life, and remained blind to God Who fills the void.

Illusion of Permance

Dearest Creator, with power infinite and wisdom profound,
I do not understand though I contemplate and have faith.
The sky, so blue and beautiful above, has been forever,
since you first set the beginning of time.

But we, people of the dust, come and go
with no power, as countless as the blades of grass.
We struggle and learn, build and work,
for a permanence that is only an illusion,
of our ignorance of the whole of You, the Almighty.

Nothing is forever, not buildings or mountains,
struggles or life. Why then, are we so
caught with meaningless, mundane illusions; houses,
cars, jobs, even the scope of an individual's life?
All that we are, were, or ever hope to be
can be gone in one blink of the Almighty so powerful.
What would you have us to do, in the here and now, that
is the present, to truly capture the illusion of permanence?

If only they would accept the truth and reject the world and its fatal charms, he thought, and humbly go to the foot of the cross to the Lord Jesus Christ, asking forgiveness for all they did and trusting forgiveness is theirs. For many, he sadly knew, to accept what cannot be seen would be impossible. So he had read in scripture:

MATTHEW 19:23-26 Then Jesus said to his disciples, "I tell you the truth, it is hard for a rich man to enter the kingdom of heaven. Again I tell you, it is easier for a camel to go through the eye of a needle than for a rich man to enter the kingdom of God." When the disciples heard this, they were greatly astonished and asked, "Who then can be saved?" Jesus looked at them and said, "With man this is impossible, but with God all things are possible."

Ken's eyes had opened to the truth, the knowledge of the Lord Jesus Christ, and his life became tolerable, even a blessing, and he experienced true joy. He sighed, thinking of the many who remained lost in the darkness, unable to see the way out to eternal life through the Lord Jesus Christ. As one who had received the Word, Ken stood in the world like a beacon of light, an extension of God's love shining into the sin-filled world of humanity.

With the touch of Joe's hand to his shoulder, Ken turned back and said, "Excuse me?"

The returned courtesy threw Joe for another loop. "Excuse me?" was not the type of question asked in the prison. Was this guy suicidal?

"Actually I wanted to help you. You need to be a little more on guard in your surroundings. In a place like this, you can't be too careful," Joe stated with more concern than he had felt in years for another person. For the first time in a long time, he felt himself wondering what one of the inmates had done to be here.

"Thank you. I'll remember," Ken replied, sensing this man's awkward concern. "By the way, I'm Ken. Nice to meet you." And he extended his hand in greeting.

Joe shook his head at the courtesy but shared the handshake out of habit, as two people would who had been introduced in more normal settings and not behind bars. The absurd situation brought a small laugh from Joe. He couldn't believe what was happening. Who was this person?

"I'm Joe," automatically fell from his lips, followed unhesitatingly by, "Nice to meet you." *Nice to meet you! Oh, my gosh! Am I dreaming?* The unreality of normal human—humane—behavior in a place that expected hostility, suspicion, and self-defense unnerved him. Joe, despite his growing curiosity, abruptly left the young man and headed into the closet to remove himself from—from what?—living?

Ken had expected rudeness to his politeness, and he sent a small prayer heavenward and continued on to fill up the bucket. The fissure of salvation had started. God would have His way. His great and glorious will be done. Hallelujah, all praise to God in His subtleties.

From that July day forward, Ken continued to be an intriguing part of Joe's day. Over the course of months, Joe and Ken would talk from time to time. It never ceased to amaze Joe how their conversation would turn to the big picture of life and what was it all for. Ken shared his insights, bringing sense to Joe's inner turmoil, and comforted him. Joe had felt so alone in his quest, and here, of all places, was one who had searched as had he. Their conversations were always interesting and never hostile. It was obvious to Joe that Ken was one of those "born again" individuals he had heard about. Every question Joe brought up for discourse, Ken showed him the truths and always pointed to the Bible for his answers. The guy seemed to literally live in his Bible. Ken wasn't pushy, just really happy and absorbed with Jesus. He seemed so sure of his salvation.

At times Joe was angry about Ken's absolute certainty that when he died he would go right to heaven. How could anyone know, really know, he was heaven bound? He knew from his past studies all would be judged in the end. He believed only then would the outcome be determined and not a moment before. The religious instruction he had received taught only God knew who would be with Him and that was after individual judgment. Ken's assuredness of no further penance for a life of earthly mistakes and immediate reception into heaven upon death maddened Joe.

Ken was not to be swayed from his view. Joe had many years of schooling to back up his own arguments, but Ken had his Bible. He would politely listen to Joe's sound reasoning and then gently offer in rebuttal a passage from scripture. His favorite passage came from John in the New Testament.

> JOHN 3:3-18 In reply Jesus declared, "I tell you the truth, no one can see the kingdom of God unless he is born again."
>
> "How can a man be born when he is old?" Nicodemus asked. "Surely he cannot enter a second time into his mother's womb to be born!"
>
> Jesus answered, "I tell you the truth, no one can enter the kingdom of God unless he is born of water and the Spirit. Flesh gives birth to flesh, but the Spirit gives birth to spirit. You should not be surprised at my saying, 'You must be born again.' The wind blows wherever it pleases. You hear its sound, but you cannot tell where it comes from or where it is going. So it is with everyone born of the Spirit."
>
> "How can this be?" Nicodemus asked.
>
> "You are Israel's teacher," said Jesus, "and do you not understand these things? I tell you the truth, we speak of what we know, and we testify to what we have seen, but still you people do not accept our testimony. I have spoken to you of earthly things and you do not believe; how then will you believe if I speak of heavenly things? No one has ever gone into heaven except the one who came from heaven—the Son of Man. Just as Moses lifted up the snake in the desert, so the Son of Man must be lifted up, that everyone who believes in him may have eternal life.
>
> "For God so loved the world that he gave his one and only Son, that whoever believes in him shall not perish but have eternal life. For God did not send his Son into the world to condemn the world, but to save the world through him. Whoever believes in him is not condemned, but whoever

does not believe stands condemned already because he has not believed in the name of God's one and only Son.

Nothing would turn Ken from what Joe viewed as a misconception. Some days when Joe felt the enormity of the time he would spend in purgatory in his own eternal destiny, he would find himself so angry at Ken's simple view and his belief in "escaping" punishment. Ken offered others in history past who shared his outlook. Joe was equally angered by—and envied—their steadfast faith in entering heaven upon death. He envied them their belief, but he didn't buy it.

"I've read *The Hiding Place*," Joe shot back at Ken. "How do you extend your belief in a direct route to heaven from its text?"

"It is the faith that Betsie had in the love her Savior had for her that allowed her to be of such quiet and steadfast use during one of the darkest hours in human history. Jesus promised life eternal if we only believe. He didn't anywhere say we would have to spend time in punishment for the wretchedness of our human condition. He knew our wretchedness, and He offered Himself for forgiveness for what we are so that we can have eternal life and love with Him."

Ken continued, "In *Uncle Tom's Cabin*, Uncle Tom was uneducated but understood the love the Savior had for him when He offered Himself as punishment for who he, Uncle Tom was, just a slave. Uncle Tom was filled with simple joy at the knowledge that he was so deeply loved by the Lord Jesus Christ. He only wanted others to know and share the joy of the Savior's love. This knowledge made him a joyous and willing servant. Uncle Tom, too, knew he would one day be free of this world, that upon death his suffering would end, and he would live eternally with his Savior. It may only be a story, but Uncle Tom's love and ability to forgive all those who mistreated him was the work and love of the Spirit of God Himself. That book opened my eyes to the depth of servitude I wanted for myself." Ken's eyes were alight with the fire of the Spirit that moved within.

"But," Joe came back, "it's just a work of fiction. There's no rational for immediate entry to heaven in a work of fiction. You can hardly use that as support for your belief."

"Isn't it true that most works of fiction are written from pieces and events of the life of the writer?"

Joe could only nod, for there was some truth to Ken's statement. But this only made him that much more unsettled. It truly disturbed him that others firmly held to such a simple belief. How could they believe something so preposterous? And why did they? Joe so wanted understanding. He groaned inwardly. God, he so wanted to see. Why was his struggle so hard? His mind was torn with all he had learned. *His* arguments made perfect sense, and Ken's just boiled down to simply believing. *Oh God, please.* The intellectual argument so tired him. Did it never end?

MATTHEW 7:7-11 "Ask and it will be given to you; seek and you will find; knock and the door will be opened to you. For everyone who asks receives; he who seeks finds; and to him who knocks, the door will be opened. Which of you, if his son asks for bread, will give him a stone? Or if he asks for a fish, will give him a snake? If you, then, though you are evil, know how to give good gifts to your children, how much more will your Father in heaven give good gifts to those who ask him!"

In the evidence of all his learning, no one went straight to heaven, except martyrs. Everyone else spent some time in purgatory to do penance for sins not yet confessed. No one was pure enough to join God immediately without atonement. His discussions with Ken would leave him so spiritually saddened and in despair at the thought that some people could feel such misguided hope. He now understood why Ken seemed so happy and at peace. He had a get-out-of-jail-free card.

Joe's seminary studies had covered theology, religious doctrine, psychology, and history, among others. Likewise, the study of the Bible came under the most careful tutelage of scholars who knew scripture. A person didn't venture into the Word of God without the guidance of theologians of Catholicism. That a layperson such as Ken knew the locations in the Bible of the answers to most every question Joe asked—and searched the book when he didn't know—amazed Joe.

In all this discourse, what Joe didn't see was his reintroduction into humanity. His quest for understanding spiritual issues connected to an interest in Ken and that, in turn, joined him to all mankind and set him on the path back into the living.

Shortly before his release from prison, Joe was finally blessed with understanding. Joe, who always relied on his intellect, finally went beyond "reason" and saw with open eyes and received.

Ken always beat Joe to the utility closet as he rose very early every-day to allow time to read God's Word. Ken truly loved the spiritual nutrition for it prepared him for his day in a world in which he did not belong. Throughout his day when the world would clamor loudly its grossness of the condition of humanity, Ken would remember the victorious love of God within him and let God be his steward. He was just an observer, a joyful witness, of God in action through his physical body.

Ken was busy when Joe approached him, and Ken turned to greet him. "Good morning, Joe. Did you sleep well?"

Always the same. Joe smiled tiredly at Ken's enthusiasm of life, and with a heaviness of soul exhaled, "No, Ken, it was just another one of those sleepless nights."

"They can be long, especially in here," Ken agreed compassionately. "When I was younger...," he smiled, for he was obviously younger than Joe, "on nights I couldn't sleep, I'd quietly get up and go outside. It used to amaze me how dark the night could be when the moon wasn't full. You could almost feel the depth and softness of the dark. It made me glad God had created the moon and the stars." He smiled at the memory. "I never minded not being able to sleep then. When I have those nights in here, I try to go back to that memory. It brings me peace, knowing God knew we needed light even in the dark of night when we should be resting. He knew some of us would be up, seeking, and He would be there for us in the dark, to see Him in the glory of the moon and the stars."

"You know, I have God in my life, too," Joe insisted. "But just what is it that you live God right here?" and Joe thumped his breastbone loudly and painfully for emphasis, almost angrily exasperated by Ken's personal absorption of his Lord, "every moment of everyday."

Ken looked at Joe with quiet compassion and answered, "We are all called by the Lord Jesus who is our good shepherd. I once was so desperately lost. When I finally heard the Lord's call for me...." Ken's voice broke at the remembered moment of his own salvation, and Joe stirred nervously, embarrassed to have brought such emotion to this young man. Ken struggled and regained his composure, his eyes intense with the passion of renewed joy, and he continued, "I clung like the dying man I was. I don't ever want to go back into such darkness, such hopelessness. I am so thankful for the eternal love that is forever mine. How can I not let that love into every aspect of my life? That is who I am. By myself, I was miserable and nothing. With the Lord Jesus Christ in control of my life and the power of the Spirit of the living God in me, I am everything in His love. He in me and I in Him. There is no other way."

At last, Ken's words had penetrated the man's defenses. Joe finally understood. So desperately had he sought clarity that once received, emotions flooded his very soul. Joe wept in recognition, in relief, in utter joy. He saw, now, because he truly wanted to see the truth. What he had been taught over the years no longer mattered; he didn't need to hold onto the doctrines anymore, and in his willingness to let go, he had received the Word. What a revelation! What a simple truth! Through his choice in what to believe, he had been condemning himself to an eternity in purgatory. He had been choosing to believe what he had been taught. Now he chose to accept and believe the truth, and he, too, would have what Ken had, the peace of God. Joe would be born again, a child of God this time, not of man, and he would have the Lord Jesus Christ as his savior. The simplicity floored him.

The acceptance of God's infinite love for him sent him into uncontrollable weeping. He was so very grateful for the gift Jesus Christ had given him, Joe, the murderer. All the conversations he had had with Ken came back in waves and washed him in new understanding. Joe now knew true forgiveness in the Lord Jesus Christ. There was no undoing the pain, the suffering, and the loss he had caused. There was no length of punishment he could do to make his error right. Joe accepted now that Jesus had suffered his punishment for him.

Ken had turned and left him, but Joe was not alone; he was in the arms of his Savior, simultaneously feeling sorrow for the wretch he was and freedom under the forgiveness God gave. He wept alone and yet in the fullness and comfort of the Spirit of God.

Joe tried, later, to thank Ken, but he would have none of it. Ken told him the thanks was not his but God's. He assured Joe that he was merely a vehicle through which the will of God was done.

Shortly thereafter, Joe carried his profound understanding past the walls of the prison to his new life on the outside.

Joe had found the path to peace; he now possessed the under-standing he had so desperately sought. No magic number of prayers or acts of goodness could ever compensate for the mistakes he had made. Suffering in the purgatory of his Church existed only in his mind, and that he no longer accepted. He, too, could go to heaven upon death because he had become a child of God. Joe accepted God's love in His only Son the Lord Jesus Christ, who had freed him from the penalty of his sins as he had hung on the cross. Through Jesus Christ, Joe was now born again, a child of God. Basking in the image of an eternity of love, Joe felt as a new person.

Ken knew Joe had accepted salvation. The glorious light on his face had given his transformation away. Joe's grief at the realization of his own previous choice of condemnation and his new insight of the depth of God's love and the true gift of eternal forgiveness had awed Ken to see grace in action.

Ken also knew the road ahead for Joe would not be easy. Salvation was a walk, and Joe would fall and stumble in his rebirth in Christ. Ken would pray for him fervently, but he knew Joe would not be alone. The Holy Spirit would be with him, continuing the work of the God of Abraham, the God of Isaac, and the God of Jacob. *How great thou art. Indeed*, thought Ken, *God is truly great.*

Chapter Eleven

Jennifer

Jennifer drove down the unfamiliar street trying to read the addresses and keep her car in the correct lane without hitting anyone in the process. The neighborhood was not the best, and she was watchful of unexpected little ones left to look after themselves. Areas like these always made her thankful for her own life. She had never felt she was rich, but when she drove in neighborhoods such as these, she felt immensely blessed and well off.

She had come in search of the women's shelter to drop off donations. After several nights of soul searching and honest reflection, she had decided to move back to the hometown she had left so many years ago. Her life had been full of so many unexpected ups and down that she was tired of toughing it out alone and wanted the support of the community she had known growing up. She didn't care anymore about being free or whatever she had thought she had needed back when she was eighteen. She had decided in the dark of her bedroom last night that life was life—here, there, it didn't matter where, life went on. She just wanted to be with those who knew her. She had lain in the darkness and let her loneliness out. God, it was so overwhelming. She was lonely, and in her loneliness she had acted so wrongly all these years. Oh God, she was such a horrible mess. All this time, she had searched, not knowing for what, and now she realized that she had only ever wanted family, her family. They could not be taken from her.

These past years she had sought comfort in flesh and had been an active partner in the destruction of the one thing she innately longed for and found she valued more than anything—family. She was thankful for the darkness of her room, for when the thought came, shame for her hurtful actions filled her with such sorrow. Yet out of the truth revealed arose plans to follow on what she truly wanted.

With her own daughter now eighteen and planning on attending the local college in the fall and living her own life, Jennifer had found the courage to face her fears. She had decided she, too, would start over again—again. Had it been that many years? *Oh God, how had life slipped by?* She drew a breath and resolved this time she would do as she wanted; the rest of her life was hers, no others to consider. She would be strong.

Jennifer had accepted her father's pronouncement all those years. Yet that had been her choice. He could say what he wanted, but she would no longer accept it. She did not have to. Why had she? She had been such a fool. Where was her strength? She had been so busy trying to be the perfect daughter, she had just done as her father had told her—go, stay away, be unworthy. No more. To hell with his idea. She would deal with whatever problems came with returning home. Then she prayed they were all still alive and well.

She had learned people are not perfect, and you work with them and their failings, or you have nothing. Whatever it took to reestablish a relationship with her family, she would do it. She was grown-up, and she would live where she wanted to. Her father couldn't—no, she wouldn't let him—stop her as she had let him in her past.

Spotting the correct address, Jennifer pulled into the small parking area and got out of her car to unload her donations. She knew how valuable good clothes and small household items were to those trying to make a new start in life.

Ken heard the car pull into the parking lot and saw the woman approach through the window. She looked familiar—but different. How? Then he recoiled at the recollection. He would never forget her face. He had given up on ever seeing the young woman who had led him to the Lord and his path to salvation. He had wanted to let her know he was okay. And, miracle of miracles, here she was; God, there was no limit to His mysterious ways.

No wonder Ken had not known Jennifer at first. The young woman from the bank was barely recognizable. Rather than joy in the light of God, her face reflected sadness and disenchantment. What had happened, Ken wondered, that he almost hadn't recognized her? What path had she chosen to live that had so hardened her appearance? There was so little softness, barely a glimmer of light left. Yet the glimmer Ken saw, beckoning to be inflamed. He held the door for her to enter with her box of items. Ken greeted this tired form of a woman and gently questioned as she set her box down to address him, "Do I know you?"

The night's ponderings had left Jennifer tired and vulnerable. She had exposed herself to herself, and she felt naked with the shame she had evidenced against herself. The question offered in quiet wondering further opened the protective fortress Jennifer had encased around herself since leaving Caroline's protective friendship. Caught unawares, her features softened to the offering of personal contact. She looked at Ken and tried to recall his features, mentally flipping through the catalogue of people she had known in her short life.

On a huge risk, Ken decided to offer the image he knew would get an instant reaction if, indeed, she was the woman from the bank. It was at this moment the Lord intervened and chose Ken's words for him to open wide the walls Jennifer had so skillfully erected in the intervening years. Ken said, "I know the way out." With tears coming to his eyes, his voice bravely continued with soft emotion, "The way out is through Jesus Christ." His hands reached out.

Those simple words melted the remaining hardness from Jennifer's features, and her eyes saw the hand extended from heaven itself. With a gasp, her tears came in a gentle torrent as she recognized the eyes of the once tormented man she had last helped so many years before. She had buried that day so deeply she had unbelievably forgotten that brief horrifying chapter. With a look of total confusion, Jennifer exhaled the words, "Oh, my God. How?" And her hands reached to Ken.

Ken took her outstretched hands and replied, "You showed me once." He gently guided her to the nearest chair.

In the great scheme of life, the miraculous works of the Heavenly Father are too varied and numerous to comprehend. He, the God of Abraham, the God of Isaac, and the God of Jacob, is the One True Living God. In the words of King Nebuchadnezzar of the Old Testament:

DANIEL 4:34-37 At the end of that time, I, Nebuchadnezzar, raised my eyes toward heaven, and my sanity was restored. Then I praised the Most High; I honored and glorified him who lives forever. His dominion is an eternal dominion; his kingdom endures from generation to generation. All the peoples of the earth are regarded as nothing. He does as he pleases with the powers of heaven and the peoples of the earth. No one can hold back his hand or say to him: "What have you done?" At the same time that my sanity was restored, my honor and splendor were returned to me for the glory of my kingdom. My advisers and nobles sought me out, and I was restored to my throne and became even greater than before. Now I, Nebuchadnezzar, praise and exalt and glorify the King of heaven, because everything he does is right and all his ways are just. And those who walk in pride he is able to humble.

For those who do believe, we are targets of the world, and he who rules now throws all doubts our way to attempt to steal that which cannot be taken from God. We are forever God's children, born again and marked by the blood of the Sacrificial Lamb. We will stumble from time to time and follow our plans instead of the Lord's, but the Holy Spirit in us is stronger than we are, and eventually we will fall back into the loving arms of our Savior, again relishing the depth of the Almighty's great love for each of us individually.

JOHN 10:27-30 "My sheep listen to my voice; I know them, and they follow me. I give them eternal life, and they shall never perish; no one can snatch them out of my hand. My Father, who has given them to me, is greater than all;

no one can snatch them out of my Father's hand. I and the Father are one."

We are here an unbreakable chain from heaven, a continuous path of light for the one who is the true light, the Christ.

Ken simply replied, "It's true. The only way out is through Jesus Christ."

With the barricades of emotional indifference shattering, Jennifer responded and began to come to grips with who stood before her. After that day in the bank, her life had tilted so far backwards that she had lost sight of the way and been sucked back into the quagmire of living her life by herself. She had forgotten to give all control and trust to the very One she herself had offered to Ken. How ironic that after so many years he was now the one showing her the way. How had she gotten so caught up in worldly affairs that she had lost the way? She saw now how dangerously confused she had been, wandering alone all these years without the Lord as her stalwart. How had it happened? When? This man was so right.

Seeing her obvious confusion, Ken offered, "It doesn't matter how or why. It doesn't even have to make sense. Let the past go and accept that which you know is true."

This simple statement brought such a wave of known relief. She let go of the shame she had unburied last night in admitting her part in the destruction of families and sobbed with all the personal anguish she thought she had carefully put from her.

Ken went to Jennifer and gave her a reassuring hug. He then gently removed himself to retrieve a box of tissues, a glass of water, and an extra chair for himself. Placing the chair a short distance from her, he offered her the tissues followed by the water and said, "It's okay. You're safe now."

Jennifer knew she was truly safe. Last night alone in her bedroom, she had realized she had done wrong, yet she hadn't truly accepted forgiveness. She hadn't let Jesus take her punishment for her wrongdoings. They were so... she could hardly say it...filthy...and the word made her shrink. She took a deep breath. Jesus loved her. She clung to this knowledge. She felt she had somehow become like the prodigal son, but she now had her eyes fully opened and saw her error. She was not only missing family, she was also missing the Lord. Oh God. And she cried. But her strength came back because she knew she could stop and leave this road and turn back to the way she now saw she had departed from. She had gotten lost in her own plans, trusting in herself and not turning to God's plan for her. And just when she thought she had it all figured out, God had dropped a signal flare as a warning—she needed Him. Thank God, she had seen. She knew what she needed to do now—and yet again, what of all the wrongs? Oh God, she had hurt so many.

Ken, watching her closely, could see the struggle she was having. The world pulls powerfully with its reasons for worries and doctrines of righteous self-criminations. And those who were once righteous feel most strongly that God could never forgive them, believing that once fallen from the true path they are now irretrievably lost. They, of all people, should have known better. But God is the righteous winner, and Jennifer only had to have faith in the gift of forgiveness to be truly free. "No, Jennifer," Ken assured her, "it's not too late. Remember you just have to have *faith* and *believe* forgiveness is there for you, too, and you won't be alone."

With shame weighing her down, Jennifer felt relieved at not having to reveal the depth to which she had sinned, and she exhaled her shame, "Oh, thank God, how right you are. How could I have forgotten and gotten so lost?"

The ageless, timeless Lord God of Hosts knew her heart. He felt her shame as His only begotten Son, the Lord Jesus Christ, hung sacrificially and so willingly upon the cross. While the world darkened with the weight of Jennifer's and the whole of the world's transgressions received by the One, His love—more than we can ever comprehend—brought light back to the world as He accepted our punishment for us. We in our own admission of guilt to Him died there with Christ, died children of this world, and are born again children of God with the Spirit of God within.

Jennifer slowly shook her head to help release the hold of the guilt within. To give all her sins and the ugliness she felt to Jesus Christ filled her with remorse and sorrow instead. Then the memory of her most recent transgression came starkly forward, and guilt made one last attempt to snatch forgiveness from her hungry soul. Her face reddened and shame slipped into her eyes. Though it had been six years since Michael had broken off their "friendship" and she had moved on to others, she had, in a moment of weakness, gone by his shop just yesterday morning to have her car tuned up before she left Cornell for good. How deep was her sin? It may have been a miracle he wasn't in, but she knew she had done a horrible wrong and so recently. Tears once again came with her shame. She felt so hideous and physically ill. How could she have done such wrong?

"Let it go," Ken gently urged. "Remember: Repent, and forgiveness is His gift. Go to your Lord and Savior. Give Him all you are feeling and accept His forgiveness. Remember, He is the victor; He willingly accepts your punishment and mine, too. He's happy to have you back in the flock."

MATTHEW 18:12-13 "What do you think? If a man owns a hundred sheep, and one of them wanders away, will he not leave the ninety-nine on the hills and go to look for the one that wandered off? And if he finds it, I tell you the truth, he is happier about that one sheep than about the ninety-nine that did not wander off."

Ken continued, "Don't let guilt draw you back. It's done. It's time to let the Lord Jesus Christ back into your life, and by the grace of God, let the power of the Holy Spirit dwell within for the work of the Most High God."

This brought new tears, but tears of self-forgiveness and acceptance of the wonderful gift of salvation and forgiveness Jennifer had lost sight of. She shoved shame away but still held a great depth of sorrow for her sins.

"What do I do now?" Jennifer innocently asked Ken after taking a deep cleansing breath, feeling freer than she had in so many, many years.

Ken patted her knee and said, "You just trust. God loves you and is in control. Everything will be all right."

"Yes, you're right. Though I must admit I'm a little scared. But I don't have to be." She tried to reassure herself as she took a deep breath and continued, "God loves me." New tears started, and Ken gave her another pat for reassurance.

"It's a miracle that God loves us wretched little humans, isn't it?" and they both laughed at his reference to their insignificance.

"I'm sorry. I don't remember your name," Jennifer stated as she tried to compose herself. "How can I thank you?"

"It's Ken, and your name is…?"

Jennifer gave a small laugh. "I'm Jennifer."

"I'm glad you came today, Jennifer. Now remember, the thanks are all God's. We are only an instrument of His peace, and I, for one, am so glad to be of His service," Ken said with joy in his voice.

"I'm still in shock at how this happened." Jennifer paused. Emotionally exhausted, she needed time to let the strength of forgiveness fill the void before leaving. "How did you get here?" Jennifer asked, moving her hand to encompass their surroundings as she remembered how she had come to give and ended up receiving far more than she had brought. She added, "God is truly awesome in His workings, miraculous indeed, but you are so far from where we parted."

Ken agreed, "In all the years since that day in the bank, one thing I have truly come to appreciate and be awed at are the ways of God. His plans are beyond words. He is truly a Master to be awed and revered. I had been transferred to a prison nearby, and during my imprisonment, I had signed up for a program in community service to help people so they wouldn't end up where I was. I believe through God's direction I came here, to this woman's shelter, after my release from prison just over half a year ago."

Jennifer silently remarked at how Ken was so filled with peace. She breathed deeply and slowly. "But a women's crisis center?"

Ken sheepishly dropped his head. "We all hope for miracles. Before I got involved in crime, my life had turned into such a mess. My wife had left me, and I had lost our little boy."

Jennifer interrupted, "I'm so sorry. I didn't mean to pry."

"No, it's okay. I guess I know what it is to be really desperate, and I felt if someone such as you had only entered my life when I was asking for help, well maybe I wouldn't have done what I had, maybe Bruce and the security guard would be alive." It was the first time he had ever fully addressed the loss of life that had occurred that day in the bank.

The thought startled him. He swallowed hard and shook it from his consciousness; it was in his past, and he could only do his best each and every day. The past would only distract him from who he was now, a willing servant for God.

Jennifer, seeing his spirit ebb, squeezed his hand.

Ken continued, "I also realized that what those in desperate need of help really want is compassion and empathy without judgment. It's hard enough to ask people for help without knowing you're being judged by them."

Jennifer silently nodded, for she remembered when she had needed help so long ago and all she had received were disapproving stares. "What you're saying is so true."

"I feel really blessed to be here. We don't have much to give in the material way, but those who do come here leave knowing they have a friend." His eyes glowed with hope.

A friend. So long ago, a friend had saved Jennifer, and she thought of Caroline. "We all need somebody," she agreed.

He continued, "I know I'm a long way from where I left my wife, but I guess I'll always hope, one day, Rachel will show up. People move. Look at you. Or maybe as I give comfort to someone, someone else will give comfort to her." He looked into her eyes, his hope shining forth, and he smiled. "God does work in mysterious ways," he said with conviction.

Rising to her feet, Jennifer again thanked Ken for the water and his time. Turning to leave, she remembered why she had come and pointed to the box she had set on the table, with a small smile. "And I thought *I* was bringing help." She shook her head and fought back tears, awed again by the gentle, mysterious, timely assistance of a loving, all-knowing God.

"You have, and thank you for thinking of others," Ken replied and added as an afterthought, "Hey, can I offer you some of our literature?" Taking a few pamphlets from the nearby table, he handed them to her. "These are from some non-profit organizations in the surrounding areas that provide assistance for various needs, for people trying to make a fresh start." He pointed and encouraged, "The one on top comes highly recommended. Two elderly ladies started this place called A Second Chance and a Helping Hand. It's not too far from here, a few towns away. I've heard great things of their offers to help."

"Thank you," Jennifer said and took the pamphlets.

He paused briefly and softly intoned, "Remember you are never alone. I don't think God intended for any of us to go it totally alone. We are here for each other, to give respite. And remember He is always with you in His Spirit. Let Him be your strength. Try to start your day with God, a simple Our Father to set you in the right frame of mind. God bless you, Jennifer."

"Good-bye, Ken, and thank you for being here for God to work through." Jennifer left the small building, slightly dazed, as someone seeing things more clearly for the first time.

Ken resumed his day's chores, again marveling at God's love for all His children. His placement in the women's crisis center upon his release from prison was truly part of God's design.

Chapter Twelve

Michael

ichael sat on the back porch, enjoying the setting sun and marveling at the beauty before him. The sounds of the evening birds mixed with those of Claire and the children from the open upstairs windows as they readied for bed.

What had started as an ordinary day had unfolded into one filled with unknown surprises. The day's turn of events left him reflective yet comforted, knowing he was not the one in charge; today had certainly settled that debate.

He had left the house as usual, telling the twins, Luke and Paul, and oldest, Sarah, to have a good day in school. A note had come home with the boys in their first weeks of school detailing their "liveliness," as he liked to call it. The note had suggested the boys be put in separate classrooms if they continued to show such enthusiasm for being friendly. They could be a bit of an uproar. The wording of the note still made him chuckle. The teacher certainly had tried to be tactful, but Claire had seemed to take her suggestion more personally and had gone a little crazy about it. But anything and everything got to her lately. He knew the boys could be a handful; they had been from birth. They had been born less than nine months after little Ruthie had so suddenly died. Then, too, she and Sarah had gotten into it last night over proper attire for school; at just thirteen she was starting to assert her independence.

Before he had left for work he had assured Claire she was doing a great job with the children and that things would work themselves out. Then, when he was going through the work orders, he spotted one that gave him pause. Jennifer Ryan had come by for a tune-up. At the sight of her name on the work order, his breath had caught in his throat. He hadn't thought of her in, well, years. He was only too glad he had been out of the shop and someone else had taken care of her car. With Claire upstairs and a moment of peace, his thoughts rolled back.

Claire had taken Ruthie's death hard. They all had, including then-six-year-old Sarah. Claire had tried so hard to be cheerful and make things normal, but Ruthie had been such an endearing little figure that everyone missed her deeply. And then they found out Claire was pregnant with twins. He had been so happy; even Sarah seemed to find comfort in the coming babies. Claire seemed reserved, but he knew hormones were involved and didn't push the subject. Thinking back now, maybe he should have.

It had been a difficult pregnancy. Michael was so thankful Claire's mom, Irene, was only a couple blocks away. He had always found her a little too bossy and controlling of Claire, treating her as if she were still a child, but during this pregnancy, he had welcomed her presence and firm hand in helping Claire. In her eighth month, she still seemed so closed off about Ruthie's death and even, he thought, uninterested in being pregnant. Her mother, out of genuine concern, had finally moved in with them. She stayed on and off until the boys were a little over six months old.

Thinking back, Michael saw now, he, too, had been in need of Irene. While Claire had removed herself from their life emotionally, he had done the same by running to another. The thoughts of the preceding years brought his head to his chest in remembered shame.

He hadn't thought the loss of Ruthie had affected him as it had Claire. At first he was sick with the stark knowledge she was forever gone. To never ever hold his sweet girl and feel her little arms around his neck saying, "I lub you, Daddy," looking at him with eyes enlarged by her thick eyeglasses. Maybe that was what made her so special.

Ruthie's innocence had been magnified because she was so painfully nearsighted. Despite the early need for thick lenses, her character had far outgrown her years and size. He smiled at the thought of her.

He remembered his panic the day of her funeral. The sight of her tiny little pink casket carried to the gravesite by her weeping cousins, full-grown men, and his stricken wife tightly holding Sarah's hand, had almost sent him over the edge. To maintain his sanity, he had mentally grabbed at the image of Ruthie being with the Jesus she so emphatically proclaimed "lubbed" everyone. He still clung to this knowledge.

Whenever he thought he would scream with uncontrolled anger over the senseless loss of someone so sweet and full of love, he felt a bolt of comfort. Ruthie was not gone. She was with Jesus. The times when his mental anguish drove him to the brink of insanity, he remembered with brilliant clarity her last morning when she had come into his and Claire's bedroom with her "Jesus lub you" routine.

Now he realized that the comfort he thought he had found in remembering her last day was an illusion. He had accepted Ruthie's departure from their lives here, but her death had presented other situations that had challenged his ability to adjust. He had dealt with those, but not, sadly, for the better. He had slipped into coping as he had before he met Claire. Old habits are always there to be reckoned with in trying times. He hadn't even realized he had slipped into his old life. Today's revelations had him recalling his own reaction to life's treacherous ways.

The day after the funeral he had tried to console Claire with the same sense of comfort he had found at the gravesite. His intended help had gone so badly. Just the mention of Ruthie's little "Jesus" routine had sent Claire into an almost hysterical panic.

She had looked at him with eyes of shock. "Michael," she had angrily whispered in their upstairs bedroom the morning after, "We just put our baby in a box in the ground. How can you be so callous?" She couldn't get the image of Ruthie in her little pink casket out of her mind. "The ground, Michael; our little girl is in a box in the ground!" she had screamed at him in whispered tones.

"But, Claire, I was just…," and he had been further interrupted.

"No, Michael, no! Just be quiet. I can't talk about…about…," and she had burst into tears and gone down the hall to the bathroom, shutting herself in and away.

Michael had stood there in shocked silence. He hadn't even finished his sentence. He had only been trying to share what had happened to him—how he had realized he would never again hold his little girl in his arms, how he had almost lost control, and how he had been saved by knowing Ruthie was with Jesus. What greater comfort could he have given?

Of course, had they both known she was already almost six weeks pregnant, and with twins, they would have realized her changing hormones were a part of her problem. She was off balance everywhere.

After his first attempt to help had failed so miserably, he was afraid to speak of their shared tragedy. Silently grieving alone, he had fallen back to the only response he had known, run; and run he did. He hadn't even realized how far he had run until he almost lost everything. The remembered guilt came in waves, pounding his heart. The sounds from the upstairs windows of his wife and children made him realize just how much he had almost thrown out.

He had thought he had handled Ruthie's departure, as he termed her death, well. He had welcomed the twin's arrival and had loved having two little boys to wrestle. When he found himself missing Ruthie, he would grab the boys and roughhouse. They were so full of life and laughter, always a handful of fun. After the difficult pregnancy and a long labor, Claire's mom had been a godsend. In reflection, her presence had enabled Michael to escape and Claire to withdraw, sending them farther from each other.

The raw wound of loss had scabbed over between Claire and Michael to fester inside them. Their love for each other and their surviving children had remained but the pain of their loss had stayed buried and unaddressed, a chest of anguish and guilt. Irene had helped Claire care for the twins, doing what Michael should have done, and the distance between Michael and Claire had unknowingly grown.

Into this pain-filled setting, life had presented Michael with the temptation of Jennifer. She had become the vehicle into which he had stepped to avoid conflict. But it cannot be avoided. He had merely substituted conflict in one relationship with that in another. However frightening and painful, dealing with conflict is a part of growing together. When managed with mutual respect and sensitivity, it helps two become one; when avoided, it pushes loved ones away while the unresolved issues lie dormant, ready to rise again.

Michael still remembered the morning Jennifer had come into his life. The shame he felt in how she had affected him had him checking over his shoulder. Jennifer had been a high school classmate, beautiful, intelligent, and kind. But none of his classmates had dared to date her. Her dad had a reputation for almost meanness in his obsessive protection of his only daughter.

The morning she had walked into the auto shop where he worked was burned into his memory.

The night before had been a long one, and he had been tired and overwhelmed. The boys both had had ear infections, and though they had been to the doctor that day, they were still fussy. He had just recently made the decision to take back control of his family. He and Irene had had words over finances, and he was tired of Claire's mother's need to be right. What a time to have gone it alone. He had forgotten the non-stop crying of a sick baby, as Irene had been doing his share of the nightly baby care. And then double that with twins.

The night had been long and sleepless. The boys hadn't dropped off to sleep until almost five a.m. Michael had groggily gotten up at the six o'clock alarm to get ready for work. Claire had asked him please to call in to let them know he was taking the day off. She had needed his help with the sick boys. Knowing there was no way in God's green earth he could survive any more crying, he had sternly told her someone had to pay for those sick boys' doctor bills. Lack of sleep had left both Claire and Michael raw and insensitive to each other. She had reminded him he was the one who had sent their "free" baby-help packing. He had hollered back, "Go ahead. Call your mother. I don't care." He had been so tired. He needed…what, exactly, he knew not… just to escape. That morning, he had gladly left that emotional mess, physically, in going to work and, emotionally, in welcoming Jennifer.

Michael had grown up with a love for vehicles and anything on wheels. The shop in which he had worked he now managed. The men he helped employ carried on the tradition of good reliable work, and his days were never slow. He loved his job and the people he worked with. The morning Jennifer had come in he had just finished replacing a radiator. He had stood up to catch the breeze coming in the open garage door when he had caught sight of a nicely dressed, shapely young lady getting out of her vehicle. One to admire a pretty woman, Michael had enjoyed watching her approach.

Only after they had discussed her car problems had Michael realized that beautiful young woman looked familiar. He had asked her if she had grown up in the area. It had caught them both by pleasant surprise to find out they had gone to high school together. They had chatted briefly, and she had said she would be back to pick up her car later in the day since his shop wasn't far from the small shopping center where Jennifer worked.

Michael had done the repair work himself, if only to have another chance to talk to her when she came back. She had brought a breath of fresh air into his life. Such a happy and carefree nature had only emphasized how his own life had become so filled with loss, frustrations, and responsibilities that never seemed to end.

What had transpired in the weeks and over most of a year, he most ashamedly remembered, had started out so harmlessly. He and Jennifer had shared jokes and daily happenings like the two best friends they were growing to be. He hadn't even been aware of when he had started to look forward to work so he could communicate with Jennifer. The weekends and long holidays had seemed never-ending. Michael had reasoned that if he only allowed himself to communicate with her from work, by phone or e-mail, he was not being unfaithful to Claire or his marriage vows.

Jennifer had respected his marriage. He had told her up front and been honest with her right from the start—he was married to a woman he loved and his children meant the world to him. He would never love another or leave his wife and children. The pronouncements he had declared to Jennifer had given him the false security the friendship he was embarking on was foolproof. He did not think failing to share this developing friendship with Claire was a signal there was something wrong with what he was doing.

It almost seemed his very declaration of his love and fidelity to his wife and children had sealed his fate and his fall. He shuddered at the memories and his own naïve ignorance of the weakness of the human flesh at the temptation of a relationship with a beautiful woman with no strings attached and none of the responsibilities of personal involvement.

In the end, it had been Jennifer's own daughter that had saved him from what he felt would surely have been the point of no return.

⁘═·═⁘

Shortly after their risky first encounter of manual and oral sexual gratification, he and Jennifer had agreed to meet at a hotel during the one business trip to Chicago he took every year. He remembered his excitement of their planned rendezvous with shame. At the time he had felt as if he had gotten a new lease on life. He recalled his feelings of being so alive, a real escape.

All their plans had gone so well. They had managed to get rooms with connecting doors, and no one was the wiser. This thought brought a wave of color to Michael's face—no one knew. What an understatement. The only one that knew was the only One that mattered, God. God, who loved him so much, had thrown Michael a lifeline in the form of an accident serious enough to injure an innocent child. Did it have to be so? He only shook his head as he remembered.

He and Jennifer had just met in his room, as they had planned, the point of no return, when Jennifer's live-in help/nanny had frantically phoned. There had been an accident. The nanny hadn't been injured, but Jennifer's daughter had been, and she was asking for her mother. Could Jennifer come back immediately? Michael had heard the nanny ask Jennifer during her cell phone call. Her daughter's injuries weren't life-threatening, but she needed surgery, and she wanted her mom.

Jennifer's departure was quick and clean. Reality had called them both back to the lives they were forsaking—and for what? The question had slammed into Michael as loudly as the door shut by Jennifer as she had raced to be with the one who she deeply loved and knew depended on her.

The realization of what had almost transpired after Jennifer had left had brought him to his knees at the foot of the bed—the very bed, just moments before, he had been lying on with Jennifer about to embark on a journey into temptation—asking for God's forgiveness.

"Oh God," he had implored with anguish and overwhelming guilt, "I am so sorry." He had finally allowed himself to see that what he had done and planned to do was so wrong. The realization of what harm and ugliness he had almost inflicted on everyone he held dear had made him feel filthy and physically ill for a few moments.

The burden of guilt rested heavily upon him. The faith he had come to accept when he had married Claire had confronted him. With tears in his eyes, fighting back the rising gall in his stomach, he had cried, "Dear Lord Jesus, I am sorry, so very, very sorry I have done so much wrong." As he had wept and reached to the Lord for forgiveness, so He had given him, and Michael's guilt and ill feeling had passed. He had known he would not tell Claire of what had happened the past months. He wouldn't punish her with his failings. He had unburdened to the Lord, and he came to know more fully of his need for the Lord Jesus.

Life was treacherous, too dangerous to go it alone. He should have sought comfort in the Lord Jesus when the nightmare had started, the day Ruthie had left. As a couple, he and Claire should have sought refuge in the Lord. They had not, and as a result, he had made some horrible decisions. He had stolen from his wife and family. A huge part of himself he had kept from them and given to someone else—the fun, the carefree, the "I love living" self that saw life as a wonder and a joy. Instead of sharing that part of himself with those he proclaimed to love, he had been giving it to a woman to whom he had no commitment, only stolen moments together. How could he have been so blind?

With those remembered thoughts and reawakened guilt, he had wept anew at what he had almost lost—his family here and his way eternally. The hurt had been so deep; he had been so sorry. He had had no words to say, only tears to shed. The comfort of forgiveness had returned as Michael had again proclaimed his sorrow to the Lord Jesus Christ.

As the moments had passed, he had come to know what he had to do. He had accepted forgiveness and would start anew with the Lord and his family. His relationship with Jennifer couldn't go on. It was wrong, and he had ended it that day. As brutal as it seemed, he had made the phone call. He had told her he realized he was wrong to have kept a secret relationship—and to have ventured beyond friendship with her and he was sorry for having taken her down a path he now knew was morally wrong. He had offered prayers for her daughter's recovery and apologized to her for any hurt he had caused her.

Jennifer had been shocked and silent on the other end of the phone. But Michael knew he was weak and had had to make a quick, clean, seemingly heartless breakup. He had hung up, not waiting for her to reply. There was no other way. It had ended.

⊹══·══⊹

"Michael, hey, Michael." Claire joined him outside and gently shook his shoulder as he appeared to have nodded off.

"Uh, oh. Sorry. Guess I was daydreaming." He clasped the hand she had placed upon his shoulder.

"Are you okay? The kids are ready for their goodnight kiss."

"Yeah, I'm fine. It's such a beautiful night."

Claire sitting down next to him, agreed, "That it is. I'll sit here, and you join me after you kiss the kids."

"Good idea." Michael rose to go to the children. "I'll be back. You want anything from the house?"

"A glass of water would be nice, please."

In mere moments, Michael returned, water in hand, to sit next to Claire, resting a hand comfortably on her leg. He settled in to enjoy the fading evening. All his previous thoughts and reflections dispersed as he relished in the blessings of his wife and family.

"Michael?" Claire began, tentatively;

"Yes."

"I want to apologize. I've done something terrible, and I'm sorry." Her tears started.

Michael wondered, *What on earth?* What could she have done? He knew she had been upset when he had left that morning, but she had seemed so different when he had come home. Everything had seemed fine just moments ago. Trying to contain the small alarm he felt, he asked lightheartedly, "What could you possibly have done?" He smiled softly to push away his fear, totally perplexed at this new development.

Through rising tears Claire's words struggled out. "I've not been here for you and the children," and she took a deep breath and finished quietly, exhaling, "since Ruthie died, and I'm so sorry."

A wave of relief flooded through Michael at her harmless pronunciation of wrongdoing. But the sudden rush of tears and visible anguish on Claire's part made Michael realize the seriousness of the charge Claire had put upon herself, and he let her continue.

"I guess when Ruthie died, I felt responsible but so helpless and scared. I was so afraid I would lose you guys, too, that I just pulled back and withheld myself." Her tears flowed freely, and the words tumbled out. "I was so afraid to continue to love you and Sarah as joyously as I had. I'd been careless, and I'd let Ruthie die." The last words were torn from her heart. Her anguish brought tears to Michael's eyes as he realized she really blamed herself for Ruthie's death.

"No, Claire." He took the water from her hand and, setting it on the ground, attempted to pull her to him.

"No, Michael, please." She gently resisted. "I need to tell you."

Michael released her and took her hand.

Claire continued, "I love you and the children so much, and when Ruthie was gone, I almost died thinking I couldn't see my precious one. She was so little, and she couldn't even see." The words brought a rush of tears. "All I could think was, *Where is she?* She was so sweet. Michael, I missed her so much. I just didn't want to love like that again, knowing one day I could lose you or Sarah or another, so I didn't. I'm so sorry. Please forgive me. Today I saw what I was doing is wrong. I'm going to stop being afraid to love fully because I'm afraid to lose. I promise."

Her anguish and rush to release years of guilt and self-denial brought a deep emotional reaction from Michael, too. How could he have not known she was struggling? He had had no idea she had felt this depth of personal guilt and had been so bereft. He had always seen what had happened as a tragic accident, never blaming anyone and certainly not his wife who was a devoted and loving mother.

"Hey, it's okay," he said, as he felt his own emotions surfacing. "You're the best mother our kids could have." To keep the guilt of his having neglected her needs in check, he asked, "What brought all this on?" And he hugged her for shared comfort, trying to diffuse the intensity of the moment.

With a little more control after having released the river of guilt, Claire began quietly, "After you left this morning and the kids got off to school, I felt so sad and empty. You know the boys' teacher hasn't been very helpful this year, and Sarah and I had words last night. I told her some of her 'friends' didn't really seem to be the friends she thought they were, and she was so upset with me. I just got to thinking life can be so mean and unfair." She sighed with remembered sorrow.

He nodded in agreement, for they'd had this discussion many times over the years. Life can indeed be cruel and more often than not unfair.

"But thinking made me even sadder, so I went for a walk to clear my head and breathe in some fresh air. Outside was so beautiful, and it made me think of sweet little Ruthie. She was so special. I'll never forget her last day. All she talked about was Jesus loving everyone. It was almost as if she knew Jesus, or saw Him. Poor blind baby." She smiled at the thought of Ruthie's thick glasses, not seeing the irony of her statement.

Michael smiled, too, as he thought back to Ruthie's big brown eyes made even bigger by her glasses.

"Claire, it wasn't your fault," he tried to reassure her.

"That's not it, Michael. It's okay," she told him, now giving him comfort and growing stronger as she remembered the gift she had received in the morning. "Once I started thinking of Ruthie, well, I just lost it. I had to sit down."

Michael rubbed her hand and she continued.

"While I was sitting, a man came." Claire still had no idea Joe had been there all along. "You know, Michael, he was probably an angel, because…well…I never saw him come. Just all of a sudden, he was there. And I surely needed one. We started talking, or he did, poor guy. I was crying so hard I could hardly see, and everything came out.

"All these years, I've felt guilty and afraid. He helped me see I needed to forgive myself for whatever I felt I'd done; even if I hadn't done anything, I felt I had. I needed to forgive myself. I loved Ruthie and would have done anything for her. I finally let go of the guilt; guilt hurts so much. It's so heavy." She sagged as she remembered how it had weighed her down. "Then," and she almost started to cry, and she squeezed Michael's hand for help and the comfort to go on. "I had to remember Ruthie wasn't 'disappeared.'"

Her choice of words made Michael laugh for the loss of Ruthie was deep.

"I finally accepted fully Ruthie is with Jesus. She is just as real today as the day she left us. I had to really focus on this and believe it so I could start loving you and the children as I used to, with joy and happiness." Her words trailed off quietly as she revealed her sin. She then continued, "The pain of not having Ruthie right here made me afraid ever to have that love with anyone else. It hurts so much to feel that close loss of love. Yet, it's even sadder not to love. I was so tired of working at not loving and trying to keep everybody alive so I could just have you and not love you too much in case someone…well…disappeared." And they both smiled despite themselves. "I was so tired of making myself sad and miserable. This world is tough, and I wasn't making it any easier."

Michael laughed softly at Claire's rationale and the picture of her struggling with her adversary, "the world." What a crazy woman she could be.

"Anyway, Michael, I'm so sorry. It won't be easy, but I'm going to try and not be so afraid of the day one of us has to leave here and return to be with God. I'll remember just to love you and enjoy you. I'll do my best and really trust that God loves us more than we love each other. I won't think about Ruthie's physical leaving. I'll hold on to the fact God is real and Ruthie is not gone; our love does not die."

"I'm just sorry I didn't know you were doubting and struggling so," Michael offered.

"No, Michael, it wasn't anything you should have known. *I* should have known better. I don't know how I lost sight of the truth." Claire shook her head in disbelief.

"I think maybe, because death came to someone so young as Ruthie and because she was so very dear and innocent, you just went into shock. And, we—your folks and I—didn't realize what had happened to you or that you needed our help." Michael tried to make sense of that dark time in their marriage, remembering how Claire had pulled away from everyone.

"I guess at the time I just didn't want to admit that I felt responsible for her death, that she was gone because of me." Claire ended in a small voice. "It was so hard to know I would never hold her again or feel her love. I just wanted her back, physically with me."

"You're right. You know the guys at the shop were talking about that movie *The Passion* and Jesus' agony and torture. I think old Mel Gibson got it wrong. I think Jesus' real agony was His knowledge that some of us would reject His offering of His own life as payment for our wrongdoings and they would remain separated from God. Jesus' true agony may have been that there would be so many who would say no to the perfect eternal love of the God of Abraham, the God of Isaac, and the God of Jacob." Michael continued, "I think Jesus wept because, even though he told his apostles he had to leave so that help in the form of the Holy Spirit could dwell in all who accepted what he taught, he knew others would come who would intellectually steal this Gift from his flock; they would mislead his followers into thinking that forgiveness comes from certain people rather than directly from Christ."

JOHN 8: 21-23 Once more Jesus said to them, "I am going away, and you will look for me, and you will die in your sin. Where I go, you cannot come." This made the Jews ask, "Will he kill himself? Is that why he says, 'Where I go, you cannot come'?" But he continued, "You are from below; I am from above. You are of this world; I am not of this world. I told you that you would die in your sins; if you do not believe that I am the one I claim to be, you will indeed die in your sins."

Michael continued, "Anyone who has buried a loved one will tell you the loss is far greater than any physical pain. Jesus knew that there would be those—who God created and loved—who would choose not to believe and accept what he had willingly given, his life for atonement for their wrongdoings, and these creations of God would suffer needlessly."

"I think you're right, Michael. I feel such relief, knowing Ruthie is not disappeared and one day we will be reunited with our loved ones and with God's perfect love. If only we can remember His gifts to us, His love for us, His full forgiveness for us, how much happier we are. So much suffering we bring on ourselves—and we don't need to." Claire sighed. "Living in God's love is all about having faith and believing, isn't it, Michael?"

"Yes, it really is. If you feel guilty, whether you've done something or not, you need forgiveness. By the way, I forgive you," and he smiled at her.

Despite his smile, Claire kept the discussion serious. "Forgiving ourselves and accepting forgiveness because we can't atone for our own wrongdoings is harder than offering forgiveness to others. It is so humbling to know we are so small and in such need of God's greatness."

"That's the truth. We sure can't go it alone," and he remembered his reflections earlier in the evening.

"Life sure is a struggle, isn't it?" Claire added. "I knew I missed Ruthie, but I hadn't realized it was bothering me so much."

"Yeah, life is a lesson, a lesson in love and trust. We learn as we live, and it isn't easy." Michael shared a smile as he pulled Claire close and added, "I'm glad we're in it together."

Claire asked as much into the darkening night as of Michael, "Do you think the man I talked to today was an angel?"

Michael responded, "Mmmm. Does it matter? Man or angel, he was filling his part in God's plan. And we do the same when we let Him work His will through us so we're at the right place at the right time, saying and doing the right thing for Him. But the man on the bench may really have been an angel. Who knows for sure? I'm just glad we have God to help guide us through this unjust world and in our lives."

"Me, too," Claire agreed and nestled comfortably into Michael's shoulder, enjoying the rest of the evening, contemplating the kindness of a stranger.